CONVICTIONS

CONVICTIONS

A NOVEL OF THE SIXTIES

Taffy Cannon

William Morrow and Company, Inc.
New York

Copyright © 1985 by Eileen E. Cannon

Library of Congress Cataloging in Publication Data

Cannon, Taffy.
  Convictions.

  I. Title.
PS3553.A5295C6 1985   813'.54   84-29468
ISBN 0-688-04343-7

Printed in the United States of America

First Edition

1 2 3 4 5 6 7 8 9 10

BOOK DESIGN BY JAMES UDELL

*This book is dedicated
to Bill
and to the memory of
Mildred Toll Cannon
and
Emily Hacker Cannon,
two extraordinary women
who lived before their time.*

ACKNOWLEDGMENTS

Many people have participated in the evolution of this book. Special thanks are due to:

—Felicia Eth of Writers House, Inc., for loyalty and persistence

—Laura Golden and Millie Loeb of J. P. Tarcher, Inc., for editorial wisdom and perception

—Jeremy Tarcher for gracious professionalism

—Sherry Arden and Laurie Lister of William Morrow and Company, Inc., for enthusiasm and determination

—Martha Craig for perspicacity and patience

—Sally Lynch, Betsy Cole and Val Alexander for criticism and insight

—and, most particularly, Bill Kamenjarin for everything.

Book One

Honesty is different things
to different people.

—Spiro Agnew
May 15, 1980

Chapter 1 _____

Prentiss Granger was featured on the *CBS Evening News* tonight for the eighth time. The first was with fist clenched high during the Days of Rage, the second was the 1972 shoot-out in Beaumont, Texas, and the third followed quickly when she was added to the FBI's Ten Most Wanted List. Then came the issuance of the New Freedom Manifesto when J. Edgar Hoover bought the ranch, followed by a long silence broken by two sudsy reports when her mother died.

But only tonight's broadcast comes close to capturing the tangled essence of her, with glimpses of the qualities that have nurtured our sixteen-year friendship. Sixteen years is half my life. There've been other friendships in that time, other loyalties, separate dreams and frustrations and goals and achievements. But no other relationship has come close to the strength and intensity and complexity of this one.

At least this long and painful day is nearly over, the reporters have finally gone, the sun is beginning to dip behind the crisp springtime green of the peach orchard.

Perhaps in the morning I'll be able to make more sense of this latest crisis and horror. But that's what I told myself yesterday, and the day before, and I feel no closer to understanding now. Perhaps time will help.

Or maybe nothing will. Ever.

When Prentiss Louise Granger first appeared at the Chadwick Academy for Girls in the fall of 1963, she certainly didn't seem a likely candidate for inclusion on the Ten Most Wanted List, though she might easily have qualified for the Ten Cutest Girls in the South. She arrived nearly two weeks late and by then the rhythms of the semester were already well established. So I was mildly surprised to round a corner and find our headmistress Miss Penelope, the sole surviving Chadwick, earnestly addressing yet another beautiful belle and her father in the dormitory foyer. A large globe of the world teetered on top of a mountain of beige luggage.

It took only a glance to identify the two as father and daughter. They shared jawlines, eyebrows, and gleaming chestnut hair, his in a bristling crew cut and hers in a pageboy, sleek as the Breck girl's. Her blue flower-sprigged shirtwaist dress was identical to a hundred others that hung in Chadwick closets and my first reaction was minor annoyance. The last thing in the world we needed was another darling daughter of Dixie.

"Naturally we are most particular about the supervision of our girls," Miss Penelope informed them as I passed by. "Chadwick young ladies are scrupulously chaperoned at all times." The crew cut bobbed twice in brusque acknowledgment, but the pageboy never moved. Then suddenly the brown eyes of our newest student met mine and rolled skyward.

By the next morning everyone was aware of the newcomer. She was Tissa Granger, a sixteen-year-old junior transfer from Miss Farnsworth's. The dorm gossip had it that she'd been asked to leave for disciplinary reasons. She seemed the type, with a pack of Kools in her purse and a box of Tampax in her closet. She never wore a circle pin or even the monogram pins we all used to clench our Peter Pan collars firmly together. But her appearance was always immaculate, and she used makeup so skillfully that not even Miss Penelope realized she was wearing mascara and blusher.

To a casual glance, she was the quintessential bratty belle, the sort of bubble-headed Chadwick twit who came in droves to our secluded conservative Tennessee campus from all over the South. We were daughters of privilege for the most part, related to governors and senators and various other pillars of the southern oligarchy. We were being "finished," readied for sedate female junior colleges, marriage to upstanding young gentlemen from respectable backgrounds, memberships in frivolous women's clubs and the rearing of a new generation of well-mannered young ladies who would one day succeed us at Chadwick.

It was quickly apparent, however, that Tissa Granger intended to be educated, not finished. There were no stuffed animals on her severe navy bedspread, no pictures of Troy Donahue or Kookie Byrnes or Bobby Rydell on her bulletin board. The entire bulletin board, in fact, was covered with a *National Geographic* map of Revolutionary War battles. She required an extra bookshelf to accommodate her collection of histories and biographies. And when the rest of us gathered nightly for gossip and silliness, she stayed in her room studying until lights out.

There were other Chadwick girls who were smart and diligent, of course. But even those who could do calculus and read Homer in the original underwent a lightning metamorphosis whenever they came into contact with boys. Their eyelids would flutter, their accents would thicken, and you'd swear when they opened their mouths that they'd have a rough time plowing through *Fun with Dick and Jane*.

Not Tissa. At the first September mixer with the Parker Military Academy, I drifted by her as she was deeply engrossed in conversation with a Parker senior, staring intently into his eyes. Two other boys stood slightly to the side, shifting their weight awkwardly. I instantly understood the reason once I heard her speak.

"The point you're missing is that the immolation of Buddhist monks represents a truly deep division in the country. There just isn't any way the Diem regime can survive in the face of that sort of opposition. Sacrificial public suicide has always been a powerful tool of protest. Just look at the Irish hunger strikes during the twenties."

The mention of hunger strikes reminded me of my primary mission, reaching the refreshment table before the pecan tarts were all gone, but as I took my glass of ginger ale punch from one of the elderly English teachers, I couldn't help feeling resentment. Tissa Granger was beautiful and suave and capable of conversing with a strange boy on a subject I knew absolutely nothing about. I had not spoken to a single boy in the hour since the mixer began, and as I leaned across the table to help myself to another cookie, the French mistress crooked her finger and whispered, in French, that my slip was showing.

"*C'est la guerre,*" I responded brightly, and headed off, absolutely thrilled to have an excuse to leave.

I felt instantly more comfortable once the locker room door closed behind me. Everybody smiled and greeted me warmly and somebody jumped to help me fix my slip. I surveyed myself in the mirror and reapplied ice pink lipstick, wondering for the thousandth time why Mama

insisted I was pretty. Clearasil only partly concealed the sprinkle of pim-
ples across my nose and despite six ounces of Adorn, my dishwater blond
hair was escaping its perky flip and starting to friz. Only my eyes pleased
me. They were dusky blue, suddenly larger and more vivid thanks to
painstakingly applied mascara.

"Eat your heart out, Liz Taylor," I announced as I snapped my com-
pact shut. I was in a comfortable niche again, everybody's favorite funny
fat girl with her pals.

Mind you, I wasn't the kind of grotesque who automatically stops
conversations and takes up two seats on the bus. At fifteen, I was twenty
pounds overweight, but that was enough to put bicycle tires around my
middle and mash up my thighs when I forced my knees together as, indeed, students at Chadwick were urged to do constantly. Chadwick was,
however, an ideal place for me to be. Girls' schools throughout recorded
history have been the perfect repository for those of us destined to ride
out adolescence feeling like inflated life rafts. We are the ones who
mimic the teachers, tack up parody notices on bulletin boards, leave toilet seats up in the housemother's apartment and always have a hilarious
idea for the Parents' Weekend skit.

The only catch is, while we're easing the pain of everybody's else's adolescent traumas, nobody's doing a blessed thing to alleviate our own.

By mid-October, I no longer paid much attention to Tissa Granger
one way or another. Because she was a year ahead of me, the only class we
had together was PE. She struck me as being snotty and smug, and she
kept to herself a lot. She seemed to study constantly and had no particularly close friends at school.

I don't even remember seeing her the night of the Secret Friends
drawing, when the whole dorm gathered in PJs and pink foam curlers in
the parlor. That night I pulled Sandy Shilton's name from the pewter urn
in which it was rumored that the ashes of Miss Penelope's Lost Love had
once rested, obligating me to perform small anonymous kindnesses for
Sandy for the upcoming ten days. It was not a prospect that much excited me. Sandy was a silly Knoxville sophomore who giggled incessantly
and never had to strain to appear dumber than the boys who flocked
around her.

Still, I enjoyed the spirit of Secret Friends, and derived a certain pleasure from evading detection as I slipped inspirational poems beneath

Sandy's door at night and arranged candy bars on her pillow during her afternoon hockey classes. Actually, my performance as a Secret Friend was upgraded a bit by shame at the way my own Secret Friend was showering me with unwarranted generosity. My favorite kinds of candy bars appeared mysteriously on my desk and moon pies popped up in the pockets of my Chadwick blazer. A charming bouquet of bronze chrysanthemums was reflected in my dresser mirror when I awoke one morning. My wrinkled gym uniform suddenly hung neatly ironed on a hanger, ready for Inspection. On various occasions I found a small bottle of Woodhue, green pearlescent nail polish, a copy of the new *Seventeen,* a cute little eyeshadow paintbox and a pack of color film for my Instamatic.

And on the morning of Revelations Day, the time of truth for those girls who hadn't yet deduced or apprehended their Secret Friends, a four-foot roll of paper had been hung outside my door. LAUREL MAY HOLLINGSWORTH was spelled out vertically in two-inch-tall black letters, and next to each of them ran a virtue beginning with the appropriate letter, from LOVABLE and ACCOMPLISHED all the way down to TRUSTWORTHY and HUMOROUS.

It was signed in neat script in the bottom corner: YOUR SECRET FRIEND, TISSA GRANGER.

Of course I felt like a prize fool. I'd guessed at least five girls who might have been my Secret Friend and hadn't even considered Tissa a possibility. I hurriedly dressed and ran downstairs, anxious to thank her at breakfast. She was sitting at the end of a table reading a history book when I arrived, breathless.

"I'm sure grateful for your generosity," I started awkwardly.

"It was fun," she answered with a warm smile. "As a matter of fact, I enjoyed it a lot more than I expected to. At first the whole thing just seemed silly. But then I figured I might as well try to do it right, and I started investigating you. It was good training in case I ever decide to join the CIA."

I blinked at the image of Tissa Granger as a spy. "You *investigated* me?"

She grinned impishly. "Well, sure. I had to find out what you were really like, didn't I? I know all sorts of things about you. You're from St. Elizabeth, Louisiana and your mother was Chadwick Class of '31. You have three older brothers. Your favorite subject is English, your favorite color is blue and you take excellent photographs. You hate PE and last year you put Jell-O in the maid's closet sink. Lime, I think, though I couldn't find out for sure. And unless I'm very mistaken, you're somehow related to Colonel Jeb Hollingsworth."

Until she mentioned Colonel Jeb, I'd been able to follow her reasonably well. But I was quite certain that nobody at Chadwick knew about my relationship to the leader of several highly colorful and thoroughly abortive Confederate raids into Southern Illinois.

"How on earth do you know about Colonel Jeb?"

"Then I'm right?" Her tone was triumphant.

"He was my great-great-grandfather. But how did you know?"

"Circumstantial evidence, which is a nice way of saying a lucky guess. I've read a lot about the War, and I knew he was from somewhere on the Louisiana instep." I listened in shock as she rattled off particulars of the notorious Ste. Marie raid and Colonel Jeb's battlefield promotions. The Hollingsworths, of course, revered Colonel Jeb's memory, but I couldn't imagine anyone else knowing or caring about him.

"I don't know what to say."

"You won't have a chance to say anything for a while. Motormouth Mary Tristan's heading our way. But listen, if we can get permission, why don't we walk into town this afternoon?"

In the days that followed I began to spend quite a lot of time with Tissa Granger, and I discovered something truly startling. She was lonely. Under all that competence and intelligence and beauty was a slightly lost and frightened girl, one who seemed almost hungry for friendship. What I couldn't understand, however, was what she saw in me.

"At first I thought you were just like the rest of them," she said one night as we sat in my room demolishing a newly arrived CARE package from my family. "You know, just interested in boys and grooming and who's wearing what to the next Parker mixer. I didn't realize till I started snooping around during Secret Friends what an individual you were. It's nice to meet somebody who has enough sense of herself that she's not afraid to be different."

I shook my head in bafflement. Couldn't she see that I was different because I had no choice? I wanted nothing more than to be truly accepted by those girls Tissa so thoroughly disdained, not as court jester, but as a pretty and popular equal. And Tissa, who could have slid effortlessly into the most exclusive cliques, wanted nothing to do with them.

"I'm no individual," I protested. "At least not on purpose."

"If you try to do it on purpose, it's not individuality, it's artificial. Take it from a born outsider. I've never fit in anywhere, really. Not at home with my family, at Miss Farnsworth's or here."

"You an outsider?" I was incredulous.

"Well, sure. Nobody understands the things I think are important. Or even the things I think are funny. Just imagine if I tried to explain about Aunt Nell to anybody but you. I'd get polite stares and then somebody'd ask if the Parker backfield would be any stronger on Saturday." Her Aunt Nell led the Missionary League in Columbia, South Carolina, where polite society had been scandalized when she kept an African minister as a house guest for three weeks. Earlier that evening I had laughed myself sick at Tissa's description of her French poodle, which had magenta toenails, a crucifix dangling from its collar and seventeen different sweaters.

"Anybody'd think Aunt Nell was a stitch," I answered feebly. Actually, I could see Tissa's point. "And you should be grateful your family has eccentricities." Her idiosyncratic kin lived in Granger, South Carolina, a town founded by her Yankee granddaddy just after the turn of the twentieth century. Her father the Major ran a textile mill, played war games, dabbled in cryptography and had lost a leg in World War II. Her alcoholic mother guzzled endless pitchers of minted "iced tea." Admittedly her little sister and brother sounded pretty dull, but they were well balanced by Aunt Nell. "The Hollingsworths may be the most boring family that ever lived."

"No family that owns a plantation can be totally boring," she argued. She had been intrigued to learn that Weatherly Plantation had been in my family since 1797 when Thomas Hollingsworth first broke ground in Piniatamore Parish, a fact that in my supreme provincialism I had more or less taken for granted. There are lots of plantations in our part of Louisiana, all but a handful still privately owned and occupied. "Not to mention old Colonel Jeb."

I shook off a heart-shaped satin pillow and brushed a sprinkling of brownie crumbs from my white chenille spread. Since getting to know Tissa, I had begun to harbor a faint suspicion that my room—with its mishmash of pennants and pompons from Parker and UT and Vanderbilt, its collection of too-cute pillows and autograph hounds—was trite and unimaginative. Certainly the Memphis blues station Tissa had tuned my radio to didn't seem to fit the decor, but maybe that was because the station seemed to be playing funeral dirges. "That was generations ago."

"Look," she said, "any family that can produce somebody with your irreverence *has* to have something going for them. I bet they're a lot more interesting than you think."

"The only thing interesting about the Hollingsworths is that they haven't been taken on tour as exhibits by the National Obesity Foundation."

She cast a sly eye at the CARE package and pulled out a praline. "Then they must put on a pretty good spread for Thanksgiving. Any chance I could get myself invited?"

On the Friday before Thanksgiving I was dozing through a session on the conjugation of irregular French verbs when the Chapel bell began to ring, the Chadwick signal for immediate assembly. We capped our cartridge pens, closed our books in puzzlement and relief, and headed for the Chapel. A few gold and scarlet leaves still dangled from the giant pin oaks that towered over the wide lawns. Levus, the old black caretaker, was lowering the flag outside Chadwick Hall. He was sobbing and we nudged each other, giggling.

Then I saw Tissa walking toward me. I waved, but she was staring at Levus as he anchored the flag at half mast. She came to an abrupt halt in the middle of the lawn and her shoulders sagged a moment. Then she drew herself up tall, ironed the expression from her face and walked on. She sat two rows ahead of me and I watched her while buzzing speculation filled the chilly chapel.

When Miss Penelope walked to the pulpit, the buzzing turned to a gentle roar. Miss Penelope was crying too, for the first time anybody could remember. She raised one hand and a shocked student body fell instantly silent. Then she choked and snuffled and told us that President Kennedy had been killed that afternoon in Dallas.

I was still watching Tissa. She never altered her expression. Other girls burst into tears and histrionics and there were a few muffled screams. There was even what seemed to be a cheer from the rear, but it broke off as abruptly as it had begun.

When we were dismissed, Tissa shot out of the Chapel, loped across the lawn to the dorm and locked herself in her room for two hours. She didn't answer knocks, but I could hear her radio playing news reports.

Miss Penelope announced at dinner that night that she was calling our families and dismissing class a week early so we could be at home in this time of national tragedy. To be truthful, though, once the initial shock passed, most girls remembered that their pro-segregationist families had trained them to hate John Kennedy and that therefore maybe it wasn't such a terrible tragedy after all.

I cried myself to sleep that night with tears of confusion and fear. What was the point of killing such a handsome vibrant man? It had to be part of a communist plot to take over our government. I was haunted by the image of poor Jackie, the epitome of sophistication and beauty and refinement, standing in her bloodstained pink suit as her husband's casket was removed from *Air Force I* in Washington. How could she tell her two little children what had happened? And what *had* happened, anyway? The world had always seemed so orderly before.

Daddy sent Jasper, our Negro handyman, to drive us home the next day. Tissa had finally gotten permission from her parents to come home with me for the holiday. Proper notes had been exchanged on proper stationery by proper mothers, but what ultimately turned the tide was Tissa's history term paper on the effects of automatic weapons on world warfare between 1884 and 1917. The Major just about busted his buttons on that one. "Cogent and concise," his letter of praise had read. "Your research is impeccable."

Tissa insisted that the car radio be on during our entire trip, and talked a lot about assassination through history. She knew all of the salient facts about Leon Czolgosz, Charles Guiteau and John Wilkes Booth, one of whose hanged comrades was an extremely distant relation on her mother's side. I listened, but all I could really think of was Jackie Kennedy watching her husband die on a hot Dallas afternoon.

What I remember most clearly about the next week is being as proud of Tissa as if I had invented her. I showed her off to anybody who would pay attention, and in a town as tiny as St. Elizabeth, that was everybody but Billy Bradley's retarded brother who was locked in the attic. She was particularly intrigued by the weapons on Grandpa's bedroom walls, and he almost swallowed his upper plate when she expertly broke down and inspected a Gewehr 98 that he had taken off a German POW in the Argonne Forest in 1918. He had no way of knowing that she was as comfortable with sidearms as petticoats, having gotten her first squirrel rifle at the age of eight.

Tissa was bright and alert and charming and asked forty million questions. The only thing she wanted was to see all of the television coverage of the assassination, no matter how wretched our TV reception might be. If it hadn't been for her insistence on that, we would have missed the death of Lee Harvey Oswald, who seemed to be gunned down in a black-and-white blizzard. Certainly the Hollingsworths had adjusted easily to the removal of what they considered an irritating wart on the American body politic. Tissa and the servants and I were the only ones around who seemed to feel at all sorry.

On the last day before we went back to Chadwick, we went out to Weatherly again. Tissa and Grandpa had just finished a lengthy rehash of Vicksburg and we took two of Grandpa's retired hunting dogs for a walk. I turned right automatically at the creek, but Tissa wanted to go down to the slave cabins again. Actual slaves, of course, had not lived there since 1865, though the cabins had been occupied well into the twentieth century.

She poked around everything. "Look at this, Laurel," she said finally. "Look at these shanties and then think about that house. What would it do to your mind to live like this while you took care of *that*? It was all so *wrong*." She sat down on the broken stone stoop of one of the rundown shacks and stared off down the creek, absentmindedly scratching one of the dogs.

Wrong, she'd called it. Wrong. Right and wrong had never entered into my feelings about Weatherly before. Only "is" and "was." Somehow she had shifted the entire focus of the place.

She was to become very good at shifting the focus of things.

Beatlemania swept through Chadwick the following spring, and Tissa and I remained pointedly aloof from the craze. Neither of us listened to records much, but when we did we liked the folkie sounds of the Kingston Trio and Peter, Paul and Mary. Tissa adored scruffy Bob Dylan, though I privately thought his voice resembled sandpaper on sheet metal, and preferred to hear Joan Baez sing his songs.

Most of that spring was consumed by Tissa's romance with Tommy Stanton, a dashing senior Parker cadet. They met at a Valentine's Day mixer and she was instantly smitten. A hidden talent for deviousness surfaced as she concocted ways to meet him outside official Chadwick-Parker functions. We often "ran into" him in the balcony of the Crest Theater on Saturday afternoons, where I would munch my Milk Duds and ignore the passionate kisses they exchanged. They would rendezvous for walks in the woods while I lay on a blanket reading a tattered and forbidden copy of *Peyton Place*. The grand finale was when they stayed out all night after the Parker prom. Returning early from my own date with a pimply, squeaky-voiced Chattanooga junior, I forged her return signature on her date pass, arranged pillows under her bedding, unlocked the hall window for her return and lay awake all night in a nervous sweat. She was back at dawn, disheveled, euphoric, and full of enigmatic smiles and silences.

A week later we separated for summer vacation, and after a few letters back and forth, she dropped me cold. I'd gone home with her at Easter and was scheduled to visit again in August, but an abrupt letter from Mrs. Granger to my mother regretted that a change in family plans made it impossible for me to come.

I was grievously wounded. I was supposed to be her best friend after all, and I'd never felt so close to anyone before. But after three anguished letters to her went unanswered, I gave up and licked my wounds in resignation. That fall when she failed to return to Chadwick, I told everyone that she'd decided to go back to Miss Farnsworth's because it was closer to home.

Almost a year and a half passed before I heard from her again. I kept myself busy, to be sure. I wrote and directed well-received Homecoming skits both junior and senior year. I talked the Chadwick administration into offering a noncredit course in photography. I reread *Gone with the Wind* and fantasized Rhett as a military school cadet. I lost nine pounds and gained back thirteen. I spent three futile summer weeks with lemon juice in my hair to develop blond streaks, finally giving up and combing in peroxide that turned my bangs orange and my mother apoplectic. I won the Junior English Award and served as Egg Chairman for the Methodist Children's Easter Party. I had lots of casual friends, but I made a point of not getting too close to anybody again.

Then, the day before Halloween in 1965, I found a letter from Tissa in my mailbox. It was short and disappointing.

Dear Laurel,

I'm sorry, terribly sorry, that it's been so long and I'm even sorrier that I can't tell you why right now. Someday I will. But for now, if we're still friends, please write me. I've missed you more than you can realize.

Love,
Tissa

I waited three weeks before drafting my nonchalant reply. I gave her all the Chadwick gossip and asked why she wasn't in college yet. Then I held the letter another week before I mailed it to her at the Greenwood Preparatory Academy in Virginia

Three days later I had another letter from her. This one was longer and chattier, but there still wasn't any explanation why she had dropped out of my life. There was, however, an invitation to come to Granger after Christmas during winter vacation. If I said yes, she'd have her mother write to mine.

Of course I went. But it was hours before we were alone. Every time I tried to ask her something she cut me off. Her brother and sister were running around being obnoxious and her mother kept rambling on about the Jackson & Perkins catalog and periodically the Major would march through the room and bark a few commands. I obliged them all by doing my imitation of Miss Penelope making morning announcements. Even the Major laughed.

Finally it was bedtime and we were alone in Tissa's room. She shut the door and I turned to her in fury. "Just where the devil have you been for the last year and a half, anyway?" I sputtered.

She sat down and looked straight at me. "I had a baby."

It's a good thing I was near my bed, because my knees suddenly didn't work anymore. "You *what?*" I couldn't believe it.

"You heard me. I had a baby. B-A-B-Y. As for where I've been, I've been pretty much in prison. You might say I displeased the Major a trifle. Andersonville was summer camp compared to what I've been through."

"But how? Who?" I was suddenly very embarrassed and terribly ashamed for her. She was just barely eighteen and for all practical purposes Ruined.

"I suspect you already know how. And as for who, I haven't told anyone."

"You don't have to tell me anything," I said stiffly. "It's none of my business."

I guess the hurt showed pretty clearly on my face then, because she came and sat next to me and touched my arm. "Silly Laurel," she chided gently. "I said I *hadn't* told anyone, not that I wasn't *going* to. Don't you see I've got to tell you?" And then we both burst into tears and hugged each other and it was a long time before either of us spoke again. I could feel hurt and anger and sorrow pouring out of her as she cried.

"You don't hate me, do you?" she asked finally.

"Of course not!" I tried to be emphatic, but my voice cracked. Of course I couldn't hate her, but I couldn't understand this, either, not really. "It was Tommy Stanton?" I felt enormous relief at her nod. At least it had happened out of love. "It must have been horrible. How did you ever tell your parents?"

She grimaced. "Well, I had a good long while to plan it. I was actually starting to show before I got up the nerve. I told Mama first, one morning out in the rose garden when she was picking flowers. That's about her favorite thing in the world to do, so I figured she'd be in a good mood. I don't think she quite believed me at first, and then she started to get a little shaky on her feet and I was afraid she'd pass out on me. I talked her into telling my father."

I shuddered. "That must have been quite the scene."

"I went up to my room after dinner and the next thing I knew I could hear the Major bellowing my name. I've never been so scared in my life. He was yelling that he'd whip the daddy's name out of me, and I think he really would've whaled me, except Mama got in between us and wouldn't let him touch me. I was confined to quarters incommunicado while they figured out what to do with me."

"You never told them it was Tommy?"

She shook her head firmly. "That would just have made it worse. Of course I was in love with Tommy, but he'd have wanted to marry me and I sure didn't want to do that. There's too many things I want to do and I'm way too young. I'd like to win the Bancroft History Prize someday, and there's no way that could ever happen if I got married and started raising a family before I even finished up prep school. I didn't even want to have a baby at all, to tell the truth, but when I started hinting to Mama about an operation, she slapped me across the face and said that I made my bed and now I was just going to have to lie in it. Which is more or less what I ended up doing, down in Brunswick, Georgia, in a horrible home. It was just like a jail, Laurel. We could never leave the grounds. No letters, no phone calls, no visitors. The only exception was parents, and I *sure* didn't feel like seeing them. I hated every second of it. I hated the baby for existing. I hated me for being so goddamned stupid. I hated the Major for being so medieval. He was sure that I'd been tricked or raped or something and he really wanted blood. I knew it was my own fault. But you know who I hated the most?" I shook my head. "Tommy Stanton, for telling me you couldn't get pregnant if it was the first time. I mean, I *knew* that wasn't true, but I wanted to believe him, and brother, did I ever pay for being so gullible." Her words hung in the air for what seemed like a very long time.

"Tissa?"

"What?"

"Was it a boy or a girl?"

Her jaw set angrily. "It was a boy. And they wouldn't even let me see him. They told me that the girls just get too attached if they see their babies before they take them off to be adopted. I spent nine months of my life making something and I couldn't even see what it was. A week after he was born, I was right back here at Azalea Acres, playing chess with the Major. Nobody has ever mentioned it again, except in kind of veiled ways, like when the Major told me that I couldn't go north to college. But I'll get to that in a minute. First let's get something to eat. Hungry?"

A silly question. We slipped downstairs and rummaged around the kitchen, and after I had demolished two large servings of peach pie and a pint of milk, I felt a whole lot better about everything.

When we were safely upstairs again, Tissa explained just what it was that she wanted from me. She had hoped to go to Radcliffe, but the Major was no longer willing to let her go unchaperoned into a land of liberal Democrats and second-generation Mediterraneans with names ending in vowels. Clearly she needed supervision in a controlled environment and his solution was that she attend either Bob Jones University or the University of South Carolina, where she could live with Aunt Nell.

Bob Jones was out of the question. Tissa Granger could never survive at a school which had, in turns, booted out Billy Graham for infractions of the rules, awarded him an honorary Ph.D. and finally denounced him as a heretic. And the state university was not much better. Tissa viewed it as simply another form of prison. Aunt Nell might have a soft spot for

Congolese ministers, but she was a priggish old bird in every other way.

"So now I move into my big sales pitch," she said with a grin. "Laurel, do you have an application in at Duke?"

I nodded. I was expecting to go to Vanderbilt with the rest of the bright girls from Chadwick, actually, but the college adviser had insisted that I file applications elsewhere too.

Tissa beamed. "Terrific! That's it, you see. Duke has the very best history department in the South. But the Major will only let me go there if you're my roommate. You know how responsible and down-to-earth he thinks you are."

I smirked. "How does he think I can keep you out of trouble at Duke? I didn't do such a great job at Chadwick."

"Does that mean you'll do it?"

I hesitated a moment to appear to be giving the matter careful thought, but my mind was already made up. Of course I would do it, if for no other reason than this was the very first time I had even been slightly excited about college. "Sure, Tissa."

She threw her arms around me. "That's wonderful! I'm so excited! And Laurel? Do you suppose you could do me just one more tiny favor?"

"I just promised you the next four years of my life. What more could you want?"

"Oh, this one's easy. I don't want to be called Tissa anymore. It sounds too frivolous."

Chapter 2 _____

Frivolity, as it turned out, would not be one of the hallmarks of our college experience. It's very murky looking back, partly because everything changes with time to fit our postconceptions. But even so, to come of age in such a marvelous period of ferment and turmoil is a privilege no other modern American generation has ever had. I think of this as my one real brush with luck, though it certainly wasn't easy. Everything was terrifically confusing and much of the time I was utterly befuddled. The world was spinning along at a brisk 78 rpm back then and I was your basic 33.

Still, anything seemed possible. The late sixties were like an Advent Calendar. Every day there was a new little window to open, whether we were ready or not. And the windows were about equally divided between the sublime and the dreadful. In one group we had Vietnam, pollution, LBJ, racism, Biafra, demonstrations, napalm, Wallace, riots, and the draft. And for each of these virtually insoluble problems there were any number of possible avenues of escape: Eastern religions, marijuana, hallucinogens and a whole pharmacopoeia of internal journey, peace marches, hitchhiking and the open road, free love, Haight-Ashbury, nature, love-ins, be-ins, teach-ins and a whole burgeoning world of music from Dylan to the Beatles to the Stones to Vanilla Fudge to Joan Baez to the Supremes to the Temptations.

So we opened those little windows, right on schedule, and the ultimate joke was on us. When we got to the big one, the twenty-fifth window, the culmination of all those wonderful and contradictory possibilities, there stood Richard Nixon, grinning diabolically with his fingers raised high in waving Vs.

Prentiss Granger was a hot commodity at Duke before she ever set foot on the North Carolina campus that fall of 1966. When I arrived for Freshman Week, the first thing I heard as I walked through the front door of Wognum House was her name, spoken reverently by three fraternity boys scouting the year's crop of frosh photos on the dorm bulletin board.

There were scads of pretty freshmen that year, and several in our dorm alone who were as good-looking as Pren. But she was more complicated than most people expected. She was the only girl in the dorm with a two-foot map of Vietnam hanging over her bed and the only person I knew who routinely read *The New York Times*. She was still hopeful that the Major would eventually allow her to transfer to Radcliffe, and toward that end she determined that academics took precedence over everything. She was barraged by phone calls from enterprising boys who swooned over her picture in *Outlook '70*, the picture manual which ruled first-year dating relationships and hung by every telephone on West Campus. To avoid the phone calls Pren studied in the library and I was faced with the thankless task of taking messages from anxious suitors.

Duke was full of surprises and revelations for both Pren and me. We discovered that northerners called us "grits," which irritated the hell out of Pren. Grits was a breakfast dish. Southerners were people. The fact that we invariably referred to northerners as Yankees did not seem to her a parallel situation. She had never attributed inflexible social characteristics to Yankees as a group and was infuriated that they presumed to categorize us as slow-moving, dim-witted, racist and (in her case particularly) just itching for Captain Rhett to carry us up that big red staircase.

But unfortunately she was always drawn to men with quick minds and facile tongues, and she admired the facility even more if it didn't drawl. She was an arrogance groupie. The easiest way to get her undivided attention back then was to be a superbly confident man and infer ever so politely that she needn't bother her pretty little head with such a complicated subject. It was a challenge she could never resist.

I once asked Pren what she considered the most significant event of her first semester in college. There were any number of possibilities: being the dorm Duchess candidate at the freshman Duke & Duchess Dance, pledging Pi Phi, dating dozens of enterprising young men, wooing and winning J. J. Webster.

She didn't even stop to think. "Ivy," she said firmly.

Ivy was a highly exclusive academic honorary for freshman girls with a 3.5 average or better. Good grades were tough to come by back then, and while any nincompoop could slither by with Cs or even Bs, a genuine A was an extraordinarily rare commodity. There were four hundred girls in the freshman class and only two dozen made Ivy.

Needless to say, I wasn't one of them. In contrast, the episode I remember most vividly from that semester was the Name Tag Caper.

It started with a panty raid, a charming anachronism that infused life into an otherwise colorless Tuesday evening as a horde of freshman boys descended on Wognum bellowing the Duke fight song and demanding dainties.

I was studying for a bio hourly with Marcy Miller and Lana Armstrong when it started. Marcy was the shy and appallingly emaciated daughter of a Pittsburgh steelworker and Howard Johnson's waitress, one of the first genuinely impoverished white people I had ever known. Not until I overheard Marcy on the phone telling her mother that a pair of loafers would be a terrific Christmas present did I grasp the depth of the financial chasm that lay between us. Lana, whose daddy was an automotive executive in Bloomfield Hills, Michigan, was unabashedly midwestern middle class, with a cheerful equanimity about almost everything but the Beatles, whom she absolutely adored. We were working with the intricacies of reproduction in ferns, and the ferns still had the upper hand.

Just as the singing began, Lana burst back into the room from her run to the Coke machine, announcing breathlessly that Mrs. Nesselrode, our house counselor, was frantically phoning the campus cops. Nessie was a scatterbrained but harmless old bird, dedicated to intricate embroidery, premarital chastity, African violets and vile herbal teas. She believed wholeheartedly in the authority of the campus cops, perhaps because they were among the very few persons on campus older than she.

But before the pair of decrepit World War I vets could trundle to the scene, somebody slipped into the Second South pressing room, gathered every scrap of underwear drying on the racks and pitched it out one piece at a time. It was an hour later before I realized that four of the brassieres wafting down to the eagerly uplifted hands of the House H freshmen belonged to me. And were clearly identifiable as mine by the name tags Mama had sewn into every item I owned.

The next evening I got a Contemporary Card in my mailbox.

SOMETHING'S MISSING!!! proclaimed a grinning ape on the front. Inside, neatly glued to the page, was a name tag reading LAUREL MAY HOLLINGSWORTH. Underneath somebody had scrawled 36C, THAT'S FOR ME! and the only signature was a giant "H."

The next afternoon I got a loutish phone call from some basso profundo who sang "Ain't got nothing but loving, baby, thirty-six C" to the tune of "Eight Days a Week." I hung up in tears and the next morning when I got off the bus at West for a bio lecture, I saw one of my utilitarian Maidenforms gracing the statue of J. B. Duke in front of the Chapel. Ordinarily I enjoyed riding the mile and a half to West Campus, which positively pulsated with energy. All the boys lived there and most classes were held on West, in breathtaking Gothic buildings with fascinating gargoyles and countless enclosed courtyards and stone steps and covered porticoes. I particularly loved the Duke Chapel, which rose gracefully one hundred twenty feet, dominating the campus effortlessly and magnificently.

But this was too unbearable. I got right back on the bus, went home to East and took to my bed, rising only for meals and the occasional Dope Shop milkshake and cheeseburger. There was nothing threatening about the bucolic tranquillity of the Women's College East Campus, with its red brick Georgian dorms and perfectly manicured grassy quad.

Three days later, as I lay in bed with my ASLEEP sign on the door and a particularly mournful Judy Collins album playing, Pren swept into the room. She turned on the lights, snapped up the shade and ordered me out of bed.

"This is ridiculous, Laurel," she said with gentle annoyance. "You're acting like a four-year-old and I really think it's gone on long enough. Nothing you can do will change what's happened, after all."

"You can't possibly understand," I wailed. "The humiliation is so awful. Bad things don't happen to you. Your life is perfect."

"That's just what I used to tell myself every night when I lay in bed at the home, wishing I could see my toes without my belly being in the way. Don't try to pull any of that 'you don't understand' garbage on me,

Laurel." Her tone softened significantly as she touched my shoulder. "I understand perfectly well, really I do. But I know this too. After a while you might just as well dust yourself off and get back up." Then she gathered her books and headed for the language lab.

She was right, of course. And over the years I have thoroughly mastered the art of dusting myself off and getting back up. What I haven't gotten used to is being knocked down in the first place.

The familiar strains of "My Girl" came blasting out of the Beta section as Pren and I ascended the stairs to their open house. Sophomore J. J. Webster met us at the door with arrogant charm. J.J. was a textbook illustration of the species Jadius Preppius, the handsome descendant of three generations of Wall Street lawyers. He had meandered through Andover under the assumption he would end up at Harvard, just like Dad and Gramps and his two older brothers. But J.J., like so many of his cohorts, had not reckoned that he would be competing with the entire Baby Boom. Shattered by his fistful of Ivy League rejection letters, he had settled into his Southern Safety School for four years of draft-evasive easy courses, sophisticated hijinks and cutthroat bridge.

"Good to see you, Laurel," he said with artful boredom, but sounding almost as if he meant it. In the Prentiss Granger Dating Derby, he had won my inside track by being invariably friendly to me, something most of the other suitors never bothered with. "Help yourself to some Purple Passion and put a little hair on your chest."

Pren and J.J. wandered off arm in arm as the Rush Chairman grudgingly handed me a name tag. I was not the sort of girl Beta really wanted at this party, which was intended to winnow out the crème de la crème of the female freshman class, in a search that would ultimately provide dates for prospective Betas during fraternity rush at Semester Break.

The Purple Passion was every bit as bilious as it looked, laced with a deadly concentration of grain alcohol and tasting faintly of gym shoes. I drank it anyway, glad to have something to do with my hands.

I could now see why Pren was so attracted to the group, insisting that I meet them even though I had a brand new issue of *Glamour* that demanded my immediate attention. The confidence level was astonishing. Charm fairly oozed up the walls as soul music blared from the jukebox. Perfectly turned out girls wearing pledge pins from the best sororities flirted effortlessly with the world-weary sons of Back Bay bankers and

Manhattan business tycoons. The jukebox poured out soul music classics. The room grew hot, crowded and stuffy, but the Betas took it all in stride, casually shedding their two-hundred-dollar sport coats, lackadaisically loosening their rep ties and generously imbibing from highball glasses filled with amber fluids. None of them, I noticed, were drinking Purple Passion.

Pren seemed perfectly at ease, but I felt like a bowl of chitlins at a French state dinner. I was just about to mosey along when Pren dropped beside me on the corner sofa where I had taken refuge. J.J. had vanished.

"C'mon," she whispered conspiratorially. I followed her into the hall where she sighed in mock relief. "I was about to evaporate from the heat. Let's go get a real drink."

I did not want a real drink. I wanted to go home. But I followed her dutifully up the stairs, in flagrant violation of half a dozen social regulations. On the third floor, as if to assure that my discomfort be as thorough as possible, a boy walked past us wearing only jockey shorts. "Ladies," he murmured with a nod.

Pren sauntered into the last room on the right, where I was amazed to find a massive Confederate flag hanging on the wall. It belonged to J.J.'s roommate, an unreconstructed lad from Macon, and it seemed wildly out of place in this Yankee stronghold. A makeshift bar was set up in one corner and J.J. was fiddling with what looked like the control panel of a Piper Cub. It turned out to be simply a record player, the first stereo component setup I ever saw. Everyone in Wognum had little portable record players, the kind that folded together into something resembling a big suitcase. Component systems were largely an item for the future back then, though naturally the Betas were on the cutting edge of sound fidelity. Where hedonism was involved, they always seemed to be in the forefront.

The wall over J.J.'s bed was hung with Oriental pictures. As I perched primly on the edge of the bed, I looked at them more closely, thinking to remark politely about how nicely the room was decorated. Two things happened almost simultaneously. I realized that the Oriental pictures were blatantly, if confusingly, pornographic, and I leaned sideways and dislodged some six years worth of stacked *Playboys*.

Four bourbons later I smashed myself into the back of J.J.'s Stingray and we drove to Chapel Hill for dinner. I was barely ambulatory by then and only semiconscious, but I revived considerably as the black waiters at the Zoom scurried past us with platters of sizzling steaks.

"So do you agree with Pren that the Betas are plastic and superficial, Laurel?" J.J. seemed very sincere and earnest as he leaned across the table, but I was just sober enough not to be totally fooled.

"No, and I've stopped beating my wife too."

They both laughed. "Don't try to bully Laurel," Pren warned him. "She's no naïve little country girl, you know."

Since when? "Your jukebox is terrific," I offered. "It's about the best I've ever heard. Y'all are real lucky to have it."

"Luck has nothing to do with it," sniped Pren. "It's just a question of money."

"And what in this world isn't?" J.J. asked with a twinkle.

"Equality. Intellectual achievement. Compassion. And me," replied the textile heiress from South Carolina.

I choked on my garlic bread.

It is sometimes hard for me to accept how tranquil and traditional that first year of college was. The biggest campus problem was apathy, lackadaisically discussed and never alleviated. And the biggest dorm scandal was the girl who was suspended for copying an article verbatim from a journal edited by her professor. She'd been up four days on Dexedrine. We played bridge, sometimes for seven or eight hours at a stretch, even while we waited for the Union dinner line to open.

Joining the springtime hordes sunbathing behind Wognum in my discreet one-piece bathing suit, I discovered to my astonishment that many upperclassmen actually planned their spring schedules around sun time. We played bridge as we sunbathed, wiping our exposed flesh with iodine-tinted baby oil. It was a very quiet, very placid, and although we didn't realize it, a very final spring of innocence.

We had no way of knowing that the next year would bring the Duke Vigil, the one following that the Afro-American Society building takeover and our final semester Kent State and Cambodia. And if anybody had tried to tell us that, we would not have understood.

We didn't believe in politics. We believed in bridge.

Chapter 3 _____

Assistant Professor Robert L. McCoy paced back and forth across the front of the classroom, lecturing intensely on slave conditions in the Old South to a generally lethargic class of about two dozen sophomores. He was short and slight and hopelessly ill-kempt, dressed as always in a ratty brown pullover sweater, wrinkled khaki pants and combat boots. His hair did not appear to have made contact with a comb for weeks and years of chain-smoking had left his teeth a dingy yellow beneath his scraggly walrus moustache. Even now he was nonchalantly dropping ash from his sixth Camel of the period.

He did not take attendance and seven weeks into the fall semester, our numbers had dwindled sharply. I could easily have cut the entire semester and just used Pren's notes, but despite my personal distaste for Bob McCoy, I kept coming back. I had never before shared a class with Prentiss Granger and loved to watch her in action, particularly since the subject, American history, was one so dear to her heart.

And active she was. Beside me I could see her hand shooting into the air. I lit another cigarette of my own. At a quarter a pack, two dollars a carton, it hardly paid not to smoke in Durham, birthplace of a fifth of the world's cigarettes. I even smoked on my way to gym class.

"Yes, Miss Granger?" McCoy sounded impatient, but he knew her name. She was one of those eager beavers who was always right up to the minute on all the reading, and it was a rare class period when she didn't pipe up about something. If she hadn't been my best friend, I'd have hated her for being such a brownnose.

"I think you've left something out," she began. "Of course heavy patrolling and lack of education and keeping out the rebellious Maroons from the Caribbean were deterrents to slave insurrections. So were severe retaliation and disproportionate punishment. But a lot of slaves really weren't all that unhappy, if you take everything into consideration."

"You mean they got their chitlins and watermelon and they just plum lapped it up?" His feigned antebellum darkie accent was atrocious, as southern black imitations by northern whites almost invariably are. There were a couple of titters from the back of the room and I saw Pren flush suddenly.

"No I don't," she answered angrily. "I mean that there were decent slave owners at least as often as hideous ones. And for that matter, if chitlings is the only food you've ever known and you're not hungry, you might just think a big porterhouse steak would make a terrible meal. Not everybody was getting whipped twenty-four hours a day. As long as there's no mass communication and limited education, a little kindness can go a long way."

"There was a book written in 1900 by William Drewry which echoed what you're saying," McCoy replied condescendingly. "Drewry concluded that none of the slave rebellions in Virginia—and this included Nat Turner, of course—resulted from white cruelty. He also said that it was abolitionists stirring up those wonderfully contented slaves. Outside agitators, if you will, the same kind Ronald Reagan thinks are responsible for student protests at Berkeley. The argument is equally fallacious in both situations. What does Aptheker have to say about slave uprisings, Miss Granger?"

"According to Aptheker," Pren answered immediately, "any time two slaves got together to complain about anything, it was an insurrection. He seems to me to exaggerate." I was impressed by her audacity in contradicting him, but even more astonished that she was familiar with the Aptheker book, which was not even required reading, but only recommended. I hadn't even cracked the main text yet.

"Perhaps you're bringing a little prejudice of your own to Aptheker, Miss Granger. He is, after all, a marxist." He pronounced the word with a deliberate sneer. Bob McCoy was a marxist too, one of many factors which made it quite apparent that he would gain tenure at Duke right after Eldridge Cleaver did.

A rattling bell sounded far off in the building. McCoy smirked at Pren. "We'll have to continue this discussion next time, Miss Granger." He turned and began to collect his papers as the room rustled into motion.

Pren and I crossed the quad and walked down to the post office. "I just don't understand what you think is so special about him," I said. "For God's sake, Pren, he looks like a rag picker!"

"Physical appearances mean nothing," she lectured sternly. She was wearing a forest green wool A-line miniskirt, matching textured tights, and a crisp white ruffly blouse, all very Carnaby Street. The previous evening she had spent ten minutes meticulously rolling her hair and another forty-five under the hair dryer. "The important thing is what he has to say."

"But it's so hard to *hear* what he has to say, because he's always so belligerent about it. All I can ever hear is *how* he says what he says. The way he belittles you infuriates me. I don't see why you bother talking at all."

She shrugged. "Oh, I don't really mind the way he talks to me. It's not like he's different with anybody else. That's just his style."

"Being abrasive and obnoxious isn't my idea of style."

"Be that as it may, he's a fascinating historian. I'm getting things out of this course that I didn't even know existed. It's far and away the best course I've had at Duke. I think it's just his politics that makes you nervous, Laurel."

"Don't be ridiculous," I huffed, though there was unquestionably some truth to what she said.

"I'm pregnant again." Pren passed me the three-pound Whitman's Sampler J. J. Webster had sent her for Valentine's Day.

I had just taken a big gulp of Tab and was saved from having to respond immediately. I was too stunned to speak anyway. I was still very much a virgin and it seemed quite clear to me that no respectable unmarried college sophomore ought to be carrying her second child. "That's just great. What are you going to do, drop out or get married? Or maybe both?"

"Neither."

I had a feeling I knew where that one was leading and I decided to evade the issue for a minute. "Who knows about this?"

"Just you. It's hardly the sort of thing I could call a candlelight for, after all."

I laughed despite myself at the image of the clustered Pi Phis in their A-line shirtwaists and arrow pins, earnestly passing the candle. Through lavaliere, pinning, engagement and even marriage rounds, as the tension and confusion escalated, the candle would continue to burn. Everybody'd be splattered with wax and the stub would be two inches high by the time Prentiss Granger took her mighty huff and started passing out cigars.

"Wait a minute. You mean you haven't even told J.J.?"

Her eyes widened innocently. "Who says this has anything to do with J.J.?"

"But I thought. . . ."

She grinned. "Relax. Yes, of course it's J.J.'s. But I'm certainly not going to tell him. I suppose I'm kind of in love with J.J., though not really as much as I used to be. But even if I did want to get married, which I don't, you know he'd make a terrible husband and an even worse father. It's all he can do to drag his body to class every third day or so. No, I'm going to have an abortion. It's all arranged for next Friday night. I know you don't believe in abortion, Laurel, but I need your help. The guy's down across the border in South Carolina and I won't be able to drive when it's over."

And so it happened that we slipped out of town on a dank winter night in a Ford borrowed from Pren's Pi Phi Big Sister, signed out to visit Aunt Nell and the Missionary League in Columbia. The oppressive burnt raisin smell of drying tobacco clung to our clothes long after we were out of Durham.

"This scares me a little," Pren confided as we tore down the highway toward our assignation with death. She was driving because I was too jittery. I was more than a little ambivalent about the whole thing. Abortion was murder. Pren was my best friend and idol. Pren was having an abortion. Elementary education majors didn't have to take logic, but even I could follow that one through.

"It ought to," I snapped back. "Do you know how many girls die from these things? What am I supposed to do if something goes wrong?"

"Hush, Laurel," she chided. "Nothing's going to go wrong. This guy's supposed to be very good and he's a regular doctor. I know for a fact that Lucy Haverford went to him four months ago and she's just fine. Anyway, it's not as if I had a choice."

"I just don't understand how this happened," I whined. "You're supposed to be so smart."

It was dark in the car but I could see tears start down her cheeks and immediately I was contrite. Maybe I had no right to be critical, anyway. Nobody wanted *my* lush young flesh, after all. It was entirely possible that one reached a point where wanton desire triumphed over all common sense and one was a prisoner of passion. It happened all the time in the soft-core porn books that circulated through Wognum, tomes with titles like *Web of Lust, Passion Pool* and *Call Me Rod*.

"Oh, Laurel," she said finally, "I don't understand either. You may not believe me, but I've only done it with two guys and ever since that awful first time, always with precautions."

I lightened my tone, remembering my role as pep squad. "Maybe the precaution you really need is a chastity belt."

She laughed. "If it's all the same to you, I'll settle for a prescription for the Pill." There was, it was rumored, a dermatologist over at Duke Hospital who would prescribe birth-control pills to any coed sufficiently cheeky to ask.

"That'll be a comfort. Just promise you won't put a sign on the mirror with Snoopy saying 'Don't forget the pill.' " There was precisely such an apparition on an engaged senior's door down the hall. The Pill was a relatively new development and only the heavily acned or soon-to-be-wed would 'fess up to taking it. Even they would soon learn to keep quiet, as the theft of birth-control pills became a campus-wide crime epidemic.

"No Snoopy," she promised, and moved abruptly to yet another monologue on the Tet Offensive. By now I knew an astonishing amount about Tet, having received countless daily briefings on the subject from my own personal military adviser ever since the first VC sapper slipped over the U.S. Embassy wall in Saigon. I had also heard Pren's end of several spirited long-distance military dissections with her father, wondering at the audacity of her attacks on General Westmoreland, a South Carolina boy and old West Point chum of the Major's. Pren found my disinterest appalling, particularly in light of my brother Lee's presence in Quang Tri Province. But somehow I knew that Lee would be just fine, returning all too soon to resume our well-established relationship. For as long as I could remember, he had condescended to me and I had cheerfully ignored him.

I hoped that Pren's abortion would go fairly quickly. I presumed that a doctor would not be using a rusty coat hanger, but beyond that I knew nothing about such procedures. We sat in a waiting room strewn with dozens of different pamphlets on baby and child care. The walls were plastered with portaits of babies, which seemed to me, under the circumstances, ghastly.

The only other occupants of the waiting room were a sobbing teenager and her martinet mother, both of whom looked very trashy. There were no ashtrays and I had to keep going outside to smoke, shivering in the chilly mist of the late winter night. I managed to stay calm until Pren was summoned inside, when I immediately got so nervous that I barely made it to the bathroom to throw up.

She was gone for forty-five minutes and when she stumbled back into the waiting room, I had to catch her to keep her from collapsing. It was long past midnight, she was clearly in no condition to drive anywhere and the doctor wanted her out of the office.

"I wish I could let you girls stay here," he said gently. I was struck by how much he resembled Judge Leslie Willoughby, back home in Piniatamore Parish. "But y'all have to leave town and find a place to stay up the road a piece. I stand to lose my license, you know, and I'm already stretching my luck scheduling two operations for one night."

Pren moaned softly in the back seat as I drove down the dark deserted highway. Finally I found a motel, roused the cranky manager and half carried her into bed. Then I sat and watched anxiously, wondering what I could do if something went wrong and whether I would even be able to tell.

At sunrise she awoke and told me to get some rest myself, promising to rouse me if anything happened. When I came to at noon, she was sitting by the window thoroughly engrossed in *The Autobiography of Malcolm X.*

Once we checked out of the Dixie Lodge, the whole episode took on a dreamlike quality. Pren turned very festive, suggesting that since we were signed out for the whole weekend, we really ought to go to Myrtle Beach and have some fun. We found a deserted motor court on the beach, where Pren read and studied while I walked along the shore pondering life and death and morality. None of the simple absolutes of my childhood seemed to apply anymore, and I had nothing concrete or specific to replace them with. The void this created was frightening.

That night at a local burger joint, a group of Clemson hell raisers attached themselves to Pren. Most of them seemed to be football players. Shortly thereafter, we found ourselves at a screaming brawl in an apartment packed with horny jocks. Doug Clark and the Hot Nuts was blaring and there seemed to be a dozen guys for every girl. Immensely relieved to have the weekend nearly over, I paid no attention to how much I was drinking.

The details are still mercifully vague, but I remember three things about that night quite clearly. I remember chugging straight from a bottle of Rebel Yell. I remember lying nearly naked on a lumpy mattress under the crushing weight of a linebacker who honked my boobs as if they were bicycle horns while ramming what felt like a telephone pole deep inside me. And I remember huddling in the corner of the front seat sobbing as Pren drove us back to the motel and spoke soothing gibberish into the black and dismal night.

The next morning we drove back to Durham. My head pounded with the worst hangover of my life, which seemed only fitting, and the excruciating pain between my legs was only partially physical. There was a ripped blouse in my suitcase and I was short one pair of underpants. The virginity I had prized so highly was gone forever.

I had lost that, but I had lost a great deal more as well. My moral indignation with Pren was laughable in the bright sunlight of that Sunday morning, a morning when gospel music poured relentlessly out of our radio and I was faced with the enormity of my own sin. I had lost my certainty that I knew what was right and what was wrong. I had lost the confidence that I could control my own actions. I suppose I had also lost my self-respect, but I was short on that to begin with. And I had lost the illusion that sex was a divinely beautiful thing, to be shared with the husband one loved. It did not seem beautiful at all anymore. It was ugly and painful and humiliating.

I steeled myself to ask Pren just what happened. "I got to you just as fast as I could," she told me, eyes straight ahead on the road in deference to my quite obvious anguish. "It hadn't been long, I'm sure. I could tell you were getting pretty loaded and then all of a sudden you were missing. I wasn't fast enough to stop him, I'm afraid, but I got you out of there as quickly as I could."

"Thank you," I mumbled meekly. I hesitated, not wanting to ask but knowing that I had to. "Pren, was there, I mean . . . Oh, dear God, what have I done?" I swallowed. "Pren, was it just that one guy?"

"Yes. Just that one."

I shuddered and closed my eyes. The sensation of movement was very strange as we sped down the highway, wind whistling through the vents. Sunlight warmed my legs through the windshield. "I guess I owe you one, Pren."

"I would say," she answered wryly, "that the events of this weekend rather cancel themselves out. And I don't think we need to ever talk about it again. But Laurel, remember this. What happened to you was an accident. It was a crime, really. It was horrible and ugly, but it doesn't have a thing to do with what sex can and should be like. Please remember that. I don't want this to screw you up and it could if you let it. Real sex isn't like that; it's very special."

"I'm not so sure I believe you," I told her, as the throbbing in my head vied with the throbbing in my crotch for attention in the Laurel Hollingsworth Memorial Pain Center. "But I'll try."

That afternoon my mother called to announce that my brother Don's wife Louella had given premature birth to twin girls, making theirs suddenly a family of seven. The news was strange, coming on the heels of our South Carolina experiences, an odd coincidence that made me enormously uncomfortable.

Since then, however, I have become a student of the Odd Coincidence and I no longer find such events too remarkable. The world is littered with odd ironies and coincidences. There is, of course, the catalog of parallels between the Lincoln and Kennedy assassinations. Susan Ford and Patty Hearst, both SLA kidnap targets, married their respective bodyguards during the same month. The high-volume champs of pederastic mass murder, Elmer Wayne Henley and John Wayne Gacy, shared the same dippy middle name. The Love Canal in Niagara Falls, honeymoon capital of the nation, brims over with one of the most deadly and virulent concentrations of chemical waste ever collected.

And *Hair* opened on Broadway to announce the dawning of the Age of Aquarius the very night that police stormed Columbia University.

Chapter 4 _____

The question of race is a curse all southerners bear, the psychological equivalent of chiggers and boll weevils and kudzu, and even calling it a "question" trivializes the enormity of the problem, suggesting that there might actually be an answer. But it's something we all wrestle with whether we choose to or not, and by the spring of 1968, I had come to believe that with due time integration might actually be possible. My family, of course, still believed that a brisk flogging might remind Rastus just how far he'd come already.

It was, in fact, only two days before the assassination of Martin Luther King that Pren and I had a long argument about him. What seemed incomprehensible at the time, however, was that I found myself taking the pro-King side, to Pren's heated pitch for Black Power.

The irony of this does not escape me. I had, after all, grown up hearing King referred to by a multitude of epithets, the most charitable of which was commie nigger. I'd come around considerably since my pubescent days when I could always get a laugh by slurring a reference to Monkey Lobster King. Actually, since the emergence of such genuinely frightening characters as Stokely Carmichael, Rap Brown and Eldridge Cleaver, I'd grown rather fond of the soft-spoken advocate of nonviolence. Even as sheltered an idiot as I could tell that the natives were very restless, and I preferred not to have them following some rabble-rouser who might suggest that they begin their search for retribution by slitting my tender throat.

"I just wish," I told her when it was clear we were at an impasse about Black Power, "that King would get off this anti-Vietnam kick. It hurts his credibility. Just because he's great at desegregating lunch counters doesn't mean he ought to be second-guessing American foreign policy."

"Twenty-four percent of the Americans dying in Vietnam are black," she retorted. "And the right to chomp chicken salad at Woolworth's is pretty useless to somebody who's dead."

"So all right, it's a problem. But you know my brother hates having all those blacks under his command." Second Lieutenant Lee Hollingsworth, U.S.M.C., was somewhere near Da Nang, gleefully zapping the Cong.

She snorted. "Your brother's a bigot and you know it. How do you think some guy from Harlem must feel having him for a CO? And having to wonder all the time if some other gung ho southern boy won't accidentally on purpose shoot the wrong guy with dark skin? We're asking black people to kill yellow people for white people."

"You sound just like Bob McCoy." I had bailed out of McCoy's class after one semester, but Pren was enrolled in his seminar, which met Tuesday and Thursday nights and generally left her frothing. "He's brainwashed you."

She glanced at her watch. "Perhaps. And it's time to go get my cerebrum sudsed out again. See you."

Any doubts I might have had about Martin Luther King evaporated instantly with the first reports of his death that April 4. I was shocked and heartsick. All we really knew was that King had been shot by a white man, which grossly magnified the guilt and pain. I waited anxiously for Pren to get back from McCoy's class so we could talk about it. But when she finally showed up, five minutes after curfew, she lay on top of her bed fully dressed and stared at the transom, ignoring me completely. When I drifted off to sleep some twenty minutes later, she hadn't moved and I had no way of knowing it was the last time I'd see her in the dorm for a week.

She was gone when I got up the next morning for my first-period art history lecture. I wondered about her throughout the day. Everyone on campus seemed somehow drugged, confused, disoriented. Finally I caught a glimpse of her at the far end of the East quad in the late afternoon. She wore a black armband and a very determined expression.

That Friday night, Marcy and Lana and I considered taking in a movie, decided that the available choices of *Gone with the Wind* and *Guess Who's Coming to Dinner* were a little too topical for our tastes and finally went down to the Ivy Room for bagels and beer.

Meanwhile, Prentiss Granger and four hundred fifty other students were marching three miles in the rain to deliver a list of nonnegotiable demands to the university president's house, a recently completed monstrosity with no less than thirteen bathrooms. There they stayed for two nights as "invited guests" of the president so that—stop the revolution while I total my late minutes—the women would not be in violation of curfew.

It was our first real campus demonstration, but nobody outside the president's house seemed terribly sure what was going on. Gradually we learned that the four demands were actually very polite, and that all could be agreed to personally by the president. The group wanted him to sign an ad in the Durham paper calling for a day of mourning, resign from the local segregated country club, press for minimum wage for university nonacademic employees and appoint a committee to investigate collective bargaining and union recognition at Duke. He refused all four.

So after two nights what had metamorphosed into the Duke Silent Vigil for Freedom relocated outside the Chapel on West Campus, just in time to greet emerging Sunday morning worshipers with a few gentle choruses of "We Shall Overcome."

News of the move reached me just after I fielded a phone call from Major Granger, who was predictably livid. "Damn communist agitators, they're everywhere! That pantywaist president of yours should have had the whole kit and kaboodle of them arrested the instant they set foot on his property."

It was the university's property, but I was not about to quibble with the Major. "I know Pren feels the same way, sir. But she's been working so hard on her independent study project, she's barely even noticed. That's where she is right now, at the library."

"Bit early for the library, isn't it?"

I laughed nervously. "That's what I told her too, but you know there's no stopping that girl once she gets her teeth into a research project. I'm supposed to meet her for lunch, and I'll have her call you."

"Tell her I want to speak to her on the double. If I thought there were one chance in a thousand Tissa was mixed up in this, I'd be on campus in three hours to take her straight to Bob Jones University." He softened his tone slightly. "And you watch out too, Laurel. Those agitators can be pretty sly. You get mixed up with any pinkos, you'll end up ruining your life."

"Yes, of course, sir. I'll give Pren your message. And please relay my very best to Mrs. Granger."

After he hung up, my hands were shaking so badly that I couldn't hang up the phone for a full minute.

When I got off the bus at West, they were singing "We Shall Not Be Moved." Pren sat in the second row between two guys I had never seen before. She wore very rumpled plaid slacks and a navy sweater, her dirty hair was plastered down on her head and she wore no makeup.

I tried to melt discreetly into the Gothic stone of Flowers Building while I listened to a series of apparent Vigil leaders deliver pep talks, lectures and diatribes. Only one diatribe, actually. It came from Bob McCoy and I later learned that while he had initially been named one of the group negotiators (inasmuch as his tenure had just been denied and everyone already hated him, leaving him with precious little to lose) he had already been replaced because even the campus radicals found him too abrasive. As he ranted that Sunday afternoon, I watched Pren's face and was shocked to witness raw and total adoration.

When they took a break, I caught Pren's eye and mouthed to her that it was an emergency. She crept out of the row and walked briskly back toward the Chapel. Up close I could see smudges under her eyes. She seemed thoroughly annoyed when she came to a halt on the Chapel steps and glared at me.

"Emergency? This better be important, Laurel, because it looks bad for people to be breaking ranks."

Breaking ranks indeed. She was the Major's daughter, for sure.

"It is, Pren, I promise. Your father called about an hour ago. He's absolutely furious."

She exploded. "Because I'm taking a nonviolent stand on a moral issue? My God, the man's demented. I swear, I'm going to call and give him a piece of my mind."

"I absolutely forbid it."

"*You* forbid it? Why does everybody think I need to be ordered around, anyway? So tell me, Miss Master Planner, what am I supposed to do next?" She was still mad, but her tone had softened.

44

"You find the nearest phone and call home collect. You burble and giggle and be the sweetest little fluffbutt who's ever hit this campus. You don't have the foggiest notion what all this nonsense is about and you can't imagine what on earth would make him suspect you'd do such a silly, undignified thing as *demonstrate*. In short, you will lie your fool head off."

She didn't say anything, just stared off at the assembled crowd.

"You have to, Pren. You know that. You don't have a choice."

She whirled indignantly. "Of course I have a choice. There's always a choice. That's what life is supposed to be all about."

"Save it for a philosophy paper. Your only choice now is to tell one small lie that will relieve your father enormously, or to go back to Wognum on the next bus and start packing your trunk. I'm not kidding, Pren. He meant it. He'll come up here and won't *that* be a dandy little scene? And then, come September, if you're lucky you'll be sitting in some stinking little Formica classroom at Bob Jones U listening to some turd who doesn't even have a Ph.D. tell you that the War Between the States happened because Abraham Lincoln developed a brain tumor and forgot to say his prayers regularly."

She laughed and I knew then that she'd call.

I stood outside the phone booth in Flowers Lounge and listened to her coo into the phone. She was sensational, a genuine dithering fool, utterly disgusting. When she hung up, she batted her lashes and simpered, "Did ah do a raht fahn job on thayat, honeh?" As I laughed she dropped the accent and gave me a list of books she wanted brought over to her on the quad. Pronto.

The week that followed was unlike anything I had ever experienced. Local 77, the unrecognized union for nonacademic employees, went on strike and certain professors and students scabbed in the dining halls. Nattily dressed heirs to vulgar fortunes joined career dishwashers in picket lines. The Divinity School faculty voted to forgo a scheduled raise. Blond Alabama coeds in monogrammed London Fog raincoats linked arms with black undergraduate boys from decaying New Jersey industrial towns. Joan Baez, passing through town with her new hubby David Harris and the Draft Resistance Movement, was publicly berated for confusing the issues and was largely ignored. Gene McCarthy and Bobby Kennedy sent supportive telegrams.

Throughout it all, Prentiss Granger maintained her second-row seat, singing when the group sang, listening attentively to any jackass who took the microphone, working Double-Crostics and studying diligently. But, partly in deference to the general strike of all classes, nobody else even cracked a book. Despite the somber nature of the whole affair, there was an underlying feeling of holiday.

More and more people moved their blankets out onto the quad. Lana went. Kitty, our FAC, went. Even J. J. Webster finally took his L. L. Bean goose-down mummy bag out there to sleep beside Pren under the stars. She welcomed him rather coolly at first, but before long the latent romance of the situation seemed to creep up on her and for a while she appeared to be thrilled to sleep beside her handsome prince in the cause of right and justice. The floodlit Duke Chapel made an extremely impressive nightlight.

Indeed, the entire event was essentially a very romantic one. We all embraced the illusion we were making a difference. We were proving nonviolence could be effective in creating social change. We were obsessed that the Vigil had to succeed, seeing it as some kind of absolute last resort.

Ghettos were in flames from coast to coast. Even Washington, D.C., was burning that week. But Durham didn't burn, as all eyes focused on the events at what I once heard a black woman near Five Points call "Mr. Duke's big school on the hill." As the leaders kept reminding us and *Chronicle EXTRAS* righteously proclaimed, if upper middle-class white students couldn't accomplish change through the system, what could poor blacks possibly expect if they tried the same thing?

It became, in a sense, a Holy Crusade. There was a thrill and satisfaction in linking arms to sing "We Shall Overcome" as the sun set gently through the Gothic towers. People became passionately committed and involved. And before it was over, at least twelve hundred hardy souls were sleeping beneath the ghostly shadow of the Chapel, watching wispy clouds drift past the moon.

I was not one of them. I came to believe in nearly everything the Vigil stood for. I was thrilled at the way it all evolved. And I was out there every day. But I was damned if I was going to sleep on the ground and swat mosquitoes for something as ephemeral as a cause. And anyway, I had other talents. I worked with the Food Committee, a very satisfying operation rather like bandage rolling or scarf knitting during a war and not coincidentally also a primarily female venture.

Of course it all had to end sometime. And it ended with a vice-president of the Ford Motor Company standing in front of the Vigil crowds in a persistent rain, hands linked to the demonstrators on his either side, singing "We Shall Overcome." The nonacademic employees, who had been making $1.10 an hour, were boosted to minimum wage, though the administration neatly skewered the previously pampered Duke boys on their own liberal guilt. They no longer got their beds made, their shirts hung and their dressers dusted daily. After the Vigil they just got their trash cans emptied, same as the girls always had.

And two weeks after we marched two abreast back to East Campus singing—what else?—"We Shall Overcome," there were violent and flamboyant demonstrations at Columbia, events which eclipsed our own small and successful scene and captured unlimited media attention. At Duke, however, it was back to Business as Usual for the traditional Joe College Weekend. I was far too hung over from Thursday night Float-building to appreciate the Friday afternoon performance in the Duke Gardens by Linda Ronstadt and the Stone Poneys. Of course there was no particular reason to pay much attention. Linda Ronstadt was just another cute young girl then.

And so was Prentiss Granger.

Chapter 5 _____

I took on a Mission that summer: I was determined to get to the bottom of the race issue, once and for all. The year had proven to me that I was appallingly ignorant and three months of otherwise dead time seemed an excellent opportunity to remedy the situation. I wasn't ready to tackle Bedford-Stuyvesant, but I had to resolve my own nagging doubts and conflicts. The death of King had touched me more deeply than I would ever have imagined. I also wanted to somehow retain the sense of meaningful accomplishment the Vigil had provided.

Pren had been enormously pleased with the plan, cautioning me not to be too blindly academic. "There's source material practically falling out of the trees in a place like St. Elizabeth. You could start right at home, for that matter. I bet you don't know the first thing about Cloretha, and you practically grew up in her kitchen." I hadn't even bothered to protest. She was dead right.

I had never done so much reading before. I plowed through *The Burden of Race, From Slavery to Freedom* and *The Strange Career of Jim Crow.* I pored over *Crisis in Black and White,* the Moynihan Report and *Rivers of Blood, Years of Darkness.* When nonfiction began to make me bleary, I relaxed with *The Confessions of Nat Turner, Invisible Man, The Fire Next Time* and *Native Son.* I was mesmerized by *Black Rage,* particularly the sections about black girls being traumatized by having kinky hair. The situation seemed remarkably akin to being fat. And my favorite of the summer was *Black Like Me,* which I read four times.

The shame of southern racism was at last within my grasp. By the middle of August, I felt like the most horrendously racist pig who had ever lived.

Pren was right. My casual strolls through town provided additional material that no case book could ever have duplicated. I had always been an inquisitive sort, if not downright nosy, because I'd learned early on that in a very real sense I was invisible in St. Elizabeth.

Yes, I was attorney Big Eddie Hollingsworth's daughter, but someone sitting quietly beneath a magnolia tree with an open book in her lap might well be an azalea bush. A familiar face on a routine stroll about town is noticed only the first two or three times, until she becomes a normal part of the landscape. And the girl who helps serve the punch at church socials or pass the sandwiches at a ladies' bridge afternoon hears many wondrous things.

I have often thought, in fact, that the possibilities for fat girls in detective work are sadly underrated.

It shocked me to realize that although I had been prowling around St. Elizabeth my entire life, even my *snooping* had been racist. It took a certain amount of painful self-appraisal to accept this, but I remedied the flaw promptly.

My major discovery might not seem earthshaking now, but for me back then it was an epiphany: Black behavior in any situaton changes when there are white people around. And these changes are profound.

Some of these behavioral variations I noted through the 200 mm telephoto lens of the Nikon F1.4 my parents had just given me for my birthday. I took so many pictures of black people, in fact, that I began sending my film away to be processed, rather than risk exciting the interest of the folks at Rexall, who routinely leafed through all the pictures returned from their Baton Rouge lab. I didn't want anybody to wonder why Laurel Hollingsworth was taking all those pictures of nigras.

Not that I wasn't shooting plenty of other things and people. This was my first single reflex camera, but in the ten years since I'd gotten my initial Christmas Brownie, I had learned that photography is a way of entering the world without really becoming part of it. I could relive bygone pleasures at my leisure and gain power over people who wanted me to photograph them. Best of all, I could shoot people the way I saw them and not as they wished to be seen.

* * *

And so I read and photographed and wandered about town in my quest for some kind of discernible racial truth. I had somehow thought, in the security of my Wognum dorm room, that I would be able to sit and chat with some of the black folks in town. I managed, with some effort, to exchange pleasantries with some and even had a few mildly enlightening conversations with the Reverend Thurman Jefferson, who evidently felt it safe to talk with a white girl because her daddy was important and he himself was bald, elderly and overweight.

Cloretha was the one I really wanted to talk to, however, and she was virtually unapproachable. We had a good deal more than four hundred years of history standing between us, after all. We had the present to contend with as well: I was the only daughter of her longtime employer, one of the town's most prominent and bigoted men. And we had our own peculiar relationship to manage as well, a relationship extending back to my earliest memories of childhood when I sat on the kitchen stool watching her roll and knead and stir and fry mysterious and wonderful things. I had undoubtedly spent more time with Cloretha than with my own mother as I was growing up, and it was Cloretha, not Mama, who cried when I was shipped off to Chadwick at the age of fourteen. So what could I say to her?

Finally I leveled with her. We were in the kitchen one muggy afternoon in early July and had the whole house to ourselves. "I feel like a real fool," I started, an opening so unusual for me that Cloretha stopped chopping okra and stared at me intently. She said nothing as I nervously kept shelling black-eyed peas.

I tried another opening. "I was in a demonstration at school this spring," I told her, annoyed at the tone of pride in my voice. Was I expecting her to get excited because I cranked out egg salad sandwiches for a bunch of guilt-riddled white kids from excessively privileged backgrounds? "It was after Martin Luther King was shot, and it mostly had to do with getting higher pay for the black employees at the school."

"Well, I 'spect them colored folk was right grateful for your help," she replied rather tartly.

"Please, Cloretha, don't make this any harder for me," I begged. "I'm mixed up enough as it is. Do you know I've been spending the whole summer up in my room reading about black history?"

"Knew you was up to something, all right. Not like you to spend so much time away from the kitchen."

Then I started to cry. She obviously noticed, but didn't say anything as she resumed her okra chopping.

"You see," I sniffled, "I feel real guilty about all sorts of things. I feel like because I'm white I'm an oppressor and it's all my fault somehow. But the worst part of it is that I don't even know the black people I know. I mean *really* know them. I just always kind of took y'all for granted and never paid much mind. And now I want to know these things and I don't know how to ask and if I can't even talk to you, what good is any of it?"

She stirred the okra into her iron kettle and brought a string bag of the previous fall's pecans over to the table. "Your daddy might not take too kindly to us talkin' this way," she said slowly. "Here, you help me shell these nuts and we'll have us a pecan pie for dessert."

"Never mind Daddy," I said firmly, having regained at least a portion of my composure. I abandoned the black-eyed peas gladly and began cracking pecans. "You'd be surprised at the things my Daddy doesn't know about me."

Slowly, carefully, cautiously, Cloretha began to tell me things. And by the time Mama got home and the pie was cooling in the window, I knew Cloretha and her family in an entirely new dimension.

Both of her parents had been dead for as long as she'd been employed by the Hollingsworth family. Now I learned that her daddy had died in a shooting accident during the Second World War. I already knew that her mama had passed on from consumption three days after Franklin Roosevelt died, and that the children together had managed to continue sharecropping their land. Cloretha, as the oldest child, raised six younger brothers and sisters on her own.

As a little girl I had wondered, quite naturally, why Cloretha had no husband. "The subject distresses her," Mama would warn enigmatically, fueling my already overwhelming curiosity. But taboo was taboo, and I would have swallowed hot charcoal before upsetting Cloretha, who held the key to a thousand spectacular desserts. I knew only that there had once been a man in her life, a soldier who died in World War II.

Now for the first time I heard the full story of Cloretha's one true love, a tall thin man with ebony skin, molasses eyes and deft slender hands that could effortlessly carve a horse or dog from a scrap of wood or swiftly fashion a doll from a husk of corn. Samuel Washington was a man for whom the local black community had held great hope. He had attended college in Tougaloo with the financial support of his church and the prayers of a hundred friends and relatives behind him.

But he left Tougaloo to enlist after Pearl Harbor, going to New York where he was finally allowed to join the air force. The "Spook Waffle," Cloretha said they'd called their segregated unit, because they were fighting the "Luftwaffe." Against all odds he finished training at a segregated camp in Tuskeegee and went to Europe as a pilot.

"Samuel was a brave man," Cloretha explained, "and he purely loved to fly them planes. Them colored pilots was called 'lonely eagles' 'count of they fly by themselves, maybe white folk figurin' nobody be safe with them or somethin'. 'Make me feel like God,' he say to me, 'up there floatin' over the land, lookin' down on my people.' 'You be God,' I tell him, 'your people be a sight lot better off than they is now.' Then he laugh and hug me and we go down walkin' by the levee talkin' about when the war be over." She sighed deeply.

The war ended early for Samuel Washington, in the sea off France, and a shattered Cloretha took refuge in the care of a gaggle of Hollingsworth children. She broke down sobbing by the time she finished the tale and we sat with tears pouring down our cheeks until the timer rang for the pie.

And ever since then, I've been haunted by that lost love of Cloretha Wilson. When I start feeling too sorry for myself, I think of her as a young girl with flashing eyes and saucy walk, strolling along the levee with her handsome young man in his air force uniform. And my own problems tumble into insignificance.

Pren had stayed at Duke for summer school, ostensibly to take some econ courses which had never fit into her schedule, but actually to be with Bob McCoy, a situation I preferred not to think about. After the Vigil she dropped hints that their relationship was no longer exclusively academic, and I steadfastly refused to ask any questions. I was afraid she'd tell me.

All I knew was that she'd dumped J.J., and that come September McCoy was scheduled to rejoin his wife in Berkeley, where she was resuming work on her doctorate in Asian affairs. I also knew that his wife had taken the kids with her when she headed west in May.

That Pren could carry on such a relationship with a married man offended me greatly. I couldn't even bring myself to think the word "affair" and the notion of sex with such an unappetizing character actually nauseated me. One might argue that this repugnance derived from my own experience with the Clemson linebacker, but that would be an over-simplification. I could still send my girlish heart into a swoon just think-ing about J. J. Webster.

Our correspondence that summer was less an exchange of mutually interesting information than reports from the front lines of increasingly divergent lives. Her letters were penned in tidy black ball-point script on lined paper torn from spiral notebooks, frequently detailing arguments with her father or possible scenarios for the upcoming political conven-tions. One letter came from Resurrection City in Washington, which she described as "dwindling dreams in a sea of mud." She never mentioned Bob McCoy.

My own notes to her were equally impersonal, rather on the order of book reports: *Tally's Corner* had opened a new world for me, I would tell her, or *Invisible Man* moved me to tears. She shot back an instant reply when I told her about Cloretha and Samuel Washington. "*Schwartze Vo-gelmenschen* (Black Birdmen) is what the Germans called them," I read "They were fighter pilots in the 12th and 15th Army Air Forces of Eu-rope. Didn't I tell you Cloretha would have a story worth listening to?" I have to admit I was furious that she could usurp even that small coup by already knowing about the Spook Waffle.

She also called me twice that summer. The first call came early on the morning after Bobby Kennedy was shot. I was plowing through an al-most unreadable history of the slave trade when the phone rang at 7:15 A.M. It was Prentiss Granger, bordering on incoherent. Indeed, I didn't even know at first what the problem was, since I'd retired long before the results of the California primary was tallied.

"Bobby, my God, how could they shoot Bobby too? Laurel, what's happening to this country? Do we all have to start carrying guns? All that promise, Laurel. He could unite blacks and Chicanos and blue-collar whites and there's nobody else who can do that. What the hell has hap-pened to America?" She'd been up all night and was more than a little soused. She rambled on about Armageddon and racial warfare and a wide range of other things that made little sense.

I puzzled over Pren's distress. She had been, consistently and for as long as I had known her, a spirited detractor of Robert F. Kennedy. Without thinking, I had accepted her views as my own. "He's a sleazy opportunist," I could hear her saying. "Anybody with those family connections didn't need to work for Joe McCarthy. Ever. There has to be a particularly high moral standard for people with inherited money. It's too easy to do harm without realizing it."

Her fury was almost uncontrollable when he entered the presidential race. "The galling opportunism!!" she yelled. "McCarthy busts his ass for months, then along comes this rotten little chipmunk and scarfs up all McCarthy's support after Gene proves it's politically safe to oppose the war. There ought to be a special place in hell for those kinds of opportunists." Somehow I doubted that Bobby Kennedy was headed for hell.

My second call from Pren that summer came the week before Kitty Moore's wedding. Kitty had been our FAC, the junior who shepherded us through Freshman Week, mixers, sorority rush and all the myriad traumas of a freshman year. She was a tiny bouncy redheaded girl with masses of freckles, sparkling green eyes and a lively but remarkably innocent sense of humor. She and her Pi Kap fiance Wayne Tehbolt had just graduated and in the fall Kitty planned to teach English to support him through Johns Hopkins med school.

The wedding was scheduled to take place in Lake Forest, Illinois, precisely as the Democratic National Convention opened in Chicago. Undoubtedly this coincidence never occurred to Kitty, but Prentiss Granger examined the calendar and wangled invitations for us both to stay with Ginger Lockford, an Evanston freshman on our hall who had pledged Pi Phi largely because she so admired Pren.

Now Pren rattled on excitedly over the long-distance wires. "Bob's going to be there for sure with Mobe, and we absolutely have to stay through the whole convention. I don't think Ginger's mother will get in the way. Ginger says she's still pretty worked up over getting divorced. And here's the best part. Her father has an apartment somewhere downtown. We might be able to hang out there if we're lucky, right by the action."

"I don't *want* any action."

"Don't be silly, Laurel. Next thing you're going to tell me is that the Yippies will be putting acid in the water supply."

"If nothing horrible is going to happen, then how come everything I read predicts anarchy?" The more information I got about the Democratic Convention, the more nervous I became. By now I was secretly hoping that some exotic disease, beriberi perhaps, would keep me from my promise to be in Chicago in August. It would be sad to miss the wedding, but I could wire best wishes from my bed of pain.

"The media don't understand anything about the movement. It's history while it happens, Laurel. There'll be hundreds of thousands of protesters there. It's like the Vigil magnified a thousand times, because this is the Democratic Party and they *have* to listen."

Which demonstrates, as I look back, a rather touching naïveté on her part, one I was not to see repeated.

Ginger had arranged to meet us at the airport, where Pren's flight was arriving an hour and half after mine. Before we even touched down, I was terrified. We flew over Chicago for what seemed like hours. I couldn't believe the size of the city. Cities were well outside my experience then, and here I was swooping down into the hog butcher of the world. I actually thought about the Sandburg poem as we were landing, never realizing how apt the pork reference would become.

Ginger was waiting at the gate, her blue-black hair a good two inches longer than it had been in May, brushing her shoulders in a sleek straight veil. Long hours on the tennis court had left her nearly mahogany and her cobalt eyes glittered against the dark skin. She looked very pretty and perky in a sleeveless white blouse, blue print A-line skirt and dainty white sandals. And she impressed me enormously by setting out fearlessly through the chaotic terminal.

Giant banners everywhere bid welcome to the Democrats from Mayor Richard J. Daley. Nobody met my preconception of Yippies, but there were hundreds of kids in all manner of political costumes, handing out buttons and bumper stickers and pamphlets. The energy level was so high that they seemed to be ricocheting off walls. Just in the time it took us to get to the Eastern terminal we encountered hyped-up kids campaigning for McCarthy, Humphrey, Ted Kennedy and someone I hadn't even heard of, George McGovern. I acquired, along the way, a totally incongruous button which read HUBIE BABY in wavy psychedelic letters. Who did they think they were kidding?

I watched Pren unpack an abbreviated linen shift she planned to wear to the wedding, then stared in astonishment as she pulled from her suitcase a pea coat, two T-shirts, boots, three faded work shirts and two pairs

of extremely weathered blue jeans. Blue jeans were still decidedly un-
fashionable attire in the South in 1968, limited primarily to sharecroppers
and mill workers. Duke students wore wheat jeans, or green if they were
adventuresome.

"So the revolution's coming home, is it?"

"I decided that two wardrobes weren't enough," she acknowledged
cheerfully. Her hair was pulled back by a scarf at the nape of her neck and
she was tanned to the exact shade of Cloretha's light gingerbread. "I bet
Mama'd be downright relieved by my miniskirts and hip huggers if she
ever saw this stuff." She stripped off her white eyelet dress and pulled on
a Berkeley T-shirt. It was much more faded than it had been at the beginning of the summer. Then she slid into a pair of blue jeans that had
been hacked off well above the knee. They were very tight, very short and
very sexy.

"I guess so! Where'd you get those, the church charity box?"

She faced me squarely, smiled broadly, then zipped the cutoffs flam-
boyantly. "They were Bob's. But he said he'd never look as good in them
as I do, so he gave them to me."

Her tone made that scrap of ragged denim sound like a diamond
bracelet.

Kitty Moore's wedding was quite the most spectacular I had ever attended. Her dress was a Priscilla of Boston original and her eight attendants floated ahead of her in lime chiffon and champagne lace with
matching mantillas and sprays of white Phaleonopsis orchids. The cavernous modern steel and marble church was completely filled. I rubber-
necked shamelessly through the entire service.

And the reception .... ah, glory, that reception! It was a splendidly
catered buffet at the Moore house, an estate comparable in size and acre-
age to many antebellum mansions of Piniatamore Parish. The main dif-
ferences were that the Moore house was newer and fronted directly on
Lake Michigan and that nearly everyone in attendance spoke in sharp,
wretchedly nasal tones. I was told repeatedly how quaint and strange my
own accent was. Coming from these folks, it was a compliment of the
first order.

I gorged myself on huge quantities of wondrous foods, but while
Pren picked desultorily at my plate through the afternoon, her mind was
clearly not on her stomach. She was barely civil to the parade of young
men who approached her automatically. She checked her watch at fre-

quent intervals and disappeared often into the house. She was trying to locate Bob McCoy, who had given her the numbers of several friends from the University of Chicago, any one of whom he might stay with.

Shortly after four-thirty, while the bride and groom were upstairs changing, Pren reappeared from one of her trips. She was beaming. "He's here," she reported excitedly, "and his wife's not. He'll be tied up with organizational meetings tonight but he's going to meet me tomorrow at the zoo. Now all I need to do is figure out a way to get downtown tonight. I want to get the lay of the land."

And indeed she did manage to orchestrate a trip to the Conrad Hilton that night. She snapped out of her lovesick languor long enough to ingratiate herself with a couple of visiting Pi Kaps from Virginia, and the five of us rode into downtown Chicago. As we sped down Lake Shore Drive, I was mesmerized by the spumes of foamy meringue which rose from the glittering licorice ice of Lake Michigan. It seemed quite unnatural to have such a vast body of water so far inland. But by then nothing seemed natural or real. I had long since passed into my own personal Twilight Zone.

Pren trotted down Michigan Avenue at such a clip that the rest of us were barely able to keep pace. I was mildly drunk and utterly terrified. Just the noise level unnerved me. I had never heard so many horns blaring and I was nearly run down by a giant chartered Greyhound which lunged around a corner unexpectedly while I was gaping upward at a building so tall I could barely see its top.

We were sweaty but respectable when we sauntered into the Conrad Hilton, looking exactly like five college students newly departed from a wedding. Everything seemed quite ordinary and innocuous despite the WELCOME DEMOCRATS banners. Later that week the Conrad Hilton would become a combination of armed camp, three-ring circus and medieval sanctuary, but on that Saturday night in August, it was just a big hotel.

Pren stayed up very late. Sated, drunk and in the final throes of culture shock, I collapsed into bed promptly on our return. Pren slipped on a Berkeley T-shirt and sat bathed in moonlight on her twin bed, under the shelves of high school basketball and swimming trophies abandoned by Ginger's older married brothers. The last thing I remember was Pren leaning on the headboard of her bed, chain-smoking and staring out the open window. When I woke at three A.M. with a splitting headache and a powerful thirst, she hadn't changed position and the room was blue with smoke hanging listlessly in the muggy air.

Ginger drove us to the Lincoln Park Zoo the next morning. I was hoping that if I could see Pren and McCoy together their relationship might be easier for me to accept. It occurred to me that perhaps I had been unduly harsh, that he might indeed be a finer fellow than I had previously thought.

I had, after all, spent the entire summer masochistically learning just what a selfish, unfeeling, racist boor I had been for twenty years. Maybe Bob McCoy had changed, or maybe I had been wrong.

He hadn't and I wasn't.

Before his belated arrival, Ginger, Pren and I waited inside the big cat house for over half an hour. We were assaulted by dreadful smells, fixed by the malevolent glares of some extraordinarily unhappy predators and treated to endless choruses of cacophonous snarls, yowls and wails. I have come, over the years, to believe in reincarnation, and I like to think that universal justice has brought deceased mass murderers, Mafia chieftains and the like back as these same zoo cats. The really horrendous ones—Jack the Ripper, Genghis Khan and Adolf Hitler, for example—are reborn in the wild where they live just long enough to experience all the joys that make freedom worthwhile. Then they are captured and shipped to zoos in temperate climates where they freeze in winter, bake in summer and are thrown a chunk of cattle lung once a day. And they pace forever back and forth in their shiny steel cages, eternal prisoners being punished for past sins.

My nose was running and my eyes were itching when Bob McCoy finally showed up in combat boots, filthy green jeans and an army jacket once issued to somebody named Kluzewski. We stood in a politically correct position by the black panther cages when he came up behind us and patted Pren patronizingly on the shoulder.

"Gotta hurry," he said, without preamble. "There's a Mobe strategy meeting in less than half an hour and I need to be there." He paused a moment, smiled lecherously at Ginger and gave me a brief glance of dismissal. It was clear that he didn't remember me at all.

"Well, see y'all later," Pren told us immediately. Alert, concerned and primed for revolution, she turned to hustle out the end of the building with her mangy mentor, never once taking her eyes off his three-day growth of beard.

I didn't see her again for two days and she didn't make it back to Evanston for four. And neither of us realized then that this week in Chicago would be one of those occasions which comes to most people three or perhaps four times in a lifetime: the life-altering experience. One cannot anticipate it and may not even recognize it at the time, but it is abrupt and final and irrevocable.

Chapter 6 ———————————————

The whine of Maxine Lockford's power sander drowned out the Doors on the portable radio Tuesday morning as Ginger and I sunbathed on the patio. I was totally overwhelmed by Mrs. Lockford's energy as she darted back and forth in her rumpled cotton Bermudas and sleeveless shell. There wasn't a spare ounce on her anywhere. Like Ginger, she had black patent leather hair and vivid blue eyes, but unlike her daughter, she brimmed over with ideas and opinions, many of them overtly political and decidedly liberal. Through the open garage door I could see AN- OTHER MOTHER FOR PEACE on her rear bumper.

Finally she shut off the sander and plopped down in a chair beside me, lighting a cigarette and reaching for a glass of iced tea filmed lightly with sawdust.

"I'll have to see about having Harriet Bell come by later," she said, changing her position again. In five days I had never seen her totally still. "She's an old friend of mine who's been teaching fourth grade for at least fifteen years. You'd like her, Laurel."

Maxine Lockford was the first adult who seemed to take my elemen- tary education major the least bit seriously. In fact, two nights earlier as she focussed in on *why* I wanted to teach grade school, I had been so taken by her obvious sincerity that I nearly blurted out it was because I expected to be a fat old maid but still wanted to be around little kids. It was the first time I had even mentally articulated this reasoning, which distressed me not just by its obviousness, but by the fact that I had never even *realized* what a pathetic stereotype my life was.

"That sounds great," I answered. "But I'm not quite sure what time we'll be back." Ginger and I were planning to drive downtown for a rendezvous with Pren, who had been gone two days now, checking in only by phone. I was worried sick about her.

"Oops, I forgot. Maybe we can do it tomorrow then. I want you girls to bring me a full report on what Blimpo McJawbones, da wonnerful mare, is doing down there. If I were twenty years younger, I swear I'd have gone with Prentiss."

The southern women I knew would have been in palpitations at the notion of their daughters visiting the growing madness of the convention, but Maxine Lockford was an entirely different breed. She did not simper or giggle or fall to pieces. She did things and organized and got people to do pretty much what she wanted. In a few months she would go to work as a real estate agent and promptly begin setting sales records. And this, mind you, was in the late sixties. *The Feminine Mystique* was still controversial, the expression Ms. referred only to a manuscript, Ann Landers was saying shut up and iron the sheets, and Gloria Steinem had recently been working undercover as a Playboy bunny.

"You've been awfully good about her leaving that way," I answered awkwardly.

"Well, it makes me a little nervous," she conceded, "but if even half of what you say about that Major character is true, I'd never dream of stopping her." Ginger had cued me on her mother's profound dislike of retired military men who refused to relinquish their wartime experiences, a reaction which had something to do with Ginger's father and the marines. And I had supplied a good hour's worth of colorful material on the Major's idiosyncrasies. Mrs. Lockford's subsequent decision to cover for Pren would ultimately involve her in deceit, prevarication and some none-too-subtle blackmail.

"Believe me," I assured her with counterfeit confidence, "Pren will be just fine."

We left the car in a lot on Wabash and walked three blocks to the Conrad Hilton, where we were supposed to meet Pren in the lobby. The sidewalks by the Hilton's side entrance on Balbo were overflowing with political flotsam and jetsam. We saw angry-looking blacks in dashikis and massive afros, bedraggled hippies with dirty hair and tattered jeans, peppy little girls wearing paper Humphrey shifts and insipid smiles, frightened women in their best Sunday suits scurrying along with eyes darting frantically about and hands clamped firmly on white envelope pocketbooks, paunchy grandfathers in plaid jackets and paisley ties feigning nonchalance, and Yippies in outlandish getups of every conceivable description.

To enter the hotel we passed through a squadron of at least a dozen heavily armed Chicago cops, all looking slightly preposterous in their delicate baby blue helmets. I did not approve at that point of the term "pig" when applied to law-enforcement officers, but to my well-trained eye, it was obvious that these were a porcine lot indeed. They had giant meaty hams, knockwurst fingers, drooping jowls, and slabs of fatback insulating their low-slung bellies. More distressing, however, was the undisguised anger and hatred in their eyes.

Inside the Hilton there were hordes of kids my own age, a larger peer group than I had ever imagined possessing. Nearly all of them managed to appear simultaneously sincere and furious, and by then they had ample reason for hostility. There had been tear gas and skirmishes with the police in Lincoln Park the two previous nights. As we pressed toward the main lobby, the only area of open space was one rendered uninhabitable by some kind of odious stink bomb.

We dashed through the stench and collided with an angry clot of middle-aged delegates from Ohio and Michigan. They wore Styrofoam convention boaters, HUBIE BABY buttons, and I'M A HUMPHREY DELEGATE pendants. Their dominant mood was impotent fury. "*Goddamned* hippie-dippie-yippie-flippies," one of them exploded in his most stentorian Rotary invocation voice as we passed. "Where the devil is that napalm when we really need it?"

This was the Democratic Party, I reminded myself, the party of the people. And the people in that summer of 1968 could not concur on anything except uncontrollable anger. I watched faces as we went along, searching for the self-satisfied smiles of those preparing to nominate their party's leader. Surely *someone* believed in old Hubert, who was at that point a shoe-in. But the folks decked out in Humphrey buttons and badges wore the most malignant expressions of all.

Suddenly we were swept up in a crush of young humanity taking positions on the curved stairs flanking the interior of the hotel's main entrance. Up the stairs we were thrust until I finally caught hold of a bannister halfway up and Ginger grabbed my arm.

A candidate would be passing through the lobby momentarily.

Rumors swept through the crowd like ripples fom a dozen rocks cast simultaneously into the same already choppy body of water. A murmur of "McCarthy, McCarthy, it's Gene" would sweep up one side, colliding with a wave of "Humpster Dumpster" coming from the other.

As the minutes slowly passed, cops cordoned off the stairway altogether and nondescript Secret Service men in drab tan suits positioned themselves at intervals, sweeping their eyes ceaselessly back and forth through the crowds. It seemed quite obvious to me that anyone with a gun and a sense of martyrdom could easily pick off a passing candidate. The rumors and noise continued their crescendo, then cut off abruptly as the candidate finally arrived.

The candidate was Hubert Horatio Humphrey, a small man with a round grinning puppet face grotesquely painted in a shade of Pepto-Bismol pink, waving and grinning as he passed, oblivious to the boos and jeers, just pleased as punch to be seeing such a grand crowd of healthy youngsters on a fine sunny Tuesday.

Within minutes it all started again, as a new corridor was cleared through the heavy crowds and the now familiar cries of "Gene! Gene! Gene!" began. This time we were even farther up the stairs, in a crowd swollen far beyond its earlier proportions. The next group of Secret Service men looked chillingly like the last bunch, automatons programmed to expect disaster. And this time it *was* Eugene McCarthy. The crowd could not have been more ecstatic had it been the Beatles, Rolling Stones and Bob Dylan all at once.

Where Humphrey resembled a ravaged relic from a defunct Punch and Judy show, McCarthy seemed calm, intelligent and reasoned. I could imagine conversing with him in a quiet book-lined study on a university campus. Never before had I seen even one presidential candidate. Now within minutes I had seen two. And could accurately report that my experience ranged from the ridiculous to the sublime.

Once McCarthy had been whisked through the lobby, the crowd dispersed with renewed reserves of energy. The war for the nomination might be near its inevitably unsuccessful end, but there was perhaps time for one last victorious battle. The peace plank was to be argued the following day. McCarthy's entire campaign had begun with the elements now comprising the peace plank, back in New Hampshire in the dead of winter. Here in Chicago in the dead of summer, the campaign would end with the same issue.

That it would end unsatisfactorily seemed self-evident that morning in the Conrad Hilton. But that it would end with a police riot just a hundred yards away seemed unthinkable.

In the sixties, of course, a lot of things seemed unthinkable. Until they happened, that is, when in hindsight they were perceived as inevitable. Because nobody had any idea of who or what to blame, everyone entertained different notions of *why,* which ranged from the military-industrial complex to nigger welfare handouts to Dow Chemical to SDS to General Hershey to Abbie Hoffman.

In retrospect, everyone was right and everyone was wrong.

It was Pren who finally found us, just outside the front doors of the Hilton. She was shockingly dishevelled, with a Band-Aid on her elbow and a peace sign painted on the back of her work shirt. She looked incredibly alive, however, with an intensity and verve I had never seen before. She was so charged up that it was impossible not to be carried along with her enthusiasm. We left the hotel and crossed Michigan Avenue, walking aimlessly toward the lake.

"We were in the park," Pren told us, with the nonchalance of someone who had spent a lifetime in and around whichever park she was referring to, "the first time I got gassed. *Gassed!* I couldn't believe it was going to happen, that they'd actually try to clear us all out at eleven for their ridiculous curfew. People were crashed already in sleeping bags and some of them had kids with them."

"*Kids?!*" Ginger was shocked. "They brought children along to something as dangerous as this?!"

Pren shrugged and grinned. "Nobody ever said revolution was easy, Ginger. Besides, nobody was making any kind of trouble. One of Bob's friends had a guitar and was playing all the verses to 'Alice's Restaurant' and then all of a sudden all hell broke loose. A photographer from the *Village Voice* was with us and he started shooting pictures of the pigs. The last thing I saw before the gas blinded me was this guy being smashed into a tree by one pig while another slammed the camera into the sidewalk."

I was now doubly glad I had left my own new Nikon up at the Lockford house. Initially I feared looking like a tourist; now I realized that to resemble a reporter was even worse. It was a value system I couldn't begin to comprehend.

"But are you all right, Pren?" I asked anxiously. "I can't believe this is all happening. It's not safe."

"Safety isn't really the issue, Laurel. We're involved in a tremendous class struggle here. You can see it all coming together in the crowds. The mule train from the Poor People's Campaign is going to march with us down to the Amphitheater."

"You're going to march to the *Amphitheater?*" Ginger stopped cold. "Do you have any idea what kind of *neighborhoods* you have to go through to get to the Amphitheater? You'll all be killed."

Pren looked angry, but she tried to keep her tone light. "By the Mau Mau, you mean? Really, Ginger, that's nothing to worry about."

Ginger was mad now too. "I happen to know a bit more about the geography of Chicago than you do, you know. I'm sure you can tell me a lot about Granger, South Carolina, but Chicago is *my* hometown and I know perfectly well which parts of it aren't safe." She paused a moment, considered, then offered the ghost of a smile. "Most parts."

"We'll just have to see," Pren replied condescendingly. "Look! Guerrilla theater!"

I think Ginger was expecting monkeys in costume. I knew better, but just barely. The performance in question involved a great deal of fake blood, some WASPs painted with Kabuki makeup to resemble Orientals, and a totally flaked-out girl in pink leotards and (so help me) pink satin toe shoes. We sat to watch.

"What about being gassed?" I asked. "You never finished that story."

"Oh yeah. I don't recommend being gassed, actually. But Bob had a rag for me with some Vaseline and we got out of there somehow. I couldn't see anything for a long time and then finally we were in an alley somewhere and there was a guy down the alley passed out or knocked out, I don't know which, and I still could hardly breathe. Bob's got asthma and he was *really* having trouble. I think I pulled him the last part of the way, and I remember a couple of pigs taking out after us but getting sidetracked when some kids threw a diversionary rock at them."

The girl in the pink satin toe shoes was now passing around the others in the guerrilla theater group. She was, evidently, a B-52 dropping napalm, a concept slightly too abstract for me. I looked around at the other people in the park. Bodies were sprawled everywhere and I would have loved to have the Johnson & Johnson concession. Everyone in sight was sporting some kind of bandage. Somewhere behind us a guitar played the familiar haunting melody of "We Shall Overcome." Despite the atmosphere of uneasiness, a lot of kids were sleeping soundly. A few photographers with suspiciously long lenses wandered about. Then a scraggly kid who maybe weighed a hundred pounds slunk by muttering, "Acid, acid."

Pren stared sharply at his receding figure. "*Acid???* My God, anybody facing the Chicago pigs on acid would freak out forever." That seemed reasonable to me. I still hadn't the faintest idea what acid did, but understood that permanent chromosome damage was only the tip of the iceberg.

"Aren't you worried, Pren? Be honest." Ginger sounded horribly concerned, as I knew she was. We had come, after all, with some hope that Pren could be persuaded to take in the rest of the convention from the Lockford rec room in Evanston, a safe, logical and politically sympathetic location. Ginger was more optimistic than I. I had a lengthy record of previous unsuccessful attempts at changing Prentiss Granger's mind and could testify that one might more easily entice Janis Joplin to sign on as WCTU poster girl.

"Of course I'm worried," Pren replied. "There's a joke going around that Leonid Brezhnev just ordered two thousand Chicago cops to be sent to Prague, and I don't find it very funny. This is a travesty of the entire American political process."

"If it's so awful, why stay? You can be just as offended up in Evanston and nobody's going to gas you there." It seemed logical to me.

"Don't criticize what you can't understand," she responded.

"And the Major's first daughter is beyond his command. Do we have to be trite?"

She started to snap back, then suddenly grinned. "I guess not. Old Hubie Baby seems to have the triteness market all locked up."

"The whole world is watching!! The whole world is watching!!" demonstrators chanted repeatedly through that fearful Wednesday night, as clouds of gas drifted over Grant Park in a melee of screams and projectiles and mischanneled furies. But the whole world never caught a glimpse of Prentiss Granger, and it is probably just as well. We were riveted to the two sets in the Lockford family room, absolutely terrified that her face would suddenly rise in screaming color.

I was in front of a television set any time that week that convention coverage was broadcast, actually. But I recall only fragments: endless choruses of "This Land Is Your Land" after a Bobby Kennedy memorial movie; the marvelously simple, achingly pure chants of "Dump the Hump!" and "Hell no, we won't go!"; Ginger announcing that she was thirteen before she discovered that Mayor Daley was two separate words. I remember strange musical juxtapositions: delegates holding candles singing "We Shall Overcome" while the band played "We Gotta Lotta Living to Do." I remember Abraham Ribicoff chastising Richard Daley from the podium and Daley's street-punk obscene response.

And I particularly remember Maxine Lockford answering the phone at nine o'clock Wednesday night. "Why, Major Granger, what a surprise!" she gushed. I spilled my screwdriver all over my plate of pizza. "I do hope there isn't anything wrong?" Ginger and I met each other's eyes in fear, then turned as one to watch her mother.

"Oh, dear, she'll be so sorry she missed you, but the girls have gone to a party tonight, over at the SAE house at Northwestern. I really don't expect them home before midnight. . . . Oh, they've been having a marvelous time. They've been playing tennis out at the club just about every day. Prentiss is just brown as a berry. She's certainly a lovely child, sir. You must be very proud." Like some kind of grotesque vaudeville act, Ginger and I gagged in unison. And after Mrs. Lockford hung up, we burst into rowdy applause.

I got very drunk that Wednesday night, largely because there was nothing else I could do to calm my irreparably jangled nerves. I could not understand how Mrs. Lockford remained so calm while Pren vanished without a trace into a woefully malfunctioning American political process. And I somehow doubt that she could have maintained such equanimity had the demonstrator been Ginger. But it encouraged me to know that at least one adult in the world considered college students to be intelligent entities capable of making their own decisions.

Finally on Thursday afternoon the doorbell rang. It was Pren, with three stitches in her scalp, a seven-inch tear in the knee of her jeans, an unrelievedly grim expression and a right wrist that resembled a Hubbard squash. It had been broken by a nameless faceless Chicago policeman who smashed his billy club into the wrist she instinctively threw up to protect her face. The first blow savaged her wrist, the second laid open her scalp.

I cried when she came in, sobbed while I hugged her and felt Maxine

Lockford wrap her sinewy arms around us both. A dark hour had ended, though its epilogue remained to be played out for another decade. Let us not forget, my fellow Americans, that what rose from the dust of the dreams that died in Chicago was the crew that brought us Watergate.

Chapter 7 _____

"You mean absolutely nobody here knows how you broke your wrist?" It seemed incredible to me. I pulled clothes from my suitcases and hung them in the closet, confident that the torpid Durham heat would remove the wrinkles promptly. Pren had already set our room up, even to the point of making my bed. She'd been back on campus nearly a week with the Freshman Advisory Council. The white cast on her wrist coordinated perfectly with her pristine white FAC dresses.

"I broke it playing tennis with Ginger," she explained sardonically. "Just like Ginger's mother told my father. I tripped sideways and smashed it into the cement." Even the doctor had lied to Major Granger about Pren's wrist. He was Maxine Lockford's cousin and she had the goods on him concerning a certain curvaceous emergency room nurse who had been along on his allegedly all-male June fishing trip to the Michigan Upper Peninsula. "And why would anybody find that strange? Do you see any clues in this room that I know the difference between George Wallace and Wallace Stevens?"

I looked around. The globe was out, but the Vietnam map was conspicuously missing. The Dylan posters were also gone, temporarily replaced by a pair of Picasso prints.

Just then two of her freshman charges burst into the room, eager to report on their downtown bedspread buying expedition. As they prattled on, I continued unpacking and marveled at the easy way Pren spoke to them. She was natural, caring and totally at ease. For somebody whose family could have given lessons in icy rigidity to the Nixons, she had come a long way in developing a warm personal style. It was clear that these girls worshiped her.

But once the freshmen were gone, she cracked off the mask of apolitical gentility. "I'm surprised I didn't kill my father before I finally got to leave for school," she said. "It really infuriates me to have to maintain all these different facades. I feel so hypocritical, but there isn't any way around it that I can figure out. It's a lucky thing we're both such facile liars, Laurel. And incidentally, speaking of lies, wait till you see what Ginger brought back with her."

What Ginger had brought back was three copies of a special White Paper Mayor Daley had just issued on the convention riots. When she returned from the Book Exchange later that afternoon, the three of us put BUSY signs on both doors of our corner suite and settled in for some hardcore hilarity.

"Listen to these so-called 'caustic items' confiscated from protesters," Ginger sneered. She sounded very much like her mother. "Band-Aids and Vaseline. You can sure do a lot of damage with those!"

"This makes everybody who was demonstrating seem so *fierce*," complained Pren. "You saw how ordinary and middle class most of those kids were. This makes it sound as if everybody under thirty-five was a ponytailed Maoist revolutionary carrying a backpack crammed with black widow spiders, nail-studded golf balls and Molotov cocktails."

"My favorite part's the injuries." By now I'd been through the White Paper half a dozen times. "It's so genuinely creative."

"You mean the injuries to the sixty civilians, grand total?" asked Pren. "I saw more than sixty injuries just the first night they gassed us in the park."

"Actually," I said, "I prefer the injuries to the cops. Chicago's finest sure are one tough bunch. Listen to this: 'split fingernail,' 'contusion to the left index knuckle,' 'abrasion to thumb,' 'bruised knuckles,' 'bruised left little and ring finger.' I wonder what kinds of weapons the demonstrators were using to inflict such horrible wounds."

"Faces and jaws, mostly," said Prentiss Granger.

Once classes started, Pren began to hang out with an entirely new group of people. She refused to see J.J. and denounced the Betas as self-serving, underachieving, hedonistic pigs. She did not seem to actually be dating anyone, which puzzled me. She had her own car at school that year, a blue Bonneville, and came and went at odd hours in frequently odder company. Her large new circle of friends included several former Vigil leaders, a smattering of *Chronicle* reporters and editors and just about everyone involved in the campus Y, which had taken the offensive on moral and political issues, be they local, national or international.

Pren's primary interest remained the antiwar movement. She would return flushed and invigorated from her evenings of heavy discussion and strategy planning. But though she spent a great deal of time with a lot of different boys, there still didn't seem to be anyone in particular with whom she was connecting. Finally one weekend around eleven o'clock, I asked her about it. We were both finished studying and she was playing *Blonde on Blonde* softly.

"I didn't really want to talk to you about it," she told me, "because I know you disapprove of my relationship with Bob. I don't want you to be any more upset with me than you already are."

I blathered on a bit about not passing judgment on her and just wanting her happiness, worrying about her well-being, and so forth. Finally she relieved my discomfort by waving a hand in mild dismissal.

"It's all right, Laurel. You certainly don't owe me any apologies. I know you're not trying to pass judgment. But of course it's not that simple." She got up and closed the door to the hall, putting out our ASLEEP sign as she did so. The door to Ginger's room was already shut. "I need to talk about all of this anyway. I think sometimes that I'm going crazy."

It was a long and slightly sleazy story, and most of it wasn't really news to me. She had fallen hopelessly in love with Bob McCoy's mind before Thanksgiving of the previous year. He was wildly intelligent and stunningly well informed about some of her favorite topics. As the year went by she found herself dating glib, handsome, socially smug J. J. Webster and wishing all the while that she was with awkward, ugly, brilliant Bob McCoy.

Then the week after she came back from her South Carolina abortion, she was alone with McCoy in his office, discussing references for her history term project. "I was standing by his desk, just ready to leave, when he offered me an Oreo. I swear to God it was an accident, but I kind of slipped and fell right into his lap. He told me later he thought I did it on purpose. Anyway, before I could even get really embarrassed, he had his arms around me and he was kissing me and I was kissing him right back. Part of me was yelling to get the hell out of there while I still could and the other part was melting. I don't know what might have happened, but then some other student knocked on the door. I split in about two seconds flat."

After that day she carefully avoided being alone with him again. "It's not that I didn't want to, Laurel. I won't try to make myself look better than I am. I wanted to ride off into the sunset with him and make love and talk about Hegelian economics. He made me weak in the knees and fluttery in the stomach. Now mind you, he's a married man with three kids and I'm dating J.J. twice a weekend and explaining every time we go out that I don't *want* his damn Beta pin. And I could hardly just forget about Bob because he was still teaching my favorite class of my entire life."

She avoided any further confrontation until the Vigil. Then the passion of politics translated itself into passion of a much more fundamental sort. "I was aware of him constantly. Every time I looked up, he was talking to somebody in front of us all and I'd catch him staring at me. I really believed in the Vigil, don't get me wrong. But having Bob there validated it all somehow. He was the one who *knew* about demonstrations, from Berkeley and the Pentagon March and all, and even after they kicked him off the negotiating committee, he was in on everything. I was going crazy. There wasn't anything I could say or do."

Eventually Bob McCoy took the initiative. During a break on Sunday evening, he slipped up to Pren and asked her to meet him in his office in ten minutes. "I won't pretend for a second that I didn't know why," she said ruefully, "and I won't pretend that I ever considered not going."

McCoy's office was on the third floor of the library, overlooking the main quad. When Pren arrived, the door was slightly ajar, the light was off, and Bob was standing by the open window surveying the crowd below. Pren moved up to join him and he stood behind her with his hands on her shoulders, beginning a back rub that ended shortly thereafter in a panting dishevelled heap on the office floor. "I could have stopped him, but I didn't want to. I figured hell, I'm on the Pill now anyway. I didn't have that excuse and I really wanted to do it. That's the part that bothered me, actually. I wanted to do it so bad."

I tried to imagine craving Bob McCoy's touch and inwardly retched. Never. Not if we were the last two humans on earth. Not to save my mother from Viet Cong torture. Not to ensure everlasting international peace. I could *do* it under those circumstances, I supposed, but I could never *want* to.

The affair with McCoy continued through the Vigil. It was an easy enough matter to slip up to his office at odd hours of the day and night. She found, to her surprise, that he was a gentle and accomplished lover, which made matters even more difficult. She found herself thinking not about nonacademic employees and human dignity and four nonnegotiable demands and Local 77 and minimum wage. She found herself thinking instead about the next chance she would have to sneak upstairs to the library.

One night the phone rang while they were just settling in and she realized with a shudder of guilt and fear that it was Bob's wife. Before he could stop her, she fled the office and took refuge in the basement stacks where nobody would think to look for her.

"The library was absolutely deserted. I found an open carrel and just cried myself sick for half an hour. And by the time I went back outside to the Vigil, I knew that I couldn't go on with it. It was just too wrong. Fortunately, J.J. was waiting on my blanket and I grabbed onto him as my way out. I knew that Bob knew exactly what I was doing and we both knew there was nothing he could do about it.

"But nothing was the same with J.J. again. I managed to put him off the rest of the semester. I hadn't been sleeping with him very much since the abortion anyway, maybe two or three times. So it wasn't that obvious. But I knew that something would have to give if we went down to the beach. And once we were on the road, I couldn't go through with it. I didn't hate J.J. or anything, but what I had felt for him was gone completely. When we got to Smithfield and passed that Klan sign, it triggered all this guilt in me, not just about Bob and J.J. but about everything. Can you possibly understand what I mean?

I nodded. I actually *could* understand what she meant. Just outside of Smithfield rose a billboard showing a hooded figure on horseback carrying a flaming cross. KKKK WELCOMES YOU TO SMITHFIELD, it read. JOIN AND SUPPORT UNITED KLANS OF AMERICA, INC. HELP FIGHT COMMUNISM AND INTERGRATION. The garbled spelling didn't say much for the merits of segregated education, but every time I saw that sign I still flinched and squirmed and wondered if God could possibly be in His heaven.

"So I made him bring me back," she continued, "and then it was summer school. Bob still had two sessions to teach on his contract and needed the bread, and I didn't want him to go anyway. Marylou, you know, his wife, went back to Berkeley with the kids and it was just us. We had to be discreet, of course, but that was fine with me. I just wanted to sit around picking his brain and hearing him say those wonderful brilliant things."

It was an odd scene to visualize: the lovely young coed at the feet of the scraggly young professor. It brought to mind *Beauty and the Beast* or *The Princess and the Frog.*

Then came Chicago and the gnawing haunting fear that Marylou McCoy might want to join her husband in the streets. Not until the afternoon of Kitty and Wayne's wedding did Pren learn for certain that McCoy would be alone. And shortly after we left her at the Lincoln Park Zoo, he informed her that the week in Chicago would be their one last fling. It was small wonder, then, that she stayed so dauntlessly in the front lines of the confrontations of that bloody, pointless week. It was her last chance to build a memory in his mind, that of a fresh and ripe and honest and persistent fighter for truth and honor. The last time they made love was in a storefront on Wabash Avenue with her wrist throbbing and the sound of one lone dispirited typewriter cutting stencils for the whirring mimeograph machine beyond the partition where they lay on some stranger's bloodied sleeping bag.

"It wasn't the way I thought it was going to end," she stated flatly. "But then again, part of me never believed it would end at all."

We didn't talk about Bob McCoy again for a long time after that night, and I kept a careful watch on Pren's social activities. She wasn't studying as hard as she had the previous two years, which puzzled me. She disappeared off campus several nights a week, joining her earnest scruffy political friends at one of the several large frame houses they inhabited just off East. I felt alienated from most of these folks, who were just barely civil to me. They seemed to make no effort at all to enlarge their narrow circle. And their arrogant self-righteousness made me quite content to be an outsider.

The 1968 political campaign continued, but from the nether reaches of Durham it didn't seem quite real and nobody seemed to notice or care.

Of course there were scattered exceptions, like Elaine Marhoefer, a plump blond DG from Birmingham who kept a Nixon-Agnew poster on her door and routinely visited every bathroom on East Campus to tape up notices of miscellaneous conservative events. She'd often drop by our room as well, aching to chat with Pren about politics or solicit a subscription to the *National Review*. I tried to be polite to her, but one time when Pren and I were both out, Ginger told her to take her fucking reactionary magazines back to her fucking Nixon shrine and never darken Ginger's fucking door again. After that she did not, in fact, ever bother Ginger again.

Not long before the election, George Wallace spoke in Durham, appropriately enough outside the police station downtown. There was an air of frenzy around the campus for days preceding his visit. Pren was going with a bunch of her new friends from the Y and the *Chronicle,* and I coerced Ginger into heading downtown on a hot October afternoon.

I gawked until I located Pren in a clot of Duke protesters. She was carrying a sign saying HITLER WAS TO JEWS AS WALLACE IS TO BLACKS and the *Chronicle* boy beside her held one which wondered BILLY GRAHAM IS FOR NIXON—BUT IS GOD? Wallaceites in the crowd had their own signs, of course, including one which begged SOCK IT TO ME, GEORGE!, a truly mind-boggling concept.

It was the standard Wallace speech, baiting the protesters and bandying the same stale proclamations that incensed crowds everywhere. There were cops galore, but nobody challenged three beehived ladies on the platform wearing dresses fashioned from American flags, even though Abbie Hoffman had recently been thrown out of HUAC hearings for wearing a similar red, white and blue shirt. Evidently it was okay to defile the Stars and Stripes as long as your heart was in the right place. The extreme right place.

Twice the speech was interrupted so that Durham police could charge into a crowd of protesters, whose offensive action was chanting, "Peace! Peace! Peace!" I saw a boy I knew from Montgomery, Alabama, pushed in the face by a cop moving through the crowd and remembered hearing him say that both his parents were fanatically loyal Wallaceites.

There was heckling, but not much. "Now I want to say a little about foreign aid," stated George Corley Wallace. "All you know is a little, George!" yelled a student near Pren. "You should be proud of your police and fire departments," drawled the candidate. "Yeah, firemen!" called a Duke coed. Even the hardcore Wallaceites didn't seem to have energy for much quibbling. And the closest thing I saw all afternoon to a violent reaction from the crowd was a local man who muttered, "I say keep families together. Bury George Wallace."

Finally the election came. I sat down in the Wognum parlor for most of the night with Pren watching the returns come in from the far West. It all seemed oddly distant at that point. Despite the fact that she detested all the candidates, Pren was busy every minute with her legal pad and lists of electoral votes.

I was surprised, actually, that Pren stayed in the dorm at all. My gut feeling was that she hoped Bob McCoy might call from California that night. He didn't. It seemed that the people had found new use for his organizational and revolutionary talents. The day after the election, students at his new place of employment, San Francisco State, began a long and bloody student strike demanding open admissions and a Third World studies department.

Bob McCoy, of course, was in the thick of the fray.

Chapter 8 _____

"Holy shit," Ginger muttered as we passed the Granger Mills complex sprawled on a hill outside town, eerily lit by floodlights. It was nearly midnight on the Tuesday before Thanksgiving. "You never told me you were a fucking robber baron."

Beside me on the front seat, I could feel Pren shift her weight nervously. "Didn't tell you 'cause I'm not," she stated flatly. Since she'd sprouted a social conscience, it bothered her enormously to think that she was part of a moneyed ruling class, though not so much that she refused her large allowance or declined the blue Bonneville.

By then we had zipped down the tiny main street and were winding up the drive of Azalea Acres. "What is this, fucking Tara?" Ginger asked. Ginger was a real sewermouth that year, delighting in particular at working scumbag, cocksucker and fuckstick into any conversation where they even remotely fit.

"Just home sweet home," Pren answered evenly.

"This place could be home sweet home for all of Wognum," Ginger shot back. And indeed she was correct about the size of the neo-Georgian monstrosity the Major had built for his bride after the war.

"Hell, this is nothing," Pren said lightly. "You oughta see Laurel's family plantation down in Louisiana." It was unlike Pren to snipe in such fashion, a clear indication of just how upset she really was. "You'd swear Big Sam was gonna lead the slaves back in from the fields down at Weatherly. Which, incidentally, Laurel seems to think is some kind of summer cottage or something."

But Ginger didn't seem to hear her. She was giggling uncontrollably as we passed the sign identifying Azalea Acres.

The next morning Ginger gawked in wonder at the breakfast spread. It was nearly ten and only our three place settings remained on the mahogany dining table. Covered dishes sat on the sideboard over sterno and I helped myself to a little of everything, with a heavy emphasis on the eggs scrambled with bay shrimp. Ginger, whose customary breakfast was two cups of black coffee, peered warily at a silver bowl filled with grits, then took some fruit salad and a roll.

"Is it always like this?" she whispered, even though we were alone. Pren was back in the kitchen saying hello to Willie Mae.

I shrugged. "Whenever I've been here it is. Willie Mae's an amazing cook. But actually, most of the family seems pretty indifferent to what they eat."

Just then Iris Prentiss Granger (Mrs. John Llewellyn III) swept into the room, a serene vision in green wool and silver filigree jewelry. Her rich chestnut hair was piled regally atop her head and her makeup was understated but flawless. I introduced Ginger, who was suddenly dumbstruck. Recalling Maxine Lockford's wrinkled dungarees, I realized how alien Mrs. Granger must seem.

Mrs. Granger poured herself a cup of coffee and joined us. "I understand the Pi Phis had a fashion show recently, Ginger."

Ginger stared blankly for a moment and I kicked her under the table. Iris Granger had no idea that her daughter had gone inactive that fall, finding the Pi Phi arrow dwarfed by the revolutionary sword.

"Oh yes," Ginger lied quickly. "It was really quite a lot of fun."

Pren pranced into the room in a beige skirt and sweater ensemble and kissed her mother. "I gather you've met Ginger. She's really an incredible tennis player."

"We were just talking about the Pi Phi fashion show," Mrs. Granger said.

Pren winked at Ginger over her mother's head as she filled a plate. "Did she tell you about the darling tennis dress she modeled?"

And so it went, gracious conversation about nonexistent events, while Ginger wriggled in her chair and nibbled at her roll, growing more glassy-eyed by the second. Not until Pren and her mother had excused themselves and we were alone upstairs did she register any real emotion. Then she collapsed onto her bed in shock.

"Is she always like that?"

I shook my head. "Usually she's a lot vaguer. She drinks on the sly, see. But I've never known anybody with a stronger sense of etiquette. Even half crocked, she can spot a social breach at a hundred yards. She lives in a little world of her own, but she's descended from three Signers of the Declaration of Independence and her pedigree goes clear back to Charlemagne."

"You're kidding!"

"Nope. Didn't Pren ever tell you she's a Daughter of the Magna Carta? Of course her mother's family lost all their money in the stock market crash, so she was dirt poor when she married the Major. And strictly speaking, she sacrificed her heritage by marrying a carpetbagger."

Now Ginger was really confused. "But I thought . . ."

I shook my head again. "The Major was born here, all right, but only a couple of months after his father came down from Connecticut and built the mill. The Granger family has a deep dark secret. At least one of their forebears was an abolitionist. With a printing press. And that sort of thing isn't easily forgiven in these parts. It probably wouldn't be tolerated at all except that the Major went to West Point, the southern snob's ultimate fantasy. And of course losing a leg in battle gains you big points in Dixie. Southerners are always into war."

She ran her fingers through her hair in wonder. "Is he really as crazy as Pren says?"

"No. But he's a bit on the brusque side. I guess he's never quite gotten used to the fact that he's a civilian again. After all, it's only been twenty years."

I kept an eye on Ginger later when the Major clomped in from the mill for lunch, issuing miscellaneous orders. He pumped my hand and nodded in acknowledgment at Ginger. He was still a handsome man, with deep-set piercing eyes, splendidly aristocratic cheekbones and silver-flecked thick brown hair which would probably have been very wavy if he ever let it grow longer than an inch.

When he learned that Ginger hadn't seen the game room yet, he insisted on giving us the tour himself. I saw her jaw drop as we passed the weapons museum, with its hundreds of hanging swords and rifles and sidearms, but she still wasn't prepared for the game room. It was a vast place, with half a dozen tables covered with mock-up battlefields complete with shrubbery and hundreds of tiny metal figures, each carefully handpainted by Mrs. Granger in her sole concession to her husband's hobby. Ginger's eyes glazed again as he went into the particulars of each individual battle scene.

"Looks like you've got more chess games going," I offered brightly. The shelves where he kept his chess-by-mail boards seemed unusually crowded.

"Thirty-seven at last count," he reported proudly. "If the damned post office were run like a regular business, I could double that. Takes forever to hear from the fellows out west these days. Fool bureaucracy."

On Friday morning Ginger stunned me by asking if we could tour Granger Mills. "When I was in junior high," she explained, "I did a big project about weaving and fabric production. I've always wanted to see a real textile mill." It seemed a nice enough idea; I'd never been inside the mill myself and Pren hadn't set foot in it for two years.

The Major beamed broadly. "The VIP tour leaves at thirteen hundred hours, ladies. Meet me in my office."

I had never heard such a din. It was obvious that the sturdy brick buildings fought an eternal battle to remain standing, what with the pounding and clanging of the looms and other mill machinery. Everything vibrated continually, including my own teeth once we were inside.

The machinery intrigued me, and Ginger seemed absolutely mesmerized by the whole operation. We stood and watched shuttles flash by on the giant looms, saw millworkers anchor threads and carry off bolts of vivid terrycloth for hemming. The Major insisted that we each take an armload of velvety towels when we left.

"My ears are still ringing," Ginger moaned as we walked toward the car when she'd finally exhausted her curiosity. "How can anybody stand that? You must pay those folks a hell of a lot to have them put up with that racket."

Pren said nothing and I was busy inspecting a loose button on my blouse. The fact of the matter, as both of us were well aware, was that Granger Mills employees were appallingly underpaid. The Major had driven union organizers out of town time and time again and paid minimum wage only to certain "skilled" laborers who were, coincidentally, all white males.

Ginger seemed to realize that Pren was consciously not responding. "Well?" she said. "What's the story?"

"The story," said Prentiss Granger, "is that you were right the other night. We're robber barons."

"Oh, come on. I was just tired and punchy then. You don't need to make a federal case out of it."

Pren looked Ginger squarely in the eye. "Making a federal case out of it is the last thing anybody in my family wants, believe you me. You think my father wants to be carted off to Leavenworth for unfair labor practices and racial abuse?"

Ginger was clearly embarrassed now and wiggling uncomfortably. She obviously wanted to drop the whole thing. "It doesn't matter, Pren."

"Sad to say, Ginger, it does matter. It matters a hell of a lot. How do you think I feel knowing that my family exploits practically everyone in this town so I can trot off to Duke and study the history of socialism and communism?"

"Duke's a robber baron school too," I reminded Ginger. "Old Buck Duke made his fortune by swallowing up all the competition and totally monopolizing the tobacco industry. And anyway, Granger Mills is the goose that lays a great many golden eggs."

Pren shook her head. "Only for people named Granger. Remember that "Tennesee" Ernie Ford song, 'Sixteen Tons'? When that was popular, my father made the radio station here stop playing it and warned the folks at the town general store that he'd be mightily displeased if they stocked that commie song. They *gave* him all the copies that they already had, and he had the kennelman hang them from a tree. Then he shot them into black confetti. I helped shoot."

"Oh, it can't be that bad." Ginger desperately wanted to get out of all this now.

"Ginger," I told her, "it's worse. But that isn't really the point. The point is that Pren isn't in a position to do a damn thing about it. It isn't her mill, it's her father's. The best she can do is educate herself and try to change things later. If nothing else, she'll probably inherit the place someday and then she can free the slaves."

"That's too long to wait," Pren said.

"So what are you going to do? Organize the folks at the mill into Local Something or Another?"

"Not a bad idea, Laurel. Not a bad idea at all. But I think that it would probably be prudent to wait until Granger Mills finishes paying for my college education."

"And graduate school too?" I realized I was baiting her, but what the hell. "We're talking about a good long while."

"I'll think of something. Just you wait and see."

I waited through the rest of the weekend for Pren to confront the Major about labor practices or minimum wage or anything to do with the mill, but she remained strangely mute. Ginger had assembled a time bomb and I had triggered it. The only question now was when it would go off.

I hoped to be somewhere else, like maybe Nairobi, when it blew.

Our junior year was filled with a wide range of minor political actions and activities. There were occasional teach-ins, miscellaneous rallies, the obligatory DOW SHALT NOT KILL signs when Napalm International recruiters showed up on campus. It was really all quite predictable.

The only real political event, a take-over of the administration by the Afro-American Society, was riddled with comedic touches. The take-over itself came at dawn, and since the colony of blacks inside Allen Building declined white company, everybody else had to hang around outside all day.

The air grew electric as rumors percolated through the huddled masses. There were the usual sorts of demands, naturally nonnegotiable, the familiar plainclothes and FBI men in ill-fitting brown suits with walkie-talkies and gun bulges. There was Prentiss Granger, bellied up to the barricades, prepared to be gassed for a black studies program. There were smug, pasty-faced *Chronicle* reporters whispering conspiratorially. There was the customary inflammatory rhetoric at a microphone on the quad.

But there was really only one question that rumbled through the day: Would the Durham police come on campus?

The answer came at dinnertime, when squadrons of Durham cops in gas masks suddenly poured out of the Sarah P. Duke Gardens and into Allen Building. They battered in doors, pitching tear gas containers onto the quad and through open windows. Then they split up, half going inside and the others turning their attention to the crowds on the quad.

The cops who went inside quickly returned to join the fracas outdoors. Under their gas masks they presumably wore very sheepish expressions, because it seemed that the Afro-American Society was no longer occupying Allen Building at all. Minutes before the invasion, the blacks had quietly vacated the building through a rear entrance.

Allen Building was utterly empty.

The main quad, however, was jammed. This was an exciting moment for cops and students alike. As the gas poured out across the quad, I saw several of the more rambunctious white radicals start to slug it out with the cops.

Alien creatures in ridiculous headgear manned giant fans, which appeared out of nowhere. It was a stunning shock. We regarded ourselves, quite accurately, as members of a privileged elite living lives of inviolable freedom while we pursued Higher Knowledge. The Durham police, just as accurately, considered us spoiled rich brats evading responsibility and the draft. Both groups had been aching for a confrontation for months.

On a purely practical level, the gas was painful and irritating and a thoroughly dreadful experience. The crowds dispersed rather quickly, with hundreds of students seeking refuge in the Chapel. The image of medieval sanctuary was quite splendid, but the fact of the matter was that the giant blowers were pumping the inside of the Chapel nearly as full of gas as the outside quad.

I hurried through the deserted dining hall kind of at a trot, not wanting to appear uncool or afraid but desperately yearning to get the hell back to East. At the far end I emerged into a covered portico and more clouds of gas. The choices were to go back inside and hope that it would end or to make a run for it. I could hear the yelling and screaming again and through the fog of gas I could barely discern the grotesque forms of masked policemen.

I decided to make a run for it. I headed out through the boys' dorms toward the Indoor Stadium and as I passed through the arches of Animal Quad, I tripped and fell. I wanted, at that point, just to stay put and die. It seemed easier. My shirtfront was sodden from the tears that had been pouring down my cheeks. When I closed my eyes I couldn't make any real progress and when I opened my eyes they sizzled in the acrid air.

Then I heard my name and felt a protective arm around me. "C'mon, Laurel, this way." It was J. J. Webster, materializing from God knows where, and if I hadn't already been dripping water down my face, I would have cried for sheer joy. I thought I might well be hallucinating, but if so, it beat reality.

I was grateful for J.J.'s lift back to East Campus, of course, but as he asked what he thought were casual questions about Pren, I could see clearly for the first time how far apart they had grown. His comments on the Afro-American Society seemed shallow and racist, and his anger at the tear gas was strictly personal.

"It was incredible," I told Pren later. "He didn't seem to have the slightest comprehension of any of the larger issues. Why, *I* had a better grasp of what was really happening than he did."

She smiled. "There's nothing so incredible about that. J.J.'s always been totally superficial. You're light-years ahead of him in political awareness and sophistication. The only thing that surprises me is that it took you so long to realize it."

Chapter 9 _____

I often used to wonder what shape sixties nostalgia would take when it finally arrived. Since popular culture managed to romanticize such lackluster eras as the Depression and the fifties, there would be no question of insufficient material. It seemed reasonable, actually, to expect the same sort of turbulent schizophrenia which made the decade distinctive the first time around.

I'd picture love beads· by Gloria Vanderbilt, stash pouches by Ralph Lauren, headbands by Calvin Klein. Tear gas cologne by Halston. Crash pad decorating featuring Indian print throws, black-light posters, cable-spool coffee tables and tie-dyed curtains. Sterling silver incense burners shaped like the peace sign. Movies about Rock and Roll Heaven with Janis and Jimi and Duane and Jim Morrison and Brian Jones.

People would give body-painting parties with acid-spiked punch and the punch, of course, would be Kool-Aid. I'd imagine how the folks at Kool-Aid must dread a sixties revival. Has ever a product demonstrated such bizarre karma? It all started tamely enough as the beverage for a generation, with fifties mommies ladling it out by the gallon to fifties kiddies. Those kiddies grew up and discovered that it made a dandy base for soluble lysergic acid diethylamide, and when its reputation was finally on a relatively even keel again, and the Electric Kool-Aid Acid Tests at last a dim memory, along came Guyana and the Prussic Kool-Aid Acid Test. And poor Kool-Aid had to take the rap for Jonestown even though the People's Temple stocked a knockoff called Flav-or-aid.

The only reasonable assumption was that nobody would know quite what to do with the sixties next time around. It would be a neat trick to deal with a period that managed to telescope the Apollo 11 moon landing, Chappaquiddick, Woodstock and the Tate-La Bianca murders into the same summer.

After the Allen Building take-over in the spring of 1969, everything on campus stayed relatively quiet. Pren had tentatively reconciled via long distance with Bob McCoy, to my sorrow, and was intending to go out and see him in San Francisco over Spring Vacation. She sold the Major on the idea that Pi Phi was having a beach week in Fort Lauderdale. The truly funny aspect of it was that shortly after Christmas, Pren had deactivated from Pi Phi altogther, a fact she somehow neglected to mention to her parents.

Pren was terrifically excited about going to California, yearning to be at last among those truly dedicated, passionate, concerned and utterly committed revolutionaries who fed their fervor on a blend of fog and potent mind-altering chemicals. Seeing Bob seemed of only minor interest, now that she had a new boyfriend who was, thank God, neither married nor a professor. He was, indeed, merely an undergraduate, a former Lambda Chi now living off campus. His name was Adam Gerard and Pren first found her way to his bed on the night of the tear gas on the quad. She swore he was an absolute genius at political strategy, with the potential to be a first-rate organizer of almost anything.

For his part, Adam was only too happy to share his lumpy mattress on the floor with Miss Prentiss Granger, who really looked terrific that year, was an asset in any social scene and could be counted on to remember the Vaseline and Band-Aids for any political confrontation. Her hair was parted down the middle and reached about three inches below her shoulders, hanging perfectly straight and eternally glossy, shimmering with just a hint of auburn in direct sunlight. She wore large slender gold hoops in her pierced ears. She had pretty much stopped wearing makeup but if anything, this enhanced her appearance, giving her a fresh, unspoiled natural glow. Plus she was trim and sexy in jeans and could wear a work shirt with such panache that you'd swear it was a designer original.

Adam was no fool. She led high and he trumped her.

Adam's good looks formed a sharp contrast to Bob McCoy. He was tall and slender, with crisp wavy black hair, large dark eyes, a marvelous peaches-and-cream complexion and exquisite ivory teeth. He was very vain, Pren told me, particularly about those teeth. He didn't even smoke cigarettes for fear of staining them, though he bent his own rules for marijuana.

When Pren got back from California, I picked her up at the airport for an immediate debriefing and drove straight to Chapel Hill. Over strip steaks at the Zoom, the story poured out of her. She had stayed in a large house in Berkeley, the kind anyone else would have automatically labeled a commune. "It wasn't really a commune," she said seriously. "More like a boardinghouse." A boardinghouse, it seemed, where everybody smoked a lot of grass and discussed Marcuse and Fanon and formulated complicated plans for redistributing American corporate wealth.

"I didn't get to see as much of Bob as I was expecting to, but there were so many other exciting things going on, I didn't really care that much. Finally it hit me. I just wasn't in love with him anymore."

I lifted my glass of iced tea. "To blessed revelations."

She grinned wryly. "You know, he was actually hurt when I told him. The male ego certainly is fragile. He kind of snapped back that in that case I wouldn't have any trouble sleeping with somebody else, just to prove that I didn't have any emotional hang-ups. I gave him a big grin and said it would be my pleasure, but actually I found the prospect just a bit scary. See, I never did anything like that before, just balling for the sake of balling. I always felt I had to be in love or something, not necessarily intending to get married, but with some kind of link other than the mattress."

I was rather appalled at the direction our conversation was taking. I chewed on yet another piece of greasy garlic bread and muttered, "You don't have to talk about it if you don't want to."

"But I *do* want to! Because frankly, Laurel, you're the only one I *can* tell. And you can appreciate what I'm going to tell you more than anyone else I know."

"Let me guess. You seduced Eldridge Cleaver."

She grinned. "Close. It wasn't a Black Panther, mostly because they're all pretty much in jail or dead by now. But it was a for real black militant revolutionary."

"You went to bed with a black militant revolutionary?!?!"

"Well, not exactly to bed. We did it on the floor. But yes, I made it with . . ." She paused, then grinned and softly sang the entire litany of racial epithets from *Hair*'s "Colored Spade."

I looked around nervously, fearful that a black waiter might slip up unsuspecting and overhear this pretty white girl vivaciously crooning racial slurs. Finally she stopped and looked expectant.

"Well, what am I supposed to say?"

"What do you *want* to say, Laurel?"

"I don't have any idea at all. I think I want to say that I'm shocked and horrified, but I'm really not. If I say I'm not surprised, maybe that's offensive. I don't know. You're the one with all the sexual experience. If it was something you wanted to do, there must have been a reason."

She grinned and held her hands some nine inches apart. "A *big* reason. What you might call an Afro-disiac."

"Pren!"

"Just wanted to see if you were paying attention."

"You're telling me about balling a black man in Berkeley and you want to know if I'm paying attention? The only reason I wouldn't be would be if I had already died of shock." Which of course wasn't what I wanted to say at all. "Pren?"

"Yes?" She knew what I wanted to ask and wouldn't even help.

"Did you mean that? I mean about . . ."

She held her hands in the same configuration, palms ten inches apart. "This?"

"Yeah."

She laughed and folded her hands demurely in her lap. "Nope. I didn't mean it. Just wondered if you'd fall for it."

"But . . ."

"But what?"

"Nothing." I paused a moment and reflected. "Pren, just *think* what the Major would say if he knew."

She grinned fiendishly. "My dear Laurel, I have been thinking of little else since the event occurred. I also thought of it almost continuously *while* the event was occurring. In fact, if it weren't for that, it wouldn't have even been a very memorable experience. I mean, the guy was a bona fide militant and all, but he was really a total jerk."

Junior year sort of slithered to an end. James Earl Ray copped a plea, Ike died, and the War went on. It was too depressing to think about, so I didn't. I mostly ignored it all, barely even reading Lee's letters from Vietnam, which Mama photocopied at Daddy's office to pass along. Pren found them much more interesting than I did, actually. Lee did not write to me, nor did I find this omission surprising. He wouldn't like what I was thinking and he most certainly would not approve of the nigger-loving demonstrations which were sweeping through the nation's universities. For all practical purposes, it was Afro-American Spring, with black studies programs being hastily assembled on campuses from coast to coast. It would have been a dandy time to be a black Ph.D. in anything.

Pren seemed remarkably quiet and well-adjusted, working hard to finish a hundred-page independent study paper she was writing on the French involvement in Indochina. She was also seeing a lot of Adam Gerard. Since Adam lived off campus and was out of town a lot on various rabble-rousing missions, Pren tended to be gone from the dorm quite a bit. A permanent note hung by the Wognum switchboard: "Do NOT tell long-distance callers if Prentiss Granger is signed out overnight. Refer calls to Laurel H." Her dorm reputation now mattered less than possible exposure to the Major.

Once a call from Bob McCoy was referred to me, but she didn't seem very interested and hardly spoke of him anymore. She did, however, love to bait me by singing "Black Boys" under her breath so only I could hear. She'd sing along out loud when Ginger played *Hair,* her current favorite album. At one point when Ginger moaned that it was getting warped, I brightly offered to iron it for her.

One quiet weeknight Pren and I were sitting on our respective beds reading. She got up, executed a perfect headstand against the wall by her dresser, then asked, "What are you going to do when you graduate?"

It was a question I had consciously avoided asking myself. "Teach," I responded. "Why the hell else would I be taking kiddie math and economic geography?"

"Well, you might be taking geography cause it's crip, like Ginger is. She takes all those easy-B courses."

"Any course that's crip is boring by definition."

Pren turned herself right side up. "Quite true," she agreed. "And of course you're going to teach. In fact, I think it's a pity that there aren't more people with your intelligence and compassion going into teaching."

I was truly embarrassed. "Why thanks, Pren. That's real sweet of you."

"Just the truth, Laurel. No false modesty, please. You have any idea yet *where* you want to teach?"

"Beats me. Why? You opening a school?"

"Hardly, my dear. I was just wondering, that's all. No big deal."

But of course it was. She had opened a whole problem area I was carefully ignoring. "What are *you* going to do?" A useful trick, one I'd learned from Miss Granger herself, was to immediately turn the tables on anyone who asked awkward questions.

"Grad school. Probably in Berkeley."

"Do you honestly think the Major will let you go to Berkeley?"

"They have an excellent graduate program in history," she said innocently.

"You'll need more than that to convince your father."

"Not necessarily," she muttered. "There's something brewing right now, actually, but I can't tell you about it for a while and it might not happen at all."

"Put me on the list when you send out the press release," I told her irritably as I checked my watch. "Gotta run. Desk girls meeting."

Pren stayed in Durham again that summer, as research assistant to a septuagenarian history professor compiling a reference tome for serious scholars in the field of military history, a project that even the Major considered amply worthwhile. And I went home, desperately trying to find myself a project to fill three empty months.

I finally came up with two. I assembled a modest darkroom and taught myself how to develop and print my own negatives, something I'd been meaning to do ever since I saw *Blow-Up* at the Rialto when I was a freshman. I had hundreds of black-and-white negatives by then and once I really got caught up in the project I began buying bulk Plus-X and Tri-X and shooting entire rolls of things like Spanish moss.

My other summer project had more immediate rewards. I had Cloretha teach me how to cook so I could feed myself properly when I had graduated, gotten skinny and begun my new life. Somewhere.

It would not be at home. That much I was certain of. I found it slightly chilling that my parents expected me to set myself down on the front porch for the next few decades. If I insisted on working, they hinted gently, there would undoubtedly be an opening in one of the parish schools for any daughter of Big Eddie Hollingsworth. But it was too late in history for me to be a spinster aging graciously beneath her father's roof.

And if I weren't living at home, Cloretha would not be fixing my meals. I wouldn't even have the comfort and convenience of Union slumgullion.

I couldn't really confront the idea of learning to cook without at least glancing at the related problem of my eternal overweight. I had all but given up on being a slender and stunning companion to Prentiss Granger in college. But I could envision myself at some future date in some unidentified faraway place, slender and sleekly attired in a tailored suit, stepping gracefully into a taxi.

Of course I tried to lose weight. Frequently. I would pick my courses carefully in the Union, eating huge salads, refusing all carbohydrates and raiding the dorm candy machine in the dead of night. One night when the choices were macaroni and cheese or spaghetti, I dumped a whole plate of noodles into the Union Suggestion Box.

To discover the origins of my weight problem, one need look no further than my parents. Mama, from birth a sweet soft round little thing, has become progressively sweeter and softer and rounder with every passing year. And Daddy has been dressed for decades by a New Orleans tailor who caters primarily to "portlies."

My three brothers are also fat. In the fine tradition of their father (and these are traditional boys, make no mistake) they have built their girth slowly but steadily. Little Eddie, fifteen years my senior and laughably misnamed, has become positively porcine. Don, four years younger than Eddie, kept his stockiness under control through athletics until a few years back when I went home one Christmas and discovered he had hopelessly blimped out. Lee is four years older than I. He was a tubby kid till the marines got hold of him and trimmed off a fast thirty pounds, but three years of French Quarter binges while he labored at Tulane Law put all that back and then some.

I suppose a certain measure of the blame for our continued family obesity must rest with Cloretha, though she herself is skinny as a pine sapling despite years of testing and tasting everything that passes through her kitchen. Nobody would ever cast Cloretha as a southern mammy. She looks more like an escapee from a backwater prison camp, somebody who will never outrun the dogs and barrel-bellied deputy sheriffs because only water and an occasional breadcrust have passed her lips for seven years.

Cloretha was, in fact, wonderfully amused when I told her what I had in mind. After the previous summer I think she was probably a little bit wary of being enlisted in any of my projects. The nation's campuses might have been sprouting courses in East African Art and Blacks in American Literature, but the rich soil of the Deep South was still producing bigots. Although Medgar Evers's brother Charles had been elected mayor of nearby Fayette, Mississippi, in St. Elizabeth, Mayor Evers was fondly known as "that damned nigger."

"What you need to know for?" Cloretha asked first.

"I may not be coming back here after I graduate. And I don't want to have to eat stew out of cans or frozen TV dinners."

She cringed. "Your daddy know you not planning to come home?" I shook my head. "Where you 'spect to go, then? Baton Rouge? New Orleans?"

Baton Rouge was out of the question. It was too close and the air stank from a glut of petrochemical plants. New Orleans, on the other hand, was well worth consideration. If I went to New Orleans, I might not have to learn to cook at all. There would always be wonderful food available. Everywhere.

"Haven't decided yet," I said. "Actually, Cloretha, I don't know what I'm going to do. Maybe I'll get a sign this summer."

"Foo on that," she sniffed. "So, what you want to learn to cook?"

"Everything."

Cloretha had almost nothing written down, judging everything by size and feel and look and taste. Even so, I quickly learned to knock out a nice cobbler, whip up a batch of hush puppies, deep fry a platter of fresh beignets. My spoonbread was nearly as good as Cloretha's by the Fourth of July and after one or two false starts, I could turn out quite an acceptable Sally Lunn. I learned the secrets of a good stockpot and how to make use of absolutely everything. I tried valiantly, though with limited success, to acquire Cloretha's "feel" for a piecrust.

Then, in the middle of summer, I got to help Cloretha really pull out the stops. My brother Lee came home from Vietnam.

Lee's return to St. Elizabeth was a momentous occasion beyond my immediate family. He was coming home from war an amply decorated hero, and if there's one thing we do well in Dixie, it's welcome returning war heroes. There were banners on the courthouse and sixty-point headlines in the *Piniatamore Rebel.* Lee had received a raft of medals and commendations in the field, including the third Purple Heart that brought him home a month early from his second and final tour of duty. I had never been able to understand why he re-upped for that second tour, but ours is not the kind of relationship where one asks such questions. Ours is the kind of relationship where one is treated like an oak armoire.

Now he was back for good, with a cast on his left ankle and a highly romantic pair of crutches. Had he not been my brother, I would undoubtedly have considered him quite attractive, particularly in uniform. He was in great shape: body trim, muscles toned, skin tanned, teeth pearlescent, eyes bright, thick dark hair growing out rapidly from the marine burr cut. That's what's recorded in my photos of his Welcome Home bash, a gala on the Weatherly south lawn attended by every important white person in the parish. What I *remember,* however, is that he still ignored me and I still didn't care.

He ate like a field hand, morning, noon and night. Cloretha doubled the morning biscuit dough and still there wasn't enough. He plowed through pies single-handedly. When Cloretha left a batch of pralines to cool on the dining table one afternoon, he wandered through and ate half of them. We fixed his favorite gumbos and jambalayas which were positively loaded with oysters and shrimp. It was all quite wonderful.

After a week his uniform didn't fit anymore. So much for the incredible discipline and willpower of the U.S. Marine Corps.

Chapter 10

"The M-sixteen's the biggest piece of shit I've ever seen, beg pardon, Prentiss." Lee spoke with smug superiority, but he wasn't about to forget his manners with a lady. "I'll never forget the time we came on a patrol that Charlie wasted in an ambush. Not a pretty sight, I tell you that. Poor suckers had been pinned down and the damn weapons failed on 'em. Charlie stripped those bodies clean, even took the C rations. But he left the guns. Hell, two of those poor bastards had started to field strip 'em after they jammed, but there just wasn't enough time. You'll have to excuse my language, Prentiss, I just get so exercised thinking about it, I forget myself."

"That's all right," she answered demurely. "No problem. It just appalls me that they won't admit that the M-sixteen was a mistake and go back to the M-fourteen. Now *that* was a beautiful piece of equipment."

"True enough. But I'll tell you, even that's a toy popgun next to the AK-forty-seven. I sure would have liked one of those babies as a souvenir. Matter of fact, one time we took one off a little dead gook, but some captain fresh out of the Pentagon confiscated it."

For three days Pren had been rehashing military maneuvers with Lee. I was accustomed to having the Hollingsworths fawn over her by now. This was the fourth time she'd been a house guest over the years, and she always received a royal welcome. Generally this pleased me, but now I was profoundly annoyed at the assumption that Lee and Pren might become a Hot Romance. Cloretha had orders to keep the cookies and lemonade coming, and I wouldn't have been surprised to find mistletoe hanging in the front hall.

For her part, Pren had so drastically altered her appearance and demeanor that I occasionally forgot it was 1969. The jeans and work shirts were back in Durham and she'd resurrected all her nice conservative summer sportswear, stuff that hadn't seen daylight for two years. What's more, although Lee was only a couple years older than she was, she never once spoke to him in the easy carefree way she'd rap with an older guy at school. She was acting like a quintessential Dixie flirt. And Lee had fallen for it. He responded like a laboratory frog's leg, all atwitch and aflutter. (I thought he was also a jerk, but that was a minority opinion.)

Since it quickly became apparent that Lee was not about to start a chapter of local disaffected veterans to oppose the war, Pren abandoned her attempts to proselytize in favor of a thorough debriefing. They spent hours together as she extracted all the myriad details of his service, and she was particularly riveted by his tales of forays into Laos during Operation Dewey Canyon.

But Lee was leaving soon for New Orleans to register for law school and find an apartment, so I just bided my time. It amused me to hear him argue against Mama's suggestion that he live at Grandma Chesterton's house in the Garden District. Lee told her, with a surprising lack of tact, that for two years he had managed successfully to avoid death or serious injury at the hands of communist guerrillas, and that he could probably manage quite nicely without a seventy-four-year-old woman to watch out for him. "The gooks couldn't get me, so no need to worry about the jigaboos," is how he put it.

Finally Lee left. After that, our schedule was wide open. We had long since exhausted the summer gossip. Pren's work for Professor Hartford had proven even easier than expected, freeing vast quantities of her summer time in Durham for other activities. The most significant of these, she felt, were New Mobe's plans for an October 15 Moratorium and a November 15 March on Washington. She bubbled over with enthusiasm discussing New Mobe, and I couldn't help but correlate that to Adam's heavy involvement. Because she had also, it seemed, enormously enjoyed spending the summer in his company.

"For somebody whose political instincts are so good," Pren said, "Adam can sometimes be incredibly naïve." We were crammed into my makeshift darkroom and I was printing some of the many negatives I had of Pren to give her father for his birthday. "You know, he was all for charging into Granger Mills and really laying into the Major—racism, unionization, exploitation of labor and resources. I had a hell of a time convincing him it would never work. So you know what I did instead? I turned that Yankee into a good ole boy."

"Adam Gerard a grit? You've got to be kidding!"

"Well, face it, if he's going to have any success at all in the South, he's going to have to speak the language." Adam's grating northeastern accent was guaranteed to automatically alienate anyone south of Baltimore. Moreover, once he translated his statements into Southern, he ran the very real risk of bodily harm. Cleaning up his communications skills couldn't help but make him a more viable organizer.

"Did you consider just teaching him sign language and having him go strictly on his physical appearance? Nobody could fault that."

"Agreed. But he really has quite a nice little drawl now, and he can 'ma'am' and 'sir' and 'y'all' you half to death. I told him it was his summer school project, and when he aced the course, I gave him a little hip flask of bourbon."

"How perfect. Here, now. You want this one printed?"

"Oh, definitely. That's just the way the Major likes to think of me, all pensive and demure."

And it was in fact that very picture which later hung in every post office in the country. In the shot her chin tilts up, her head is cocked slightly and a ghost of a smile seems just ready to break loose. Her eyes stare forward with clear intensity, her hair sweeps in a loose veil down both sides of her face and she is quite incomparably lovely.

In the years since that picture was first printed, I have seen it a thousand times, staring at me from newspapers, magazines, post office walls and my TV screen in the late night when they run FBI Most Wanted blurbs during public service time. "She should be considered armed and dangerous," they somberly intone, and I think of her clowning for the camera in the rose garden of Azalea Acres.

The strange thing is, I feel as if that picture were my kidnapped child. When it was wrenched from me and thrust into the public eye, I felt utterly betrayed and exploited. I hated myself for creating such a flattering likeness and wished I had never gotten my first Brownie. The possibility that somebody might recognize and apprehend her on the basis of my photograph has been one of the nameless dreads which haunt my adult life. And every time I see that photograph, my stomach knots.

* * *

One of the memories I most cherish from that visit of Pren's was of our plantation visits. We drove all around three parishes touring plantations with blue-haired midwestern schoolteachers and station wagon loads of supremely bored children whose parents hoped in vain to bring history alive for them.

But even better were our visits to the privately occupied plantations which were open to the public only during the Camellia Festival and sometimes not even then. These visits were incredible time warps. We were admitted as old family friends, and by old I mean dating back for centuries. Genteel but fading Daughters of the Confederacy, most of whom had known me since before I could walk, served us delicate tea-cakes and fresh-fried peach pies.

As my friend, Prentiss Granger would have been welcomed politely had she been rude, abrasive, ugly, slovenly or almost anything but Negro. Her insatiable historical curiosity was a source of delirious joy to our hostesses. We would trail behind these dear little old ladies as they unfolded the pedigree of every hand towel, curtain rod and drawer hinge. We didn't often encounter men on these little tours. By and large the husbands of these ladies had predeceased them, gratefully in many instances. A few had never married at all, moldering in genteel fragility through the decades, changing their lacy white collars and cuffs frequently throughout the steamy days to remain ever fresh as they waited in vain for a gallant knight or dashing roué or maybe even Mandingo.

We spent a lot of time at Weatherly too. Pren never ceased to be fascinated by the place and was still willing to spend hours at a stretch discussing obscure aspects of the War Between the States with my grandfather. He lay propped up by pillows in the massive four-poster bed where he had been born, clearly in failing health but coming strangely alive during their discussions.

On these plantation days at Weatherly and elsewhere, Cloretha packed picnic baskets and we lunched outdoors in the shade of live oaks on beautifully manicured lawns. The weather was horrendously hot and muggy, but we availed ourselves of siestas, slushy bottles of Coke, and six packs of Jax and Dixie we kept in a cooler as we drove around. And once again we smoked marijuana together.

Pren brought a small amount with her in a little Baggie. We went out one day for our customary afternoon drive and she inquired sweetly whether I'd mind if she got stoned. Of course I didn't. Ever the gracious hostess, I even asked if I might join her.

I didn't expect much. I had clear memories of my only other attempt to get stoned, the previous Christmas when a lid of grass arrived in a package from Bob McCoy along with a STRIKE! poster from San Francisco State, a FUCK THE DRAFT/HELL NO, WE WON'T GO! poster, a FREE HUEY poster and a handful of assorted political buttons. We had waited till three A.M., stuffing towels under our locked doors. But while Pren and Ginger both got dreamy and giggly and mildly withdrawn, I had remained bright and alert and totally unaffected, coming to feel after a spell like the guard at the loony bin. The main joy of the experience for me had been the hilarity with which they greeted my every utterance.

That first afternoon she got high and silly and giggly again, just as she had before Christmas. I choked and coughed again, just as I had before Christmas. "Don't give up so easily," she begged me. "It takes a couple of times before you really get stoned."

And so the next afternoon we set out again and repeated the performance. We were at Weatherly down by the slave cabins and I was leaning on the stoop. I was prepared to be polite and smile and say it didn't matter, just like some inorgasmic housewife from the fifties. But then I found it easier to keep the smoke down and suddenly I noticed that my body felt different. I seemed to be under the force of ten Gs taking off in a rocket for Mars, or else have gained a fast two tons. I could barely move. I turned my head slowly to look at Pren. She was staring quizzically at me.

"Did you notice the way Grandaddy drinks through that straw?" I asked her. It took me a long time to get the words out and for a moment I forgot how I intended to finish the thought. "He looks just like a chipmunk." I stuck my little finger in my mouth and puckered my lips to demonstrate.

Pren roared and I howled and it honestly seemed that Grandpa Hollingsworth drinking a pear malted through a striped plastic straw was the funniest thing we had ever witnessed.

I had finally gotten stoned.

"What an adventure!" Pren shivered with delight beside me in the front seat as we drove out to Weatherly. Outside the wind howled and occasional spurts of rain smashed into the windshield. Down in the Gulf,

Hurricane Camille was gearing up for a full-fledged assault on Louisiana and we were right in her projected path.

"More like a family reunion or house party than a real adventure," I corrected with worldly superiority. This might be Prentiss Granger's first hurricane, but I was an old hand. I couldn't even remember all the times the Hollingsworths had gone through hurricane drill. By now nobody even needed to be reminded of their assignments. Jasper had just finished boarding up Daddy's office and the house in town and Cloretha was already out at Weatherly with Little Eddie, supervising the plantation weatherproofing. Plywood sheeting was stored in one of the outbuildings along with the rest of the disaster equipment.

"Y'all are so calm," Pren marveled. "Even your mother. My mama'd be in full-blown hysterics by now."

"Not if she'd been through it as often as mine. The names to remember are Betsy, Hilda and Flossy. Betsy was the worst, back in 'sixty-four. She practically wiped out New Orleans and Placquemines Parish. Grandma Chesterton lost most of her rental property in Betsy. And dozens of people were killed. Thing is, New Orleans is already about five feet below sea level. Once the flooding starts, it gets grim in a big hurry. But we'll be fine out at Weatherly. It was built to last forever, and it's on some of the highest ground in the parish."

Sure enough, the general atmosphere was festive and gay when we reached the plantation. The weatherproofing was finished and Cloretha was starting to set out trays of food on the big mahogany dining table, covered by a plastic lace cloth in concession to the children. Little Eddie and Glenna Anne had brought their brood straight from church, stopping only to secure the storm shutters and empty the fridge in the big house they'd recently built in St. Francisville. Don and Louella and their five kids had driven up hours earlier from Baton Rouge. The children careened around the house in dizzy glee.

I could hear Daddy yelling into the phone in the library. "Forget your damn hurricane party! I don't care if you have to chloroform her, son, you just see to it that you and Grandma are on your way out of town in twenty minutes. Understand?"

Mama dashed to greet us. "Everything's all right at the house? I thought we'd never find Lee, and Mama was flat out refusing to leave town. Was Jasper finished with the house when you left?" I nodded. "Then where on earth can he be?"

"He was going by to pick up Mary and the kids, remember?" Even as

I spoke I could hear the elderly Weatherly servants begin to gush out in the kitchen, a sure sign that the six missing Wilsons had arrived. Jasper and Mary's kids loved Weatherly, and the lavish attention they got from the servants was unquestionably part of the reason.

The storm grew through the afternoon and before long the wind was howling so loudly we sometimes couldn't hear each other speak. Now and again a loud crash came from outdoors as a tree limb fell. It rained in fits and spurts, then more steadily.

Sometime in the middle of the afternoon, the power blew out. The phone went soon after that. We were cut off from the world ... which was not, historically, a very significant occurrence at Weatherly. The difference, of course, was that my eighteenth- and nineteenth-century forebears had not been able to tune in emergency broadcasting on a battery-operated Japanese transistor radio.

The more we heard about Camille's progress, the more worried Mama and Grandma became. Lee and Grandma Chesterton were out there somewhere on the open road, assuming that they hadn't already been forced to seek refuge, perhaps in so unseemly a location as a sharecropper's shack. But by and large the atmosphere was very jolly. Everyone bustled about lighting candles and kerosene lamps, snacking enthusiastically off platters which kept appearing on the dining room table and emptying the Weatherly liquor closet at a phenomenal rate.

By 3:30 the sky was streaked green-black and the light which filtered through gave everything a sallow cast, as if the world were bathed in olive oil. Pren and I went out to watch on the gallery outside the second-story bedrooms. We weren't really sitting; we were smashed into the floor with our hands tightly clasped to the spokes of the railing. It was too noisy to speak, but there was really nothing to say. The wind whipped through the live oaks on the Weatherly lawn. Now and then a mass of Spanish moss would tear loose from a tree and snap across at us. It was a scene to inspire enormous awe in nature or God or whatever else one chose to believe in.

Under the circumstances, it seemed prudent to believe in something.

Our contemplation was interrupted by a full-scale crisis. My eleven-year-old nephew Jimmy and our handyman Jasper's ten-year-old son Rufus were missing. The two boys had always played together at Weatherly, and had not yet grown into the patterns of local racism which would shortly sever their lifelong friendship. The house was in an uproar over their disappearance and a systematic search had determined that they were nowhere under the roof.

The kitchen bustled with frantically worried women, momentarily terrified children and impotently raging men. My father was too old to go out searching, of course, and Jimmy's dad, Little Eddie, was too fat and too winded from having put up the storm shutters. With Lee still somewhere out on the road, that left only Jasper and Don out searching in the storm.

Pren led me onto the service porch, where the dogs lay whimpering and moaning in fear. "We've got to do something," she said. "I can't bear just sitting around and worrying, as if we were the same as all the rest of those 'helpless' females."

"It's too dangerous," I argued.

"Why is it more dangerous for us than for Jasper or your brother? We're younger and in better physical shape than either of them."

"Listen, Pren, I'm worried too. But that's a *hurricane* out there. You don't have any idea what that wind can do to you."

She was angry now. "If you won't go, I'm going out to look by myself. Do you want it on your conscience that you let those two kids die because you were too chickenshit to go look for them?"

I sighed deeply. I could tell she meant it, no matter how naïve she might be about the force of the storm. And my pride wouldn't let me confess my own fear. "All right," I said finally. "But we can't let my mother know before we leave. Go see if you can get Cloretha out here without tipping off anybody else."

While she was finding Cloretha, I dug through a chest of drawers and found three lengths of clothesline. I had just finished knotting them together when they returned. Cloretha was upset when I told her our plan, but she didn't try to stop us. Like me, she had a nephew out there in the storm.

We skinned our hair back with rubber bands and buckled ourselves into two of the yellow Sears slickers which live at Weatherly for just such occasions. I was frankly terrified.

"If you were a kid and got caught outside, you'd try to get back to the house," Pren said. "Or if you couldn't, because the wind was too strong, you'd take cover. Where would you go?" Even as she spoke, I saw a glimmer of an idea brighten her eyes.

"The garages?"

"Maybe. Or the kennels, but I think Don went to check them. What about the slave cabins?"

It seemed as likely an idea as anything else. We tied the clothesline to a column on the back porch and headed off. The idea was to anchor the rope on one of the trees down by the creek. Getting to the creek and the cabins would be no problem. We had a 75 mph wind at our backs. But returning to the house would be another matter altogether. We would need to pull ourselves along the guide rope every inch of the way.

It had been raining spasmodically for hours, but now the sky opened completely. We scuttled like paper cups across the wide back lawn. Despite our slickers, we were immediately drenched. Once we reached the creek, we had to turn right into the wind. From then on we had to hold hands and move from the support of one tree trunk to the next.

The rain had swollen the creek beyond recognition. Ordinarily it is a pokey little thing, meandering down through the woods, stopping here and there to form ponds where tadpoles and mosquitoes breed. Now it was a little river, roaring and rushing and remarkably ferocious. At several spots it overflowed the banks.

We knew that the cabins were only a few hundred yards from the house, but it was impossible to judge distance or progress. I couldn't tell how far we had gone and there was no way to see through the rain. Most of the time I kept my eyes closed. Tree branches crashed down on all sides of us. Twice I tripped and fell headlong.

Then Pren knocked me hard in the ribs and pointed. Up ahead we could see Rufus's red T-shirt.

He was just outside the first of the slave cabins, where a large branch had fallen, crashing through the rickety old porch. He seemed to be sitting on the ground and had one arm tightly wrapped around the branch. His eyes were closed and his slight body shook. Ten yards away the creek had overflowed and was inching toward the cabin.

It took us five more minutes to reach him. By then I could see Jimmy too. Jimmy's legs seemed to be pinned beneath the branch, and Rufus sat with my nephew's flaxen head in his lap, keeping his face out of the mud. When Rufus momentarily opened his eyes and saw us, his face broke into a brilliant smile of relief.

Pren started scooping out the mud under Jimmy's trapped legs with her bare hands, while I shouted into his ear. He seemed to be in shock.

His eyes were half open, but he gave no sign of recognition. Rufus clung to my arm. I stripped off my slicker, but the wind whipped it out of my hands and it vanished. Pren saw what happened and pulled off her own, handing it to me in a ball. I straightened it out and slid it under Jimmy's face.

I pulled Rufus into the cabin. *"Stay here,"* I shouted. *"Till we get him out. Are you hurt?"*

His small black head shook from side to side. He didn't want to let go of me and I could hardly blame him. I hugged him hard. *"I'll be right back, Rufus. I'm so proud of you!"* That he seemed to hear. I set him in the most sheltered corner. Part of the roof had blown away and it was nearly as wet inside as out. *"Don't move!!"*

Back outside, I could see why it was taking Pren so long to free Jimmy's legs. The soil was so supersaturated that it was almost impossible to remove mud without more immediately replacing it. And whenever she did manage to clear some out, the branch just settled in deeper.

"We'll have to lift it," she shouted in my ear. *"Slide the slicker under him as far as you can."* By now Jimmy had passed out, so I didn't need to worry about causing him pain as I wrestled the yellow rubber through the mud under his body. He was a Hollingsworth, all right. He was heavy.

Pren was dragging over a large stone, moving on her hands and knees to avoid as much wind as possible. She gestured with her hands and I saw her plan. She had set the stone directly beside the branch. We would attempt to lift the branch and then she'd push the stone under with her feet. If all went well, we could then slide Jimmy the rest of the way out with no difficulty.

It worked. The branch was incredibly heavy, and I have no idea where the strength came from, but we managed to get it a few inches off the ground, enough for Pren to kick the stone underneath and prop it up. The branch teetered there just long enough for us to pull the unconscious boy from underneath. Seconds after we had him free, the weight of the branch pushed the stone aside and the length of wood settled flat into the mud.

I had thought I was scared before. But even as we hugged each other and sent our cheers of relief flying soundless into the din of the storm, I thought of what we now faced.

We had one unconscious eleven-year-old with what even my untrained eye could diagnose as a broken leg. We had an utterly terrified ten-year-old huddled inside the cabin.

And we had hundreds of yards of windswept lawn to cross.

As Pren buckled the slicker around Jimmy's limp body, I went back inside and retrieved a trembling Rufus. He wrapped his thin arms so tightly around my waist that I could hardly move. We'd obviously have to figure out some way to keep his tiny body from being swept away by the wind as we struggled back to the house carrying Jimmy.

I don't know whether Pren could hear my shouting or not, but she quickly understood the problem and knit her brow in concentration. A moment later she started yanking at the belt in my Bermudas. Confused but compliant, I slipped it from the loops and handed it to her. She tested its strength, then rolled up the right leg of her shorts and slipped the belt through from waist to hem. By looping the belt through a second time and fastening it, she was able to make a firm strap for Rufus to hang on to as we walked.

And then we set off. Pren led, walking backward with Rufus appended to her right hip and the leg end of Jimmy in the slicker in her hands. I came behind holding Jimmy's shoulders. The wind was partly with us till we reached the clothesline. We stopped and rested there a minute, then started out again, each of us with an arm wrapped around the rope.

Somewhere on the lawn we encountered Don, who grabbed Jimmy up, slicker and all. By now Pren was near collapse herself, Rufus was falling more than he was standing, and it was up to me to get us to the house. Somehow I got an arm around Pren's waist and the other one around the clothesline. I couldn't see Rufus at all on Pren's other side. Finally, what seemed like hours later, we neared the back porch and Jasper came around the corner of the house. He grabbed Rufus and pushed Pren and me into the kitchen.

Mama fainted when she saw us, and when I caught our reflections in the front hall antique mirror, I could understand why. The rain had washed away most of the mud, but we were soaked to the skin, with water pouring from our hair and squishy puddles appearing everywhere we stepped. While Don brought out his medical bag and started working on Jimmy, we were taken upstairs, stripped of our sodden clothing and thoroughly dried off.

"You know," Pren said, when we were alone in the bedroom putting on dry clothes, "you were right. We were crazy to go out in that. I had no *idea....*"

"It was worth it," I told her. And it was. I had no doubt that we had saved Jimmy's life. At the rate the creek was rising, he'd have drowned within an hour. And Rufus could never have made it back to the house on his own.

Which everyone downstairs seemed to realize too. We were heroines. And I won't pretend that I didn't enjoy having everybody fuss and marvel at our foolhardy courage.

Shortly after we came down to find Rufus safely wrapped in a blanket in his mother's arms, Dr. Don announced that Jimmy would be fine. His sedated and splinted young body was tucked into the massive four-poster bed beside his great-grandfather, and everybody went back to gushing over our bravery.

Finally, when I was just starting to feel uncomfortable about the continual effusiveness, the front door burst open with an incredible crash. Lee and Grandma Chesterton burst into the room, drenched but in surprisingly good spirits. Lee was full of stories about stopping to clear road debris and other adventures of the open road. Initially he seemed rather baffled that nobody was particularly impressed.

But as everybody babbled at once, spilling out the story of our daring rescue, his eyes narrowed and he looked at me with an expression I had never seen before.

It was respect.

Chapter 11 _____

A hurricane was the appropriate end to that summer and a fitting prelude to a tumultuous fall. The complacency of the previous six months had merely been the eye between the madness of 1968 and the stormy finale of the fall of 1969.

The semester was barely a week old and Pren was up to the gold peace signs in her earlobes with New Mobe plans when suddenly the entire character of the fall changed dramatically. Bob McCoy blew into town.

His tale of woe warmed my girlish heart. The long-suffering Marylou had finally reached her limit. She had kicked him out and was now living with a Chinese lesbian, giving new depth and meaning to her doctoral program in Asian Affairs. Meanwhile, San Francisco State, under the new leadership of Sam the Tam Hayakawa, had discovered no further need for Bob McCoy's services. He was footloose and fancy free, and Prentiss Granger was one of the fanciest freebies he had ever encountered.

He was no longer interested very much in New Mobe or the upcoming Moratorium demonstrations. What he wanted now was blood. His career was in shambles, his wife had replaced him with a dyke Chink, he was flat broke and Ho Chi Minh had just died. It was almost enough to make me feel sorry for him, but not quite. I have a natural affinity for underdogs, but a rather marked disinterest in curs.

Prentiss Bleeding Heart, however, took instant pity on him. Fate (or karma, as I preferred to view it) had dealt poor old Bob a pretty miserable hand. Ever generous, he wanted to spread his misfortune around and thought Chicago would be a nice place to start. The Chicago Eight Conspiracy Trial was just beginning and Weatherman had unfolded a scenario of nifty demonstrations. The word from the Bay area was that blood would flow.

"You know, I could probably have you committed for this," I remarked conversationally as Pren tossed a change of jeans and an assortment of adhesive tape and gauze into her smallest suitcase. "People with your intelligence level don't willingly fly a thousand miles to have their heads beaten. Surely you haven't forgotten the last time you tangled with Chicago's finest."

"We've been over this before," she replied irritably. "What I choose to do with my time and money is my business."

"If you choose to buy that jerk an airplane ticket, that's true. But when your father calls, it turns into my business and you know it. I thought you didn't *like* Bob McCoy anymore. Remember the epiphany in Berkeley?" I sang a few lines of "Black Boys."

She slammed the suitcase shut and glared at me. "I'm not accomplishing anything here. This is a chance to be where things are really happening again. I'm sick and tired of sitting around this two-bit town waiting for all these polite little boys and girls to get political. I want *action,* dammit. Everything here is so bloody genteel it makes me want to scream."

"For God's sake, Pren, he's just using you. You're rich and he's broke. You think he'd be here if Marylou hadn't finally wised up to him?"

"I told you, it's none of your business."

"You're just like your goddamned father, you know that? The two of you, always worrying about the front lines and battle plans and strategy. Has it ever occurred to you that it's just as difficult sometimes to have to sit around and wait? The people who get left behind suffer plenty too. We build aircraft carriers. We hoe victory gardens. We lie to our roommates' fathers. We have all the worry with none of the excitement. We're always underestimated and once the dust settles after the big battle or riot or whatever, nobody pays any attention to us."

"You have my deepest sympathy," she sniffed. "Maybe you could join the ladies auxiliary." And then she was gone.

Of course I followed the news from Chicago religiously, and so it happened that I saw Prentiss Granger in the crowd outside the federal courthouse in Chicago, waving her fist vehemently. Her hair was pulled back and her face so contorted that at first I didn't recognize her. The little weasel at her side, however, was unquestionably Bob McCoy. My stomach began churning and it took me quite a while to remember that the Major never watched the CBS news because he considered Walter Cronkite a trifle on the pink side, despite the fact that Walter was a war games aficionado.

For the next several days I read about rioting and vandalism and some yahoo who managed to trip, fall and break his neck chasing the Weathermen through the dark deserted Chicago streets. I was terrified of what might happen to her, and the violence of the demonstrations seemed pointless. I couldn't talk to anybody but Ginger about any of it, and Ginger was interested only in her latest boyfriend.

When Pren returned from the Days of Rage, she embraced a position of artful nonchalance, but it seemed to me that beneath her worldly boredom, she was genuinely troubled. "It wasn't the way I expected," was all she said at first. And for the first few days, while she busied herself with Moratorium plans, that was all. But then I asked her the wrong question one night and got to see another side of her, one that scared the hell out of me.

I thought I was being innocuous enough. "It sounds pretty counterproductive," I offered innocently. "Nobody's going to want to cozy up to a bunch of thugs who run around smashing windows and destroying property."

"You'd best not cozy up to me anymore then," she snapped. "When I threw a brick through that first plate-glass window, it was one of the most exciting and revelatory moments of my life."

"I bet it was pretty exciting for the person who owned the plate-glass window," I replied irritably. "Did you get together for a little chat about it? Maybe lunch on top of the Prudential Building?" I could hear a snicker from the next room. The suite door was halfway open and Ginger was out of sight, lying on her bed studying for a psych hourly. Pren heard the snicker too, looked in annoyance at the suite door, started to say something and stopped. She turned back to me instead.

"So I broke a few windows. So what?"

"A few? Now it's a few? Just exactly how many windows did you break? If I'm not prying?"

Pren looked away from me and pulled her laundry bag out of the closet. "I'm not exactly sure."

"What do you mean, you're not exactly sure? I can't believe I'm having this conversation. You just wandered around throwing bricks through windows and you don't know how many? Okay, try it this way. Was it more or less windows than there are in the executive offices of Granger Mills?"

This time Ginger didn't snicker, she laughed out loud. Pren glared angrily at the suite door. "Either come in where I can see you laughing at me, Ginger, or fuck off."

Ginger appeared in the doorway, hair in rollers, wearing a ragged navy blue Pi Phi sweatshirt and wheat jeans. "I'd love to stick around for the fireworks," she told Pren, "but I haven't read one word for this test and I think it's half the grade. Laurel, I'll have to count on you for the details, I guess. See you later." She closed the suite door and Pren muttered something angrily under her breath. I flipped another page in *Time,* trying to find the movie section.

By now Pren had taken time to collect her thoughts. "Item. I was not throwing bricks through windows. I threw one brick through one window. It was a shoe store. Item. I also broke four other windows with a baseball bat. Item. It was a Louisville Slugger. Item. They were all stores that cater to wealthy people, leg-waxing salons, imported handbag boutiques, that kind of shit. And final item. The insurance companies will pay for the stupid windows. It was a statement, Laurel, that's all."

"Well, what ever happened to the kind of statement that was words on a sheet of paper? Or spoken through a microphone?"

"That kind of statement," she said, picking up her laundry bag and a box of Tide, "is gone with the wind that swept through Georgia." And she stalked out of the room.

The Moratorium on October 15 seemed to mellow her, however. She'd been involved in the planning from the beginning, and Bob McCoy stuck around long enough to teach a seminar on imperialism in the Third World. Pren reported later that he was brilliant, but I'd have worn the VC flag to dinner with the Major before I'd go hear Bob McCoy discuss anything but his own imminent suicide.

Once he left town to go rouse rabble in Washington with the planners of the November 15 March, however, I found it much easier to get along with Pren.

"If I hear one more word about how David and Julie and Tricia are the true spokesmen for our generation, I think I'm going to scream." I hurled a copy of *Newsweek* across the room. I had never realized I was capable of such blind fury. "The only thing that makes me madder is that goddamn 'Southern Strategy.' It makes the whole South seem ridiculous."

"I know," sighed Pren. She set aside a history text. "But I never realized their secret weapon was going to be Agnew and *Roget's Thesaurus*. 'An effete corps of snobs who characterize themselves as intellectuals.' What bullshit! You sure you can't get away early for the March on Death?"

I shook my head. "I don't dare miss a day of student teaching. But Lana doesn't mind waiting to leave till Friday night." I honestly believed that if enough nonviolent protesters appeared in Washington, Nixon and Congress would have to pay attention. And I was exhilarated at the prospect of seeing Democracy in Action on my maiden visit to the nation's capital. Our door had been covered by a poster showing starving Vietnamese babies for over a month now and their hunger touched me deeply each time I passed into the room with a Milky Way and a Tab.

"They're up to something, I just know it. Like the way they fired that senile old goat General Hershey from the Selective Service Commission right before the Moratorium. I wonder what little Hershey kiss they'll throw us this time."

"Maybe they're counting on the Silent Majority."

"The only thing they're counting on the Silent Majority to do is keep their mouths shut, so all those Republican goombahs can 'interpret' what they're thinking. I just hope that nobody's really fooled by all that talk about Vietnamization. You know, they're projecting a million people to come to Washington. Once that hits the network news, I don't see how they can claim the antiwar movement is just a handful of troublemaking commie agitators."

But of course they did have something up their sleeves, a tidy plan to sidestep that nagging little question of the First Amendment and effectively assure that the American public wouldn't see the march at all. Even as we spoke, Agnew was making his media power speech to Des

Moines Republicans. The TV news media have too much power, Spiggy said, and though the networks responded swiftly with denials and rebuttals, old Spig had a point. And sure enough, coverage of the March on Washington all but evaporated. Half a million people came to the seat of their government to protest and the TV medium gave the whole thing less attention than Smokey the Bear's birthday.

The walk down the mall Saturday morning filled me with awe and wonder. It was cold and crisp and lovely and a sense of carnival euphoria filled the air. The assembled protesters were all ages, sizes, shapes and colors, though admittedly leaning toward the young and white. The D.C. cops seemed only slightly nervous and if there was a preponderance of suspicious-looking "marchers" aiming 500 mm lenses at the crowd, it was nothing I hadn't seen before in Chicago and Durham. I never saw Pren, and I didn't really miss her.

Richard Nixon might well have announced that he'd be too busy watching the Michigan–Ohio State game to pay any attention to the half million visitors in his back yard, but I didn't care. I was so thrilled to know that I had a half million compatriots there that even the old Trickster couldn't put a damper on my day.

We sang of peace and love and freedom. As the American flags around the Washington Monument whipped in the wind, I was proud to be an American for the first time in a long time. If these wonderful people were *my* fellow Americans, perhaps there was hope for the country after all.

Those twenty-four hours in Washington are among the most genuinely pure memories of my lifetime. The drama of the situation overwhelmed me. I had never seen so many people in one place for any purpose before. That the place was incomparably lovely, the weather gorgeous and the people gathered because they were in agreement with me was almost more than I could comprehend.

The romantic sense of community I derived from being part of that massive gathering has stayed with me through the past ten years. It's a memory I bring out periodically. I close my eyes and put myself back on the Mall with the sky clear, the air cold and a feeling of passionate warmth radiating out from my heart. And suddenly I am reminded that there was a time when I was gathered with half a million kindred spirits and truly believed for a few golden hours that anything was possible.

Chapter 12 _____

There was no mention of labor unions or the textile industry that Thanksgiving when we went to Granger. Which was just fine with me, because there were so many other delicate subjects open for discussion that it threw me off my feed. I distinctly recall declining a second slice of Willie Mae's notorious whipped cream banana pie.

Ginger was with us again, but most reluctantly. "I would rather suck slivers of cold dry turkey in the closet of my room," she sniffed, "than listen to Prentiss do her revolting debutante act one more time."

So we were the same merry trio as the previous year, and Lord knows there was no dearth of controversial conversational topics. The most palatable of these, at least to me, was the recent rejection of Clement Haynesworth, a South Carolina boy, for the Supreme Court. The Major was predictably furious. He and Haynesworth went way back together and the Major considered the defeat of his nomination to be a personal loss. I guess it *was* a personal loss, actually. Who wouldn't like to have an old buddy on the Supreme Court?

The Major's argument in favor of his friend was simple: Judge Haynesworth was opposed by the AFL-CIO and the NAACP. Anyone those commies disliked was acceptable by definition. It was all part of an international conspiracy to make things tough for Richard Nixon, that well-known enemy of communism. The Major spoke with a certain measure of authority, since he numbered among his friends some extremely well-known professional communist haters. He was always pressing copies of *The Gravediggers* or *None Dare Call it Treason* on me.

Pren called him on that one, and they went a few brisk rounds on the subject of influence peddling and the ethical implications of ruling in favor of firms in which one owns stock. After a thorough dissection of Judge Haynesworth's investment portfolio, they finally dropped the subject.

Alas, we were not able to dispose so readily of most of the other knotty little topics which hovered over our holiday weekend like a Huey loaded with white phosphorous grenades. And one of those grenades blossomed into destructive horror on Friday night as we sat around the living room with after-dinner coffee.

"It's downright treasonous the way some of those senators talk about unilateral withdrawal," the Major said. "Now's the time to really beef up our forces and wipe that yellow communist slime off the map once and for all."

"It's not treason, it's just plain common sense," Pren retorted. "In fact, a unilateral withdrawal is really the only logical strategy at this point."

I could see the Major choke on his cookie and recalled the NUKE THE GOOKS bumpersticker on his Eldorado. "What in the devil has gotten into you?" he roared. "If we pull our boys out of Vietnam now, all of Southeast Asia will go down in weeks." He couldn't have been more upset if he'd just learned that a battalion of crack East German troops was creeping up on Granger Mills.

"There's no way to win with conventional weapons, and there's no way they'll ever get approval to use atomic ones. So why postpone the inevitable?" Pren spoke nonchalantly, and out of the corner of my eye I saw Ginger slip from the room.

"Who in the devil has been putting these ideas into your head, young lady? There better not be some pinko professor feeding you this propaganda, or there'll be hell to pay!"

Even as I wondered where Bob McCoy was hanging his greasy sweatshirt these days, the phone rang. Pren was smart enough to make a dash for it. It was some old crony of the Major's calling long-distance from San Antonio, and by the time he rang off, the three of us were safely closeted in Pren's room upstairs.

I couldn't help but marvel, however, at all that Pren had successfully concealed from her father. She had been injured at the 1968 Democratic Convention, procured an illegal abortion, fornicated with a left-wing professor, broken Chicago store windows, picketed on countless occasions, laid a black man in Berkeley, organized Mobe activities, marched on Washington and been gassed half a dozen times.

Yet somehow she managed to sit snugly in the bosom of her family, as if she'd never done anything more controversial than return a library book two days late. She'd perch primly on a Chippendale chair in a heathery blue skirt and sweater ensemble, her hair demurely pulled back into a gold barrette at the nape of her neck. Little cultured pearls nestled in her dainty ears. It was both hilarious and nauseating.

It would have been quite bad enough just to watch her simper and twit about in those clothes, clothes which actually gave off a faint aroma of mothballs. But Ginger's premonition had been correct, and Mrs. Granger wanted to discuss nothing so much as Pren's upcoming bow to society. It would run through most of the summer of 1970, as Mrs. Granger envisioned things, and of course Ginger and I would have to come to South Carolina for as much of it as possible. I had to bite my tongue not to ask if we'd get to meet Judge Haynesworth.

On Saturday night the Major began to deliver his theory on antiwar protesters. "Those commies are sly," he explained, "and a lot of folks are stupid and gullible enough to believe anything. Those so-called antiwar protesters, they're just professional rabble-rousers. Couldn't tie their own shoelaces without detailed instructions from Hanoi. Hanging's too good for them."

The atmosphere had grown unbelievably charged, as if a massive thunderstorm might break loose any second. In desperation, I decided to clear the air.

I twisted a linen napkin into a headband and pulled my shirttail out. Then I leaped to my feet and everybody stared at me blankly. "I'm Obadiah Blowhard," I announced, "from Rent-a-Radical, and have I ever got a heavy deal for you!" I could see out of the corner of my eye that Pren was not amused, but she gave a little chuckle anyway and the tension was broken.

I paced back and forth across the room, the undisputed center of attention. I emulated Bob McCoy's walk—slouched beneath the weight of the world's problems, head thrust forward belligerently. "Mr. Communist Agitator, we've got all the models you've been looking for, at a price even a Russky can afford." I flashed the peace sign and grinned. "Wanta off some pigs? Then you'll want our Radical Fanatic model, complete with hard hat, gas mask and semi-automatic weapon."

Ginger started to giggle and I knew I was all right. I invented a Rap

Brown model, inwardly flinching at my own hypocrisy. But I simply couldn't bear another evening listening to Pren and the Major argue. "But hey, you say you want a mellower demonstration? Then our Heavy Hippie's just what you've been looking for. He's a little hard to talk to, 'cause he spends a lot of time shooting up marijuana, but you can lay this fellow down in front of a troop train and he won't budge till the cops cart him off by the heels."

By now they were all laughing. Mrs. Granger tittered merrily, Ginger was convulsed, and a series of staccato guffaws came from the Major. "The Heavy Hippie model's on special this week only, two for the price of one. All our radicals come complete with blue jeans, protest signs and hair you could raise a family of robins in. What's more we absolutely guarantee that any radical you rent will not have bathed in at least a week. So don't wait a minute longer, Mr. Communist Agitator, just head on down to Rent-a-Radical today, and there'll be a full-scale disaster in your community tomorrow!"

I sat down, suddenly exhausted. Everybody was still laughing and now they were applauding too. The Major, in fact, laughed so hard that he choked and had to be smacked on the back. Pren performed this function with enthusiastic vigor.

And then at last it was Sunday afternoon and we were finally able to get the hell out of Granger. I didn't want to hear one more word about the Silent Majority or strict constructionism or Clement Haynesworth or peace with honor or communism in any shape or form.

All I wanted to hear was Janis Joplin. Loud.

The prospect of student teaching had gripped me in cold terror through the first half of the semester, but for once my fears were unfounded. The following Monday when I was back in my classroom at the DeWitt Clinton Elementary School in Raleigh, I thanked my lucky stars that on this front at least, everything was working out fabulously. I was loving every second of teaching. Admittedly I was in a special school. It was white, suburban and amply funded. Our second-grade classroom had twenty-seven students, a part-time aide and a wealth of educational materials. The teacher was Mrs. Lucy Warner, a Duke graduate who had married her Carolina boyfriend and settled in Raleigh five years earlier. She had everything set up with learning centers and group rotations and individually paced workbooks and assignments.

"It's a lot more work to keep up with," she acknowledged one day after school as we corrected workbooks. "Sometimes I wish I were the old kind of teacher who had everybody sit at desks in rows and do the arithmetic problems on page forty-three. But then I get somebody like Roy. Roy's reading at an eighth-grade level and he's got that freaky math aptitude that doesn't really test but just lets him spit out the answers to really complicated problems. In a regular classroom Roy would be bored out of his skull and he'd be a real discipline problem. But here I can keep him busy, going at his own pace. And I can think that maybe he'll grow up and cure cancer."

I had no idea whether Roy would grow up and cure cancer, but I did know that Lucy Warner's students were getting a splendid education. And each moment I spent in her classroom was a joy. When I broke through the concept of subtraction with shy little Jennifer, I wanted to set off a twenty-one-gun salute. It was exciting to watch Freddie rip through his workbooks, never making mistakes, and gratifying to read the simple children's stories about me, written in large clear letters on lined composition paper. I took a short breather from my growing agnosticism to thank God or anyone else who might be listening for having this all work out so well.

An evergreen wreath covered with gold pipe cleaners twisted into peace signs hung over a neatly typed list on the door of our room. I stopped to proudly read the list when I got back from student teaching on the last Wednesday before Christmas. After weeks of random angry jottings on scratch paper taped to Pren's closet door, we had finally compiled a complete lexicon of descriptive terms for Spiro Agnew, who had recently identified us as "nattering nabobs of negativism." All who passed our door could now learn that Spiggy himself was an agonizing advocate of asininity, a blubbering buffoon of Babbitry, a chattering cheerleader of churlishness, a dastardly dragoon of dementia and so on, clear through to zestful zero of zealotry.

I was surprised to find Pren in the room, and I was absolutely flabbergasted when she suggested that we go to Chapel Hill to the Zoom for dinner. I knew she still had two papers to finish before leaving for Christmas. I would have expected her to be buried over in the West Campus library stacks, surrounded by dusty old volumes on obscure subjects, scribbling furiously on yellow legal pads.

"How come? Is something the matter?" I was exhausted, but not too tired to notice how out of character her behavior was.

Pren shrugged. "Just going a little crazy, that's all. The usual December crunch panic. I thought it might be nice to get away from campus. Maybe we could walk around a little and do some Christmas shopping while we're there."

She was right. She clearly *was* going crazy. Prentiss Granger never suffered from December crunch panic. She'd never even gotten an extension on a paper.

And of course she had an ulterior motive in suggesting the dinner, but she didn't tell me until I was midway through my hot apple pie à la mode. By this time I would probably have agreed to chain myself to the White House fence if the pitch were made adroitly.

"What you got planned for Christmas vacation, Laurel?"

"Nothing. Just the usual at home. How about you?"

She poured herself more iced tea. "We're having something of a family reunion this year. Rare public appearances by aunts, uncles and cousins."

"Aunt Nell?"

"Oh, definitely. She always comes for Christmas. No, I mean more than usual." She looked carefully around as if to see whether anyone was listening, then leaned across the table and whispered, "We've got *Yankees* coming in, Laurel. From Connecticut."

"Oh my God!" I swooned in mock horror. "You mean real baby-eating, mongrelizing, nigger-loving Yankees?"

"The genuine article."

I returned my attention to the remains of my apple pie. "So what's the problem with that? I'd think you'd welcome having other people there. Take the heat off you and all that."

She sighed. "Unfortunately, it doesn't work like that. It's the Major's sister and her family. Aunt Anne's a minority stockholder and director of Granger Mills. She approves wholeheartedly of the way her brother runs the company, except that she thinks the wages he pays are maybe a bit high. And she's married to a reactionary idiot who owns a silver company. Serving trays, water pitchers, that sort of thing. Aunt Anne's very southern, make no mistake. But Uncle Peter is a real rock-ribbed New Englander. And a galloping fascist. When he and the Major get to chatting, it's like being in the bunker with Adolf and the boys."

"Sounds like fun."

"Yeah, like spending the holidays in a Con Son tiger cage. A real bundle of laughs. How'd you like to come visit?"

So that was what she was after. I quickly sketched out the possibility in my mind. There was no real reason not to. Nothing remarkable was happening in St. Elizabeth over the holidays and I'd be back there again at the end of January for Grandma Chesterton's seventy-fifth birthday. "You make it sound so appealing, how could I possibly say no?"

She beamed across the table. "Does that mean you'll come?"

"Oh, hell, what am I getting into?"

"It's okay, Laurel, just say yes. It won't be bad if you're there, honest. They'll leave us alone then."

"You mean they'll leave *you* alone. I'm the one who'll have to be nice to everybody."

"They'd love to have you there. You know my mother thinks you're my last chance of ever being a proper lady."

"Which shows just how in tune with reality your mother is."

"Yeah, we're on exactly the same wavelength," she said wryly. "I think she has a mind to do some serious debutante planning over this vacation."

"You'll make a lovely bow, my dear. I think you'll be quite a delightful deb, and I look forward to your round of parties immensely."

"Fuck off, Laurel. You know perfectly well that I don't have the slightest intention of going through with any of that."

"Then you'd better tell your mother, because I think she's already planned about eleven different parties and balls, down to the color of the after-dinner mints."

Pren grimaced. "I know. I guess I'll have to break it to her over this vacation. Or else she'll start ordering invitations to things."

"Wonderful. I get to sit around and mop up after you break your mother's heart. I think I'm changing my mind."

"It won't be that bad!"

"Then why do you need me?"

"Because somehow when you're around, it always seems more bearable. Because you can make me laugh at myself when I start taking myself too seriously and get all huffed up at the Major. Because we can take day trips and only show up for meals. Because ..." She stopped and grinned at me. "Listen, I'm willing to grovel if it'll help."

I laughed at the mere thought of Prentiss Granger groveling. "All right, you win. But I can't come until at least the Monday after Christmas. My family would have a fit."

She beamed as she picked up the check and pushed back her chair. A cane syrup drawl flowed from her lips. "The Monday after Christmas will be most delightful, Miss Laurel. We're all just thrilled and we're certain that you'll have the most wonderful time celebrating the birth of our Lord at Azalea Acres." She switched abruptly from the drawl to a brisk, clipped Yankee accent. "Flak jackets and hard hats will be issued upon arrival."

Chapter 13 _____

"Are you sure it's all right for me to be here?" I asked as we rode in from the airport. Pren was a nervous wreck.

"All right?!?! You must be kidding! I think of myself as a beseiged outpost and you as my own personal cavalry."

"Oh drat, and I forgot Rin Tin Tin."

Pren laughed. "Funny you should mention old Rinty. Aunt Anne and Uncle Peter just happened to bring along their dogs. They have a pair of the most neurotic—and racist—miniature collies you've ever seen in your life. One of them bit the daily cleaning lady and she's refused to come back till they leave. Anytime Willie Mae comes into a room, Flopsie and Cottontail start to howl as if the moon were full and Dracula were slinking around the corner."

"Flopsie and Cottontail?" I queried, in a dreadfully neutral tone. She nodded grimly.

I shuddered and lit another cigarette. I was chain-smoking already and I hadn't even set foot in Azalea Acres yet. I decided on the spot that this time I was going to have to smoke in front of Major and Mrs. Granger. "What about your cousins?"

Pren opened her mouth as wide as it would go and let out a piercing scream of frustration.

"What's the matter with them?"

"Nothing that about five years of forced labor wouldn't solve. Their main objection is that the quality of television is so inferior in Granger."

"How old are they?"

"Brian is fifteen, and he's actually not too bad. He's been playing games with the Major. And so have I, God help us all. I've been sitting around in the game room playing Waterloo and Gettysburg and Blitz-krieg with the two of them. Brian's real nice and sincere and all, a Youth-for-Christer type. But his sisters drive me bananas. They're seven and nine and they whimper constantly. I've never seen such insufferable children. They didn't *like* some of their presents, so they tossed them aside. Spoiled little monsters! When I think of all the kids who don't get any Christmas at all. . . ."

"Now, now," I soothed. "Everything will be just fine. You want to turn around and drop me at the airport? I think I forgot my hairbrush and I'd like to run home and pick it up."

She had absolutely nailed the Peter Leach family. Mr. Leach was tall, thin, balding and exceedingly acidic. He fussed and fidgeted constantly. Mrs. Leach resembled the Major physically, though her hair was still chestnut brown while his was getting tweedier by the minute. The dogs followed her everywhere, whimpering. In fact, everybody in that family whined about everything. Incessantly.

On Tuesday Pren and I went into Columbia so Pren could deliver a treatise she had written for some antiwar group or another on the role of France in Indochina. I wasn't quite sure how that was going to bring the boys home any faster, but the girl in Columbia seemed very excited to have it. We wandered around the university campus awhile, ate lunch, and headed home.

When we got back to Granger it was around three. The Major met us on the front porch, furious. I had never seen his face so red. Blood vessels bulged on his forehead and he was actually shuddering in anger. He stalked menacingly across the porch toward Pren.

"*YOU!!!! Into my office on the double!!*"

Pren looked at him, glanced at me, and tried to smile. "What's the matter, Daddy?"

He stared malignantly at her for a moment. Then he bellowed, "The matter, you little Judas? What is the matter? I'll tell you what is the matter. I was visited by the FBI this afternoon. On your account. Now *inside*! *ON THE DOUBLE!!!*"

Pren cast one last anguished glance at me, then was swallowed by the house. I stood there with my mouth gaping. I had created lots of scenar-ios in which Pren's father found out that she was involved in one demonstration or another. I had covered for her so often that I routinely worked out every possible way any given situation could go wrong.

But it had never once occurred to me that anybody—particularly the Federal Bureau of Investigation—might actively intervene. And every repercussion I could think of from this unexpected turn of events made my flesh crawl.

I finally braced myself and walked into the house, prepared to act as if nothing out of the ordinary had happened. Mr. and Mrs. Leach sat in the living room with those damned collies and for the first time he looked like he was actually enjoying himself. I nodded to them and walked on through the house to the kitchen. Willie Mae was sitting at the kitchen table, staring out the window onto the back lawns. She was a huge woman the color of Hershey's syrup. Her hair was completely covered by a bandanna that matched the shapeless blue cotton uniform she wore. She jumped when the door opened, but actually seemed relieved to find it was only me.

"Hep you find somethin', Miss Laurel?" She started to stand up but I waved her back into her chair.

"My lost youth."

Willie Mae let that one go right by. "There be cookies in that tin over by the counter," she offered a moment later. Without thinking I walked to the counter and helped myself to an apricot jam bar. "Good," I mumbled, my mouth full of cookie.

"Please you like it, Miss Laurel."

We heard a crash from the wing of the house that contained the Major's study, library, game room and arsenal. Both Willie Mae and I jumped nervously. I decided that for the moment, Willie Mae was my best possible information source.

"When did the Major get home? Very long ago?"

Willie Mae hesitated. Clearly she was figuring out how to put me off. Willie Mae had been with the Granger family for a long time and was fiercely loyal.

I leaned forward across the table. "Willie Mae, please. It's very important that I have some idea what's going on here. The Major told us that the FBI had been to see him. Did they come here?"

Willie Mae looked at me suspiciously. "I be in the kitchen, Miss Laurel. I don't hear no thing."

I made my tone as conciliatory as possible. "Please, Willie Mae, it's important. I'm very worried about Prentiss."

"That girl give her daddy a heart attack."

"Quite likely," I agreed. "Did the FBI come here?"

Willie Mae shook her large head. The corner of the bandanna was starting to come loose where it was tucked behind one ear. "They go to the mill."

"Oh, dear God." No wonder the Major was so apoplectic. G-men had invaded his mill to announce that his oldest daughter was trying to over-throw the government. "Where's everybody else?" It suddenly occurred to me that save for the Leaches, I hadn't seen a single soul since we came in.

Willie Mae ticked them off on her fingers. "Miss Shirley, she take the little Leach girls over by the Burtons. The two boys, they go squirrel hunting out to the woods. Miz Granger, she lay down up to her room."

That didn't surprise me. With her good buddy Jack Daniel's, no doubt.

I stood up. "Damn, damn, damn!"

"No cussin', Miss Laurel."

"Sorry, Willie Mae."

She smiled at me expansively. "You take that tin with you, why not. And here, some milk to go with." She lumbered over to the large refrig-erator and poured me a tall glass, set it on a tray and put the tin of cook-ies beside it. I was touched and grateful.

Pren stayed closeted in the War Wing with her father for more than two hours. Because his office was directly beneath the room Pren and I shared, I could periodically hear him yelling, though I could never make out any of the words. I pulled an armchair over to the window and stared out across the orchard of leafless peach trees through my vigil. I saw Shirley and the girls come up the driveway in Mrs. Granger's baby blue Lincoln Continental and a little later watched Llewellyn and Brian come loping across the fields with their rifles. Nobody came to my room and I wasn't about to leave its sanctuary. Fortunately Pren shared a private bath with Shirley and it opened directly off the bedroom.

By five o'clock it was pitch black and I felt truly trapped. A veil of gloomy silence had settled over the house and the unnatural quiet was nerve-racking. I longed to hear something rough and rollicking, the Rolling Stones, perhaps, or Janis, or maybe some hard-driving Aretha. Anything to lift that scrim of silent fury which engulfed Azalea Acres.

At 5:15 Pren stumbled into the room. I jumped up to greet her and held her tight. She was quivering and I led her over and deposited her in an armchair. As she sat down I saw that her lip was puffed up and that she carried an ugly red welt across her left cheek.

"My God, did he *hit* you?"

"Only perfunctorily." She smiled, wincing slightly as the puffed lip stretched. "And it was nowhere near as rough as the inquisition I've just been through."

"You're experienced now," I offered lightly, "in case you ever get caught behind enemy lines."

"I just was. And we're now both prisoners of war." She crossed to the mirror and inspected her face casually. "You have any ice here?"

"No, but I'll run down—"

She cut me off. "Forget it! If you got waylaid downstairs, I couldn't exactly ride to your rescue. The Major is not a stupid man, Laurel. It didn't take him any time at all to figure out that you've been lying your head off to him for years. I'd steer clear." She went into the bathroom and rinsed her face. "It's nothing serious anyway."

"My sainted Aunt Petunia, it isn't serious."

Now she sounded mad. "I mean it, Laurel, just forget it. It's the least of our problems."

"What's the worst?"

She sat down again and looked pensive for a moment. "Hmmmm. The absolute worst or one of the five worst?"

"Get to the point, for God's sake. What happened?"

"Two men from the Federal Bureau of Investigation stopped by Granger Mills today to pay their respects to an old war hero. And to bring him photographs and excerpts from the dossier compiled by the FBI on one Prentiss Louise Granger, a senior at Duke University."

"Holy shit! *Pictures?!*"

"Uh huh. Some real charmers too. They were even generous enough to leave the Major copies. There's a shot of me sitting out during the Vigil and another from the Allen Building take-over. And one taken outside the New Mobe offices last summer with Rennie Davis. You can imagine how *that* went over. Then there's a couple from last October in Chicago, picketing outside the courthouse. With Bob, who was identified as a 'prominent anarchist agitator' and also as a former professor and lover of mine. I must have left something out. Let's see. Oh, yeah. There are a couple of real beauties from the March on Washington last November."

"Holy shit," I said again. "But why would they bother with you? You're such a little fish and the radical left is such a great big sea."

"I've been trying to figure that out. My guess is that it's just a shotgun assault. It can't take that much time and effort for them to go visit the parents of people who are stirring up trouble, even if they aren't so terribly important. It certainly worked with the Major. Half an hour of government time and my whole world gets turned upside down. Incidentally, we're confined to quarters. In the morning, the Major will call your family and inform them that you're on your way back to Louisiana, posthaste."

"Oh no! He wouldn't do *that*, would he?"

"Would and will. He feels terribly betrayed, Laurel. I kept telling him that you had nothing to do with my politics, but he wasn't listening. A quisling, he called you."

I lay down on my bed. This didn't seem to be the kind of nightmare that one woke up from. Several minutes of silence passed, interrupted only by the muffled yapping of those wretched collies.

"What are you going to do?" I asked finally.

"I'm thinking it through," she said. I cocked my head up from the bed and saw that she was sitting with her eyes closed in apparent deep concentration. "Leave me alone for a little while."

So I shut up and went back to staring at the ceiling. I felt quite comfortable in Pren's room, actually. Not only did it have that wonderful view across the rolling peach orchards, but it was tasteful and quietly decorated, almost to the point of austerity. Shirley's room, by contrast, was a veritable sea of pink and lavender ruffles, the kind of room where you always feel certain you're tracking in mud.

We stayed in that configuration for at least forty-five minutes, me on my back on the bed, Pren in the chair with her eyes closed. When there was a quiet knock on the door, both of us jumped.

"Got yo supper, girls," Willie Mae announced through the door.

Pren got to her feet and unlocked the door. Willie Mae stepped in carrying an enormous tray and Pren shut the door behind her. Willie Mae set the tray down on Pren's desk. "I be back with the tables," she said on her way out, "and I get you some ice for that lip." A moment later she reappeared with two wicker snack tables and a bowl of crushed ice. By then, of course, I had already inspected the tray pretty carefully. Willie Mae had been more than generous.

"Thanks, Willie Mae," Pren said, hugging her. Willie Mae hugged Pren hard, then turned and left the room without saying a word. I noticed that she never once met either of our eyes.

"Good old Willie Mae," Pren said fondly after she was gone. "It's been a few years, but she hasn't forgotten the drill. The last time she brought me trays when I was 'confined to quarters' was when I was pregnant. She'd only been working here about six months then and it really shook her."

I didn't answer this. I was already biting into my first sandwich. Pren picked a bit at the meat and cheese tray. I plowed through two sandwiches and three slices of pie before she spoke again.

"I've finally got it figured out. Here's what we're going to do." Then she outlined a course of action for the next twelve hours that boggled my mind.

"You can't be serious."

"Of course I can. I hadn't planned for this to happen so soon, but the fucking FBI forced my hand. There might not be another chance."

"You'd actually do it?"

"You bet your ass. We're talking about the rest of my life right now, Laurel. It's a subject that's rather dear to my heart." We argued it back and forth, but the more we talked about it, the more she convinced me that her plan was the only feasible alternative.

Willie Mae brought a pot of coffee and more cookies when she returned for our dishes. Nobody else came to the door, though Shirley knocked at the bathroom door once to ask if Pren was all right.

"I'm just fine, honey," Pren told her, unlocking the door. "Come give me a big hug." Shirley stepped forward awkwardly. She wasn't the least bit comfortable with displays of emotion and small wonder. The Granger family didn't offer much precedent for them. Shirley stood stiffly while Pren hugged her. "Don't worry, Shirl, everything will work out fine," she promised. "We'll talk about it all tomorrow, okay?" Shirley nodded and retreated hastily into the bathroom.

I'm sure she didn't have the slightest idea that she would never see her sister again.

Pren and I used the radio as cover for our preparations as I worked my way systematically through two packs of Winstons. We heard Shirley shower and periodically there'd be a torrent of canine yapping, but in general the place was remarkably quiet. The Leaches were probably glued to the television. Mrs. Granger wouldn't emerge from her room for two more days, Pren prophesied. And the less we heard from the Major, the better.

Finally after midnight there were no more noises from the house. We lay fully clothed on top of the bedspreads in total darkness. I watched the second hand sweep around the luminous alarm clock dial.

At one-thirty Pren rose silently from her bed and slipped over to the door. Opening it, she stuck her head into the hall, looked both ways, then disappeared. I couldn't hear her at all and hoped that everybody was sleeping as soundly as Pren claimed they did. She was gone for a long time, nearly twenty minutes, and I began to worry. Finally the door swung open soundlessly and she slipped back into the room. At that precise moment the collies started to bark.

"Oh, shit," Pren whispered. We listened close to the door. The Leaches and the collies were down at the far end of the hall, across from the master bedroom. The dogs kept yipping away and we heard doors open. Then came the Major's voice. "Anne, those dogs go to the kennel *now!*" Silence. "Anne, I mean it. Immediately. They're bothering Iris." Next we heard the dogs whimper along the hall, with Mr. Leach admonishing them to be quiet. A few minutes later we heard them barking distantly outdoors and heard footsteps in the outside hall again. Then the dogs stopped barking and all fell silent again.

"Did you get it?" I whispered.

Pren held up the manila envelope. "Right here. It took a lot longer to get into the safe than I expected. And there was more shit to go through in there than I thought. But we're set. Now we just have to wait till about three-fifteen before we make our next move. Everybody's so jumpy that they might not get back to sleep for a while."

We sat there in the silent dark for the next hour and a quarter. I was absolutely terrified. I didn't have the slightest hope that we could actually get away with the stunt Pren had dreamed up, and I knew that when we were apprehended it would not go well for us. I could already feel the bamboo shoots sliding under my fingernails.

At last it was time to go. Our winter coats hung in the hall closet downstairs and we didn't dare stop for them, so we bundled in as many sweaters as we could. Then we picked up our bags and slipped out into the hallway. "No more than you can carry," Pren had warned. "And carry *easily*. I'll replace anything you have to leave, don't worry." She herself had finished packing her one small suitcase in about two and a half minutes. I noticed how lovingly she handled the manila envelope and peeked while she was in the bathroom to make sure she hadn't brought any souvenirs from the Major's weapons museum.

Pren propped the envelope containing her note on the desk beside the empty cookie canister and coffee pot. Then she looked around the room one last time, blew a kiss into the darkness and slipped into the hall. I followed, terrified but somehow mobile.

Pren led the way down the hall. There was enough moon so that we could see the stairway fairly clearly in the light through the tall windows. I stumbled slightly on the landing, but recovered without making too much noise. Pren glared furiously at me. We reached the kitchen quickly. Pren set down her bag and slipped off for a second to disconnect the alarm system. Why the Major found it necessary to wire his house I had never quite understood, but even the old fallout shelter in the back yard was hooked up to the alarm system. Pren was back quickly and we slithered out into the night.

It was cold out there, a lot colder than I had expected. Pren's car was parked in the front of the parking area, since we'd been the last ones out before the pyrotechnics began. She opened the passenger door and carefully hoisted our bags into the back seat, then slid in herself. "Don't slam the door," she whispered. "Just hold it." I made it catch silently.

"What time is it?"

She peered at her watchface. "Three-thirty-five. The train should be through here in ten minutes."

We sat shivering and waiting. An eternity later we heard the faraway whistle of the nightly freight train. I tried to remember the details of the Doppler effect and couldn't. Just as the train approached, when it was its loudest, Pren started the engine of the car. In the silent night, it boomed like the explosion of an oil refinery. Wasting no time, she slipped the car into gear and crept down the winding driveway. We went slowly without lights but she knew the drive well, and once we approached the road, it would be almost impossible for anyone in the house to see us.

We reached the road, driving along without lights till we were clearly away from the house. Then Pren switched on her headlights, thrust back her head and gave an enormous Rebel yell. I didn't say anything. I was still in shock. Pren glanced at me. "You okay?" I nodded. "Well, *good*!!!!

We did it, Laurel. We got away. Free at last, free at last, thank God almighty, I'm free at last."

"We're not home free yet," I reminded. "In fact, we have a whole hell of a lot farther to go before we can start to feel safe."

"But we did the hardest part. We escaped."

My mind was reeling as we hurtled through that late December night. I was absolutely terrified of being caught. Never had Duke seemed quite so far away.

By sunrise we were approaching Raleigh and I was frozen solid. The car's defective heater was no substitute for a good winter coat, like my new gold wool one that hung in the hall closet of Azalea Acres, probably forevermore.

We reached Pren's Durham bank just after it opened. "No hitch at all," she told me as she slipped back into the driver's seat. "I left ten bucks in the joint account with the Major and opened myself a new one with the rest of it. Also, I got a safe deposit box."

"For what?"

"For the stuff I took from Granger," she explained patiently, as if addressing the addled. "My stock certificates and savings passbooks and the savings bonds. No point in carrying them around right now. When I work out the next part, I can always come back. It made me too nervous to be carrying my whole financial life around that way."

We breakfasted at the Toddle House, then drove to a large white clapboard house near East Campus. Suddenly I was exhausted. And Pren was right. Being back in Durham did make everything seem more plausible and reasonable. As soon as we hit the city limits, I had relaxed perceptibly. Now the yawns came faster and faster, till I barely had time to close my mouth between them.

Nobody seemed to be around the house when we got there, but the door was unlocked and Pren seemed quite at ease. She led me into what she identified as Adam's room and we both crashed immediately on his double mattress on the floor. I had been curious about Adam's house for a long, long time. But I was sound asleep before my head hit the pillow and the next thing I knew it was dark again and Pren was shaking me, telling me to call my parents. Fortunately the Major hadn't gotten to them first, so I just explained that Pren and I had come back to school a little early. It was a snap.

I had completely forgotten that it was New Year's Eve. And we were not going to be nibbling finger sandwiches and sipping champagne in Granger after all. We would be celebrating in a whole new world, at least for me. Except for my adolescent visits to Granger, every New Year's Eve of my life thus far had been spent in St. Elizabeth.

But tonight, to celebrate the beginning of a new decade and the estrangement of Prentiss Granger from her family, I would be at my very first genuine New Year's Eve party. We went to a pleasantly funky party over in Chapel Hill. It was held at a large old house out in the country and I never did figure out exactly which of the three or four dozen people at the party actually lived there. There were a lot of folks with very long hair and headbands and overalls. I overheard one lengthy nostalgic conversation about what Woodstock had *really* been like, and listened to a guy with a lot of wild fuzzy hair explain that Joni Mitchell was the incarnation of all that was wise and true and beautiful. He was so eloquent and persuasive that I went out and bought *Clouds* the next week. There were a few of Pren's radical friends there, but mostly it was a less political group of people. This suited me just fine. It was a pleasure and a relief to be with nice silly folk who shot screwdrivers into each other's mouths with squirt guns and smoked what seemed like pounds of grass and played Creedence Clearwater and the Grateful Dead. There was lots of good stuff to eat too, very health foody sorts of things like carrot cake with cream cheese icing and raisin nut mix.

Pren had decided not to announce her sudden independence now. "I'll tell people soon enough. Very soon, in fact, probably tomorrow, because my friends need to know about this FBI shit. But not tonight. It would spoil everyone's fun."

The night that brought us the seventies was another one of those occasions where the details of how I got home are still a little vague. I smoked vast quantities of dope, overate shamelessly, drank several Seven-Sevens and talked for a long time to a UNC sociology major. She wore white overalls, long braids, a beaded headband and a pin that proclaimed IF YOU ARE NOT PART OF THE SOLUTION, YOU ARE PART OF THE PROBLEM. She was planning to go into VISTA after graduation and work in Appalachia. I was pretty impressed, and I guess I must have carried on at some length. Finally she looked at me oddly and said pointedly, "You could do exactly the same thing, you know. VISTA needs teachers desperately. In fact, VISTA needs everything desperately. That shitface Nixon has practically cut every cent. You could teach on a reservation or in Appalachia or in the inner city."

The girl drifted away not long after that and the next time I saw her she was out on the back porch locked in a torrid embrace with some guy whose hair was in an honest-to-God ponytail, still a very rare phenomenon. His hand was in those overalls clear up to the elbow and I scooted back inside, embarrassed.

Pren seemed to be in fine spirits throughout the entire evening. She looked beautiful. Her hair hung like chestnut satin down her back, at least two feet long, parted on the side and clipped back with a large tortoiseshell barrette. She wore just enough makeup to camouflage her recent injuries and most of the glow she radiated seemed to come from deep inside her. She looked very much alive, vibrant and vivacious. She wore faded blue jeans and a dark green ribbed turtleneck sweater, long dangling earrings and a button that read FREE THE CHICAGO SEVEN. She floated around on what seemed to be a private little cloud, and it seemed odd to me that she didn't have a date. She could easily have hooked up with one of the stag guys at the party, and several of them came on to her pretty strong, but she really did seem to want to be alone and nobody much minded. A lot of folks at the party didn't have dates.

At midnight everybody screamed and yelled and kissed everybody else. I was kissed by a lot of men that night, including the guy with the ponytail and the Joni Mitchell fan. I was even kissed, accidentally no doubt, by a *Chronicle* editor. It was without question the most men I had ever kissed on any one occasion and perhaps in my entire life.

During the round robins of kisses and hugs at midnight, I encountered Pren unexpectedly. "Happy seventies, Laurel," she told me with a wonderfully warm smile. Then she gave me a big long hug.

At that moment the decade seemed filled with promise. I would not have believed how soon it would disintegrate around us.

Chapter 14 _____

The science of earthquake prediction is at best an inexact one, but seismologists generally agree that any quake of great magnitude will be followed by a series of jolting aftershocks. So it was with our hasty departure from Granger. There were at least a dozen messages for Pren to call her father when we moved back into Wognum, all of which she pitched into the trash.

There was also a message for her to come to the Dean's office as soon as possible. It turned out that the Major had already tried to withdraw her from the university and had been told, very gently, that his daughter had achieved her majority nearly a year earlier and consequently could be withdrawn only by herself.

The deans of the Women's College were quite fond of Prentiss Granger, politics notwithstanding. She was one of only seven coeds initiated into Phi Beta Kappa on completion of junior year, with an overall average that still soared above 3.7. Once Pren assured them that she could finance her final semester, she emerged triumphantly from East Duke as what they called an "emancipated student." The only thing they wouldn't let her do was move officially off campus.

The Major called the dorm frequently during the first week we were back. Pren refused to take his calls and I wasn't about to talk to him either. Unfortunately, the sly devil finally called me directly. Once I realized who was on the other end of the line, I was absolutely petrified. But it seemed that the Major didn't particularly want his pound of flesh from me. He just wanted to be absolutely certain that Pren got his message. She'd already sent back four letters marked REFUSED. "You can tell Prentiss that she is no longer welcome in my home," he thundered. "Ever again. As far as I am concerned, she is no longer alive. I did not raise my daughter to be a communist traitor and a common thief."

I relayed the message verbatim, but it didn't seem to much faze Pren. She had taken nothing that wasn't rightfully hers and had accepted from the beginning that any break would have to be total and irrevocable.

She wouldn't talk about the estrangement from her family, except in passing, but I could see that it bothered her. Even in a family as formal and unemotional as hers, there's a certain amount of love floating around. So sure, her relationship with her father had always been strongly intellectual. And yes, her mother had a totally remote set of values and ideas. I was even willing to agree that Shirley and Llewellyn were extremely irritating annoyances.

But the sum total of those people was family. Had they been wiped out in an auto accident or killed in an early morning fire sweeping through Azalea Acres, I know she would have grieved. And it seemed to me that beneath her exterior of giddy nonchalance, a subtle grieving process was occurring almost despite her wishes. Now and then I'd catch her looking sadly pensive, though she always bounced right back when I spoke to her.

But any remote possibility of reconciliation was totally eliminated seven days after we got back to Durham, when she arranged to sell her stock in Granger Mills to what was then called a New York limousine liberal. He thought it would be wonderful fun to meddle in a southern textile mill. Pren flew to New York to handle the sale of stock to Murray Levin, the middle-aged ne'er-do-well heir to a New Jersey electronics business.

Until Pren sold her stock, Granger Mills had always been totally owned by members of the Granger family. The company was founded by Pren's great-grandfather in 1873 in Connecticut, where it operated until her grandfather relocated to South Carolina in 1911. The majority of the stock passed to the Major on the death of his father in 1958, with lesser portions to his sister Anne and their combined six children. In addition, the Major had transferred some of his holdings into his children's names over the years for tax purposes. So when Pren cleaned her stock certificates out of the safe in his office on that late December night, she held 13 percent of Granger Mills in her own name.

Now that 13 percent belonged to Murray Levin. And Prentiss Granger had salted away nearly a quarter of a million dollars in certificates of deposit in five New York banks. She had also immediately donated some $50,000 to Mobe, the Chicago Seven Defense Fund and the Black Panthers.

Oddly enough, the money didn't seem to matter that much to her, though hers was the indifference possible only to those who have never gone without. "I'll probably give most of it away," she announced grandly. "But what *really* satisfies me about all of this is knowing that Murray Levin will aggravate the Major mercilessly. His very existence will be a constant irritant. I only wish I could be a fly on the wall at that maiden board meeting where Murray meets the Major. If I'm not mistaken, it will be the first time a Jew has ever set foot in Granger Mills. Or Granger, South Carolina, for that matter.

Pren's grandfather had arranged the corporate structure of the company with cumulative voting so that minority stockholders would be assured representation on the board of directors. This provision was not, God knows, out of any concern for minorities of any conventional sort. What it was designed to do was assure that the female stockholders, who by virtue of sex held lesser shares of the company, could sit on the board. What the old man had been aiming at was a seat on the board for his daughter Anne. And what his son was now getting was a New York Jew. There was a delicious irony to it all.

Mrs. Granger sent me my abandoned suitcase and miscellaneous possessions by Railway Express, which I thought was actually quite sweet of her. I wondered if perhaps I ought to write her a note and thank her. I still felt a little uneasy because I hadn't written a proper bread-and-butter note for my brief visit. But what could I say in it? I mentally drafted a note:

> Dear Mrs. Granger,
>
> I'm so sorry I didn't have a chance to say good-bye in person, but I certainly enjoyed the cold tray in Prentiss's room on my recent visit. Please give my regards to the Major, and tell him that I hope he's gotten over his blind rage.
>
> Sincerely,
> Laurel

Obviously it was hopeless.

I went to New Orleans as planned over Semester Break for Grandma Chesterton's seventy-fifth birthday. There were forty-three of us there, gathered in a private room at Antoine's for one of the most memorable meals of my life.

I was seated directly across the table from Grandma, so I got to talk to her quite a bit that night in between pig-out sessions. She had lived and eaten in New Orleans her entire life, and it showed. She was a soft, pillowy lady with gentle silver curls and clear, gray blue eyes. Despite her weight, she was pretty and I realized that night that in another twenty years, Mama would look exactly like her. I didn't take it the next logical step: One day I too would look exactly like her. It was several more years before I made that connection. Sometimes we just aren't ready to assimilate information.

Grandma wanted to know my plans following graduation and it didn't seem an appropriate response to tell her that I was pretty curious myself. I'm sure she was hoping that I'd suddenly spring a handsome beau and surprise engagement. My whole family was beginning to be a little alarmed, I knew, that I had no eligible suitors hovering on the horizon.

So I just told Grandma that I planned to teach first or second grade, but wasn't exactly sure where yet. When she suggested that I might come to New Orleans and live with her, I had a forkful of Baked Alaska en route to my mouth. It hung suspended for a few moments while I thought through the culinary possibilities of living with Grandma Chesterton, who no longer went out to restaurants much but employed a superb cook.

I seriously considered her offer. There was enough room in her large Garden District house to assure my privacy, and she even arranged an interview with the principal of a nearby parochial school. "You'll want a private school," she explained. "So there won't be any *problems*." Problems, of course, was her euphemism for Negroes.

The interview went well. I could probably have a job, Sister Marie Lousie told me, though she wouldn't know for certain until July.

But did I *want* a job at Queen of Angels, a school with no problems? I wasn't quite sure. I kept remembering the sociology major from New Year's Eve and her VISTA plans. I thought about all of my accumulated racist guilt. And it didn't seem that Queen of Angels was a very promising location to start obliterating racism. If my long association with Prentiss Granger had taught me nothing else, it was that one could not sit back and expect somebody else to solve problems. Unless one really didn't care whether or not they were solved.

"There's going to be another Orangeburg," Pren said. "I can just feel it coming." A few months earlier at South Carolina State in Orangeburg, police had shot and killed three black students and wounded twenty-seven others during an alleged riot.

She sprawled on her bed on a glorious spring afternoon, chain-smoking and reading *New Left Notes*. The windows were wide open and our curtains blew gently in a warm spring breeze. Our room had been through a lot of different incarnations over the past four years, but now for the first time it seemed more my place than Pren's. Her books were still there, and most of her other stuff, but she was living off campus most of the time in a house half a block off East, down the street from Adam's place. Her room there was small and bright, opening onto a little balcony overlooking the back yard. The Vietnam map, now yellow and tattered, hung over her bed there. But the only other significant decoration was an artistic arrangement of her FBI surveillance photographs, which she took on impulse the night we fled Granger. (They were not, I should note, particularly good-quality prints.) She slept on campus only rarely these days.

"Of course there will," I answered. "That's like prophesying that next week will start with Monday. They've been bumping off blacks in the South for centuries."

She shook her head. "I'm not talking about blacks. I'm talking about students. White students. The political climate's changing, and a lot of people who started out nonviolent are getting frustrated because nothing ever happens. The establishment is paying more attention now, and you know why? Because college students are beginning to really enjoy destroying property. The one thing corporate America can't tolerate is the destruction of *things*. And that's going to keep right on happening. I don't think you'll ever understand how satisfying that can be until you do it."

"I'll take your word for it. I couldn't pitch a rock more than two yards. And if I ever tried to use a bomb, I'd blow us all up."

"That's not funny," she said shortly.

I felt instantly contrite. It was only weeks since a few scattered bits and pieces of three Weathermen had been picked out of the rubble of a Greenwich Village town house. "I know. I'm sorry. But bombing doesn't solve anything, Pren. Any more than your running around breaking windows in Chicago solved anything."

"We've been through this a thousand times. It's the symbolism that matters. There's no other way you can hit IBM or the phone company or a bank besides symbolically. But actually, what worries me a lot more than police overreaction is all this hard-hat violence Nixon's stirring up. Those guys are dangerous. And there are plenty of students furious enough to take them on. My God, there could be blood in the streets like nobody's ever seen before."

But the blood, when it came, was on a hill in Ohio, in the very heart of Middle America. The students who died weren't radical revolutionaries and their killers weren't angry construction workers. In fact, the only thing about the murders at Kent State that made any sense at all was the timing. I don't mean that they followed so close on the heels of the Cambodian invasion (or incursion, as the Trickster was calling it, hopeful perhaps that folks might confuse it with the special economy Trailways fare). Any fool could have predicted that protest would follow the Cambodian invasion.

No, the fascinating thing about the timing was that the student deaths occurred close enough to semester's end so that all across the country, colleges simply closed down early for the summer. It was as if the Trickster had *willed* disaster when all else failed, seeking any desperate measure to shut down those burdensome hotbeds of radical fomentation.

Duke didn't shut down, but we could change all our courses to pass-fail with professorial permission and most profs were extremely understanding. Or maybe they were just worn down themselves by then. It had been a hell of a year.

And the Trickster was able to get away with merely appointing a commission, that splendid sixties governmental panacea for societal ills. By the time any of those commissions reported, the dust had long since settled on the atrocities in question. They produced fat unreadable volumes that nobody in power ever paid the slightest attention to. So it didn't make any difference if the Walker Report blamed Mayor Daley for the police riots in Chicago. The Chicago Seven were convicted nevertheless and charges were dropped against eight cops who were briefly indicted in an alleged show of judicial impartiality. And it didn't matter in the slightest that the Scranton Commission pronounced the killings at Kent State to be "unnecessary, unwarranted and inexcusable." It was still three years before the Nixon administration got around to a grand jury investigation, and nine years before the last legal remedy was exhausted. Unsuccessfully.

So our four years in college ended with both a bang and a whimper. There were lots of demonstrations and marches and events, of course, first for Cambodia and then for Kent State and then for Jackson State. Pren went back up to Washington after the Kent State shootings, but she was only gone three days. Pass-fail or no, she still had papers to write and the concept of writing a paper merely for a passing grade was quite alien to her. Whether she was breaking windows or falling in love or analyzing the impact of the Chinese Cultural Revolution on the future of Maoism, she always gave it 500 percent. So she came back to campus and holed up in the library and wrote and wrote and wrote.

Then she packed her books and blue jeans, gave all her old clothing from the Granger wardrobe to our dorm maid Loretta, and loaded the Bonneville. A week before graduation, she hugged me good-bye and hit the road for California. I was left to take apart our college room for the last time before heading out into the Real World.

There was only one problem. I no longer had the slightest idea what reality might be.

Book Two

Get tight with a Southerner
and he'll step in front of a car for you.

—*Duane Allman*
1971

Chapter 1 _____

I sat cross-legged on an old braided rug in blue jeans, eating turkey, whole wheat raisin stuffing, broccoli stir fried with beansprouts and a strange lentil rice curry. On either side of me, with similarly groaning plates, sat Prentiss Granger and her current boyfriend, Wilt Bannister. We were at a potluck Thanksgiving dinner in the Berkeley hills with a dozen of Pren's friends. Several guys were clustered around a black-and-white portable TV watching football, a three-year-old boy lackadaisically smeared cranberry relish on his arm and a Japanese baby crawled determinedly toward a big black dog of indeterminate parentage. Behind me the FM radio was playing "American Pie."

I had been in California less than twenty-four hours, but I could already understand what Pren had told me repeatedly about the seductive freedom of Berkeley. These people seemed to dress, speak, think and act precisely as they pleased, but without the self-consciousness of Pren's activist friends at Duke. And there was a gentle sort of joy in this group, a sense of fellowship I could never recall experiencing at Thanksgiving dinner before. These refugees from odd corners of America projected a stronger sense of family than any of the gatherings of Granger and Hollingsworth relatives I had ever attended.

It pleased me that they had accepted me in such a casual, friendly and immediate manner. This was partly, of course, because I was Prentiss Granger's friend. But it was also because of my present occupation, inner-city teacher in the high-rise slums of Chicago. And I was not about to blow my political image by confessing that it hadn't been my intention to teach in the ghetto at all. Alas, there was a hideous glut of newly certified teachers, more than ever before in history, and jobs in well-heeled suburban school districts simply didn't exist for us. I was teaching at the McLaughlin School, a horrid hellhole sandwiched between the Dan Ryan Expressway and a twenty-three-story project, because it was the only job I could get.

"I just can't picture Ginger Lockford in law school, no matter how hard I try," Pren said.

"I know. But she figures that anything, even going back to school, has to be better than what she's doing now." What Ginger was doing now was working as a minor administrator in her father's sporting goods company, chasing down lost orders and placating irate customers. I knew just exactly how much she hated her job because since I'd moved north after teaching a year in New Orleans, we were roommates, sharing a fifteenth-story apartment overlooking Lincoln Park and Lake Michigan.

"But why law school? I never suspected she was even *interested* in law, unless you count that she used to watch *Perry Mason* a lot at school. And dated that law student from UNC, though he didn't last long, if I remember correctly."

"It was typical Ginger logic. Last year she took law boards, grad records and business boards. She scored highest on the law boards."

"In the old days," Wilt said wistfully, "I could have said that sounded just like a woman."

I laughed. I genuinely liked Wilt Bannister, even as Pren had promised I would. He was a warm, solid fellow with pale blue eyes and a springy mane of soft antique-gold curls. At twenty-seven, he had a good five years on me, but he looked younger and never acted patronizing. He and Pren seemed well suited to each other. His genial good nature tempered her intensity and it was obvious that he adored her. They even held hands in public.

"Don't let Mona Ritter hear you say that," Pren warned. "I'd have to sign an affidavit in blood that you were only kidding."

"Hey," Wilt said. "I'm tough. I was in the First Air Cav. I don't hide behind my old lady's skirts."

Pren grinned. "Your old lady doesn't own any skirts."

"That's okay," he said. "But I still think you're missing a bet. You'd look awfully cute in one of those ruffleduffle Tricia Nixon numbers, with a bunch of little bows in your hair."

I chuckled at the image. At the moment, Pren was braless in a gaily embroidered Mexican skirt, faded denim bellbottoms and handmade leather sandals. Her hair was parted down the middle, then swept back into a single molasses braid down the center of her back. She stuck her tongue out at Wilt, then turned to me.

"This is a terrific salad, Laurel. I knew it was a good idea having you come out. You saved me from public humiliation, trying to come up with something edible."

"There's always your Chef Boyardee ravioli," Wilt said. "That's a guaranteed crowd pleaser."

Pren lunged at him in mock anger. "At least I know how to open a can, smartass."

"Oh, God," he sighed in mock resignation. "Here we go." He made his voice all high and squeaky. "What have *you* done around the house lately, you vile male chauvinist pig? Sisterhood means never having to do the dishes."

As it happened, however, it was only the ladies who bellied up to the sink half an hour later. Susan Yamaguchi, an Oakland sixth-grade teacher with whom I'd been swapping ghetto horror stories before dinner, washed. I dried with a hefty brunette named Roxanne. More than once I thought wistfully of past southern Thanksgiving feasts where the dishes all vanished and were taken care of by somebody else.

"So what kind of community organizing is there in the neighborhood where you teach, Laurel?" Roxanne asked. She was a big-boned girl with piercing dark brown eyes set a little too close for her wide forehead. Black hair drooped lank and lifeless to her narrow shoulders. She was a painter friend of somebody's, visiting from Portland.

I was much too embarrassed to tell her that my only contact with the neighborhood surrounding McLaughlin was the terrifying interlude between my car and the school building. I laughed a little nervously. "The kind that keeps you alive until tomorrow. These people are just trying to survive. They can't even let their kids out except to go to school, and then they have to walk them across the street and hand them over to somebody. Usually after they've walked down around sixteen flights of stairs. The elevators are always broken."

Susan shuddered. "At least here the kids can go outside and play. I can't imagine what those poor kids must be like if they can't even play."

"Picture tightly coiled springs," I answered. "We do jumping jacks and toe touching and running in place every morning, just to settle them down enough to start the day."

"We've got to pay more attention to organizing welfare mothers," Roxanne said. "They're victimized by everybody."

"Where I teach, they're not just victimized. Sometimes they get killed." I felt almost as if I were bragging, playing some sort of Top-This-Atrocity game. But these girls seemed genuinely interested. "About a month ago the mother of one of my kids was raped and beaten to death in the project lobby. In the middle of the morning."

"How horrible!" Susan said. "Did they catch the guy who did it?"

"Guys. One of the teachers saw four of them come running out of the building just before the body was discovered. She'd just gotten back from the currency exchange from cashing her welfare check and they jumped her. But no, they didn't catch them and they probably won't. She left six orphans." I could practically feel seven-year-old LaWanza clinging to my hip, as she had for weeks following the murder.

"What happened to the kids?"

"They finally shipped them back down to their grandmother in Alabama. There didn't seem to be any shortage of daddies, but nobody looking for six mouths to feed. Papa wasn't just a rolling stone in this outfit, he was a goddamned avalanche." I turned to find that Pren had quietly entered the kitchen while I spoke. I felt an odd pride that I could converse so easily with her friends.

"What perfect timing," Pren said. "Everything seems to be just about done. Who wants to take a walk with us? If I don't start moving pretty soon, I may never walk again."

And so it went for four glorious days. Actually they were four rather cold and foggy days, but they seemed quite splendid anyway. Pren and Wilt lived in a big clean second-floor apartment with a wonderful bay window and lots of motley Salvation Army furniture covered with Indian print throws. There were stacks of paper everywhere from their work with VETRAGE, an organization of antiwar veterans Wilt had cofounded. What had once been the dining room was a blizzard of papers and cardboard boxes crammed with files, all part of the manual on veterans' rights that Wilt was writing in his spare time.

The back bedroom was occupied by a Texan named Randy Hargis, a strapping six-footer with broad shoulders, a sparse beard and an equally scraggly ponytail. His twangy accent was the kind one rarely heard anymore now that LBJ was back at the ranch, but he didn't speak much. For that matter, he didn't do much either. He seemed to spend most of his time in his room, watching TV and drinking Coors. Pren warned me not to go in his room or mess with his guns and I willingly agreed. I wasn't about to annoy anybody who kept an Uzi in his nightstand.

Pren and I walked down to the VETRAGE storefront office on Friday morning while Wilt stayed home to work on the rights manual. The venetian blinds were drawn and the office dark until Pren unlocked the door and threw a switch. There were a couple of battered wood desks, several tables, three file cabinets, half a dozen folding chairs and an ancient brown overstuffed sofa spilling stuffing from a dozen wounds. The walls were papered with antiwar posters and the entire place was pretty thoroughly trashed.

"Damn!" said Pren. "These guys can certainly be pigs. There've been a couple of fellows from Detroit crashing here the last few days and every morning it looks like Omaha Beach. I used to try to keep it together, till I realized that they expected me to be doing the cleaning, being the only lady around and all. So I gave it up and now nothing ever gets done." She kicked a military sleeping bag angrily against the wall and opened the blinds to the street. In full light, the place looked even grimmer.

"Well, I'm afraid I'll catch a disease from this floor. Isn't there a broom someplace?" She pointed at a closet and I began sweeping up a small mountain of cigarette butts, fuzz balls, moldy Kleenex and crumpled telephone messages dating back to August. This was the first time we had been alone since my arrival and there was a question I'd been burning to ask. "Doesn't it bother you having Randy living with you? I'd think that you and Wilt would rather be alone. At least I'd rather be alone, if I had a guy like Wilt to live with."

She smiled. "And so would I, when you come right down to it. But until Randy gets his act together, which looks like maybe never, he'll be sitting in that back bedroom oiling his guns. There's a reason, though, and it's one I really can't argue with. Here, come look at this."

She stood beside a framed eight-by-ten glossy of Wilt and Randy in front of a grass hut, each stripped to the waist and grinning broadly. Randy was holding a rifle. Their hair was much shorter and they both looked very young. "This was taken in Binh Tri in 1969. Wilt was

Randy's platoon leader, but they were a lot tighter than officers and grunts usually get. About a week before this picture was taken, Randy saved Wilt's life. Wilt was pinned down on the side of a hill and Randy managed to sneak around and pick off the sniper. Randy's a hell of a shot. But the real reason that Wilt feels so guilty about Randy is that he sent him on the patrol where he stepped on the mine that blew off his foot."

I was reeling from the sudden knowledge that Randy Hargis was an amputee. It surprised me that Pren had never mentioned it, but I guess she took missing limbs for granted, what with the Major and all. I wondered what foot it was. I couldn't recall any limp on his frequent trips to and from the refrigerator for more beer. "And they've been together since then?"

She shook her head. "No. Randy was medevaced out immediately, of course, and Wilt didn't hear from him for more than a year. By then Wilt was back home in L.A. working for a tile company. Randy just showed up one day, broke and sick. His family had thrown him out and he had a recurrent infection because he couldn't get a decent prosthesis out of the VA. So Wilt started hassling the VA on Randy's behalf and while he was doing that, he started to run into a lot of other vets who were having trouble. Their problems seemed more important than deciding whether the bathrooms in some office building ought to be blue or yellow, and before long he quit his job. He had a girlfriend in San Francisco, so he came up here and got involved full time with VVAW."

"I take it the girlfriend is out of the picture."

"Oh, they broke up right after he moved here. She thought he was crazy to give up a promising career to hang around with a lot of unemployed bums. That's a quote."

"But why didn't he stay with VVAW?"

The phone rang and she walked over to the desk to answer it. "VET-RAGE. . . . No, Mike's out of town. He won't be back till Tuesday. . . . Sure, Eddie, I'll tell him to call you . . . . Bye." She hung up. "Where was I? Oh yeah, VETRAGE. Wilt got crosswise with a couple of the top VVAW guys and decided he could get along just fine without them. It wasn't nasty or anything, but there's a lot of heavy ego tripping that goes on. And God knows there's enough war for everybody, and an incredible number of furious, fucked-over vets. Your brother may be the only vet in the country who got a Welcome Home celebration. So Wilt and Mike

Donovan and Randy put together VETRAGE after everybody got back from the VVAW protest in Washington last April."

"It must be quite a strain, having to switch allegiance every time your boyfriend gets mad at somebody."

She laughed. "You think I'm doing this because Wilt's my boyfriend? Hell, I signed up before I ever even met Wilt. I'd been doing a lot of different things with a bunch of antiwar groups, spread kind of thin. But it seemed like we just kept doing the same old shit, over and over, and nobody was really listening anymore. I was a lot more impressed with the guys at VVAW. When *they* said the war was all fucked up, people were more likely to listen, 'cause they'd been there. That seemed like the best way to channel my energy effectively. But there wasn't any way I could get involved in strategy and organization at VVAW. There were too many guys and most of them just figured I was good for coffee or an occasional fuck. I knew Mike when he was with VVAW, though, and once the spring semester ended, I decided to find out what was happening with this VETRAGE group he'd helped start. Wilt wasn't even here at the time."

"I thought he was a founder."

"Oh, he was, but he was off in Washington, hassling the VA and congressmen as a kind of informal ombudsman for some of the guys. By the time he got back a month later, I'd reorganized the entire office. He had to like me or he'd never have found anything again."

"I haven't heard him complaining."

"And I hope he never will. Listen, why don't we toke up and go down to Telegraph Avenue? It's really quite a zoo and I think you'd get a kick out of it. Go lock the door and draw the blinds."

She took a hash pipe out of a locked file drawer and filled it from a film canister. It was real lungbuster stuff, and by the time we stumbled outdoors, I was so stoned that I had to concentrate to move. There was a quality and intensity to the street life here that I had never dreamed possible. Everybody seemed to wear faded patched denim and the hairstyles were right out of Ripley's. Mimes vied for attention with guitar players doing bad Neil Young imitations. The walls were thick with faded political posters, announcements of Grateful Dead concerts and graffiti exhortations to free everybody from David Hilliard to the Catonsville Nine. Before long I even got used to being accosted by miscellaneous waifs and wastrels begging spare change.

Street vendors hawked the *Berkeley Barb* and sidewalk stands offered the produce of the Greening of America. Half of California, it seemed, was busily producing leather belts, fringed vests, phony Indian jewelry and Con Three candles in a hundred different styles.

As we headed home after lunch and a tour of the Berkeley campus, Pren said it would be at least a year before she got back to school full time. The previous year she had carried a full academic load, but now she was down to one course and considering skipping the spring semester altogether.

"I'm burning out on school," she explained. "It just doesn't give me that old pure knowledge kick the way it used to. And anyway, the stuff I'm doing with VETRAGE seems so much more immediate to me. I've spent so much time just protesting that it's good to be working on something more constructive. Sooner or later the damn war is going to be technically over, but it won't end for these guys who can't get jobs because everybody thinks Nam vets are junkies and baby killers. Every day I spend with VETRAGE, I feel like I'm genuinely accomplishing something."

"Well, you are." We were huffing up rather a large hill and I stopped for a moment to catch my breath and admire a psychedelic mural painted across the front of an otherwise unremarkable building. "And whatever you're doing, it seems to agree with you. I haven't seen you this happy in years."

"You've never seen me this happy," she said with a warm gentle smile. "It hasn't happened before."

Chapter 2 _____

April 6, 1972, changed all that forever.

Late that afternoon, in the muggy spring heat outside a convenience store in Beaumont, Texas, gunfire roared for a few brief moments. When the shooting stopped, Prentiss Granger squealed away with a seriously wounded man in the passenger seat of her blue Bonneville. Two men lay dead on the ground behind her. One of them was an off-duty police officer.

I would like to be able to report some sort of prescience, some kind of preternatural awareness that elsewhere on the planet someone I loved was in desperate trouble. But try though I may, I've never had much luck with extrasensory anything. And so I learned all this at the same time millions of other Americans did: twenty-four hours later on the *CBS Evening News with Walter Cronkite*.

"What at first appeared to be a routine Texas convenience store robbery took a bizarre twist today," intoned Walter. "Richard Lyons reports."

Suddenly a photograph of Prentiss Granger filled my television screen. And not just any photograph either; it was *my* photograph, the one from Thanksgiving of junior year. I dropped my glass of burgundy on the white shag carpet and screamed for Ginger, completely forgetting that she hadn't gotten home yet.

I gripped the arms of my chair and watched in horror. "State and federal officials tonight are searching for antiwar activist Prentiss Granger in connection with the fatal shooting of a Beaumont, Texas, police officer yesterday afternoon," said Richard Lyons, as the scene switched to a dusty little Minute Mart with a solitary gas pump out front.

Numbness spread rapidly down my arms and legs as I learned that two men and a woman had robbed the Beaumont store of $62 the previous afternoon and that on leaving the store with drawn guns they encountered an off-duty cop who pulled his own weapon. In the gunfire that followed, the cop and one of the robbers were killed. The dead robber had been identified as William Bannister of Berkeley, California, a founder of the antiwar organization VETRAGE. Shortly after daybreak the getaway car was spotted by Texas police off a side road in the Big Thicket area; inside they found the other male robber, unconscious and in shock from bullet wounds to the side and upper arm. He was identified as Randolph Tyler Hargis, also a Berkeley VETRAGE leader, presently in critical condition.

The blue Bonneville, which I recognized immediately, was registered to Prentiss L. Granger of Berkeley, California. Two elderly female passersby had positively identified photographs of Pren as the woman who waited restlessly beside the car outside the Minute Mart, then jumped behind the wheel and sped away with the wounded robber. "I particularly noticed her," one of the old ladies told CBS, "because I thought what a terrible shame that such a pretty girl should be wearing such unsightly clothing." The clothing in question, an army fatigue jacket with the sleeves ripped out and a pair of extensively patched blue jeans, had been recovered from the back seat of the Bonneville.

And there was a film of the manager, a florid good ole boy in a string tie, talking to what appeared to be dozens of uniformed cops carrying shotguns. Behind them, a covered body was being lifted into an ambulance.

There was only one thing missing. Prentiss Granger had vanished. A warrant was immediately issued for her arrest, but she was long gone. The FBI was joining in the search because of her California residence, the proximity of the Louisiana state line and the extreme likelihood that she had fled the state. Richard Lyons concluded by returning to my photograph of Pren and warning that the FBI considered her armed and dangerous.

I smashed the off button on the TV and collapsed in my chair, oblivious to the spilled wine at my feet and the shadows of fading light coming through my apartment window. It had to be a bad dream, a hallucination, a short circuit somewhere in my brain that had caused me to imagine this grotesque nightmare. Wilt Bannister couldn't be dead. I had spoken to him only two weeks earlier, when I called Pren for a long rambling chat one Sunday afternoon. "Remember how you didn't believe there was a table under all that paper and crap in the dining room?" he asked. "Well, there was a geological breakthrough just last night. There *is* a table, Laurel. It's blue." Then he turned me over to Pren, who was full of plans for their projected reconnaissance trip to Miami. They were going to scout locations for protest activities during the upcoming Republican and Democratic national conventions.

But it seemed they'd been permanently sidetracked in Beaumont. There weren't going to be any political conventions for Wilt Bannister, and there wasn't going to be any veterans' manual either. It didn't sound like anybody was going home to the airy apartment with the big bay window. I threw myself onto the sofa and sobbed.

Finally I heard Ginger's key turn in the door. She bounded in all cheerful and peppy after several exhilarating rounds of Harvey Wallbangers at Wally's Tavern, a slick local singles hangout. It took me several minutes to report what I had seen on the television news and even longer for her to believe me. Not until we walked down for evening newspapers and saw it all in cold clinical print did the situation take on any vague resemblance to reality.

And there was nothing we could do but wonder and worry and agonize and question.

Throughout that long eerie evening, however, I was haunted by information I could share with no one, but which made the entire situation even more nauseating, grimy and sordid. A month earlier, as she changed planes at O'Hare, Prentiss Granger had given me a children's shoebox neatly wrapped in brown paper and twine, with instructions to surrender it to someone who would contact me regarding investment in a Wisconsin apple orchard. I balked, but she assured me that there was no danger, and gave me permission to inspect the box once I got home. She warned me to tell nobody I had seen her.

Back home, I had carefully unwrapped the box. Inside, packed in tissue paper, were eight neatly banded stacks of twenty- and fifty-dollar bills. I counted it twice, and each time it came out to $100,000.

The following morning I had put it in my safe deposit box at the La-

Salle National Bank, far too nervous to keep such a cache at my apartment. And there it still was. There had been no calls regarding investment in Wisconsin apple orchards, and when I made oblique reference to this in our last phone call, Pren had seemed unconcerned, saying only that some things took time.

One thing, however, was quite clear. If she could afford to drop off a hundred grand in one month, she certainly wouldn't need to rob anybody of $62 the next.

The weekend that followed was a swirling, horrifying blur. The FBI came for Ginger and me on Saturday morning and took us both downtown to a dreary impersonal office full of scarred gray metal furniture. They talked to Ginger first, while I fidgeted in a small green anteroom with a very suspicious mirror on the wall.

Ginger was in with them for over an hour before Jim Evans, one of the agents who had picked us up, came out to fetch me. He was around thirty, with extremely intense steel gray eyes and closely cropped hair that was starting to turn prematurely silver around the temples. I loathed him instantly, partly at least because of his unnerving resemblance to a supercilious New Orleans import broker I had several times gone to dinner with. On two of those occasions we had ended up in bed, strangely unsettling experiences that at least tempered the fear and ambivalence toward sex I had felt ever since my unfortunate encounter with the Clemson linebacker. Even if he hadn't been a bit of a dolt, his obvious preoccupation with Grandma Chesterton's wealth had cooled my ardor. His memory predisposed me from the outset to dislike Jim Evans.

"Where's Ginger?" I asked. I didn't like the idea that people could just disappear into the bowels of this building, particularly when they were my only link to the outside world.

"She's waiting just down the hall, Miss Hollingsworth," drawled the older G-man, who had to be at least fifty. I was intentionally thinking of them as "G-men" partly because that was what Pren always called them, voice dripping with scorn, and partly because it made them seem slightly less intimidating. But this guy didn't really seem intimidating at all. "I'm Melvin Sanford, and I'd like to visit with you a spell, if you'll be so kind as to have a seat."

His gracious manners and unmistakable southern accent took me totally by surprise. As he smiled in greeting his ruddy face crinkled into well-worn lines. I decided I might as well try to be civil to him, which turned out to be a sound decision in the long run, since he ended up as head of Operation Prentiss Granger.

It was obvious from the questions they asked that Major Granger had spilled absolutely everything he knew about Pren's political activities long ago. I doubted very much that so complete a dossier could have been compiled in the thirty-six hours since the Beaumont shooting. Pren had never spoken to her father again after leaving in the dead of that December night, though she had recently begun a clandestine correspondence with her mother. I had resumed an exchange of Christmas cards and notes with Mrs. Granger myself. But the Major had apparently not softened a bit. I was furious that he could side so unequivocally against his own flesh and blood.

I was there for hours, trying to be polite but ignorant and finding it a much simpler task than was flattering. I had never been arrested, questioned, or even stopped for speeding. But they knew a disturbing amount about old anonymous me already.

They asked endless questions that I couldn't answer about Wilt and Randy. They wanted to know everything I knew about Prentiss Granger from the name of her baby's father to the subjects of her independent study projects to why I had lied to the Major for so many years. Of course I told them nothing about the apple orchard funds. I answered "I don't know" and "I don't remember" a great deal, setting a savvy example that Bob Haldeman would follow barely a year later.

Then they brought out the pictures. There were hundreds of photographs of young men and women, mostly mug shots but others which I recognized as having been taken at considerable distance with a very long lens. All of the fugitives one might expect turned up in this rogues gallery, folks like Bernardine Dohrn and Mark Rudd and Kathy Boudin and the Armstrong brothers. Even Bob McCoy had made the portfolio, and I happily identified him. To liven things up, I sometimes said that one picture or another looked vaguely familiar, and mentioned having possibly spotted the subject in New Orleans, or at the Lincoln Park Zoo. They took detailed notes of everything I said.

Then suddenly I came upon a picture I most certainly did recognize. It was Roxanne, the visiting painter from Portland with whom I'd dried Thanksgiving dishes in Berkeley.

"This looks like a girl who was at Chadwick," I said casually. I'd spoken up often enough before so that I figured it wouldn't hurt to find out who she was. "Carolyn Armstrong, I believe her name was."

Mel Sanford smiled. "This girl was born and raised in New York City, Miss Laurel. You sure you didn't run across her somewhere else?"

I shook my head. "No, I'm certain of it. You mean that's not Carolyn Armstrong?"

"That's Peggy LaFeure," he answered. "She jumped bond on a bombing charge in New York in 1970."

I shrugged. "Oh, well." I started flipping through the pictures again, throwing up a smoke screen as I pretended to recognize several other people from far-flung times and places. So Peggy LaFeure had shared my Thanksgiving dinner, had she? It was unthinkable that Pren wouldn't have known who she was. So if Pren was involved with Peggy LaFeure, she was also involved with the political underground. Suddenly the $100,000 apple orchard made a lot more sense.

They seemed to assume that Pren would be in touch with me, and asked repeatedly if I correctly understood my patriotic duty. I was reminded at depressing length of the legal penalties for aiding or harboring a fugitive and assured unctuously that any cooperation I might render would remain strictly confidential. After a while, I began to wonder if my watch had stopped.

And then, finally, it was over.

I was reunited with Ginger, who'd been cooling her heels in that drab little anteroom for hours, with nothing to read but an office copy of *Masters of Deceit*. She was plenty annoyed, and curtly declined the Bureau's offer of a lift. We said little during the cab ride home and I, for one, was fervently hoping that J. Edgar Hoover and all of his underlings would immediately contract debilitating and mutilating venereal diseases.

As we let ourselves into the apartment, the phone was ringing. It was my parents, getting a day's jump on their usual Sunday call because they too had been visited by the FBI. "They were really quite lovely gentlemen," Mama said, "but I told them it had to be some kind of dreadful mistake. Prentiss might be headstrong, I told them, but she couldn't possibly be mixed up in anything like this."

"Of course not," I assured her. I was shocked that anyone would bother the Hollingsworths, pillars of the parish. But it would have been a very genteel visit. I could picture Cloretha carrying in a tray of coffee and cookies and wanted to scream.

"Laurel, they told us that she was seen right near the Louisiana border and might be coming this way."

"That's preposterous, Mama! And it can't be Pren anyway, no matter what they say."

Just then Ginger emerged from her bedroom with a very frightened look on her face. She came over and took the pencil from our phone pad. On the top sheet she wrote, "Don't say anything you don't want Big Brother to hear." I was alarmed to see her so upset. Ginger was the original Miss Unflappable.

Two minutes later I hung up the phone, heeded Ginger's finger across her lips and followed her silently to her room. She pointed at the dresser, orderly as always, except that on top of her hand mirror rested a neatly sealed Baggie of marijuana. Beside the Baggie, which held a quarter ounce at most, lay her red plastic rolling machine and a package of cherry-flavored papers. I regarded Ginger with some confusion, since all this paraphernalia was quite familiar to me, but she put her finger to her lips again. I stood at the bathroom door while she flushed it all, even the rolling machine. Then I followed her out of the apartment, down the elevator and into the street.

It was getting dark and starting to feel chilly, with a brisk wind off the lake. Nevertheless, Ginger headed off in that direction, stalking so rapidly and furiously that I could barely keep pace with her.

So I just kept chugging along and pretty soon she turned into the Rookery. We went off and sat on a bench while ducks and geese squawked nearby. Then she told me about the dope. "It wasn't out there when we left, Laurel. When the doorbell rang, I was in my bedroom and saw it on the nightstand. You know how paranoid I am. So I stuck it in the toe of a pair of out-of-season shoes in a box in my closet."

"And somebody moved it while we were gone. Welcome to 1984."

"They didn't have to let us know they'd been there, remember. I've read enough detective stories to know that you can search a place without leaving a trace. They left it out as a message. They're telling me that I could have been busted and I'd better cooperate. I can't be a lawyer if I have a felony conviction for possession of marijuana, you know. Shit, I wish I actually knew something, so I could get them off my back!"

"You can't tell them what you don't know." I was glad that I had long since stopped reporting everything I heard from Pren. But that feeling was almost immediately replaced by a crawly awareness that strangers had been pawing through my possessions, prying into the most intimate details of my life. There are items in even the most circumspect life that one would like to remain private. I had a sudden strong and nauseating realization that my privacy might never be sacred again. "I feel so violated."

"So do I. Our phone is bound to be tapped from now on, and I bet they bugged the place too. First thing when we get back, I'm searching the whole apartment."

"Don't you think that's a little melodramatic?"

"Not a bit. And you know what else? There's a guy over by those swans there, in a sheepskin jacket. He followed us down here. When we leave, he'll wait a moment or two, then nonchalantly follow us, probably on the other side of the street."

Which is exactly what he did.

It was a slow news week, unfortunately, so the Prentiss Granger story got a lot more attention that it really warranted. On Monday J. Edgar Hoover placed her on the Ten Most Wanted List, denouncing her as an armed and dangerous terrorist. That the Ten Most Wanted List now numbered fifteen did not elicit much public notice.

There was a profile of Pren on the CBS news that night, with film of Granger Mills and a brief interview with the Major and some stock footage of miscellaneous antiwar demonstrations, most notably the previous year's VVAW Washington protest when disaffected veterans had hurled their medals back at the government which awarded them. Ginger and I were staying at her mother's house to avoid the press. We had been tracked down at our respective jobs by three different TV news camera crews and a gaggle of newspaper and magazine reporters, but both of us stood by our decision to say absolutely nothing to the press. Even so, there was film of me walking to my car outside the McLaughlin School saying "I have nothing to say." They found us quickly at Mrs. Lockford's house, so finally we just went home. Reporters kept leaving messages for us at work and slipping their cards under our door and calling late at night. Outraged, Ginger unlisted the phone and changed the number. Eventually the reporters went away and things settled down a little.

Until *Life* magazine hit the stands the next week, that is. With a five-page photo essay entitled "The Debutante Revolutionary."

It was all there: her expulsion from Miss Farnsworth's, her illegitimate pregnancy, her associations with Bob McCoy, New Mobe and VETRAGE. There were lots of photographs of Pren as a child and Granger Mills and the Major in his game room. There was even a picture of me and Pren together one vacation or another in Granger, one that I had never seen before and which had to have come from the Major. Wilt Bannister and Randy Hargis were profiled in sidebars, brief bios which told me nothing now.

But they'd gotten something else, something that had not previously surfaced in the media. *Life* told the story of how Pren had left home in the middle of the night with her roommate and stock certificates, recounted the sale of her stock to Murray Levin and reported that she had cleaned out her New York bank accounts the previous March. The FBI had located California accounts holding some $143,000, but the rest of the money had vanished into thin air. *Life* announced that she was on the lam with a hundred thousand dollars, which made the convenience store stickup seem even more appallingly senseless and evil.

I was angry that they brought up the money, but even more furious at the asinine name they gave her. Debutante revolutionary indeed! It was a little flight of creative fancy based on a quote from Iris Granger. I didn't doubt that the quote was genuine, that Mrs. Granger had indeed confided to the reporter that she was already immersed in plans for Pren's debut when the rift with her family came. And of course Mrs. Granger meant no harm. I guess you can't blame *Life* for it either, though I took secret delight when the magazine went bankrupt at the end of the year. It's just that as soon as I saw that name in bold script that way, I knew it would stick. And it seemed as unfair a nickname as it was inaccurate.

I spent the following weeks in rather dim shock. I knew that the G-men had been correct. At some point in some fashion, I would hear from Prentiss Granger again. I was, after all, holding a lot of cash for her. And there was always somebody watching me, following me, trailing slowly behind in a white Chevrolet or a navy blue Ford. Sometimes I didn't notice them and sometimes I couldn't help but noticing them, like when they parked across the street from the McLaughlin School all day every day.

I became even more passionately embittered against the FBI, a feat I would not have thought possible, when two agents actually sat there in their white Chevy and *watched* some black teenagers steal my spare tire in the school parking lot. I know they saw it happen because I saw it happen too, out the window of my classroom. I saw two punks jimmy open my trunk and lift the tire out, then dart off down the street with it. And by the time I got outside, screaming in rage, they were gone.

Only the two guys in the white Chevy remained, impassive. I marched straight to their car and confronted them directly. "Sorry, lady, didn't see a thing," the driver muttered. He was a new one that I didn't recognize, about thirty-five with an absurd little pasted-on moustache, and I suppose he thought he was already endangering himself needlessly simply by his continued presence in such a dangerous neighborhood.

Then they pulled away and drove around the corner. I didn't bother to follow to see if they stopped. I just assumed that they would. And I didn't bother to call the police about my car, or even to tell the officer assigned to the school. I figured that the way my life had been going lately, I'd be arrested for driving with insufficient emergency equipment.

Chapter 3 ─────────────

But where was Prentiss Granger?

The question obsessed America in that quiet spring of 1972. During the first month of her disappearance she was spotted in hundreds of locations from Missoula, Montana, to Havana and Bartlesville, Oklahoma, to Algiers. But nobody could find her. As more time passed, I grew increasingly confident that she might outwit the bastards after all.

Then J. Edgar Hoover died.

The cantankerous old goat managed to hang on long enough to avoid the embarrassment of dying on May Day, but not by much. I can't remember feeling so excited about the death of any other human being in my lifetime. I make no apology for this reaction either. I only wish I'd been there to drive the stake through his heart.

Hoover's death prompted the first public statement by Prentiss Granger since her disappearance a month earlier. The New Freedom Manifesto was delivered simultaneously to five Los Angeles radio stations on cassette tapes. The voice on the tapes was unmistakably that of Prentiss Granger, speaking on behalf of something she called the United New Freedom Revolutionary Liberation Front.

She sounded very calm and self-assured and persuasive. Over the previous several years she had winnowed all traces of her South Carolina accent from her daily speech.

We claim no credit for the death of J. Edgar Hoover. But his death will benefit us as it benefits all true American patriots. Systematic programs of sabo-

tage and harassment by the United States government in the guise of preserving national security have made it unsafe for any American to express dissident ideas and opinions. We celebrate the death of an evil man because the abuses of the FBI go far beyond suppression of free thought.

She then listed an exhaustive catalog of various atrocities perpetrated on the Black Panthers, the Berrigan brothers, Angela Davis and a host of miscellaneous other revolutionaries.

The rest of the tape was taken up by a man with an irritating nasal delivery who identified himself as Lonnie McWhirter, a Boston radical who had slipped underground after a botched 1970 explosion in his Philadelphia apartment. Lonnie McWhirter railed about the death of Che Guevara and CIA involvement in Latin America, subjects which seemed unrelated to J. Edgar Hoover's death to me. But after all, what did I know? I just taught second grade. *They* were the revolutionaries.

Excerpts from the tape ran on national network news as well as various radio news programs. CBS, which referred to Pren as the Debutante Revolutionary, once again used my picture behind a crawl of snippets from her statement. The tape probably wouldn't have gotten so much attention if there hadn't been minor disturbances at several branch FBI offices that day. Six different revolutionary groups were claiming credit, but it was Prentiss Granger who had so recently captured the public imagination. So it was our own Debutante Revolutionary who got the air time.

I listened to the tape in its entirety at the FBI office. Twice, in fact. Mel Sanford wanted to pick my brain about Prentiss Granger's connections with the miscellaneous revolutionaries and troublemakers mentioned on the tape, so he stopped off in Chicago on his way to Washington for the funeral.

Ginger was asked to listen to the tape as well, and though she agreed, for her it was the last straw. She was beginning to feel extremely cramped and victimized by the surveillance. Her father was enraged that harassment of his daughter continued despite his attempts to wield his relatively minor clout and call off the hounds. As a Cook County Republican, he obviously had no local recourse, and it had developed that his connections to the national Republican party were not quite as firm as he had envisioned, despite the fact that Lockford Sporting Goods had slipped a generous CREEP contribution to Maurice Stans just before the campaign financing law changed the previous month. Ginger herself made no secret of her fury and disgust with Prentiss Granger.

Nevertheless, it was a severe jolt when she announced that as of June 1, she was moving into an apartment of her own. "It's nothing personal, Laurel, you know that. They'll probably tap my phone there too. But face it, there are only so many gumshoes to go around, and if they have to concentrate on just one of us, it won't be me. I just happened to be Pren's sorority sister for a while. You're the one who's been her friend for nine years."

And she was right, of course, although her defection hurt quite a lot at the time. I was the former roommate, the frequent family guest who so boldly flouted hospitality. I was the girl with a well-documented record of lying to authority figures about the activities of Prentiss Granger. I was the quisling.

I was actually starting to *feel* like a criminal by then. I guess that was what they wanted. Sometimes when you erode somebody's confidence in herself as a rational law-abiding citizen, you can cause that person to make mistakes. In my case, it merely hardened my resolve not to let the bastards get the better of me. And it was involving considerable self-sacrifice. I was still being hounded by persistent media yahoos anxious for my exclusive story. There was still a white Chevy parked outside the McLaughlin School all day every day and a navy blue Ford parked across the street from my apartment building all night every night. I assumed that my mail was being read and that every word I uttered in my apartment was heard by strangers. It made me just a little bit crazy to feel so closely observed.

When I learned that the other teachers at McLaughlin had been visited at home and questioned about me, I applied for a transfer, hoping to regain some of my former anonymity. Perhaps by fall, things would let up and nobody at the new school would be aware of my connections with the fugitive world. I hated McLaughlin anyway, hated the pompous little principal, hated the ubiquitous corporal punishment, hated the broken windows that remained unfixed in my classroom and hated the wretched projects that hovered over and around the school, huge malignant perpetuators of poverty and crime and fear and disease. I hated everything about the place except my students and I grew markedly less fond of some of them when they started asking me why the POleece were watching me.

I shouldn't have cared about it, I suppose, but I did. And while I doubted that any other school would be better, at least it would be *different*.

I moved into a one-bedroom apartment on the same floor of the same building, assuming that the government would handle additional wiring promptly. It was quieter at home with Ginger gone, and I had to buy a new stereo because hers had spoiled me. My old fold-up Motorola just didn't cut the Mean Mr. Mustard anymore. On the assumption that any wiretap would probably be voice activated, I kept music on whenever I was around the house and often left the radio running when I went out, hoping to bore the government into leaving me alone by forcing them to listen to hour after hour of the sound tracks from *Shaft* and *Superfly* while they waited for another juicy exchange between Subject Hollingsworth and the Lincoln Park Dry Cleaners.

I practiced losing my tails, but it wasn't easy and took a lot of energy, forcing me to go places I didn't want to be at times I didn't want to go. Still I knew I would someday have to get that money to Pren, and I had to acquire the skill. It pleased me to drive out the Stevenson Expressway, then suddenly cut across three lanes and dart up an off ramp, while the navy Ford hurtled on toward Cicero.

Finally the academic year was over and I retreated home to Lousiana for a vacation. I felt I would finally be safe in the sanctuary of my childhood home. My brief flirtation with fame had worn me out. It wasn't really fame, even, merely notoriety, and I yearned even less for notoriety than fame. Fame must seem very different to those who seek it, but it doesn't seem to accrue a lot of benefits for those who find it accidentally. Were it possible to poll Karen Silkwood, Karen Anne Quinlan and Mary Jo Kopechne, I suspect we'd find them all opting for obscurity.

My relationship to my family had changed a bit since my graduation, even before Pren was accused of armed robbery. During the fall of the year I lived with Grandma Chesterton in the Garden District of New Orleans, she quietly rewrote her will. When she passed away on St. Patrick's Day the following spring, the Hollingsworths learned with some shock and consternation that I was her primary heir.

So now I wasn't just fat little Laurel anymore in the eyes of the Hollingsworth clan. I was a Very Wealthy Woman. (Who was now paying a lot of taxes, which were being used to spy on me and search for my best friend.) And nobody except Cloretha seemed to understand at all when I insisted on moving north despite my newfound means.

Of course it was *because* of the money that I went, but they couldn't understand that. And I only really came to grasp the true meaning of my decision years later, when I realized that without the significant cushion of my inheritance, I might not have had the gumption to go to an alien city in a hostile land that way. Leaving Louisiana was an act of survival.

I dropped off one tail at O'Hare Airport and picked up another in Louisiana. The interesting question of how an FBI agent might possibly hope to camouflage himself in St. Elizabeth had already been resolved. I'd made my reservations by phone from my apartment and talked freely to my parents about my plans. Two G-men had visited my father's office and explained they were assigned to watch me for my own protection.

And so a couple of agents out of New Orleans took up the vigil in town. Daddy didn't like it much and all my relatives were alarmed that the government considered me to be in danger. I couldn't argue without casting doubts on my own wide-eyed innocence, so I had to let it ride. But their presence made me so uncomfortable that I would almost certainly have cut short my visit even if nothing noteworthy had happened.

However, there were more surprises than the FBI waiting for me in Piniatamore Parish. I had not been home even twenty-four hours when I learned that I would not be escaping the ghosts of Prentiss Granger by fleeing to Louisiana.

We had just finished lunch and I was getting ready to drive out to Weatherly and see my grandparents when Cloretha asked if she might ride along with me. It was not a particularly unusual request and so I didn't think much of it. We had quickly reestablished our relationship with a steaming vat of filé gumbo the previous evening. Cloretha wanted to pick artichokes for dinner from the stand at Weatherly, a remnant from the days when Louisiana was a significant force in national artichoke production.

She seemed preoccupied during the ride, and I noted grimly that a tan Ford was following us at a discreet distance, though the car remained outside the Weatherly highway gate, on Daddy's orders.

I spent an hour and a half with Grandma and Grandpa, sitting first in his bedroom for a stiff obligatory chat and then sipping mint tea with blackberry tarts on the front gallery with Grandma. I didn't see Cloretha again until I excused myself to take a turn around the grounds, but evidently she was keeping track of my whereabouts. No sooner did I set off for the stream than I heard her thin voice and turned to see her striding down the path in my direction.

At her suggestion, we walked to the kitchen garden to check the artichokes. It was there, as I lustily inspected the firm young buds, that she shattered my afternoon.

"She was here, honey. You know that?"

I looked up in genuine mystification. "Know what? Who?"

"Your friend." The response was so circumspect that at first I still didn't understand. And then in one heart-gripping moment, I realized that Cloretha was talking about Prentiss Granger.

"Oh my God. No." My knees buckled. I sat down abruptly and smashed a young pepper plant.

Cloretha helped me to my feet, muttering softly. "Now just you act normal, hear? I got things to tell you. No tellin' who might be watchin' out of what tree."

And so I learned that during the first week of her exile, Prentiss Granger was holed up in a burned-out hunting cabin only four miles from Weatherly as the crow flies. While I was being interrogated in a ratty federal office in Chicago and the WANTED posters were being dispatched to every post office in the country, while *Life* magazine was snooping around the town of Granger and the fugitive was spotted in countless locations around the globe, Cloretha and Jasper were slipping off into the woods to feed the friend who saved the lives of two little boys during Hurricane Camille.

She appeared two days after the Beaumont shooting, Cloretha said, just after sundown out at Jasper's place. She would not say how she had gotten there. She was tired and hungry and cold and penniless. Coming to Jasper was a calculated risk, I suppose, but I guess she figured he was her best hope. They'd gotten along well ever since that first long night ride from Chadwick Academy to St. Elizabeth in 1963 and she knew that he credited her with saving Rufus's life.

Jasper brought her food and a blanket and left her in the woods while he pondered what to do with her. She was alarmed to learn that only a few hours earlier the FBI had been to see my family, and had no idea how extensively she was being sought.

Once it was pitch black, the two of them drove off, with Pren under a blanket on the floor of the back seat. Jasper often hunted possum on the grounds of the old Merrivale Plantation, which had been vacant for as long as I could remember. It would be too risky for her to stay in the plantation house itself, since kids from town sometimes went out there to drink beer and party. But far back in the woods behind the house there was a burned-out hunting shack which seemed to suit Pren's purposes ideally.

Cloretha saw her the next afternoon. Jasper led Cloretha back out through the woods and she cried even now as she spoke of it, the frightened girl shivering in the marginal protection of the burned shell. But however frightened Pren may have been, she had already orchestrated her escape. During the next four days, Jasper carried food out in the pre-dawn hours and informed her she had made the Ten Most Wanted List. Meanwhile, he and Cloretha quietly gathered the materials she requested. A trip to Baton Rouge was required but eventually they assembled everything.

And Cloretha went back out that final afternoon, to help dress the Debutante Revolutionary. She wore an old long-sleeved dress of mine, cut down to fit her and dyed a dowdy brown. She wore black stockings with her own battered loafers and carried a cheap little plastic shopping bag.

She also wore a demure afro wig and a great deal of nut brown pancake makeup over the dark brown shoe polish she rubbed into her face, hands, neck and chest.

Then Cloretha hugged her good-bye and Jasper drove the quiet young Negro woman clear over to Hattiesburg, where she stepped automatically to the rear of the night bus for Atlanta.

Chapter 4 ──────────────────────

She had left a letter for me, which Cloretha retrieved from deep inside a fifty-pound flour sack where it had been warding off weevils for three months. I took it to my room and read it a dozen times. It was written in pencil on a scrap of brown grocery sack. There was no date or salutation, but every word seared into my brain as if she stood before me speaking.

> If I haven't been captured by the time you read this, I won't be. Someday in some unexpected way I will be in touch with you, and sometime we will see each other again.
>
> I didn't intend for any of this to happen and I couldn't stop it, but there's no way to change anything now. So I'll have to build up a new life and find alternate channels for the work that remains to be done. I have a feeling that my misadventure will complicate your life. I'm sorry, but there isn't any way around that either. Whatever else happens, you *must* keep up your work. There's so much to be done and so few with the willingness and ability to do it properly. Don't give up, whatever you do.
>
> I had to borrow some money to get away, and I wish there were some way I could repay it tenfold. It would be nice to have that tenfold amount myself, but I'll manage somehow.

That was all. It wasn't signed, but it was her neat familiar script and the message was unquestionably to me. The part about borrowing money puzzled me. Cloretha hadn't mentioned money at all. But when I was able to get her alone away from the house and ask about it the next day, she explained that she had scraped together some $528 to give to Pren for her journey. I think this touched me more than anything, this strange and pathetic sum. I was personally capable of spending as much in an afternoon without thinking about it. But I was well aware that Cloretha's paltry salary did not allow her to buy a new dress every year, much less finance the escape of a white girl charged with murder.

Once I had Pren's letter, I wanted nothing more than to return to Chicago immediately, not just to repay Cloretha but also to get the hell away from St. Elizabeth and the absurdity of having FBI agents parked outside my various ancestral homes. Everyone in town knew the FBI was there, just as everyone in town had a theory on Prentiss Granger and Why She Did It.

I didn't need every bozo in the parish offering his nitwit opinion on communist infiltration of our universities or mistaken identity or (my personal favorite) the Manchurian Candidate theory, espoused by the Misses Micholet, who emerged from their mauve drawing room to announce that she'd been programmed for revolution while under the influence of "LDS" at Berkeley.

But I had to stay awhile, or arouse suspicion. I gleefully watched the Democrats refuse to seat Mayor Daley and heard an appalling number of bad jokes about Thomas Eagleton and electroshock therapy. I also fielded a lot of crap from everybody about how I really ought to come back home to live now that I'd gotten this silly notion about wanting to live in Chicago out of my system. Where they got the idea it was out of my system I cannot imagine; I struck myself as nauseatingly enthusiastic about my life in the Windy City. But of course that wasn't the central issue at all. The central issue was a good deal more fundamental, as I realized after dinner one night when Daddy exploded at me, a rare and shocking occurrence.

"Don't you see," he roared, "that it just doesn't *look* right for a daughter of mine, for a Hollingsworth lady, for somebody whose family has been an important part of the life of this parish for over two hundred years, for somebody like that to be teaching Yankee pickaninnies? You're liable to be killed in those slums, Laurel, just up and have your head bashed in one day by some dope-crazed buck, and for what purpose, I'd like to know? So's you can teach the ABCs to some little pickaninny leaches off the welfare state!!"

Generally we didn't discuss my work at all. It was a big ugly minefield we tiptoed carefully around. This little speech, however, didn't merely end our voluntary cease-fire. It also absolutely infuriated me. I yelled right back at him, something I had never done before.

"I do it because I *want* to, Daddy. I love to teach." Gone and forgotten were all the horrible memories of the McLaughlin School and my agonizing year there. "And they aren't really Yankee kids anyhow. Half of them were born down here and just went to Chicago because their parents were trying to get away from the racial oppression of the South."

Mama tried to stop us before things got too heated. I could see her out of the corner of my eye, wringing her hands anxiously, bobbing her little head back and forth to watch us both. Just about the only thing Mama detests more than a family scene is being the last to hear a truly juicy bit of gossip.

"Now y'all just behave and don't go spoiling our lovely time together," she cooed. "Let's just all have some of Cloretha's delicious blackberry cobbler and hush this ugly talk at the supper table." She dished out two substantial servings and passed them to us.

But Daddy was not going to be stopped by anything so trivial as blackberry cobbler. "She's disgracing the whole family, Mama, apart from what I would think you would understand immediately about the danger to her own physical well-being. Why, those little pickaninnies'd be happier and better off being taught by their own kind. I didn't send my only daughter to a fine educational institution like Duke University so's she could throw away that splendid education this way, just squander all that learning on a passel of pickaninnies."

"I took a degree in elementary education," I replied stiffly when he stopped for air. "I teach second grade. I don't see how that does anything but *utilize* my 'splendid education.' "

He didn't seem to hear me at all. I noticed that he wasn't really looking at me either. He was playing to the jury here, and the jury was obviously Mama. "Of course most young ladies the age of Laurel would be more than happy to stay away from such unpleasantness, particularly if they happened to have inherited a nice little fortune from a very understanding grandmother who's more than likely whirling in her tomb to know that her precious granddaughter, her *only* granddaughter, is up in a hostile northern city risking life and limb every day when she might just as easily have a perfectly lovely position teaching respectable little boys and girls right here in Louisiana where she belongs. And you know, Mama, I would think that Laurel would understand that she's taking a job away from some deserving colored woman who could go off welfare if'n she got a nice job teaching her own kind."

I couldn't let it go by. I just couldn't. But where the hell do you begin to refute a cockamamie speech like that one? I particularly liked the part about me stealing some black woman's job. Every black teacher at McLaughlin School wanted nothing so much as a transfer to some pleasant middle-class neighborhood where they wouldn't need to worry about having their tires or throats slashed. It wasn't one teensy bit safer for blacks than whites, but that hardly seemed a sensible or soothing rebuttal.

I kept my voice calm and thickened my accent considerably. "I'm teaching in Chicago because that's what I want to be doing, where I want to be doing it. Daddy, I love teaching those kids. Honest. And I feel like I'm doing something important, really significant, whether or not you want to try to understand it. I don't want to spend all my vacation here arguing, but I'll tell y'all right now, I *am* going back and I'll be teaching in the fall in Chicago. I'da been doing that no matter what happened with Pren, and nobody's going to tell me that I can't."

Then I got up and fled the room. As I hurried through the kitchen, I noticed Cloretha standing by the sink and realized that she had to have overheard everything. But all I told her was "Good cobbler" before I pushed the screen door open and headed into the steamy evening, still light and hot despite the late hour.

I walked clear through town formalizing plans for my return. I would have to just grit my teeth and serve my sentence, preferably easy time. The year in Chicago had changed me in a lot of ways that I hadn't previously recognized, one of which was a vastly intensified sense of independence. True, when my world started to self-destruct, I wanted nothing more than to fall into the warm folds of the bosom of my family, but that desire lasted only until I actually did so. Then I was able to see for the first time just how smothering that family bosom could be and how poorly I now fit into it.

We didn't allude to the argument again, but two days later I told

Mama I'd be going north in early August. Her only response was a deep, heartfelt sigh.

And go north I did. The euphoria I felt on returning to my place over Lake Michigan surprised even me. I knew I wanted to go back, but I hadn't realized how much. St. Elizabeth did not offer gyros around the corner, lovers watching swans in the Rookery at sunset, crashing waves on sandy shores, bars on every block or delis open past midnight. I knew when I returned that August that I'd changed my core of existence, transferred it away from my family into an area that was murky and unfulfilled, but wholly my own.

Except for Ginger and the Lockford family, nobody in Chicago knew I had money. Nobody knew about my family plantation or my grandmother's will or my father's formidable legal reputation. Nobody knew, thank God, that I was a Daughter of the Confederacy.

In Chicago I was a second-grade teacher in a ghetto school. I wore loose smocks and carried a camera almost everywhere. I was a familiar face at every eatery within the radius of a mile. I had a southern accent, sure, but I was trying to ditch it as soon as possible. I was neither fat enough to turn heads in incredulity nor thin enough to turn them in wistful lust. I was a rather ordinary and unremarkable character, and I loved the anonymity. I didn't want opportunistic goombahs like that jackass New Orleans import broker making passes at me because I was rich. I didn't want my students to realize that the interest on my investments in one year was more than their entire family income. And I didn't want anybody's damn deference because I was privileged.

I'd been back in Chicago only a few days when a slender dark-haired woman in large sunglasses and a beige linen shift sat down on the stool next to mine at Naturally Yours, where I was waiting for one blueberry Smoothie to go. She placed a *Daily News* on the counter between us, then suddenly knocked it to the floor with an apparently accidental flip of her wrist. It landed at my feet and I slid off the stool to pick it up. As I handed the paper to the woman, I looked straight at her. She was in her early twenties, lightly tanned, and her loose dark curls seemed to be Dynel. I was sure I'd never seen her before.

She slid a scrap of paper into my hand when I gave her the newspaper and I realized in a heart-stopping moment of panic that I was being Contacted.

"Thanks ever so much," she told me.

"No problem 'tall," I replied. Then my Smoothie was ready and I paid for it and left. My tail was leaning across the lightpost across the street, positioned to have witnessed the entire newspaper drop through the window of Naturally Yours.

I continued on casually toward the beach, but curiosity soon got the better of me. I ducked into the Lincoln Park Zoo, scooted into a ladies room and in the relative sanctity of my own bolted stall, I pulled the slip of paper from my pocket. It read, in its entirety, "At precisely 9:30 tonight, call 834-7293 from a pay phone. Lose your tail first."

Better my tail than my head, I thought giddily as I emerged from the rest room, trying to appear relieved. I went about my planned activities, walking along the beach for an hour or so, taking a couple of pictures, nothing much to exterior appearances. Inside, however, I was in overdrive.

By 8:15 when I left the apartment, I was a bundle of jangling nerves. The navy Ford slid smoothly into traffic behind me and followed a discreet two cars behind me down Lake Shore Drive and onto the Eisenhower. I went through the Spaghetti Bowl to the Dan Ryan, noting in relief that traffic appeared light enough for me to be able to execute a quick cross-lane maneuver. I exited abruptly at Sixty-third Street, cutting across three lanes, then hopped back on the expressway and headed back north to my own neighborhood. I parked in a supermarket lot with time to spare, bought myself a bag of bing cherries and sat in the car nibbling till 9:25. I felt extraordinarily foolish when I entered the booth, but what the hell. This was it. Naturally I dropped my dime.

The phone rang twice. Then an unfamiliar male voice answered. "Yes?" His tone was anything but affirmative.

"I was supposed to call this number," I said. "This is—"

"No ID," he cut me off. "We know who you are." Which gave them a decided advantage, since I hadn't the foggiest notion who *they* might be. "Did you lose your tail?"

"Yes, definitely."

"Good. You're followed all the time, of course."

"I know."

"There's somebody who wants to see you. It isn't possible for that person to be here right now."

How coy. "Give that person my regards," I answered wryly. Or at least I intended to sound wry, but I was pretty nervous.

He ignored me. "Say nothing that isn't essential. This person hopes to be able to see you on August seventeenth. That's ten days from now Six days from now, on Monday the fourteenth at eight-forty-five P.M. call this number for further instructions." I wrote the number down. "Is this clear?"

I read the number back.

"There's one other thing," he said. "There was a financial request. It should be honored at this meeting."

That had to be the note left with Cloretha. *I wouldn't mind having that tenfold amount myself,* Pren had written. In ten days I could easily find time to drop my tail and visit the safe deposit box. It suddenly occurred to me, however, that I was taking an awful lot for granted. I had no idea who was on the other end of the line. They could be extortionists just after money, making a vague reference they hoped I'd pick up on. They could be kidnappers after *me*. In fact, it might even be the FBI, trying to sucker me into spilling how much I knew by involving me in an ersatz cloak and dagger rendezvous.

"How do I know I'm talking to the right person?" I asked.

"If you asked that question, I was told to respond with a name and a date. Dr. John Robinson. February twenty-first, 1968."

The South Carolina abortionist. A sudden flooding memory of that horrible evening swept over me and collided head-on with a countering wave of relief. Only Prentiss Granger and I knew about that weekend of anxiety and humiliation. I had never told a soul, it hadn't surfaced in any of the publicity about her, and it was not the sort of thing Pren would blab around either. So these folks were for real, then. I was in Contact with the Underground.

"That's fine," I said.

"Any questions?"

"No."

"Next week then." I heard a click, followed by a dial tone.

Six days later I went through the whole lose-my-tail business again and spoke to the same guy again at the new number. I was told that I should lose my tail on August 17, go downtown, and be in the paperback section of Kroch & Brentano's main store at 5:15 P.M. I was to bring the money with me, tell nobody my plans and be prepared to stay away overnight. I didn't like the sound of this too much, but on the other hand, it could mean that I would actually get to see Pren.

"Will our mutual friend be there?" I asked.

"I'm authorized to tell you only what I must. Will you be able to get the money?"

"Yes, dammit! Will she be there?"

He hung up and I cursed him blue.

At last it was actually D-day. I'd retrieved $10,000 from my safe deposit box downtown after losing a tail in Marshall Field's the previous Tuesday. I had mentioned my plans to nobody and my toothbrush was in a Baggie in my purse. Now it was 5:45. I had the money strapped around my waist in a preposterous jerry-rigged money belt and I had never felt more frightened or ridiculous as I perused the education section of Kroch's paperback department. It worried me that nobody had showed up yet. It was nearly half an hour after they were supposed to meet me.

Then the woman who had slipped me the phone number in Naturally Yours suddenly appeared beside me. She wore a scarf this time and in the fluorescent light it was quite clear that her brunette bouffant curls were phony. She wore a yellow shell, a polka-dotted black and yellow skirt and the same oversized sunglasses. But once again I was struck by how little she resembled anyone I'd ever seen who was part of the New Left. I could picture her hosting a Tupperware party.

"Are you sure you lost your tail?" she asked without preliminary.

"Positive."

"How?"

"I went out the back way from a dressing room at Carson, Pirie, Scott."

She looked pleased. "I'm glad that wasn't a problem. I'm going to leave you now. In exactly ten minutes, be on the southeast corner of Wabash and Lake streets. The car is a pale green 'sixty-four Impala and both sun visors will be down. Be ready to jump into the back seat. Clear?"

I nodded and she drifted away. I loitered a few seconds longer, then paid for a copy of *Bury My Heart at Wounded Knee,* newly out in paperback. If we were delayed for some reason, I could learn something and appear properly concerned about oppression at the same time.

The green Impala appeared as promised and I slid hurriedly into the open back door, pulling it closed as we peeled around the corner. Lady Dynel was in the back seat with me. The driver's long shaggy brown hair poured out from beneath a jockey cap. He reminded me of Ringo Starr.

"Where we going?" I inquired brightly.

The guy turned on the radio and Rod Stewart explained that every picture tells a story. It seemed that visuals might be all I'd get.

Lady Dynel shifted around so she could look sideways out the window. "You don't need to know," she told me. Friendly bitch.

"I'm Laurel," I offered.

"We know. Brown LTD, Mike."

So his name was Mike. We weren't making a lot of social progress. Mike looked in his rearview mirror, then unexpectedly crossed two lanes and turned right instead of left onto Lake Shore Drive.

"Gone," he said. "Went north."

We continued south in silence. Lady Dynel searched my purse and I decided against attempting any further small talk. We took the Dan Ryan to the Chicago Skyway cutoff, then drove high above the city in almost total isolation.

Lady Dynel spoke abruptly. "I'm going to have to ask you to put on these sunglasses."

"Sun doesn't bother my eyes," I answered brightly. "Anyway, I have my own."

She handed me a pair of very black wraparounds, a style that had been passé for quite some time. "Put these on," she ordered, and disobedience didn't cross my mind again.

As I took the glasses I saw that they were lined with adhesive tape to allow no light through the dark lenses. Once they were on, I was effectively and efficiently blinded. These were clever folk indeed. Almost immediately my other senses seemed to shift gears in compensation for my lost sight. I noticed for the first time that Lady Dynel was wearing Jean Naté and that Mike could do with a shower.

We exited not long thereafter and I could tell from our reduced speed and frequent stops that we were on surface streets again. The air smelled horrible, full of noxious gases and vile chemical fumes and all manner of foul stuff. East Chicago, probably, or Gary.

Five or ten minutes later, the car stopped and Mike turned off the engine. "I'll come around for you," Lady Dynel said. I sat there terrified, pumping adrenaline by the quart.

I managed to get up the front walk and negotiate seven stairs without tripping or making too much of a spectacle of myself. Then we entered a building where the omnipresent aroma of noxious chemicals was enhanced by a few more ghastly odors, most notably liver, cabbage and

Raid. By the time I huffed up the fourth flight of stairs, I deduced that we were in an apartment building.

They led me down a hallway, around a corner, then finally stopped. I heard six staccato taps on a door.

"Yes?" came a muffled male voice from inside. Three more knocks, a pause, and then two knocks. Then the door opened and I was led inside. Here, thank God, somebody had taken the only sensible approach to the hideous odors. Sandalwood incense was burning. Almost as soon as I realized this, Lady Dynel removed the glasses from my face and I looked around, blinking rapidly.

We were in a small room, furnished only with a cable-spool coffee table and three beanbag chairs in purple vinyl. The cheap yellow carpet had gone without benefit of shampoo since at least the McCarthy hearings. The walls showed clear outlines of pictures which no longer hung. A long-haired guy in jeans and a khaki T-shirt lounged in the kitchen doorway, cradling an Uzi.

But I caught all of this in one glance. And after that, Uncle Uzi would have had to start firing to draw my attention away from the young woman sprawled in one of the purple vinyl beanbag chairs. Her chestnut hair was parted in the middle and hung gracefully past her shoulders. She wore blue jeans and a dashiki and she showed perfect teeth in a lovely gracious smile.

"I'm glad you could come," she greeted me warmly.

There was only one problem. She wasn't Prentiss Granger.

Chapter 5 _____

"Who the hell are you?"

She rose to her feet and extended a hand which evidently I was supposed to shake. I dreaded this, wondering what kind of complicated forty-three-step soul shake she had in mind and hoping that I wouldn't botch it too badly. One of the more amusing minor annoyances of the Age of Aquarius was the interminable ritual handshake where one clutched, twisted, clenched, slapped and otherwise diddled away several minutes before getting down to business. I got lucky. Her shake concluded with a quick thumb twist and that was it.

"Who are you?" I repeated. Clearly this was going nowhere. The door to the hall had immediately closed and my surly friends from the green Impala were standing behind me. The guy in the kitchen door hadn't moved an inch and looked like he'd enjoy nothing more than getting a little close-range target practice.

"You may call me Mimi," the girl in the dashiki said. Then she looked at Lady Dynel. "Any trouble, Jackie?"

I turned to see if I'd proven more difficult than I thought. The woman shook her head and for the first time removed the oversized glasses, disclosing bright green eyes. "We staked her apartment all day," she reported. This was hardly cheering news. It did not enhance my rapidly waning sense of privacy to learn that there were people following the people who were following me. It was like one of those optical-illusion pictures where somebody holds a picture of herself holding a picture of herself, etc., etc. "Mongo and Mike tailed her, Mongo on the bus she took downtown and Mike after the cab her tail got into. She gave Mongo and her other tail the slip in Carson's. Mike was sure that nobody else was on her."

Mimi looked questioningly at Mike. He nodded. "Just one thing, though. Mongo said some kind of house pig came along after she went into the dressing room and the pig started talking to her shadow. Almost like he was hassling the guy, till the shadow flashed a shield."

I laughed despite myself. Everyone looked at me expectantly and with no small degree of concern. "The saleslady was a nice sweet God-fearing lady. I asked her to help me and let me out through an employees' door in the fitting room because I was being followed by a hooligan who kept trying to make me take drugs. She promised she'd have him arrested, soon as I had time to get away."

Mimi laughed then and everybody but Uncle Uzi at least smiled. I felt as if I'd crossed an invisible hurdle.

"Nice work," Mimi said. "Of course it draws more attention to the fact that you cut loose, but I like it anyway. I was told that you were a very bright, capable woman, which makes things a lot easier for all of us. You're going to be under a lot of heat for a long time."

We were all still standing stiffly around this crummy little room with the drawn shades. I was every bit as nervous as I'd been before. I also desperately needed to pee.

"Is there a bathroom?" I inquired meekly. Uncle Uzi looked skeptical, but Mimi took my arm warmly and led me out of the room.

Inside the bathroom, I peed frantically, then checked my "money belt," four stacks of twenty-dollar bills wrapped in a continuous long tube of plastic wrap which tied over my belly button. I wore an old pantie girdle to hold the money in place and the plastic wrap left odd patterns of welting on my flabby white skin.

When I went back into the hall, Mimi was waiting for me. She led me into the bedroom, which was totally empty except for two grimy green sleeping bags and a backpack which lay open in the corner. A sheet was tacked over the only window.

"Do sit down," she told me. "I'm going to call you Penny, if you don't mind. Please don't use anybody's real names as we talk. I know this may seem silly to you, but security is absolutely crucial. Even here, in this apartment that we're virtually certain is safe. One thing you must always remember, if you decide to cooperate with us, is that you cannot *ever* let your security precautions down. One little slip can mean disaster for somebody else. Is that clear, Penny?"

It seemed odd to hear myself called by another name, but I nodded nevertheless.

"You won't be told anything you don't need to know," she continued. "This is for your own protection as much as ours. You can't possibly be tricked or duped into revealing information that you don't have. You're under continuous, twenty-four-hour surveillance right now. After a while, it will probably be cut back to random, spot surveillance, but you can't count on anything changing and you still will need to act as if every move were being watched."

We were cross-legged on the floor and I was getting so hot I thought I might pass out. The window was shut and there wasn't even a fan to disturb the air, which seemed to cluster around us in oppressive globs. I could feel wet circles under my arms and the plastic-wrapped money under my pantie girdle was swimming in sweat. Mama would have called it perspiration. She would probably have also called the four folks in the apartment desperadoes.

Mimi regarded me quizzically for a minute. "You okay?" I nodded weakly. "Want something to drink?" I nodded again. She went to the door and called down the hall. "Hermit, bring us a couple cold Cokes, would you?" I didn't hear an answer, but a minute later Uncle Uzi handed her two chilled cans, already dripping condensed air from the torpid apartment. I could feel the frigid liquid plummet toward my stomach and almost instantly the sugar and cold and caffeine began to revitalize me.

I decided to take the initiative. "Where is she?"

Mimi stared at me blankly. "I'm sure you realize, Penny," she started, emphasizing the name enough to make me remember that I had to always obey their stupid security regulations, "that I couldn't possibly give you that information. Even if I had it, which as it happens I don't. You can be certain, however, that Jeannie is all right. I saw her three days ago and she gave me a message for you."

So they were calling Prentiss Granger "Jeannie," were they? It seemed a dumb, cheerleader sort of name. Maybe that was her penance for having been named the Debutante Revolutionary by *Life*.

"What's the message?"

"The primary message is on a cassette tape," she answered. "My instructions were to deliver this tape directly into your hands. I haven't listened to it and neither has anybody else here. You're to take it directly from here to someplace where you can listen to a sixty-minute tape without being disturbed. Is there such a place?"

I thought for a moment. In Louisiana, it would be no trouble at all. But in Chicago, the only possibility was Mrs. Lockford's house in Evanston, which seemed like a lousy idea. "No."

"We'll take you to a motel then. Do you have enough cash to pay for a room and a cab ride home?"

I had left home with fifty dollars, paid one bus fare, bought one cheeseburger and invested in one paperback book. "If the cab ride doesn't last forever."

"It won't." She smiled at me again and I thought she certainly seemed like a nice enough girl. Until I flashed on old Hermit with the Uzi out there in the hall. I couldn't afford to forget just how serious these people were.

I hoped that Pren hadn't let them know how wealthy I was. I didn't want to become a sitting duck for any left-wing wacko wanting to finance a private revolution. But perhaps they knew I had Pren's money. In which case I was hardly any safer. It was very unappealing all the way around.

"Did Jeannie send any other message?" I asked, giving the name Jeannie with just a faint sneer. I wanted to seem tough. It seemed important not to let these people walk all over me, though Lord knows why. The opinion of a few scraggly radicals had never mattered to me before. Of course my best friend had never gone underground fleeing murder charges before, either. These seventies were not promising to be a very pleasant decade.

"She said that you would have some cash to send her."

"Did she say how much?"

"Five thousand dollars. In cash. Don't you have it? What's this little game about, anyway?" Mimi sounded annoyed.

"How do I know she'll get the money?"

"You don't. But you're just going to have to take my word. Someday you'll receive another communiqué from Jeannie and I'm sure she'll mention it if we shortchange her. Do you think I'm going to rip off a sister underground?"

"Of course not." This was all getting off on several wrong feet. I didn't want to alienate anybody who might be able to keep me in touch with Pren, and I didn't want to make this Mimi person angry with me. "I'm sorry. It's just that I've been nervous about that and I thought she'd be here and I've never seen you before. I didn't mean to be rude." I smiled, hoping to erase previous churlishness.

"I have enormous respect for Jeannie," Mimi replied rather stiffly. "I wouldn't do anything to endanger her safety and I wouldn't dream of ripping her off."

"Well, I've got the money, don't worry." As I reached beneath my blouse, I saw Mimi tense. "Relax. I'm just getting you your money." I pulled the damp plastic out triumphantly, unrolled it and stacked the four small piles of bills neatly on the floor. "Here it is. But it isn't five thousand dollars."

"Jeannie said—"

I interrupted. "I know what Jeannie said. I was afraid that wouldn't be enough. There's ten thousand here."

This brought me a very strange look from Mimi. Clearly she wasn't used to being around people who could cough up an extra five grand on the spur of the moment. And her expression suggested that she *didn't* know it was Pren's own money she was delivering. I realized that I was setting myself up as an incredibly soft touch.

"I'm sure she'll be delighted," Mimi told me.

"When will you see her?"

"I can't answer that. But I will be seeing her soon and I'll get the money to her intact, don't worry."

"That wasn't what I was thinking about. I was just wondering how she is."

"Healthy. Dedicated. And very, very busy."

This wasn't much of a report, but it was obviously all that I was going to get. "When can I see her?"

"Maybe never. It's far too hot for her to travel for a long time."

"I could go to her."

"And lead a trail of pigs right to her? Not fucking likely, Penny. Not fucking likely."

"Well, is there some way I could get a message to her? Or write her a letter?"

"I'll see what I can do."

Then Mimi asked me for details of every encounter I'd had thus far with the FBI. She paid close attention, nodding frequently, hanging on every word, altogether the perfect audience. She was particularly interested in Ginger's reactions to all this. I was so into my role as underground courier/rebel by now that I automatically referred to Ginger as Betsy. Mimi smiled the first time I did this and I could see that she knew my roommate wasn't named Betsy at all. It pleased me to score a few points with her. But it also disturbed me when I'd finished to have her focus critically on Ginger.

"Jeannie suspected that Betsy might be a problem. Does she know that you've been in contact with us?"

"No."

"That you're sending money to Jeannie?"

"Absolutely not."

"Good. Keep it that way. She's too weak a link to be involved here."

I resented this a little. After all, I'd known Ginger for five years and Mimi for an hour. But I had to admit that I was a little worried about Ginger myself, though I didn't think that she'd ever consciously sell out Pren.

Mimi finally brought me out and took Mike and Jackie into the bedroom for a brief conference. Hermit sat at a battered linoleum kitchen table eating pork and beans straight from a can he'd heated in a pan of water which still simmered on the stove. He fished a hot dog out of the water and ate it plain, right off the fork. I was pretty disgusted, but I don't think I would have wanted to cozy up to Hermit if he'd just finished correcting the seasoning on a tureen of boeuf bourguignon. He was a pretty unsavory-looking character and I expected little crawly things to come wandering out of his filthy scalp and make a break for his bushy eyebrows.

"Ready to go," came Mimi's voice from the doorway. Behind her, Jackie had her dark glasses on again and I suddenly realized that the brunette bouffant wig and huge glasses gave her a very strong resemblance to Jacqueline Kennedy Onassis. Did somebody in the underground actually have a sense of humor?

They put the dark glasses on me again and led me outside. When Jackie let me take the glasses off, we were on the Eisenhower heading west. Somewhere out by O'Hare we pulled into a quiet motel.

"We'll wait in the car till you're registered," Jackie told me. "Stay here tonight. Be sure to burn the tape before you leave the room in the morning. Did Mimi show you how to do it?" I nodded. She surveyed the lot critically. "See that Dumpster back there? Check out tomorrow morning at quarter to eleven and leave the tape recorder behind that trash bin. We'll pick it up."

"Will you pick me up too?"

"No. Take a cab home. You can afford it." The last was sneering and crude, but I restrained my anger.

"Thank you for everything," I said, as I stepped from the car, clutching the brown paper bag which held my cassette recorder and the tape. Then I walked inside, paid cash for a single room away from the road, and registered as Penny Pauper from Peoria. I took the key to Unit 11, nodded good-bye to Mike and Jackie, then let myself into the first total privacy I had experienced for a long, long time.

For the first five minutes, I just sat weakly on the edge of the bed, reconstructing the past several hours. I was fairly certain that I'd been accepted, or at least tolerated, and I was immensely relieved. I wanted word to get back to Prentiss Granger that Laurel Hollingsworth was one tough cookie. Why, she even managed to make a joke about using Brand X plastic wrap when she unstrapped her money belt, that Hollingsworth girl did, about not using Saran or Handi Wrap and supporting old Napalm International.

I wondered who Mimi was and who Mike was and who Jackie was. I wondered what Hermit was.

But mostly I wondered about the contents of the brown paper sack I still clenched tightly in my right hand. In just a few moments I would hear the voice of Prentiss Granger again. Unless this was all a cruel hoax. It seemed unlikely, but the Major had warned me often enough that you couldn't trust the commies any further than you could throw Granger Mills. I hoped that the reactionary old fart was having a lot of trouble sleeping as I switched on the tape recorder and heard the clean clear voice of his oldest daughter once again.

For some reason, it's very hard for me to talk to you through a machine this way. This is the third time I've started and I'm just going to go ahead with it and hope that the awkwardness will go away. It feels like years since I last saw you, even though it's really less than five months. The life I'm leading is so quiet that there's too much time for introspection. It annoys me not to be able to move about and do things as I want.

I feel terrible about the inconvenience that I know I've created for you. I can't understand the fuss that the media have made about me, far more than I deserve. I could keep telling you over and over how sorry I am to have fucked around this way with your life, but it would waste precious time on this tape. I do hope to get word back about the kind of harassment you've had to handle, however. This is important to me because it can help me assess just how intensely they're looking for me. I hope you'll cooperate with the people I send to you.

I was hoping that with J. Edgar finally in Fag Heaven that the heat would let up on political fugitives, but it actually seems to be getting worse. Just remember not to give the FBI an inch. The more you say to them, the more likely you are to slip something that they might be able to use. Of course I don't mean that you'd ever consciously do anything to give me away. I know much better than that.

But you've got to figure that they probably have your apartment bugged. Which could be embarrassing even if nothing political ever gets said! Do make sure your roommate realizes how serious this is. I have a feeling she probably has brushed the whole thing aside as some kind of silly game I'm playing. Well, it's deadly serious. I face a capital murder charge in Texas. and that carries the death penalty. You can't get a whole lot more serious than the electric chair.

The future at this point is very hazy, of course. I don't know where I'll be in a year or a month, or even a week. I feel a kind of pressure and tension I didn't know were possible. Maybe this fear will subside with time, but I doubt it. I've been in touch with people who've been underground a long, long time and the way they seem to survive is to develop about four additional senses, all to register danger.

Since I'm so hot now, I've been lying very low, but the danger still feels real all the time. It's discouraging to think that I'm going to have to live this way for the rest of my life. There are so many things that you just take for granted till you lose them. But I don't mean to go into a self-pity rap here. What's done can't be changed. Now I just have to make the best of it.

Which brings me to one of the primary reasons for sending you this tape. The person who gives it to you will be supplying very precise instructions for when and how to listen to it. It's imperative for my safety and your legal purity that the G-men never know about this or any other tape. Which means you'll have to develop your capability for subterfuge and evasion. I hope you won't take this the wrong way, but I've always thought you had a rare talent for being sly and sneaky. Bet you never realized you'd have to put that talent to work to keep me out of the hoosegow, did you? What a ridiculous, upside-down situation this is!

But I was going to tell you about what happened in Beaumont, wasn't I? So fasten your seatbelt, kid, and I'll tell you the whole grim story. Since Randy seems to be playing mum, nobody really knows what happened or why. I'm not sure I can answer the why part myself, really, but at least I do know what hap- pened and I think that if you can understand that, perhaps you won't be so angry with me. Oh yes, I know you're angry with me.

The press has made a big deal out of me and my background, which is just ridiculous. It doesn't make me feel any better to see how fully the Major's been cooperating either. Imagine turning my baby pictures over to Life *magazine! Nothing would please me more than to be able to give him a piece of my mind for about ten minutes. Maybe I'll mail him a tape someday. I mean, Jesus Christ, you wouldn't think he'd be so eager to deliver me to the electric chair, would you? I may not have ever been the kind of person who gets herself named Daughter of the Year, but I don't think I deserve this.*

But back to Beaumont. Everything seems to go back to Beaumont, doesn't it? The rest of my life will go back to Beaumont. In fact, the life I'm leading now only really began in Beaumont. I'm four months old in this new life, but I think that one ages a lot more rapidly under these conditions. I feel like I'm about ninety.

And I keep avoiding telling you what happened, don't I? Okay. We were on our way to Miami and Randy began to act real strange while we were in Texas. He'd been more withdrawn lately, but the prospect of the trip seemed to cheer him up. Actually, we hadn't planned to bring him along at all. It was supposed to be a kind of private vacation for Wilt and me, but then one day Randy just an- nounced that he was coming too. I wanted Wilt to tell him he couldn't, but he had his guilty conscience all revved up. And it killed him.

Here her voice cracked, there was a moment of silence and I could hear the machine click off. When she spoke again, it sounded as if she'd been crying.

It's strange, but telling these things to you makes them somehow more real to me, and it's harder than I thought. I've relived every minute of that day in Beaumont a thousand times, and I'm still not used to it.

Randy got weirder as we crossed Texas, and it takes a long, long time to cross Texas. He was hassled by a gas station attendant out in Odessa and it really pissed him off. And when we stopped for lunch at some burger joint, a couple of rednecks gave him a wolf whistle. He was ready to go beat them up, but Wilt calmed him down. So I guess by the time we hit Beaumont, he was spoiling for a fight. Maybe we should have recognized that he was ready to crack. I don't know, it's impossible to say even in hindsight. If you did something every time a friend started acting peculiar, you wouldn't have many friends for very long.

I really only have Randy's word for what happened inside the Minute Mart. He said there was some crotchety old fart behind the counter who started giving him a hard time, telling him to get a haircut, hippie, all that Easy Rider sort of stuff. They were buying a six-pack and Randy gave the guy a twenty.

"Don't change no twenties for no hippies," is what Randy said the guy told him. And Randy just snapped. He said he didn't even know what he was doing, but the next thing he realized, he had his gun on the guy and was telling him to just give him the fucking beer. He said he never asked for the money in the cash register, just told the old fart that he didn't have a goddamned foot because he was off making it safe for the fart to be an asshole. Randy said Wilt tried to stop him but it didn't matter.

I suspected something was wrong when they were in there so long and as soon as they ran out, I knew we were in real trouble. Randy was waving his gun around and screaming with a six-pack of beer in his other hand. Then this old geezer ran out carrying a sawed-off sixteen-guage shotgun.

Meanwhile, this other guy pulls into the parking lot and hops out of his truck waving a forty-five and yelling for them to hit the deck. There was no way to tell he was a cop and I didn't find out he was until much later. Anyway, this new guy, the cop, had on a T-shirt and cowboy hat just like every other redneck in the state.

Randy goes to fire at this new guy and Wilt dives on his gun hand. As nearly as I can tell, what happened was that Randy's first shot winged the cop's shoulder and made him drop the gun. Then the Minute Mart guy fired one barrel of the shotgun and blew Wilt's head all over the lot.

Her voice faltered again and I switched off the tape. I had never heard anything about the nature of Wilt's fatal wound, and had somehow assumed it was a clean shot through the heart, like in a John Wayne movie. I thought of those beautiful blue eyes, that springy gold hair, the mouth that had kissed me good-bye at the San Francisco airport. Suddenly I gagged, and barely made it to the bathroom before I was violently ill. It was a good ten minutes before I felt well enough to start the tape again.

Once Wilt went down, Randy was incredibly fast. The shotgun had gotten him some in the right arm, but even as the cop was going after his gun, Randy switched the three-fifty-seven to his left hand and wasted the guy. The Minute Mart guy tried to fire the other barrel and I guess it jammed. Which is the only reason I'm here to make this tape, probably.

Randy kind of catapulted into the car, screaming at me to split. I panicked. Maybe we should have stayed, I don't know. Under the circumstances, maybe it wasn't so strange that I did panic. I didn't know who else was going to start firing and I was absolutely terrified. It was cowardly of me to leave, I know. But by the time we were on the highway again, it was too late.

Randy was covered with blood and bleeding some himself, but he really didn't seem to be hit too badly. He caught some of the blast that killed Wilt, mostly in his arm and side. I found a shopping center and drove to the back of the parking lot. Randy was sure he could get help if he could just get to Dallas and frankly I wanted to be rid of him. So I tied his wounds up as best I could, changed my clothes and left him the car. The last I saw him, he was driving out of that shopping center. I wandered around till I found a car with the keys in it and then I split. I was in shock by then, I suppose. I don't really remember anything about the drive, and it went on quite awhile. All I remember is seeing Wilt's head blow up, over and over again. I couldn't get it out of my mind, and I guess I never will. I have nightmares every night where it all happens again, in slow motion. There just aren't words to describe the horror of it.

The entire thing was so pointless. *Nobody was trying to stick up that wretched Minute Mart. Nobody took any money from it. I have no idea what happened to the six-pack of beer that started it all. And now I'm charged with capital murder as an accomplice to an armed robbery which never really took place.*

But most of all, Wilt is dead. And I loved him more than I've ever loved anybody in my life. Knowing that he's gone has left a huge pit open inside of me and sometimes I think it would be a lot easier just to fall into that pit than to go on.

I don't know if this clarifies anything for you or not. But I did want you to realize that all was not as it seemed. And that I'm suffering more than I would ever have thought possible.

As you've undoubtedly surmised, I'm with some people who are very, very po-

litical. It's a lot different from the kind of situation I was in before, but I'm not really in a position where I can be too picky about my friends. And like it or not, my notoriety can be used effectively. I've discovered that one way to sublimate my own pain is to become more immersed in other problems, and the world is full of problems. My first instinct is to simply find myself a new identity and retire, like some mafioso stoolpigeon. But I keep remembering Wilt and how much he wanted to accomplish. I'm not sure what use I can be under all these constrictions, but I don't feel I can stop. I'm still alive, after all, and while I've lost one form of freedom, I've come into another. Perhaps one day it will all make sense.

I hope it will be possible for you to continue to help me. It's much too risky for me to try to see you now and it might stay hot for a long time.

There's one other thing I hope you'll be able to do for me. It won't be long before they try Randy and I don't think he's got any money for a defense. Legal Aid is fine, but I'd feel much better if I thought that Randy had the best lawyer he could get and wouldn't have to worry about paying for it. Why don't you call Mike Donovan in Berkeley and see how much it would take to rustle up some first-class legal talent? Mike may have suggestions for who to hire, and you can also call Jason Abernathy in San Francisco to see if he's willing to take the case or knows somebody who would be good. This needs to be handled pretty promptly, since justice moves swiftly, if not surely, in Texas.

Try not to let all this interfere too much with your own life. Perhaps that's impossible, I don't know. But once again, thank you for everything, and I'm sorry. It means everything in the world to have you handling this stuff for me.

Hasta la vista, amiga.

Chapter 6 _____

I listened to that tape five times. It seemed strange to have Pren's disembodied voice and presence in the room, but I felt better than I had since April 6, now that I understood more clearly just what had happened. I never wanted to believe she was guilty of murder, but it helped a lot to hear it from the lady's own lips.

After I burned the cassette, stashed the borrowed tape recorder behind the Dumpster and checked out, I had the cab driver drop me four blocks from home, per Mimi's instructions. Then I got a fistful of change and stepped into a pay phone to call VETRAGE headquarters in Berkeley. Mike Donovan himself answered the phone.

"I'm a friend of a friend," I began obliquely. I was assuming that this fellow would be fairly savvy about telephones and security; there wasn't one chance in five million that VETRAGE's lines weren't tapped. "I'm interested in making a contribution to the Randy Hargis Defense Fund."

His voic̄ was very deep and sounded oddly familiar. "I'm a bit tied up rig⌐   ⌐s there a number where I can call you back in a couple of
ⴈ ̄

                    ⵊ number of the next booth over and hung up. Five
                    ⵊone rang and I lunged for it.
               ⵊere."
               ⵊline?"
                    I suppose. Are you Laurel?"

I was shocked. "Why do you ask that?"

"Southern drawl, Chicago area code, offer of money. Uncle Sam don't let no dummies be officers in military intelligence, ma'am. Or so Uncle Sam do claim."

I laughed. "You nailed me. And it sounds like you were expecting to hear from me."

"True. I heard a rumor that I might. I've been shopping for lawyers and I think once we have the money straightened out, we can get Randy a pretty good defense. Jason Abernathy thinks it would prejudice a Beaumont jury if he went down to defend him, but he knows a good criminal attorney in Houston who'll take the case for fifteen big ones. Is that a possibility?"

I thought about the piles of Pren's twenty- and fifty-dollar bills lying in my safe deposit box alongside Grandma Chesterton's pearls. "It's no problem at all. How do I get the money to you?"

"Is this contribution above the table?"

"No."

"That complicates it a little bit." He thought a moment. "I'm supposed to leave tomorrow for Miami. What if I stopped over in Chicago on the way?"

I was carrying the safe deposit box key. "That will work just fine. Where shall I meet you?"

"Hmmm, let me think. Okay, let's do it this way. I don't know what time I'll get into O'Hare yet, but I'll call you at home tonight and let you know. It will be a station call and I'll asked for Jeffrey. You say there's nobody there by that name and ask what number I'm calling. The last four digits of the number I give will be the time you should meet me. Give yourself plenty of time to get there and be sure you aren't followed. Maybe it would be easiest if you lost the tail downtown and took a hotel limo out to O'Hare. There's one from the Palmer House, I know, and another from the Conrad Hilton."

"Sounds like you know Chicago pretty well."

"Born and raised in Bridgeport." So that was why he sounded so familiar! It was those nasal A's creeping into his speech now and again, linguistic sewage seeping to the surface of what was otherwise a very pleasant voice. "My folks still live just a few blocks from Mayor Daley. Anyway, go to the airport and find the cocktail lounge nearest to the United ticket counters. I'll meet you there. Let's see. I have black hair, shoulder length, parted to the right. I'll be wearing tan cords, a white shirt and a button in the shape of a stopsign saying STOP THE WAR! There'll be a pack of Salems on the bar or table where I'm sitting and I'll be drinking beer. How will I recognize you?"

Whew! His immediate control of the situation impressed the hell out of me and I was determined to match his professionalism.

"I'll be wearing a dark blue skirt and a blue-and-white striped blouse. I'm five feet five and my hair's short, light brown and real curly, kind of in a natural." I just couldn't bring myself to give him the most obvious clue, that I was fat. He'd fine out soon enough.

"Okay, then. I'll call you at home tonight. And if there's going to be any kind of problem so that you won't be able to meet me or bring the money, let me know when I call. Say there's no Jeffrey there and hang up immediately. Then call me tomorrow morning at eight-thirty your time at this number."

I wrote down the number, gave him mine and hung up. Then I hopped on a downtown bus and removed another $15,000 from the safe deposit box. At this rate, it wasn't going to last long. By the time I got back home, I was utterly exhausted. An enormous amount had been telescoped into the twenty hours since I left the apartment and I had hardly slept at all the night before.

I dead-bolted my apartment door, put the key back in my jar of Major Gray's chutney, stuffed the money up into the box spring of my mattress and fell asleep almost immediately. It was dark when the phone woke me and I felt slightly disoriented. Still, the moment I heard Mike Donovan's distant voice ask for Jeffrey, everything came tumbling back into focus and I followed instructions perfectly. The designated time was 1645.

At 4:45 the following afternoon, I wandered as nonchalantly as possible into the cocktail lounge by the United ticket counter. And there, in close promixity to a bottle of Michelob and a pack of Salems, sat a dark-haired lad in tan cords and a white shirt with a stop sign pinned to the collar. And he was gorgeous. Maybe Jesus really did love me after all, and had just been taking a prolonged nap.

He rose to greet me as I walked nervously across the room. "Welcome to the world of intrigue, Laurel," he said, pulling out a chair for me. The waitress asked for ID when I ordered my bloody mary, which made Mike wince slightly. He asked for another Michelob and paid for both our drinks. It was as close as I'd come to a date for quite some time and I rather savored the entire experience.

"Ready for heavy action in Miami?" I asked, immediately kicking myself under the table for banality. I sought to recover. "But I guess you've probably been to plenty of conventions." That was even worse, and sounded as if he were off to join the Jaycees or the American Association of Hardware Retailers.

"Nope, this is my first convention," he answered with a grin. His right upper canine was slightly crooked, but he had a wonderful smile. "Got tied up in July and never made it to the Democratic carnival. And I missed 'sixty-eight altogether, I'm afraid, when it was right here on my own turf."

"It was a dilly," I assured him.

"You were here?"

I nodded smugly. He didn't need to know that I'd been chewing my nails to the elbow out in an Evanston rec room during all the action. I had memories of the 1968 Democratic National Convention that I was quite confident I would carry to my grave. "Where were you in 'sixty-eight."

"Saigon."

"Ah, yes. Military intelligence, isn't that what you said?" I wasn't quite sure how to keep the conversation going without mentioning Prentiss Granger or gunfire in Beaumont, Texas. And once I gave him the money, there'd be no reason for him to hang around. Mike Donovan seemed to be quite a spectacular fellow, all told, and my hyperactive fantasy elves had already settled the two of us in a rose-covered cottage, till death do us part.

"What I was doing had precious little to do with intelligence, Laurel. But that was what they called it. In fact, what they actually called it was 'area studies,' if you can believe that. You just can't beat Uncle Sam's army for euphemism. You know, I almost met you over Thanksgiving, when you came to visit Prentiss. I should have stayed in town." He gave me a smile and leaned closer across the table.

I felt suddenly weak and slightly dizzy. He was *flirting* with me. This handsome black Irishman with the versatile eyebrows and warm brown eyes was focusing all of his considerable charm on me. I gulped the rest of my drink. I fumbled with my cigarettes and he took the matches from my hand. I almost swooned and my hand shook as he lit my cigarette.

"Are you all right?" he asked, with what sounded like real concern.

"Just having a little nervous breakdown." I wanted to sound flip, but I knew it wasn't working. "I'm worried about Pren and I'm scared about what's going to happen to Randy and all this cloak-and-dagger stuff scares me half out of my mind."

He took my hand across the table and spoke soothingly. "Don't worry, Laurel, everything'll be all right, just wait and see. We'll get Randy a good defense and you know Prentiss is going to be all right. She's about the most capable girl I've ever known. Have you heard from her?"

I didn't know what to do. I said nothing.

He smiled gently. "No answer seems like yes to me. You can trust me, you know. Wilt was one of the best friends I ever had. I'm on the same side you are."

"I know," I answered quietly. "This must be just as hard on you as it is on me."

"Now don't go trying to outsuffer an Irishman. It'll never work. Here, let me buy you another drink." He signaled to the waitress. "Now, let's see if we can't cheer up a little, all right?" He gave a silly grin and I smiled almost despite myself. "There, that's better!"

He took his hand away to pay for the drinks and by the time I was sipping mine, I felt much more in control of myself. I also was aware that this would be ending much too quickly. In the space of five minutes I'd developed an infatuation suitable for the *Guinness Book of World Records*. Suddenly I had an idea.

"I'd like to be able to talk to you about Randy's trial without going through all that hocus-pocus about pay phones. What would you think if I made another contribution to the defense fund above the table? Like maybe a check for five hundred dollars?"

He stared at me intensely for a moment, then smiled. "We could use the bread, no question about it. Why don't we do it this way? I'll be back in Berkeley on the twenty-eighth. Call me sometime the next day during normal working hours. You might as well be open about it and call from your own line. Just introduce yourself as if we'd never met and say you want to contribute to the defense fund. Then you can mail me a check. And naturally you'll want to keep informed, if you have an investment and all."

"Sounds fine to me. You know, that's a great button." I pointed at the stop sign on his collar.

He smiled. "Prentiss designed it."

"Really?"

"Un huh. It was one of half a dozen projects she was working on last spring. Before." He paused a moment and finished his beer. "Sure do miss that girl. And Wilt and Randy too. It tore the heart and guts right out of VETRAGE losing all three of them."

"You're left," I reminded him gently.

He shook his head and I could almost watch the wave of pain sweep down his body. "Just barely." He pulled the stop sign from his collar and handed it to me. "Here. This ought to be yours."

He needed to catch his plane to Miami then. So I pulled the money from my purse, neatly gift-wrapped in a thin box. Mike slipped the "present" into the soft battered tan zipper case at his feet. Then, unexpectedly, he leaned across the table and kissed me full on the lips.

"That's in case anybody's been watching us," he murmured. "A fellow always kisses a pretty girl who's just given him a present." He leaned back while I basked in the blarney. "Now I think you'd better go. Take a cab home, or to your neighborhood, rather."

"Why not the Palmer House limo again?"

He grinned. "Because anybody who can decide on the spur of the moment to fork over half a grand can afford to take a cab driven by some vet who can't get another job. And lives on his tips."

Meeting Mike Donovan gave new purpose to my life. To say that I was smitten puts it far too mildly. I was head over heels in love with this Irish boy from Bridgeport, this former military intelligence officer, this mild-mannered crusader against injustice to the American veteran.

Unfortunately, there wasn't a damn thing I could do about it.

To begin with, anybody who looked like that could undoubtedly have his pick of girlfriends. Maybe (and this was a particularly depressing thought) one of them had been Prentiss Granger, before she met Wilt Bannister. Mike had, after all, been her first connection with VETRAGE. And what sort of connection had never been specified.

I wore the STOP THE WAR! button he had given me every single day, as a pledge of love and adoration. Meanwhile, I discovered that there were no fewer than eleven Donovans within a five-block radius of Mayor Daley's Bridgeport bungalow, and drove past each and every one of them in a futile search for further clues.

Amidst interminable hours of CREEPs at the Republican National Convention, there was film of a VVAW parade down Main Street. I was quite certain I made out the face of my One True Love. It happened quickly and I couldn't actually be sure, but it looked enough like Mike Donovan to jolt me three feet in the air.

I was watching at Maxine Lockford's house that night, flattered to be invited. Ginger wasn't interested in the slightest and didn't bother to even come for dinner. It seemed wonderful to me that her mother and I were comfortable enough together not to need Ginger as a bridge. I brought my portable out and she carried her bedroom portable down and we were able to monitor all three networks, which mostly allowed us to watch the likes of Strom Thurmond in grim dull triplicate.

She agreed with Mike Royko that politics in Chicago was as much a spectator sport as football, and she'd been sitting on the fifty-yard line her entire life. She told tales of manipulation and boondoggling, of secretaries of state and shoe boxes full of cash. She spoke so matter-of-factly of gargantuan corruption that if I hadn't been raised in Louisiana, I probably wouldn't have believed her. But we have our own traditions of political hanky-panky. I'll match the Longs against the Daley Machine any day. Charlie Chaplin, Zasu Pitts, Babe Ruth, Clara Bow and Charlie McCarthy have been on the Placquemines Parish voting rolls for years. In a political sense, I'd been training all my life to move to Chicago.

Once the convention was over, I couldn't wait for it to be Tuesday the twenty-ninth so I could call him. I thought of very little else through the weekend except that I was going to have to get skinny in one hell of a hurry. I plunged myself headlong into *Dr. Atkins' Diet Revolution*.

Nobody answered the VETRAGE phone for a solid week after Mike had claimed he'd be back. Then, finally, I got a busy signal. I did a dozen deep knee bends and hyperventilated five minutes, then dialed again.

When he answered my mind went utterly blank. A moment later, I recovered. "This is Laurel Hollingsworth. I'm an old friend of Prentiss Granger's and I'd like to give some money for the defense of Randy Hargis. Unless of course his legal expenses have already been met."

"Miss Hollingsworth," spake my true love, "we'd be delighted to have your help in paying for Randy's defense. I was just down in Houston meeting with his attorneys and we're definitely short on cash. You couldn't have called at a better time."

"Good. Who's representing him?"

"Martin Wheeler. He's about the best criminal attorney in Texas for this kind of thing. He does a lot of dope cases and has a really fine reputation. I think he'll give Randy a good defense."

"I'm glad to hear that. It seems like they're ready to lynch him."

"Ready, willing and able. I'd guess the only thing that's kept him alive this long is that his family is fairly prominent. Of course they've publicly disowned him, but still you don't go around stringing up the sons of wealthy oilmen at least until after they've had some facsimile of a trial. We're hoping that this will be better than a facsimile, though. I'm impressed with Martin Wheeler. Now tell me, Miss Hollingsworth—"

"Please call me Laurel."

"Laurel. Laurel, how large a contribution would you be able to make?"

"I was thinking maybe five hundred or seven hundred fifty dollars. I mean, I hardly know this fellow and I certainly don't hold with killing policemen, but he ought to get a fair trial."

"Laurel, we can use every penny we can get. I sure hope you'll decide to make it seven fifty. Do you want to send us a check?"

"Well, you'd hardly expect me to have that kind of money in cash!" This line came out of nowhere and I was particularly proud of it. All through the conversation we'd been speaking on two levels, of course. But now I'd found a way to remind him again about the cash I'd handed him and perhaps he'd even recall the kiss that went along with the package. Lord knows I hadn't forgotten it for more than ten minutes at a stretch since it happened.

He laughed. "Of course not! You can make it out to the Randall Hargis Defense Fund and mail it to me here at VETRAGE. Do you have the address?"

"Yes."

"Great. You wouldn't happen to have any ideas where we might be able to scare up more money, would you?"

"You might start walking the streets of Berkeley asking for spare change."

He laughed. "That beat's pretty well covered, I'm afraid. Keep in touch, Laurel, and I'll let you know what's happening with the trial. It's been good talking to you."

I decided, as I replaced the phone, that it was time I became much more involved in veterans' affairs.

* * *

The mysterious Jackie popped back into my life a few days later, suddenly materializing beside me as I picked through the produce at Jewel. "Don't look at me," she murmured. I would have recognized her voice anywhere. "I need to talk to you for a few minutes. Can you be at R. J. Grunt's later this evening?"

I nodded, casting aside a blemished artichoke and critically appraising another.

"Fine. Meet me in the ladies room at eight-thirty."

Since there seemed no reason not to, I invited Ginger to join me for dinner. It was a school night, but she needed little coaxing. I hadn't seen her for several weeks, since before she started classes. There were bags under her eyes and she chain-smoked, trembling.

"Honest to God, Laurel," she moaned, once we were seated in the restaurant, "I've never had to work so hard in my life. I feel as if everybody's out to break me and I don't dare stop paying attention for a second or I'll be left behind forever."

"Come on, Ginge. It can't be that bad."

"It's worse. Law school's like a giant window fan. Turn it one way and it sucks, turn it the other and it blows. Plus I think they're harder on me because I'm a girl."

"But you were expecting that, weren't you?" Funny how we took it for granted back then.

"I sort of expected it. But I have this one torts professor who says Misssss Lockford and makes it sound like a snake. He always calls on me and he's always finding fault with my answers and I'd swear he's trying to get me to quit."

"It's just because it's new," I reassured her. "A couple of months from now you'll be laughing about all this."

"I will never in my life laugh about this," she vowed, and I was impressed by her fervor. After all, she had never really worked in college and claimed to have been scarcely more motivated in high school. Maybe this actually *was* the first time in her life she'd been forced to buckle down. If so, I decided, it was about time. I wasn't as forgiving of Ginger or as conciliatory about her moods since she'd moved out on me.

At eight-thirty I went to the ladies room. And there was Jackie, Dynel and all. I wondered what color her hair actually was. She was wearing horn-rims instead of shades this time.

"Any problems?" she asked. I shook my head. "Good. Now here, pay attention. This is a list of telephone numbers in your neighborhood. You tend to take a lot of walks anyway, so there won't be abnormal suspicion when you check these out. You'll see that the numbers are in five groups of no more than three each. That's because some of the locations have several phones at the same place. These are the ones that are easier to use. If one line is busy or out of order, there's a backup. The others were chosen for their privacy. Memorize the locations and then tear off that part of the list and burn it. Tonight. Following me? Good. Now, the code word is 'Moustached.' "

"Moustached?" Maybe I hadn't heard her properly.

"That's right, hairy on the upper lip. Each letter corresponds to a digit, beginning with one for M, two for O, down to zero for D. And you read all numbers from right to left. Okay?"

"Sure."

"Now, if you should ever encounter a string of meaningless letters, like on a piece of paper somebody slips into your pocket or something, it will mean you have an incoming call. The code will be the same. The first number is the grouping on your list. The next four numbers are the date, with zeros where necessary. And the last four numbers are the time of the call, Central time. There will always be nine letters on such a list and they'll always read from right to left. Repeat it back to me."

I concentrated a moment, then gave it back flawlessly.

She smiled proudly at me. "Fine. Now, here's your first incoming call. Translate, please." She handed me a slip of paper which read "DUTMC-MEDU."

I took my time to get it right. "List three on September seventeenth at three-thirty in the afternoon."

"Perfect. Be there. That's when your call will come. Remember to memorize and burn that list of locations before you go to bed tonight. Also, if for some reason it's impossible for you to meet a phone assignation on the specified date, another attempt will be made to reach you at the same location exactly twenty-four hours later. Any questions?" I shook my head. "Great. That's it, then. But I'm curious about one thing, Penny."

"What?"

"Remember when you lost that tail in Carson's by telling the saleslady he was trying to make you buy drugs?"

I nodded. Forget a moment of glory? Not this cowgirl.

"What if she'd been young or black or something?"

I smiled. "Well, if she'd been either one, it would actually have been easier. I would have said that the guy was my sister's husband who kept beating her up and that he was after me because I'd turned him in to the cops."

She grinned broadly. "It's nice to have you on our side," she said, and it was the closest thing to praise I'd had yet.

Later that night I memorized and burned the list of locations. I guess by then I had come to terms with this strange new life. Not until I was in bed did it occur to me that I ought to feel ridiculous.

On Sunday the seventeenth, I took a ride in the country to exercise my G-man, then lost him on a cloverleaf somewhere around Belvedere. I was left with several hours to kill, so I went to the public beach up in Evanston and wandered along the shore for a while. It was a beautiful day and I felt tremendously excited. There could only be one reason for all the shuck and jive about this call. There was only one person in the world who would need to go to so much trouble.

At 3:30 I was shifting my weight beside the booth. When the phone rang at 3:34 I snatched it up. "Hello?"

"You would think," drawled Prentiss Granger, "that a charming little daughter of Dixie like yourself might be able to muster a trifle more enthusiasm for greeting a long lost friend."

"Insufficient enthusiasm has nothing to do with it," I shot back. "Just wanted to be sure it wasn't some drunk lugan trying to get through to his wife."

"Logan? What did you say? It's a bit hard for me to hear you."

"Lugan. L-U-G-A-N. It's my favorite new ethnic slur. It means Lithuanian. Before I moved to Chicago, I never even knew there *were* Lithuanians. Now I can insult them."

"Penny."

I stopped short. "Yes?"

"You're babbling."

"I'm sorry. You're right. But I've just been so nervous about this call, about actually hearing your voice again. Are you all right?"

"Oh, I'm fine. A bit bored and I don't have any freedom of movement worth mentioning, but I'm free and I'm alive."

"I'm glad you sent me that tape. I needed it more than you might know."

She sighed deeply. "This is really ridiculous, isn't it? You know, sometimes when I first wake up in the morning, I think I'm back in Berkeley, with my honey right there beside me. It only lasts a few seconds, but it's the best part of my day."

"Chin up, Jeannie." I wanted to keep it light if I could. "Is there anything else I can do to help you? More money, or anything? I took care of the defense fees, by the way."

"I know, I heard. I really appreciate that you could do it so quickly."

"It wasn't any trouble at all. Matter of fact, it was a real pleasure."

Her tone was wry. "Do I detect an odd note in your voice?"

I never had been able to fool her for long. "You mean that breathless catch, that faint girlish glee?"

"Yeah, that. What's the story?"

"Nothing really. Just that I liked, um, Errol Flynn."

She laughed. "Errol Flynn, eh? I might have guessed. Isn't he a honey?"

"Quite." I hesitated a moment, then decided to get it out in the open and find out once and for all how jealous I needed to be. "In fact, I'm surprised you didn't take a crack at him yourself. Or did you?"

"I was friends with his wife," she answered. "It seemed a little too sleazy."

His wife. Two simple words that sliced me neatly into vermicelli. No reason for him to have mentioned being married, after all. It was hardly necessary to chat about your marital status with the girl who brought money for your friend's murder trial. It had never once occurred to me that he might be married. And I was being quiet too long.

"Hey," she said gently, "you really like him, huh?"

"Nonsense," I responded with bright, utterly counterfeit cheer.

"The last I heard they split up," she said easily. "That was around January or February. I was siding with his wife, actually. He's a terrible tomcat. He'll fuck anything that moves and he swept rather a wide swath through her circle of friends. Finally she had enough. I guess there's a chance they're back together, but I suspect I'd have heard somehow."

"It's like having a direct line to Louella Parsons. You ought to start a New Left gossip column."

"The New Left is starting to get a little creaky and arthritic," she said.

"And it would be a trifle difficult to manage from underground in any case. And I'm afraid this call can't go on much longer. It's too risky. I probably shouldn't be calling you at all, but I wanted so much to hear your voice again."

"Likewise," I told her, trying to sound tough. I felt like crying. This brief conversation reminded me with dreadful clarity of how irrevocably our lives and friendship had been altered. "Jeannie? Can't you just turn yourself in? You really haven't done anything that wrong."

Her voice tightened. "That's not what the indictments say. Penny, the political climate's all wrong and it's *Texas*. It doesn't matter what I did. It's what they *think* I did. It would never work."

"Don't you think you're exaggerating a bit?"

"I wish I were. But I'm not making a move till I see what happens to Randy. As a matter of fact . . ." She hesitated.

"What?"

"Do you suppose you could go to the trial and be my witness on the scene? That way you can tell me exactly what happens."

"But I have to work."

"Take a couple of days off. Call in sick."

"Long-distance?"

"Why not? I really wish you'd go. Errol Flynn will probably be there," she teased.

"I'm sure I couldn't care less."

"I bet. If he's there alone, you might just as well have an affair with him. He'd probably be agreeable. Just don't go falling in love with him. You'll end up being very sorry. In fact, if you can't handle just having a sex thing with him, maybe it isn't such a good idea after all."

"It's all preposterous," I said huffily. "I'm sure he doesn't have the slightest interest for me. Or in me. But all right. I'll go to the trial. So I can tell you about it."

She laughed. "Whatever. Okay now, you know the code?"

"Yes ma'am, and I have my Dick Tracy Superspy Decoder wristwatch running twenty-four hours a day. Just in case."

She laughed again. "Damn, I miss you! I know this all seems silly, but it's important for security. Now listen. When I intend to call you, if I have time I'll send you a book through the mail. It will always come first class. Count the words in the title. If it's five, say, then count five chapters from the back and five pages forward from the end of that chapter. The next page on the left will have pinpricks under letters, in order, that are the code for when and where I'll call you. Don't forget that the numbers read from the right. Now tell it back to me."

I did, feeling fairly foolish. "Anything else?"

"Nope. Except that if I don't talk to you before then, and I probably won't, have a good time at the trial."

"You bet. Bye, then. And thanks for calling. It means a lot to me."

"Likewise, chum. Be careful."

Then she was gone again, vanished back into the mysteries of whatever life she was leading wherever. And I started planning what to wear to Randy Hargis's trial.

Chapter 7 _____

I arrived in Beaumont for *The People of the State of Texas* v. *Randall Tyler Hargis* on a chilly October Tuesday night. The trial was scheduled to begin the next morning and the newspaper I picked up at the airport announced that the prosecution predicted a conviction in no more than two days. I pitched the paper in a trash can and pointed my rental car toward the Beaumont Bar-None Motel, where I had reservations. When I checked in, the codger at the desk leered while confiding that Mr. Donovan wanted me to know he was in Room 214.

Which made me so nervous I could barely get to my own room. I dumped my bag, changed into jeans, combed my hair, applied fresh makeup and hyperventilated awhile. Then I walked the seemingly endless balcony to Room 214.

Mike Donovan answered the door and my heart started going through the kind of maneuvers generally associated with the Flying Angels air team. He was even more beautiful than I remembered. But this time he was very depressed and not a little bit drunk.

"Welcome to the wake, Laurel," he greeted me. "Make yourself a drink. We have Scotch and water or water and Scotch."

"Either one is fine," I told him. "How are you doing?" I walked over to the dresser and plunked a couple of cubes into a plastic glass. Given my nervousness and the fact that he was clearly far ahead of me, I made mine Scotch and Scotch. He had the radio playing softly and had apparently been sitting on the bed, which was mussed slightly with the pillows bunched at the head. It was hard to avoid the bed, actually, since the room was fairly small. I sat in the only chair with my drink and he sat opposite me on the bed.

"To acquittal," I said, raising my glass.

"To old friends," he responded, raising his. "And to new friends. I'm glad you're here. I was feeling very alone."

"You're by yourself?"

"Nobody else could afford to come out. I couldn't really either, but I had to."

I didn't say anything, just gulped convulsively at my drink. I had to forcibly restrain myself from tilting the glass and pouring the whole thing straight down my throat. We sat there in silence for several minutes, waiting. Finally he looked up.

"They say," he remarked wryly, "that God invented whiskey to keep the Irish from ruling the world. I'm sorry to be such lousy company, Laurel. But I saw Randy this afternoon and he looks just terrible. He's lost forty pounds and he seems to have stopped caring what happens. Now Wheeler says he doesn't think we can get in any of the psychiatric evidence. In which case Randy might just as well have hugged that claymore in Dak To. They've got a brand new capital punishment law and it fits him like a wetsuit." He fell silent again, reached over to the dresser and poured more Scotch into his glass.

"Have you eaten anything?" If he didn't start sopping up that alcohol with something, he'd pass out momentarily.

"Not since breakfast. Hungry?"

I shook my head. "I had dinner on the plane. The same kind of mystery meat they used to serve in the Duke Union. But I think you ought to eat something, don't you?"

He smiled a thin half-smile. "I suppose. C'mon, there's a steakhouse just down the road. We won't even need to drive."

So we walked through the cool October night to the Cattle Rustler, where Mike put away a large medium rare T-bone and I ate a salad. It took every ounce of discipline I could muster not to plunge across the table and snatch the meat off his plate.

"So you want to know how I got from Bridgeport to Berkeley?" He had polished off the entire steak and no longer seemed quite so smashed. "I wonder about that myself, sometimes. By all rights it should never have happened. My parents are one generation out of County Cork and

I'm an only child, one of the great sorrows of my mother's life. She wanted a dozen kids and couldn't have them, so she used to take in foster children. She hasn't missed a morning of mass in twenty years. My father's a political slave to Mayor Daley. He's been a supervisor in the Sanitation Department ever since the late fifties, when his plumbing business went belly up. I grew up going to ward picnics and selling chances for the parish raffle and believing that Protestants were going to have to sit out on God's porch when they got to heaven. *If* they got to heaven. Went from St. Ignatius to the university down in Chambana without missing a beat or changing any of my friends. I was so straight I actually enlisted."

"You're kidding!"

"Oh, I wasn't being heroic or anything. But it was 'sixty-seven and I figured I'd be drafted. I enlisted so I could get into intelligence, believe it or not. I wanted to go to Nam. I thought it would be real exciting to be at war. And I absolutely without question believed that we were doing the right thing to be there. So did all my friends. We couldn't wait to zap the Cong."

"So what happened?"

He grinned. "Drug abuse. I was stationed in Saigon, working in a nice air-conditioned office with a lot of time on my hands. I met this French chick, a free-lance photographer, and through her I met a bunch of hippie journalists, mostly Americans. They were the mavericks, the ones who didn't show up at the Five O'Clock Follies to get their official handouts and weekly kill-ratio charts. They were in and out of town all the time, doing crazy-ass things like flying into Khe Sanh when it was under seige. Two things happened once I started hanging around with those guys. They had enough firsthand information about all sorts of different things to make it absolutely clear to me that we could never win that war, that it could go on another thirty years and the only thing that would change would be the dog tags in the body bags. Also, I started doing a lot of drugs. Acid mostly, but a lot of grass too. You could just get amazing quality marijuana over there, everywhere. Toward the end of my tour, I was getting stoned each morning before I went to work, and I tripped all the way across the Pacific on my way home. Needless to say, I didn't fit into Bridgeport anymore, and my parents had a fit when I moved out to the Bay area. My father intended for me to sign on with City Hall, soon as I could get my law degree. He hasn't forgiven me yet for not going to law school. And his friends all think that I sell insurance in San Francisco. But hey, I'm talking too much about me. What about you, Laurel? All I really know is that you're some kind of rich southern aristocrat."

"Don't be silly," I scolded, trying not to think about Weatherly Plantation. "I'm a schoolteacher and I work with ghetto kids in Chicago. That's all."

"And you happened to find fifteen thousand seven hundred fifty dollars lying in the gutter one day, so you said, 'Hey, why don't I give this to a defense fund for some guy I met once?' Give me a little credit, please. Remember my cloak-and-dagger background."

"I'm not rich," I replied shortly. Nor am I fat or nervous, I thought. Who was I trying to kid?

"All right. You're not rich. You know, Prentiss used to be touchy just the same way. There's nothing to be ashamed of about having money, you know. A lot of us would love the opportunity."

He rested a hand on my shoulder as we walked back to the hotel. Neither of us said anything until we were back in the neon glare of the motel parking lot.

"Come in for a nightcap?"

"Of course," I answered suavely, Nora Charles to his Nick.

And so we went to his room and had a couple more drinks and became very drunk indeed. Mike got very melancholy again and I didn't know whether or not he was going to make a pass at me. This was a matter I had given much thought, resolving finally against Pren's suggestion that I have an affair with him. Even as I had fantasized how glorious it might be, I kept coming back to what I perceived as three immutable realities. First, I did not want him to see my Pillsbury Doughgirl body. Second, if I ever did go to bed with him, I would probably do something very wrong and consequently never see him again. And third, there was no earthly reason to assume that he'd be interested.

Now that I was actually with him, however, the prospect of his rejection was suddenly more than I could bear to contemplate. And so I forestalled the question. I rose shakily to my feet, waved a feeble goodbye and told Mike I would meet him for breakfast at eight. He tried to stand up but I waved him back and slipped quickly through the door.

By the time I reached my own room, tears were pouring down my face. I didn't even turn on a light. I just collapsed on the bed and sobbed my heart out.

When we arrived at the courtroom the next morning, we immediately ran into Mel Sanford, who greeted us both like long lost friends. "Well, my goodness gracious," he drawled, his accent considerably thickened in this setting. "I didn't realize y'all knew each other." He couldn't be *that* far behind in reading his phone transcripts. "You're looking good, Miss Laurel. I didn't realize this was a school holiday."

"You know perfectly well that it isn't," I snapped at him. "But it's hardly worth getting me fired. It's a terrible job and nobody else wants it, I can promise you. Most of the time it makes me thoroughly miserable, so it's actually to your advantage to have me stay there."

Mike took my arm and led me away, none too gently. "You don't need to talk to that asshole," he lectured sternly.

"I wasn't talking to him," I offered meekly. "I was just wishing I had the guts to look him in the eye and tell him to go fuck himself. It's just barely possible that the shock would kill him."

"I'm sure he's heard it before."

"Not from a southern girl."

"Well, then, by all means give it a whirl."

As soon as I saw the judge, I knew Randy Hargis was a goner. Judge Wayne Carrington looked like somebody my father might sit and drink bourbon with on the front porch while they worked out a solution to the nigra problem, something like injecting cyanide into watermelons. In fact, he looked a great deal like one of Daddy's old friends, Luke Pickard, a dentist who continued to maintain separate and distinctly unequal waiting rooms for his patients. You could still read the outlines of the plastic letters which had spelled out COLORED on the door to the smaller and infinitely less habitable waiting room. The plastic letters disappeared one night during the summer after Charles Evers was elected mayor of Fayette, Mississippi.

Judge Carrington had the same slick prematurely bald pate, the same steel-rimmed glasses and the same supercilious attitude as Dr. Pickard. This did not portend well for poor Randy Hargis. We'd been warned by Martin Wheeler that our chances of acquittal in the courtroom were almost nonexistent. Judge Carrington had already denied several crucial pretrial motions and excluded evidence Wheeler hoped to introduce showing a correlation between Randy's Vietnam experience and his overreaction to the storekeeper's behavior.

I'd lately been nursing the romantic notion that perhaps the tide was turning for the American judicial system. Angela Davis had been acquitted and so had the Berrigans. Maybe justice wasn't dead after all, but merely comatose.

In that Texas courtroom, however, they'd already pulled the plug and wheeled away the life support system.

It took barely an hour to seat a jury of ten men and two women, all white, all middle-aged, all exceedingly somber. It took even less time for the Judge to exclude the defense's psychiatric evidence. By then I had reached the stunned realization that Mike and I comprised the entire defense support team. The Hargis family was conspicuous by its absence and the courtroom was packed with police officers, more than I'd seen in one place since the 1968 Democratic Convention. Their malevolent stares bored holes in the back of my head.

Randy, however, was oblivious. When Mike and I first spoke to him during a recess that morning, he was gaunt and sallow and seemed permanently dazed. He didn't even remember me after I reminded him of Thanksgiving, less than a year earlier. Up close his eyes yawned with a blankness normally seen only in those blind from birth.

We had lunch with Martin Wheeler that first day. His forty-five-year-old face was heavily lined from a lifetime of fighting creeping fascism in one of its more fertile breeding grounds. I liked him, but he sure didn't have any good news. "We might as well expect the worst, gang," he warned, "and figure it'll be set right on appeal." This fit with my well-established notions about southern justice. In Piniatamore Parish in 1947 a man was lynched for "acting sassy" to a white woman.

After lunch the prosecution began its case. I watched as if in a dream as the little old ladies related their version of the shooting and the florid cracker store manager told his. I heard the deceased police officer described as a good-hearted family man and watched his sobbing widow escorted from the courtroom. I wanted to scream.

We had to brush off a bunch of reporters to get away that afternoon, and it gave me great pleasure to rudely direct them to Martin Wheeler with brusque "No comments." I noted, with distant but considerable pride, that Mike was pleased by the way I handled the press.

By now, of course, Mike and I were all but welded together by the brutal force of community hatred for the friends of Randy Hargis. But I needed no excuse to hover near Mike. I was so madly in love that I could grow faintly dizzy merely by glancing sideways at him in the courtroom and seeing the shape of his fingernails or the scuff pattern on his shoes.

When we left the courtroom that afternoon, we drove to the Minute Mart where it all began and parked across the street. It looked smaller than I had imagined, dustier, more defeatedly decrepit. Neither of us said a word. Then Mike gunned the motor and we peeled out, both acutely aware of the green Ford behind us. We went directly to a redneck bar and ordered a pitcher of Lone Star beer.

We sat in that dark, odd place and drank beer and ate fried pork rinds and talked about all kinds of odd and crazy things. We both ignored the FBI man who sat just inside the door drinking Coca-Cola, and I did my best to be funny and vivacious. I told some Prentiss Granger stories from way back and did my imitation of the Major. Mike loved it and kept making me repeat it. I was happy to oblige.

Three hours later when we got out of the car with a bag of burgers and a six pack of Budweiser from the 7-Eleven beside the DQ, Mike turned to me. With an exaggerated leer and a big grin, he asked, "Your place or mine?"

"Yours," I answered firmly. To be able to boldly enter a man's room created the illusion of a good deal more experience and worldliness than I actually felt. I actually felt as if I'd spent the past twenty-four hours in the spin dry cycle.

He had clothes and junk all over the chair, so I sat on the bed as we ate our dinner. He turned on the radio and found a Houston station playing a lot of Carole King and James Taylor and Joni Mitchell, soft comfortable music for a soft comfortable time. We both kept drinking.

I'd pushed up the forearms of my sweater as the room grew warmer. I suddenly realized that he was running his fingers lightly up and down my left arm, just barely skimming my flesh, sending tiny jolts of electrical shock through me. I decided that I probably ought to be paying closer attention to what was happening and discovered that had I been any more relaxed, I would have been melted butter.

So I didn't make any attempt to stop him as he rubbed along the back of my forearm. It had never previously occurred to me that the back of one's forearm could be an erogenous zone, but clearly I had plenty to learn. I was tingling in places I didn't know I had.

Then he slipped his arm around my shoulder and went to work on my right upper arm. Damned if that didn't turn out to be an erogenous zone too, even through a cableknit sweater. At this point half of me was terrified and the other half was screaming for more. Any minute now he would make another move. I wondered what it would be, in a sort of floating, detached fashion. Then it happened, and it turned out to be that he brought his right hand up my arm, across my shoulder and onto the side of my face, which he turned gently as he leaned down.

It was a little wet initially, as kisses go, but very, very nice. It was no trouble at all kissing him right back and it went on for quite some time as our tongues carried on a dialogue of their own. Then he moved his lips and started kissing across my cheek, moving down my throat inside my collar, making me so suddenly weak and lascivious that I realized I had only a few moments left if I wanted to back out of this. The character of the evening was about to change dramatically and permanently. And as I thought that, I felt his lips moving back up my neck. His tongue flicked gently all around my ear.

"You know what would be awfully nice," his voice came softly, and I was glad I couldn't see his face, "would be to make love to you and forget everything else in the world." He swept his left hand gently along the not inconsiderable curve of my body.

I was out of my league, I knew it. But how often does a Little Leaguer get to pitch to Mickey Mantle, anyway? Still, I was damned if I were going to put on a sexual performance for Special Agent Melvin Sanford.

"Isn't this room bugged?" I whispered back to him.

He pulled his head gently away, flashed me a big crooked grin and held up a finger to assure me he'd be right back. Then he burlesqued tiptoeing across the room to the telephone. He turned over the phone, pulled out a Swiss Army knife and unscrewed the base. He removed a little silver box, opened the door of the room and pitched it as hard as he could into the night. I heard a distant plunk as it crashed to the asphalt of the highway.

And then the door was closed and he bolted it and came back to me, turning on the bathroom light and closing the door partway, killing the other light and then sitting beside me on the bed, facing me and leaning down, the way I'd seen in a hundred movies. Except that this movie was actually my life. I was stiff and nervous for a couple of minutes, I'll admit it. But he was slow and he was very gentle and he acted as if we had all the time in the world.

And I learned that night that Prentiss Granger had been right about still another thing. Sex could indeed be a very wonderful activity.

Chapter 8 _____

I was determined to be hip and modern about this. I wasn't going to make him declare his love or expect his hand in holy wedlock or otherwise make a fool out of myself. I would be just as cool and together and seventies about him as any other woman he might meet. We were two people thrust together by fate. We needed to exist solely in the present through our brief interlude together. There was no past and there would be no future.

Sure.

I floated through Thursday on memories of the night before and anticipation of the one to come. The trial went badly that day, and we reenacted the night before with little change in detail, save that the outcome was no longer really in question.

Friday afternoon, the jury returned its verdict of guilty. Judge Carrington recessed the trial until Monday for the punishment phase of deliberations. Martin Wheeler had explained that he would try once again to get in some of the psychiatric evidence and would also put Mike on the stand. But I faced a fact more personally horrible to me than the verdict. I could not possibly stay through the rest of the trial. I would have to go back to work on Monday.

And that meant I would have to leave Mike Donovan.

Court recessed by three-thirty on Friday. Mike and I went again to what I was beginning to consider "our" bar, accompanied by our inevitable shadow. We were both pretty disconsolate, and I hated the prospect of parting on such dreary terms. Suddenly an idea hit me.

"How would you like," I asked him, "to go to New Orleans for the weekend and forget all about this?"

He looked at me oddly and raised one eyebrow.

"There's a place we can stay," I continued. "We could take my rental car and you could drive it back and I'll fly out of New Orleans. I have to be back in Chicago Monday. It won't cost more than gas and a couple of meals and we could have a lot of fun." To my relief, he didn't seem to be automatically dismissing the idea.

He worked his eyebrows for a moment, then nodded thoughtfully. "It probably will be pretty grim around here. Maybe that's not such a terrible idea. I always did kind of want to see New Orleans, and I don't get down to this part of the country very often, thank God."

"If you've never been there, then we *have* to go. It's a wonderful city!"

"How long would it take to get there?"

"Maybe three and a half hours."

"Then let's get the fuck out of here."

I drove, and was thrilled by his approval when I ditched our tail and called New Orleans to make sure no relatives were at the house. As we roared across the dark swamps and bayous of southern Louisiana, I felt more worldly than Marie Leveaux. There was still one enormous hurdle to be negotiated, however. I could only hope that Mike wouldn't freak altogether when he saw the house.

Because the same Laurel who had so piously denied her wealth was taking this boy from Bridgeport to Grandma Chesterton's massive Victorian home in the Garden District. The house was currently inhabited only by two elderly black servants, except when my relatives stayed there on visits to town. I decided to warn Earline and Claude never to let anyone know we had been there and if necessary I was prepared to order them to remain silent. They were there at my sufferance, you see. I owned the house.

Mike gave a new meaning and focus to aspects of New Orleans that were already very dear to me. He was intrigued by the French influence, likening it to similar elements in Saigon, a comparison that had certainly never occurred to me. He found the Vieux Carre charming, and I was able to steer us unerringly toward the best tucked-away gumbo shop and Adelaide's for crawfish and the Morning Call for café au lait and beignets.

"Southerners have always used New Orleans as a safety valve," I explained over a dozen freshly shucked oysters. "It's designed for temporary insanity. Say you're an abolitionist senator on vacation. Nobody in New England's going to know you're with an octoroon in lace pantaloons. You're a backsliding reverend from Georgia? You can be sloshed for four days and the Baptists back home will never know. Everything's available. If you wanted, you could buy a carload of coffee, a Louis XIV dining table, a sixteen-year-old hooker, and still make it to Brennan's for breakfast by noon."

"It reminds me," he answered, "of Disneyland. It's Fantasyland for grown-ups."

I know that I put Earline and Claude, two people I truly love, in an awkward position by showing up with a young man and ordering secrecy, but I couldn't really help that. Actually, they seemed glad to see some romance in my life.

Naturally, Earline made up two bedrooms for us. Mine was the room where I had spent that odd and lonely year, the room with the gold velvet chaise longue and the intricately carved four-poster bed one of my ancestors had ordered from Paris. Many nights I lay awake in that enormous bed and fantasized about having a rakishly handsome pirate slip into the room to make wild and passionate love to me.

Mike Donovan wasn't exactly a pirate, but he was indeed rakishly handsome and I found that for once the reality surpassed the fantasy. He'd leave the lights on in his room down the hall each night until after Earline and Claude went to sleep in their apartment over the carriage house. But by then he'd have been in my room for hours, with me an active star in all my favorite dreams. I was every princess who'd ever been locked in every tower in every fairy tale throughout history.

But there was an edge to the passion, an urgency to the sex that belied the holiday atmosphere we so carefully nurtured during the daylight hours. It was a denial of reality, a refusal to accept the truth behind our hastily planned trip, and a frenzied attempt to forget the horrors of murder trials and electrocution and a gaunt Texan with empty cavernous eyes.

I tried, with occasional success, to separate both my rational thought processes and galloping fantasies from the two physical organisms which were starring in this wonderful weekend. I would detach my spirit and hover around us as we walked the streets of the French Quarter or sat beside each other to eat or lay in a sweaty tangled heap on fine white lace and linen sheets with moonlight streaming through the window, tracing patterns on the wall as the magnolia branches stirred gently in the cool fall breezes.

Neither one of us ever mentioned love. I knew he was a Berkeley tomcat with a wife and a string of girlfriends worthy of any Arabian sultan. I knew that it would take me a bloody long time to recover from the pain of losing him, even though I was all too acutely aware that I never had "had" him in any but the most fundamentally carnal sense. He could not know that no other man had ever made me writhe and moan in such exquisitely ecstatic rapture. He would accept my behavior as standard for a lover.

And then there was his final gentle kiss before I boarded my plane for Chicago, his final strong tight hug before he turned and went away. "Thank you for helping me forget," he told me. And I thanked him for the same reason and pivoted smartly to board my plane. I was a big brave girl and I didn't cry at all until I reached my seat in the rear of the plane and realized with sudden shattering clarity that it was all over. Finished. Completed. Then I sobbed my heart out.

That night I paced from room to room in my lofty perch above Lake Michigan. Fifteen stories below me sat a white Ford with an FBI agent ready at the wheel. A thousand miles to the south, Mike Donovan was in a motel room at the Beaumont Bar-None. Somewhere out in the universe, Prentiss Granger was living the cautious life of the fugitive.

And here I was, nursing a hopelessly broken heart. First love is a tough one, whether you're thirteen or twenty-four. And while I didn't have much choice in the matter, I think I'd have preferred to get that particular pain over with as an adolescent, when one expects to be miserable anyway.

But even as I paced and sobbed and listened over and over to "You've Got a Friend" and "So Far Away" and "Fire and Rain," I knew that nobody could ever steal my memories of the brief affair with Michael Brian Donovan and nothing would ever diminish the beauty of those few days we had spent together.

I was the proud owner of one Golden Moment.

At five o'clock the next night, I went out to a pay phone and called Mike at the booth outside the Beaumont Dairy Queen. He answered on the second ring and his voice dragged with despair.

"They gave him the chair," he said without preamble. "It took all of twenty minutes. Wheeler couldn't get any of the psychiatric stuff in. And the prosecution kept objecting to my testimony about Nam as hearsay, since I wasn't with Randy there. What could I say? The one who was there was Wilt Bannister and he's dead."

"Dear God." It was all I could think to say. I'd spent so much of the day worrying about what was happening, devising scenarios around my hero Michael Brian Donovan, and all for naught. It seemed that the decision had already been made by a redneck judge and cracker jury, a bunch of narrow-minded idiots determined to make the South safe for autocracy by systematically annihilating anyone who disagreed with them.

"It's pretty depressing," he said finally. "But at least there's the appeals process. I keep reminding myself of that."

"I wish I could be there."

"So you could be depressed too?"

"I'm already lower than a bassett's belly. You don't have to be in Beaumont to feel rotten, you know."

"No, but the Chamber of Commerce guarantees that if you are, you will."

I laughed. "There were times when I wasn't." Instantly I regretted my loose tongue.

"Booze and sex," he responded, "have a way of taking the edge off almost anything."

Oh, God. There it was, an out-in-the-open reference. "They took the edge off me," I said quietly.

"That was the idea." He reported the day's events in detail and then he was gone.

It had all been a dream, I realized. I would never see Mike Donovan again and I might as well start getting used to the idea.

Two days later Randy Hargis was being transferred from Beaumont to the state penitentiary when he was shot and killed by sheriff's deputies who reported that the prisoner had attempted to escape. The Randy Hargis I had watched in that musty courtroom did not seem to have enough spirit to finish breakfast, much less make a break for freedom.

But there were no other witnesses.

I tried to call Mike the next morning from a pay phone at a nearby drugstore on my way to school. There was no answer at his home number in Berkeley. In desperation I called VETRAGE, waking some guy who had been sleeping in the office. He told me that Mike had left town permanently. There seemed little else that I could do, so I sent a short note to him at VETRAGE, marked PERSONAL. Then I plunged headlong into the vast abysss of loneliness and despair which suddenly surrounded me.

I knew that I would never cross paths with my beautiful Irish Pirate again. My purest Golden Moment was over.

Since I have never really lived any other way, I tend to think of time in terms of academic years, by winters and summers. I am not sure how the unemployed or people with jobs in the business world view the calendar. Perhaps time is as much a blur to them as it is to me.

In any case, the year of 1972–73 hit an all-time low. I had a broken heart. I gained back every ounce of weight I had lost in my short-lived tryst with the Atkins diet revolution. I had nobody to talk to about the things which bothered me the most. And all around me, the world seemed to go into decline.

A lot of it had to do with Nixon's landslide, carrying every state but Massachusetts. And with four more years stretching ahead of him, the old Trickster wasted no time in dismantling any vestigial remnants of the Great Society. OEO was to be phased out immediately. Millions of dollars of antipollution funds were impounded, a quaint new improvisation on the Constitution worked out by a slimy little weasel we'd all be meeting shortly, John Dean. Any funding even remotely related to health, education, welfare or any other sort of social improvement was certain to be vetoed automatically, and a few trial runs determined that Congress lacked the votes to override.

So social progress was going right down the toilet, while the Nixonians in their white sidewall haircuts and three-piece suits stood gleefully flipping the flush lever. Just about the only bright spot on the horizon was the overturn on appeal of the Chicago Seven convictions, though it certainly came as no surprise to those of us who had followed the trial that Judge Julius Hoffman was a prejudiced old nincompoop.

I threw what was left of me into my work. By now I had two solid years of classroom mistakes to learn from and I decided that if all else failed, I would develop a professional life I could regard with pride. It seemed to be the one aspect of my existence over which I still retained control.

And actually, I felt quite lucky. My desperate transfer out of the prefab squalor of McLaughlin might have landed me elsewhere in the projects, but instead I'd been sent to the Fletcher Primary Center in Lawndale on the West Side. Make no mistake about it, we were still in the ghetto. But it was a different, more habitable sort of ghetto.

The James D. Fletcher School had been built to endure, as had the surrounding two-flats and apartment buildings where my students lived. The neighborhood had changed dramatically over the decades, of course, but there were still occasional patches of lawn and some oak trees and a less intensely magnified sense of community fear and danger.

To begin with, at Fletcher I felt reasonably secure physically. Every day I had spent at McLaughlin, I felt quite certain that I would be winged by a stray bullet fired out of one of the project windows or assaulted on my way to my car by vicious street thugs. At Fletcher there wasn't that immediacy, the smell of fear that drifted down the halls and seeped through the ill-fitting doorjambs at McLaughlin.

Fletcher was no Chadwick Academy, to be sure, but it marked an enormous improvement over McLaughlin and the children whose miserable lives were spent in those horrid little warrens overlooking the Dan Ryan. Even the G-men seemed more comfortable there. I sometimes wondered just who those guys were and who they worked for. I always thought of them as G-men, but they could easily have been Red Squad members from the Chicago Police Department or representatives of some obscure government agency I had never heard of or even private detectives hired by Major Granger. I was careful to exercise them at least once a week so they wouldn't get stale and also, of course, so I wouldn't be so obvious when I had genuine need to lose them.

I had already done rudimentary things to open my classroom, but now I set about creating the most exciting learning environment on the West Side of Chicago. I built study nooks and fitted out two packing crates as quiet areas, lining them with carpet scraps and pillows. I stocked the science table with white mice and a bunny, surrounding them with feathers and pine cones and seashells and smooth, pretty rocks. I beefed up the library and math corners.

I papered the classroom with images of significant blacks from Crispus Attucks to Muhammad Ali to George Jackson to Aretha Franklin. I hung model biplanes and rocket ships from the light fixtures. I took pictures of classroom activities and printed them, mounting them behind plastic on big red poster boards. I found a marvelous series of baby animal photographs and hung them all around the science table. I brought in all manner of plants, some flowering, and replaced them promptly when they died. I put labels on everything.

Many of my students seemed to have learned nothing in first grade except that Miss Burton brandished a mean ruler. Several could not even write their names and one nine-year-old girl had never been to school before because nobody realized her blind grandmother was keeping her home. I worked out individualized programs for everything and everybody and almost immediately could document changes in the kids' performances. And of course there was also a significant change in my own performance: I was working at least five times as hard.

I spoke with Prentiss Granger three times that year, odd conversations that keyed me up tremendously yet really accomplished very little that was meaningful. The first of these conversations took place in two parts. It was very soon after I got back from the trial in Beaumont and my nerve endings were still very raw. As I talked about the trial and my broken heart, I broke down sobbing.

"I'm all right," I kept blubbering, as Pren tried to calm me down. But I wasn't all right at all and both of us knew it.

"Penny, honey, don't *do* this to yourself," Pren soothed. "Don't let yourself be miserable this way."

"I'm not *letting* myself, for Chrissake," I wailed. "This isn't *voluntary*. I can't do anything to stop it. I've just never hurt like this before."

"It'll get better, babe, honest. You'll see. After Wilt died, I didn't think I'd ever be able to function emotionally again, but even that's healing."

"But I'm being rational! That's what's so hard about it. I *know* I'll never see him again and I knew it all along, but I didn't think anything could hurt like this. If only I thought—"

She cut in and her voice came low and fast. "Penny, I have to hang up. Same time, same place tomorrow." And then there was a click and she was gone, so abruptly that it took me several moments to realize that the connection actually was broken. There I stood, on a frigid street corner by a darkened Shell station, wind howling off the lake and tears pouring down my cheeks.

The next night at the same time, Pren apologized. "Somebody came by," she said succinctly, "and there was no way in the world I could continue talking. Were you all right? I felt horrible just cutting you off like that. This life has all these minor aggravations and fears that normal people don't even have to think about. It would be a lot easier to cope with the big stuff if it weren't for all these little nuisance things."

And of course by then I was fairly well recovered, having cried long and hard the previous night. I gave Pren the rest of the details about the trial and Randy's death and Mike's disappearance. She took the disappearance in stride.

"He'll be back. He's got too much conscience not to keep going, even after something like this." And long after we had hung up, I took that as a comfort. He might indeed turn up again someday.

Pren sent me a copy of *Fire in the Lake* to set up an assignation in March and by then I had recovered pretty well from my devastation at the hands of the Irish Pirate. I was pleased to be able to joke about Watergate and make her laugh, and tremendously excited when she suggested that perhaps sometime over the summer we would be able to meet. It was a very tentative thing, she warned, but it just might work if I were willing to go to a little trouble.

"Trouble?" I responded breezily. "I eat trouble for breakfast. Also lunch, dinner and a variety of between-meal snacks. Set it up."

Chapter 9 _____

On the appointed hour of the appointed day in June, I boarded a Rock Island commuter train heading south at the height of rush hour. It was a miserably muggy Monday afternoon and there hadn't been a breeze for days. I wore sturdy walking shoes and carried a small navy blue canvas tote bag and a large straw purse. Around my middle, swimming in sweaty plastic wrap, was strapped $10,000.

I was on my way to meet Prentiss Granger.

I was terrified. I didn't feel any personal danger, really, but suddenly I was in a position where I might directly affect the safety and continued well-being of my oldest and dearest friend. If I messed up, as my students always put it, it was the slammer for Pren. Ordinarily the stakes are not quite so high when I have to worry about messing up, though I guess that the fear is universal enough. I once saw Barbara Walters interview Diana Ross in a palatial Beverly Hills mansion which had been redecorated expressly for the occasion. Diana was slim and rich and beautiful and talented. "What are you afraid of?" queried Barbara. "Messing up," replied Diana.

The train passed McLaughlin School and a vast glum skyscape of high-rise slums on the near South Side as we whizzed through those nasty neighborhoods without stopping. I had intentionally boarded at the very last minute as the train pulled out of the station and had not walked forward seeking a seat until after the train was barreling along too fast for anyone else to jump on. I was quite certain that I hadn't been followed, but I was prepared to abort the entire trip if things got hairy.

There were no hitches, however. I left the train at 111th Street and walked west, climbing a huge hill, then scooting around the corner into a branch library. I cooled my heels in the stacks for fifteen minutes, one eye on the door, then left the library, turned right and meandered through a neighborhood of massive shade trees and lovely old brick homes.

There was an infestation of seventeen-year locusts in the area. Huge numbers of large, atonally shrieking bugs with formidable shells hung from trees and shrubs and littered the sidewalks. A few kids rode bikes and one old codger was mowing his lawn, but nobody showed any interest in the woman with the navy tote bag stepping gingerly around the little bug bodies. When I was satisfied that I was alone, I crossed 111th Street and cut through the modest grounds of the Morgan Park Academy to 112th Street.

There, as expected, I found a dark green Mustang with Pennsylvania plates parked beside a large shrub which dripped with screeching bugs. Behind the wheel sat Mimi, who had delivered the money to Pren a year earlier.

I didn't start breathing normally until we were past Aurora. Mimi explained that we would travel exclusively on secondary highways, avoiding interstates and large cities. We would obey all the relevant traffic laws, even if it meant going half the speed of everyone else. All of our purchases would be paid for by me in cash. Next she put me through a rigorous cross-examination about my activities for several days prior to departure and on the first leg of my journey.

Finally she relaxed. I seemed to have made no irreparable blunders.

We were obviously heading due west into the sunset, but I was supposed to ask no questions about our route or destination, one of many predetermined restrictions. In fact, when you added up all the things that I wasn't allowed to discuss, you destroyed every inch of common ground that seemed to exist between Mimi and me.

Had we been men, we could have shot the breeze about baseball, but the only sports news I'd paid any recent attention to was the upcoming Billie Jean King/Bobby Riggs tennis match and we disposed of that almost instantly. I was not about to attempt any small talk about other current events. There was no way in the world to guess Mimi's politics, save that she would be a leftist, in some presumably exotic fashion. Even

Watergate might not be safe; there were undoubtedly revolutionaries of various odd stripes who wanted Nixon to retain power until the proletariat uprising, scheduled soon.

So we listened to a Beatles retrospective out of Chicago and made only perfunctory conversation, all the way through dinner at a drive-in in western Illinois. As the sun disappeared in a breathtaking vista of tangerine and cerise stripes, Mimi spoke abruptly. "Ready to drive through the night?"

"Sure," I replied, a great deal more eagerly than I felt.

"Terrific. Do me a favor now, Penny. Reach behind me in the bag on the floor and find the empty Pepsi can." Mystified, I retrieved a surprisingly heavy Pepsi can from a garbage sack of assorted fast food wrappers and soda cans. "Twist the top to the right," she instructed. When I did so, the can separated into two pieces. In the base rested a Glad bag of grass, a pack of wheatstraw Zig-Zags, and two rolled joints.

"Well, I'll be damned! Is this what they mean by the Pepsi generation?"

Mimi laughed. "Coming at you, going strong. I'm rather proud of it, myself. No cop is going to bother with an empty soda can. Or anyway that's been my experience. Light one of those jays and put the can back in the trash."

"Is it cool to smoke on the road?"

"Cool enough. I carry a can of Lysol to spray the car if I get stopped, but that's never happened yet. Some of the heavier political types don't like it that I blow dope on the road, but they need me more than I need them. You couldn't do as much meaningless driving as I do without dope. Last year I logged seventy-eight thousand miles. At that, I have it a lot easier than messengers of yesteryear. Back in ancient Egypt, they'd shave somebody's head, tattoo a message on it and send the guy along as soon as his hair grew back."

"Yuck!" I responded sincerely. "Seems like it would limit your usefulness too. Once they used up all the different parts of your skull, you'd have to retire."

"And hope you never went bald! Say, what happened to that jay?"

So I lit the joint and got stoned for the first time in over a year. As we drove through the dark night across the endless rolling hills and plains of Iowa and Nebraska, Mimi loosened up a little.

She explained that she was sort of an unofficial courier for and among different loosely allied groups of political people. She herself had neither police record nor living relatives and was on no wanted lists, which gave her great flexibility and freedom. She seemed to thrive on the excitement and adventure, the unpredictability and danger, the illicit thrills and nameless palpitations. Her tale was so plausible that it was weeks before I realized it was quite possibly fictitious.

We switched places and I drove, cruising through the warm clear Great Plains night with Mimi asleep beside me. I sang along softly with the Beatles, remembering fondly the litter of Beatles paraphernalia in Marcy and Lana's room at Duke and the anguish with which they had faced the possibility that Paul was dead. Lana was married to another chemist, a humorless bespectacled young man who seemed born to the Bunsen burner, and they both worked for a paint factory in Detroit. And Marcy was a rabid feminist in New York, an editorial flunky at a large publishing house. She seemed to think I should abandon my traditionally female career in favor of something more exciting, such as pipefitting or driving a bulldozer. I missed them both. I had never really appreciated how special the Duke student body was until I found myself alone in the Real World. And now it was too late.

Early the next afternoon we arrived in Estes Park, Colorado, the touristy home base for Rocky Mountain National Park. I was puzzled when Mimi pulled into a travel court outside town and disappeared into the office.

Five minutes later she was back with a key. We drove around to the very rear of the complex in search of our cabin, which nestled into the side of a hill. It was set far back from the road in a pine grove so dense it was difficult to hear the highway traffic. Thoroughly confused, I followed Mimi into the cabin, which was very rustic but clean and charming, with knotty pine walls and furniture.

Mimi brought my tote bag inside and stayed just long enough to determine that the room was empty. "Wait here," she ordered. "And I mean don't leave this cabin for *anything*. Don't open to anyone unless they give this knock." She rapped twice on the dresser, paused, then rapped three times. "I have business to attend to, but I should be back before dark. If anything goes wrong and I don't get in touch with you by tomorrow night, go to Denver the next morning and fly to Chicago under a fake name. Go home and wait. Got it?"

I nodded, locked the door behind her, and collapsed trembling into a knotty pine armchair.

Two hours later the code knock came. I opened the door cautiously and in walked Prentiss Granger.

She strode past me, stood in the center of the room with her hands on her hips, and surveyed the cabin critically. "Not bad, not bad at all," she stated definitively. I shut the door and leaned back against it weakly. Pren turned to me. "And as for you ... you look *wonderful!*" She broke into an enormous smile, spread her arms out, and the next thing I knew I was hugging her. We held each other hard a long time. Tears poured down my cheeks. It had so often seemed that I would never see her again, that we were permanently parted. Her disembodied voice on the telephone never quite seemed real. To be with her again was almost more than I could comprehend.

When finally I broke away and blew my nose, I took a long hard look at her. What I saw was heartbreaking.

Her beautiful long chestnut hair was all hacked off. She wore a feathery pixie cut and what little remained of her hair was dyed an uninspired shade of dishwater blond. She wore horn-rimmed glasses in an unbecoming style. She was dressed all in doubleknits, wearing a baggy, rump-sprung pair of salmon pants and a scoopnecked lemon-and-white checked shell. Combined with the hair, the glasses and a plain gold wedding band, the effect was perfect. Nobody would give this rather unattractive young woman more than a casual glance and nobody would think for a second that she was a radical fugitive on the FBI's Ten Most Wanted List.

"You look horrible," I told her.

She grinned. "Thanks! It hasn't been easy developing this Sears Roebuck look, let me tell you. I never realized just how vain I am until I had to start looking crappy all the time. Most of the time I'm tucked away out of sight and I can wear jeans, but when I'm out in public I have to go into my turista disguise. All I lack is a couple of squalling kids with runny noses and a paunchy balding husband with an Instamatic hanging around his neck."

"What happened to Mimi?"

"You mean now that she's delivered the goods? She's on her way to Boulder right now. Something about getting laid, I believe she said."

Pren laughed and I tried to join in, though talk about getting laid made me very nervous.

She walked into the kitchenette, then emerged with one hand on her stomach. "Do you suppose I could talk you into making a grocery run? I haven't eaten since yesterday. Here." She tossed me a set of keys. "It's the tan VW Beetle."

I caught the keys but didn't move. "Uh, Jeannie?"

She caught the ironic tone in my voice and matched it. "Yes, Penny?"

"I don't know how to drive stick."

So we both went into town for groceries. It seemed that Prentiss Granger had become an ardent vegetarian, so serious about her diet that she actually arrived bearing her personal bottle of tamari. I went along without a fuss as we bought all sorts of veggies and didn't even bitch about the brown rice, a grain I find nearly as tasty and appealing as sautéed sneaker soles. I wasn't going to carry this health nonsense too far, however. I made certain that we also stocked up on soda pop, potato chips and Pepperidge Farm cookies.

It was as if we had never been separated and we both yammered so much that my jaw grew sore. That first night we sat cross-legged on our respective beds, very much as we had sometimes done in college when we talked clear through until dawn. It was an enormous relief to find that we were the friends we had always been, with a rare chemical bond that linked us more closely than blood sisters.

"I'm always scared," she explained intensely. "I feel frightened every minute. Even when I'm in an utterly secure place where nobody knows who I am or why I'm there, I feel the same anxieties. When I'm alone in the woods I think I'm being followed. I spend half my time avoiding eye contact with anybody and the other half looking over my shoulder. I'm not taking chances either. I've been so cautious and careful that I think I'd have a more active social life in a Carmelite convent. It's so *unlike* me to be this way, to have to stop and ponder every single move I make in advance, to always know where the exits are and think of every stranger as the enemy. I'm even scared of children. Who knows what kid's been studying the junior crime-busters manual of identification and cramming on photographs of notorius fugitives? If I get popped, I don't want it happening because some nine-year-old wants a junior G-man trophy."

She refilled both our wineglasses and resumed her lament. "You know what I was thinking not long ago? It would really be a kick to play chess with the Major by mail."

"You've got to be kidding!"

She laughed. "I guess I am at that. But it would be fun, in a way. To better him at his own games. Anonymously."

"That's just the sort of jackass grandstand play that gets people caught. If he ever figured it out, he'd turn you in. You know that."

"Yeah, I know that. I've thought about it a lot. He was always so competitive with me in those games. He never let me win, not even at the very beginning. The first time I ever beat him at chess I felt as proud as if I'd leaped across the North Atlantic in a single bound." She shook her head sadly. "I'd never have thought that he'd sell me out like he has."

"You're wanted for murder," I reminded her.

"Yeah," she snorted. "For somebody who's spent so much of his life figuring out better ways to kill more people, he's taken a pretty peculiar position, I'd say."

"We don't know what position he's taken. Neither one of us has seen him for three and a half years. Except on TV and I don't think that counts."

"I never saw it, thank God. I was too busy imposing on Jasper and Cloretha."

"They didn't think it was an imposition."

"Well, they were wrong. It was and any idiot would agree. God, it makes me so angry the way I have to keep imposing on everybody now. I'm like the guys who came back from Nam in chairs and just can't get used to the idea that the world is going to be different forever. I can't go anywhere or do anything. I'm absolutely helpless."

"You? You're as helpless as a water moccasin!"

"Well, thank you, I guess," Prentiss Granger answered. "But I'd like to think I'm a little less lethal. I *didn't* kill anybody, remember."

"Keep up the good work," I told her.

We talked endlessly. She led me through every second of Randy Hargis's trial, a recounting which lasted hours even without the more intimate details of my nocturnal adventures with Mike Donovan. And we reminisced interminably about Wilt Bannister, claimed by the forces of fate and history at the age of twenty-seven, at the very apex of Pren's love cycle.

In her memory, I realized, he would remain forever twenty-seven, forever a love object, forever slightly larger than life. I tried not to draw the all-too-obvious parallels with myself and Mike Donovan, who was presumably still alive somewhere but as eternally lost to me as if he had also perished in Beaumont. In a sense, I suppose he had.

She was extremely ambivalent about her life underground and her political activities since becoming a fugitive. "I don't think I'm really cut out for this," she said the second night as we finished dinner. I had stir fried quite a creditable vegetable medley and we were eating in the tiny kitchenette of our cabin.

"So what does cut out have to do with it? It's a little late to change your mind now, you know."

She grimaced. "I know. Do I *ever* know! No, what I mean is the underground terrorist business. I'm not certain I understand what's being accomplished by my increasing expertise with plastic explosives."

We were rapidly moving into areas I wanted to know nothing about. "You probably shouldn't talk about that," I cautioned. "Sounds like you're compromising security to me."

"To hell with security! Remember a bombing at the Presidio in San Francisco right after Nixon started the Christmas bombings last year?"

I nodded, though in fact my memory of miscellaneous bombings was sketchy at best and the Presidio meant nothing to me.

"I was in on that. Specifically on the construction, since for some reason I ended up with a bunch of jokers whose technical expertise doesn't extend beyond pop-top cans, zippers and a little basic credit card breaking and entering."

"Are you sure you ought to be talking about this?" She didn't seem to notice how acutely uncomfortable she was making me.

"Of course I shouldn't be talking about this. And I shouldn't be here and I shouldn't ever have been in touch with you at all. I'm fed up with *shouldn'ts*. I'm only twenty-five years old, Penny. A mere quarter of a century. If I live out a normal life span I have at least forty-five more years to go. Forty-five years is a long, long time."

"Simply because you can't live openly under a certain identity doesn't mean you have to run around blowing up buildings."

"This was a specific act of retaliation. And nobody was injured or killed. That bomb was set off because American B-fifty-twos had leveled Bach Mai Hospital in Hanoi. Completely annihilated the place. Do you have any idea how many bombs were dropped in those Christmas raids?"

"I suspect I'm going to find out."

She ignored me. "A single B-fifty-two holds thirty tons of bombs. To save you the trouble of multiplying in your head, that's sixty thousand pounds. In twelve days, something like a hundred thousand tons of bombs were dropped on Hanoi and Haiphong. That's two hundred *million* pounds. That's more than the Nazis dropped on England in all of World War II. That's—"

"That's enough," I cut in. "I get your point. And I'll be the first one in line to disapprove. But I still don't see why that means that you have to do the same thing. Two wrongs and all that."

She shrugged her shoulders. "I guess I don't either, really. I think that's the point I was trying to make. Penny, I don't know what to do. I have to figure out some kind of plan for my life. Sometimes I like that kind of unformed visceral rush there is to being a fugitive. But mostly I can't stand it. I always admired the Weather Underground for the way they were able to seize upon any political situation and dish up a retaliatory bombing within twenty-four hours. I was damn proud that we could do the same thing. But dammit, those bombings don't *do* anything. They don't slow down any kind of imperialist aggression, they don't even really put the tiniest dent in the military. So a wing of the Presidio gets blown apart. What does that prove? That military security wasn't as tight as they thought. That any half-wit with proper instructions and materials can build a functional bomb.

"But what have we *accomplished*? In practical terms, absolutely nothing. The military will dip into one of those bottomless slush funds and fix up the place that got bombed. Security will be tightened at the location where it happened. And maybe a few clerks will have to move to different offices while they repair the damage. You can't do anything to stop the United States military with a handful of fugitives as your army. It's like a gnat on an elephant. You can be just active enough to stay in the public eye and mind. You can make symbolic gestures like crazy. But symbols aren't worth shit in any practical sense."

"So what are you going to do?"

She shrugged again and threw her hands upward. "I haven't the vaguest idea. I was hoping that maybe you could help."

There were, of course, plenty of options, and the next day as we hiked in the park we began to systematically evaluate them. For starters, she could always turn herself in, an option which seemed to me to offer the most long-term promise. But Pren flatly refused to even consider the idea. "I ran," she argued. "They'd take that to mean I was guilty. From what you say about those eyewitnesses, they wouldn't be able to read their own names if they were tattooed on their forearms in sixty-point type. But they'll identify me anyway, and they'll tell the same ridiculous story they gave at Randy's trial. The only witness I have is Randy, who just happens to be dead. And he died after they found him guilty. Guilty, *guilty, GUILTY*! That's felony murder and if I were real lucky, they'd commute it to life because I was only driving what they call the getaway car. It's just hopeless. Texas is like the Dark Ages in penology. The last spring I was with VETRAGE I was assembling information on vets who'd gotten into trouble with the law after getting back, trying to find out their crimes and sentences and that kind of stuff. The guys in Texas were put away for longer than anybody else and usually with a lot less reason. You know, stuff like ninety-nine years for two seeds. No way do I ever turn myself in. Period."

There was also the very real option of changing nothing in her current life. She could stay underground, remain involved in various guerrilla activities and continue to make random public political statements. Practically this made sense, particularly if she could extricate herself from the realm of high explosives. She had a complicated web of associates and companions, a certain measure of built-in security and, most important, the financial means to guarantee her continued acceptance.

But Pren was no longer very keen on maintaining her current situation. "I told you, I just can't take the group paranoia for the rest of my life. Of course I'll always have to be paranoid for myself. But worrying about these other people is too much responsibility. And sitting around earnestly dissecting miscellaneous Marxist doctrines turns into mental masturbation pretty damn quickly. We're drafting a written public manifesto and you wouldn't believe the infighting that goes on. And what's been written is virtually incomprehensible. Even if the damn fool manifesto ever gets finished, nobody is going to read it. Except masochistic theorists who routinely devour impenetrable philosophical treatises. And the FBI. If I'm going to put my energy into writing something, I'd like to think that I'm persuading or informing or converting somebody, not just serving up scripture to the converted. Does that make sense?"

"Absolutely," I assured her. "But if you're not going to turn yourself in and you're not going to stay in the political underground, what *are* you going to do?"

"Damned if I know," she replied cheerfully. Just then we approached a couple of teen-agers sitting by the side of the trail smoking a joint. They were comically furtive, tossing the roach to the ground, covering it with a hiking boot, even (I swear) whistling. We were silent till we were long past them. Then Pren spoke up again.

"I could always leave the country. It's easy enough to get a permanent Canadian identity and just start over. Of course then you have to live in Canada, and I'm not too terribly keen on that idea. I guess I could go to Cuba, but what's going to happen when I'm there? I don't care to be a sugarcane field hand, frankly. I may not be able to use my education very efficiently now, but trying to avoid clipping the next worker over with my machete wouldn't be much better. Algeria used to be a possibility, but they kicked the Panthers out a couple of months ago."

"There must be someplace you could go besides Algeria and Cuba, for crying out loud. It's a big world, Jeannie."

"Yeah, but what's safe, anyway? They popped Timothy Leary in Afghanistan, of all places. And anyway, the only language I really know is German. That isn't going to do me a lot of good outside of Europe, except maybe in Argentina. I really don't want to leave the country, when you get right down to the nitty gritty. Fucked up as America is, it's still the best place in the world."

"I'd love for your father to hear that impassioned statement of nationalism."

"I'd love to say it to his face!"

The only option really left at that point was really the easiest, too, at least on the surface. She could leave the political underground and assume a new identity somewhere in the United States.

"It wouldn't be so hard to do that," she said thoughtfully that night as we lounged around our cabin.

"Well, of course it wouldn't," I answered irritably. "I mean, particularly since you already seem to have about forty-three different aliases and identities anyway. Jeannie."

"The identities are the easiest part," she responded easily, ignoring my irritation. "I'm better documented now than when I was Prentiss Granger." I jumped in fright at the four familiar syllables and she grinned. "See the power of a name?"

"Uh huh. But if it's that easy for you to become somebody else, then it seems relatively simple to me. You go to some other town and stay there. You've got enough money, after all. You're really quite secure, all things considered. The only question left is what do you want to do?"

"I don't know," she wailed.

"There must be community type things you could do. What about something like a Head Start program or a day care center?"

"I haven't the patience. Kids in bunches give me the screaming willies. On the other hand, I'm sure you don't need any credentials to do day care and it *is* an important social function."

"Well, isn't there some way you could get involved with labor organizing? I always kind of figured that's what you'd come back to eventually. It *is* your heritage, after all. Granger Mills and all that."

She stared at me. "You can't possibly be serious. Of course I'd love to do something like that, but I could never get away with it. Union organizers are always under incredible scrutiny. I'd be busted in an hour."

"You're right," I admitted. "I don't know, Jeannie. I'm running out of ideas. Unless you want to learn a new skill?"

"You mean like shorthand, maybe?"

"Actually what I was thinking of was more on the order of data processing."

She shuddered. "I'd rather be in jail in Texas than programming computers."

The world was hopping that summer. Indeed, our reunion occurred during the summit meeting between Nixon and Brezhnev. The Senate Watergate hearings were adjourned for the week while the Trickster was occupied with détente, probably a wise move diplomatically. We'd just learned of Gordon Liddy's plans to kidnap political activists and employ double-agent hookers and John Dean was the next scheduled witness. It clearly would be imprudent to showcase such a potentially damaging canary while the Trickster was yukking it up with his old pal Leonid. He might start hurling about bowls of cottage cheese and catsup.

Pren was surprisingly blasé about Watergate, I thought. To me it was a series of glorious revelations, which would only end with the Trickster being driven away from Washington in humiliation and shame. I saw the scene rather in biblical epic scenes: a lone figure in a tattered three-piece suit being driven out of the White House into a howling desert dust storm. Of course, being the Trickster, he sneaked right back around the Rose Garden to steal a little food in the next scene, but what the hell. And I'd already made it a point to learn what was involved in the impeachment process. A teacher has a responsibility to be informed about such matters.

"It hardly affects *me*," Pren explained, when I puzzled over her general indifference. "Of course I'm fascinated by the idea that the walls are caving in on them, slimy bastards that they are. If I thought there were a real chance that the wretches at the top would get it, I'd probably be more enthusiastic. But it's just the little fish that'll get fried and none of them will do any time anyway. He fired Haldeman and Ehrlichman. That'll be enough."

"But what about John Dean?"

"Can a clerk bring down a king? Forget it."

"What about Indians?" Pren asked suddenly one afternoon as we sat on a scenic trail overlooking the Rockies. She was fingering a beaded leather pouch which hung from the belt loop of her lime polyester pants. "That could be the answer."

"The answer to what?" I asked in some confusion. The last thing we'd been talking about was whether or not Pren's sister Shirley was still a virgin at twenty. (Our decision was yes.)

"A community I can work with!" she responded enthusiastically. "Indians! There's a lot of heat on right now because of Wounded Knee, but it shouldn't take too long before the feds back off. I could do something on a reservation, maybe."

"Like what? Lead the rain dance?"

She glared at me. "I'm better at survival skills than you think, smarty. I'll have you know that I've worked on a fourteen-acre farm."

"You're kidding!"

She looked a little sheepish. "Security breach. Well, so what. Yeah. I was all involved in stuff like hoeing and harvesting and killing bugs without poison. I milked a cow and goats and mucked out the barn and gathered eggs from some surly Rhode Island Reds. Can't say that I *liked* it very much, but it's a useful skill to have and I bet I could learn a lot more about it if I tried.... Indians.... it really *could* work, I think."

Two days later when she drove me to Denver, she was still enthusiastic about the idea, and the more I thought about it, the likelier the prospect seemed. There was hardly, after all, a more thoroughly neglected segment of American society. And if the Indians themselves were so thoroughly forgotten, it seemed unlikely that anyone would pay much attention to anybody attempting to help them. The only real obstacle was that Indians were momentarily too much in the public eye. But that, we'd agreed, wouldn't last long under the Nixon administration. They'd already learned plenty about squashing obstreperous minorities. When the Indian leaders were dead, jailed or driven underground, their followers would disappear with depressing rapidity. It had certainly worked well enough with militant blacks and white radicals.

I started to cry as she pulled up outside the hotel where I'd be catching the airport limo.

"What's the matter, Penny?" she asked with genuine concern.

"I'm just wishing this didn't have to end. I hate it so much that you have to live this way."

She was silent a moment. "I hate it too," she said finally. "I should be excited about going back and fighting the good fight and all that, but I'm not. I wish I could just get on a plane with you and fly backward through time, to 1971 and Berkeley. Back then it seemed like anything was possible. And now it seems like nothing is."

There were tears in her eyes too when she hugged me good-bye.

Chapter 10 _____

There was nothing the least bit illicit or clandestine about the excursion, but nevertheless I found myself ten times more nervous going to visit Major and Mrs. Granger in South Carolina than I had been sneaking off to meet their daughter in Colorado. Pren was itching to know what had happened to her family in the four years since we had last seen them.

As I drove my rental car into Granger on a cold December afternoon, I decided that I had been smack out of my mind to think I would be able to carry it off. As I passed the Granger Mills complex nestled in the hills outside town and felt my heart plummet, I knew there was no way Pren could ever repay me for this. And when I drove up the long winding front drive of Azalea Acres and glimpsed the huge holly wreath on the front door and the massive Christmas tree glinting through the living room windows, my sense of déjà vu became so strong that my hands started shaking. The very last time I had come up this drive was also on a late December afternoon. Twelve hours later, I was sneaking down the stairs with Pren, quite certain that I would never darken the door again.

Mercifully it was Shirley who first came out to greet me. I gasped when I saw her. She was a knockout. Her rich deep glossy chestnut hair curled and swirled around her shoulders. Her skin was fair and flawless, her rosebud lips and fingernails a rich deep burgundy and her toffee-colored eyes made huge by artfully applied liner, shadow and mascara. She wore tailored wine wool slacks with a gray and white cashmere pullover.

From a gangly teen-ager, she'd metamorphosed into the variety of southern beauty who routinely wins the Miss America Pageant singing "I Enjoy Being a Girl."

I got out of the car, leaving it in front, and Shirley floated down the steps, a girl clearly well trained in the art of Entrances. I made the first move to hug her hello, an instinctive southern gesture of ersatz affection, and she responded politely but with little enthusiasm. "You look beautiful, Shirley," I told her. What I didn't say was that she also looked so much like her sister once had that I thought my heart would break.

"And so do you," she cooed back, ever the gracious lady. She stepped back and we were both grateful to be separated.

"Is everything okay?" I asked nervously. "I mean, about me being here and stuff?"

Shirley nodded. "Just please don't bring up Prentiss in front of Daddy. Her name isn't ever mentioned here."

"You're kidding!"

She shook her head. "I'm hoping that having you here will maybe change that. But they don't *ever* talk about her. Daddy's last word on the subject is that he only has one daughter. It's really kind of creepy."

My plane was scheduled to leave for Atlanta the next morning at eleven-thirty, a time span that suddenly seemed adequate for reaching Jupiter by spaceship. I had spent a lot of time wondering what I could say to the Grangers about Pren, but I really hadn't concocted a game plan for the eventuality that they wouldn't want to discuss her at all.

There had been no hint of such a situation in Iris Granger's response to my early Christmas card. I had fabricated a Virginia wedding and wondered if I might drop in afterward to pay my respects on my way home for the holidays. By all means I should come, she had written in royal blue ink on monogrammed ivory vellum. I would always be welcome.

As we walked into the front hall, my trembling increased. Everything looked *exactly* as it had before. Had four years actually passed? If changes had been made, they eluded me. The only difference I could find was that no photographs of Pren hung anywhere.

Iris Granger glided gracefully out of the living room as Shirley closed the large front door. I was shocked by the change in her. Her face was slightly puffier, that dead giveaway of too much alcohol over too many years. But even while she was puffier, she was also thinner and very, very drawn. She looked more frail than I remembered, and as I touched cheeks with her in embrace, I noticed that her skin seemed somehow detached from her bones.

Mrs. Granger dispatched Shirley to get my bags brought in and led me into the living room. By the time Willie Mae trundled in with a tea tray and cookies, we were settled deeply in our armchairs by the fire and I had reported on the excellent health of my family, the hideous Chicago winter weather and Ginger's enrollment in law school. Willie Mae greeted me warmly.

Once we were alone again, Mrs. Granger leaned forward in her chair and whispered, "Is my baby all right?"

I knew just which baby she meant, of course, but I played dumb and offered her a puzzled expression.

"My little Tissa," she said.

Her little Tissa. Little Tissa had disappeared the instant Prentiss Granger first set foot on the Duke campus. "I honestly don't know," I murmured quietly. "But deep inside me I'm sure she's fine."

Mrs. Granger leaned back. "I hoped you'd be bringing news, Laurel. That was why I was so glad that Major Granger was still at the mill." She began to cry quietly and I felt like a prize fool.

"It wouldn't be safe for her to contact me," I explained gently. "Most of the time I'm being watched by FBI agents and I know that my phone is tapped. She's too smart to try to get in touch with me."

She just sat there crying quietly. She brought a lovely lace handkerchief out of a pocket and dabbed at her eyes. I suddenly realized that Iris Granger had probably been sobbing on the sly for most of her life.

"I'm sorry if I've disappointed you," I continued when it seemed clear that she wasn't going to blow her nose and toughen up. "I didn't mean for you to think that I had news of Pren. But I did want to see y'all again. Y'all were like family to me while Pren and I were in school, and I hated to lose you too just because she was gone." It was a pretty sappy speech, but not all that far off the mark and certainly I wasn't worried about Iris Granger finding me insincere.

Luckily Shirley reappeared just then. She cast a side-long look at her weeping mother, crossed to take a cookie off the already depleted tray, then settled in a wing chair beside the Christmas tree. When I pulled out my cigarettes, she got up and brought me an ashtray, then silently resumed her position by the tree.

I learned that Llewellyn would not be home for several more days. "He's very happy at the Point," Iris Granger recited mechanically, "so proud to be serving his country and following in his father's footsteps." I doubted very much that it ever occurred to Llewellyn Granger not to seek an appointment, and I realized I probably wouldn't even recognize him anymore. The picture of him on the grand piano looked like every military portrait since time began, all hat and chin.

And then we heard the purr of the Eldorado outside the window and looked at each other in mild trepidation. It was not exactly like hanging around with the Anderson family, waiting for Robert Young to breeze through the doorway dispatching warmth and wisdom.

I watched Major Granger get out of the car through the window. He still wore a Bob Haldeman brush cut, though it seemed now to be more gray than brown. He still strode forward with a brisk no-nonsense pace marred only by the slightest limp. He still slammed the car door far more heavily than necessary, and as I heard his footsteps clomping across the front porch, I realized he still scared the bloody blue hell out of me.

I stood as he entered the room and he jerked his head in acknowledgment of my presence. "Good to see you again," he told me brusquely, in a tone that fooled nobody. Then he nodded curtly to the three of us and disappeared in the direction of the War Wing. Shirley and I exhaled slowly in unison.

He didn't come out again till dinner, a splendid golden roasted goose stuffed with figs and chestnuts. But the atmosphere around the table was far less convivial than such a feast deserved. Nobody said a word about anything but the meal. After our plates had been cleared away and we were waiting for Willie Mae to bring in the Scripture Cake, the Major launched a diatribe against excessive government regulation by inexperienced imbeciles who wouldn't be able to manipulate dental floss without an instruction manual.

I gathered that OSHA had recently paid an unannounced visit to Granger Mills.

He spewed and sputtered through dessert and coffee, then suddenly pushed back his chair and looked directly at me for the first time all evening. "Come to the game room, young lady," he ordered. It never crossed my mind not to drop my fork and obey.

The game room seemed unchanged to me, though I find the Battle of the Bulge and Gettysburg virtually indistinguishable when the protagonists are all an inch tall in a giant sandbox with trees and shrubs fashioned from green sponge. Probably the only scenario I'd have been likely to recognize would be a Minute Mart with one gas pump and a miniature blue Bonneville parked out front.

"You are here because my wife insisted," the Major told me without preliminary. "Mrs. Granger has been ill lately and I'm more inclined to indulge her. But I trust that you haven't been upsetting her."

I was livid. *Me* upsetting *her?* "I most certainly haven't been upsetting her," I answered, doing my best to keep my anger under control. "But I'll be happy to leave immediately if you'd rather I didn't stay."

"The arrangements have been made. I believe you leave in the morning?"

I nodded.

"Then that will be a reasonable departure time. Why are you here?"

I ran through the same line I had given his wife two hours earlier, and this time it sounded preposterous. I was shocked, however, to see him raise a hand and order me to be silent when I referred directly to Pren.

"I will not have that name mentioned beneath this roof," he barked. "You may inform her that nothing will ever make me alter that position."

"I can't tell her anything," I told him. I'd been inching around the back of the sand tables to keep a good distance between us. This gave me a little more nerve and allowed me to speak more firmly than I might have face to face. "I don't know where she is."

"I don't believe you. There was a time when I trusted you and learned later that my trust had been badly misplaced. You may lie yourself blue in the face, young lady. I don't care. I don't know what she sent you here to do, but you may inform her that I have only one daughter and her name is Shirley. That will be all."

Shaken by my dismissal, I marched out of the game room as briskly as possible and took refuge in a nearby bathroom. But when I emerged a few minutes later for my next bout with the family Granger, the Major was gone and Mrs. Granger had retired, no doubt with a nightcap. Shirley's suggestion that we might be more comfortable in her room sounded like a first-class idea.

The room was still a nightmare of pink and lavender satin, and sure enough, once we were alone, Shirley wanted to know how Pren was.

"I don't know," I answered patiently. "I haven't heard from her and I haven't seen her. I don't know where she is. I don't see why nobody believes me."

"We were so sure," Shirley explained woefully. "Mama and I had it all figured out, that Prentiss was sending some kind of message to us."

"I'm sure she wishes she could. But honest, Shirley, I just came to go to a wedding in Virginia, exactly like I wrote your mother."

Shirley shook her head patiently. "There wasn't any wedding, Laurel. We all know that. Daddy checked with the FBI. You came straight here from Chicago."

I was shocked. I didn't know who to get mad at first, the Major or Mel Sanford. "Shit," was all I could think to say for a while. No wonder Iris Granger had been so tense and had broken down so completely. "Shirley, you're right. There wasn't a wedding. But apart from that, my story is true, I swear it. I wanted to see your family again, that's all. I'm kind of a sentimental jerk, I suppose, but y'all were once very special to me. Just like Prentiss was."

"Daddy would never believe that. He still calls you the quisling."

It was hard not to laugh out loud at the realization that a girl like Shirley Granger had a word like "quisling" in her vocabulary.

"Well, how sick *is* she?" Pren asked impatiently. I had skipped our prearranged phone assignation in St. Elizabeth over the holidays because I considered it too risky, given the Major's collusion with Mel Sanford. Now it was January and I was back in Chicago.

"I don't know," I answered for the third time. "And I can't really tell how much of it was the booze either. I pumped Shirley as much as I could, but I honestly don't think she knows either. All Shirley knew was that Mama had been having problems with the change."

Pren snorted. "She's been having problems with the change for ten years now. Every little twinge and ache, she puts it down to the change. Has she been to a doctor? I mean a real doctor, not old Doc Minton."

"I didn't check her appointment book. For crying out loud, I did all I could. I told Shirley I thought she ought to be under medical supervision. There isn't much I can do beyond that. And I know that the Major knows, because he specifically referred to her illness as why I was allowed to come."

"Damnation!"

"I know. It's tough not to be able to go there and check it out yourself."

"I'm sorry to be such a baby. But I've been horribly worried, particularly since you didn't take the call last week."

"That's why we have backups, remember? And what about you? I thought you were going to strike out on your own."

"So did I. But there isn't any way I can do it yet."

"Unless you're in a body cast, it ought to be fairly simple." I was getting a little tired of hearing how much she yearned to abandon her warren of radical fugitives. "You put one foot in front of the other and walk out the door."

"Would that it were so simple."

"Am I supposed to be urging you to leave? Or just saying, okay, do whatever you want?"

"Urging me to leave, I suppose. But there's a minor emotional complication right now."

I could smell this one clear across the continent. "Is that supposed to mean you're in love?"

She laughed. "I think 'in heat' would probably be more precise."

"Spare me the details of your wanton desires."

"I'd have to anyway. You know, security."

"Fucking security!"

"Precisely what I'm doing, my dear. Several incarnations ago, he was an MP."

I went directly from my phone assignation to cooking class. The previous fall I had decided to enlarge my culinary repertoire by studying Italian cuisine. But four months of pasta and butter and cream had proven too depressingly fattening. When it came time to enroll in the second session, I opted instead for a Chinese cooking class. The class began just before the holidays and my new diet began just after. I was hoping to combine the two into a new svelte me.

I was a little bit late arriving, and I slipped quietly into my seat beside Annie Vanderwoek. Annie was a bright, friendly woman I met in the Italian class. She was in her late twenties, with blue-gray eyes, wide cheekbones, a pale complexion and thick dark blond hair the color of buckwheat honey, cut blunt to her shoulders.

I'd seen quite a bit of Annie through the fall, as part of my conscious effort to expand my circle of friends. She was most impressed by the photographs of children on the beach that I entered in a local exhibition and came over several times to use my darkroom equipment. I was delighted to teach her how to develop and enlarge her own prints and she proved to be an excellent student. Her photographs were usually of trees and buildings and only rarely had people in them. Her sense of composition was pretty lousy, but we managed to correct that in the darkroom.

Annie worked for an insurance company downtown and had been in Chicago about four years. Her family lived in Holland, Michigan, and she fascinated me with tales of tulip festivals and picturesque canals. For Christmas she gave me a planter of forced red tulip bulbs in a pottery wooden shoe, and kept saying that come spring we would have to visit her family's bulb farm. I felt very close to her in some ways. She had been through an extremely nasty divorce and didn't want to talk about her ex-husband at all. I respected this reticence without question. After all, I had a few secrets of my own.

"Egg rolls," Annie whispered excitedly to me, and I settled in with great anticipation as Madame Chin began waving a wonton wrapper.

It was Annie Vanderwoek who first told me of the kidnapping of Patricia Hearst. I missed the morning paper because I was out in a predawn snowstorm, waiting in a gasoline line that snaked for six blocks down Belmont. At five A.M. it was still pitch black, thanks to the combination of winter and emergency daylight savings time. I anticipated an hour-and-a-half wait. Under such conditions, Billie Holliday seemed more appropriate than Elton John, so I listened to a cassette instead of the radio. My only real teacher friend at school was out sick with the flu that day and on my arrival home, I decided to catch a quick nap before Annie arrived for dinner and the movies. So when Annie burst into my apartment with the news, it came as an enormous shock.

My immediate reaction was a bottomless fear that somehow Prentiss Granger might be involved. Patty Hearst had been seized by something calling itself the Symbionese Liberation Army, a name which had the ring of many of the crackpot organizations Pren had been entangled with. I told myself firmly that it was absurd for one rich girl to kidnap another, but stranger things had happened and some of them were in my own personal experience.

Annie and I had tempura at a nearby Japanese restaurant and went to see *American Graffiti*, a movie I had never gotten around to largely because it seemed to have nothing to say to me. Sure enough, it revealed an alien culture of cute boys and pretty girls riding around in souped-up cars, a scene which seemed less comfortable and logical to me than bandits stuffing a half-naked heiress into an automobile truck. For perhaps the thousandth time, I wondered what it was about California that fostered such strangeness.

I pleaded a headache to get rid of Annie early that night and sat staring out over the lake, my favorite position for purging my mind of excess turmoil. The problem, of course, was more complicated than whether or not Prentiss Granger might be involved in this particular terrorist outing.

I was no longer able to make any sense of the far left at all. The war was theoretically over, the POWs were home and various congressional investigating committees were exhibiting great skill at chopping up the Nixon administration. All manner of nefarious CREEPs had been subpoenaed out from under their various rocks and everybody but the Trickster was currently under indictment. Guys who had never anticipated greater social embarrassment than spilling a drink at a country club bar were falling all over each other to cop pleas and get into Danbury. Tony Boyle had been convicted of killing Jock Yablonsky and eight National Guardsmen were indicted for murder at Kent State.

Speaking as one who had personally polished off an entire magnum of champagne on the night of Spiro Agnew's resignation, I was prepared to say that the system worked just fine.

I couldn't understand the type of international terrorism that resulted in airports shot up at random, jets hijacked to Algeria, hostages seized by South Moluccans, and Italian industrialists "kneecapped," a graphic new entry into the lexicon of terrorism. I couldn't keep track of all these different groups of radicals and their various gripes and I certainly couldn't figure out what a preppy nineteen-year-old California girl had to do with anything.

I was turning into a reactionary old fogy right in front of my own eyes.

Or maybe I'd never stopped being one, deep down inside. The conditioning of my Louisiana youth ran down through me like the mycelia which permeate the horse manure in which mushrooms are grown. So perhaps it wasn't surprising that an occasional toadstool of conservatism popped up now and again.

Sure, I'd made giant strides toward understanding and condemning America's folly in Vietnam, but so had everybody else. Somehow or other, all those vociferous hawks seemed to have transmogrified into pristine doves carrying olive branches in their dainty little beaks.

I could make a more convincing claim for my efforts toward the goal of racial equality, but I didn't deserve any particular recognition for doing what was so obviously right. And anyway, that was probably just an overreaction to the massive cargo of guilt I carried because my ancestors actually *had* owned slaves. After all, most white people in America could say, hey, slavery was really a bummer, sure, but during the Civil War *my* family was digging potatoes in Ireland. Or tending sheep in Greece. Or working twelve hours a day in a New England mill or New York sweatshop.

I had no such excuse. At the time of secession, my family owned 431 men, women and children. The Hollingsworths had a whole hell of a lot to feel guilty about, but I was the only one really shouldering any blame. In a very real sense, my work was penance. I would atone for the sins of my forefathers against *their* forefathers by teaching them to read and figure and become effective members of an integrated society.

But I couldn't do that by myself. Nobody could. The problems were too overwhelming, too far out of control. All the turmoil and demonstrations and picketing and anguish of the Civil Rights movement had wrought very little change. We had moved from *de jure* to *de facto,* that was all. Ten years after the passage of the Civil Rights Act of 1964, some of my students had never seen a white person in the flesh before they entered my classroom. Something was still horribly, terribly wrong, and I no longer felt I had any notion of what it might be.

Prentiss Granger called on schedule the following week, ten days after Patty Hearst disappeared into the Berkeley night. She immediately announced that she found the entire Hearst-SLA episode to be a real cliffhanger and claimed to know nothing about the SLA, in a tone which actually sounded miffed. She'd grown so accustomed to feeling she was at the heart of the radical action that it was tough to be displaced in the public eye by a bunch of strangers and a silly little heiress who probably thought Mao Tse-tung was a Cantonese pancake.

"I'm pretty close to leaving here," she confided.

"That's not good enough," I countered. "It's kind of like saying you're a little bit pregnant."

I heard her breath suck in sharply. "How did ..." She stopped abruptly.

I had forgotten the famous fertility of the Debutante Revolutionary. "You can't be serious."

"Wanna bet?"

I was totally taken aback, but recovered quickly. "I'm sure you can find an abortion without any trouble. It's legal now, after all. And you're experienced in the field."

"I may not do that."

"What do you mean? You're going to settle down and raise a baby? I thought you were running for your life."

She was silent for a moment. "I haven't decided what I'm going to do. Nobody knows except me. And now you."

"Some secrets are harder to maintain than others. Along around your seventh or eighth month, people are likely to catch on." I was surprised that I could be so flippant about the whole thing. It seemed like several lifetimes since I'd first learned of her teen-age pregnancy and nearly as long since our trek to the South Carolina abortionist.

"How soon do you have to decide?" I asked.

"Not for a while. In fact, it's so soon I might just have a bad case of nerves. I'm only a couple of weeks late. And I'm not as regular as I used to be."

"Or as careful either."

"Spare me your condescension, thank you. I'm as careful as a body can be. The only way I could be more careful would be to tie my tubes."

"Or stay celibate."

She laughed. "Out of the question, I'm afraid. There may be folks who can tolerate abstinence, but I've never been one of them."

I didn't answer.

"Don't worry about it," she soothed. "I have a while yet to decide what to do. And it may even force my hand. If I stay where I am, I'll be forced to get rid of it. Very strict rules about that sort of thing. So maybe this is an act of God to make me get my ass in gear and split."

"Won't it be awfully hard to go off alone that way?"

"Not really. It might even simplify things. I can afford to just go someplace and indulge myself while I wait, after all. It could turn out to be the perfect cover."

"I think I wish I hadn't heard any of this," I said. "Though I'd rather have you sleeping around than kidnapping people."

"Sleeping around? Did I hear you say sleeping around? Listen, I'm not exactly your basic suburbanite playing swap the hubby, chum. I pick my lovers pretty damn carefully."

"I wish you picked your contraceptives as carefully."

"But I *do*." She sounded very hurt. "I just seem to be in that two percent that gets pregnant no matter what. You know, every method has a certain margin of error. Well, that's me. Your friendly neighborhood margin of error."

"Enough. I don't think I can handle any more."

"Don't kid yourself. You can handle damn near anything by now and you know it."

"Only from trying to keep up with you," I retorted.

But long after the conversation ended, I kept thinking about what she had said. *You can handle damn near anything by now.* I was strangely proud of that pronouncement. Somehow I had passed over any number of peculiar hurdles and emerged as a functional, coping member of society.

Was it possible that, at the age of twenty-five, I was actually starting to grow up?

Chapter 11 _____

Annie Vanderwoek and I lived and breathed the Patty Hearst story all through the spring, dissecting it from every conceivable angle and perspective. We analyzed the middle-class, middle-western backgrounds of the SLA members in excruciating detail. We took a certain perverse pleasure at the preponderance of women in the group and marveled at the intriguing sexual permutations. We did, however, find it difficult to understand the heavy militarism, outrageous Radical Stew rhetoric, and the inexplicable devotion of the entire SLA to General Field Marshall Cinque. We thought that General Field Marshall Cinque sounded like your basic garden variety thug.

We watched the food giveaway program disintegrate into roaring chaos and took careful note that all those canned beets and black-eyed peas were tax deductible as a Good Work through the Hearst Foundation. We listened in fascination as Patty's reedy little voice denounced her fiancé as a "sexist, ageist pig" and by then we'd seen enough of Steven Weed to agree. After we heard Tania announce her decision to "stay and fight," we debated for hours over her sincerity.

In all this discussion and analysis of revoluntionaries and life underground and FBI evasion, it would have been quite natural to disinter the skeleton of Prentiss Granger. Several times I was tempted.

But I never did. It was Ginger Lockford who let that particular cat out of the bag.

Ginger and Annie came to dinner the Friday after the SLA stuck up the Hibernia Bank in San Francisco. Ginger had met Annie several times and they seemed to like each other. I had grown fonder of Ginger once again too. As the end of her second year of law school approached, she seemed to be loosening up just a little.

"We're having coq au vin," I announced. "It's my concession to the meat boycott. And they only marked the chicken up twice on my way to the check-out counter."

"I tried to buy a can of peaches the other day," Annie said, "and they didn't have *any*. I simply don't understand how all of this goes back to the Russian wheat deal. I mean some of it's obvious, like rye bread tripling in price, but peaches?"

"It's that elusive Middleman," Ginger explained. She wore a black blazer and red plaid skirt, her close-cropped patent leather hair combed sleekly behind her ears. Her jeans had all gone to Goodwill the day she made Law Review. "I keep thinking that one day I'll meet one, driving a truck of dollar-a-pound hamburger, chuckling fiendishly."

"It isn't middlemen at all," I snapped. "It's greed, pure and simple. American business watched the gas crisis, and they figured out that people will pay *anything* for something they think they need. Earl Butz suggested the other day that everybody exercise before meals. Well, I'll tell you, the exercise that appeals to me most is running in place on Earl Butz's stomach."

After dinner we lounged around the living room, listening to the new Paul Simon album, finishing our second bottle of Beaujolais, and once again discussing Patty Hearst. Suddenly Ginger looked straight at me. "Wouldn't you love to know," she asked. "what Prentiss thinks about all this?"

This was clearly not the time to reveal that I knew precisely what Prentiss thought about all this. She thought it was a crock of shit and the Symbionese Liberation Army a passel of morons.

"I would imagine," I began carefully, "that she'd probably be very indignant because Patty is such a revolutionary-come-lately."

Ginger giggled. "You mean because she hasn't had time to really master all the nuances of Marx and Engels yet?"

"Something like that."

Annie cut in in some confusion. "What are you guys talking about, anyway?"

Ginger shot me a puzzled look. "You mean she doesn't know?"

"That's right," I answered evenly.

Ginger shrugged and poured herself some more wine. "Oh, well, I can't see what difference it makes anyway."

"What difference *what* makes?" asked Annie.

"Your ball," Ginger told me.

I looked at both of them and planned my words carefully. "It isn't really that big of a deal, Annie. But when Ginger and I were in college, we knew somebody who got pretty involved in radical politics."

Ginger snorted. "You make it sound as if we once caught a passing glimpse of Bernardine Dohrn. What Laurel's trying to say, Annie, is that she used to room with Prentiss Granger. You know, the Debutante Revolutionary."

Annie looked at me in some confusion and I could see that her feelings were hurt. "You never said a word."

"There was nothing to say," I answered rather shortly. "It was all long ago and far away. I've been kind of trying to forget about it."

But Ginger just wouldn't quit. I yearned for a dart gun loaded with tranquilizers. "Come on, I don't see why it has to be such a big horrible secret, Laurel."

"It doesn't," I answered. "But it's something I try not to think about. I don't see why we have to talk about it."

"We don't," Ginger agreed. "But it sure looks like Annie'd like to."

And indeed Annie Vanderwoek was on the edge of her chair. While Ginger obligingly ran through the history of Prentiss Granger for her mesmerized audience, I opened another bottle of wine. I visualized Mel Sanford and his cronies sitting around a table watching the tape reels spin as they heard Ginger Lockford denounce her one-time idol, mentor and Pi Phi Big Sister as a "misguided kneejerk radical."

Annie was too drunk to drive home to Rogers Park, so she spent the night on my sofa. And the next morning, moaning loudly about her incredible hangover, she brought up Prentiss Granger again. "If you don't want to talk about her, I can understand," she told me. "I guess I'm just curious because I never really felt like any of those people actually existed. They seemed so unreal to me."

"Prentiss Granger is very real," I assured her, as I whipped up a Spanish omelet. "Reality was never one of her problems."

Despite her hangover, Annie managed to keep up a steady barrage of questions. It was nothing compared to my FBI interrogations, but annoying anyway. I was absolutely furious with Ginger. Finally I fabricated a dental appointment just to get rid of her.

After Annie left I cleaned up a bit and critically surveyed my furniture. I had bought new modern furniture when I first moved to Chicago, clean Scandinavian pieces in light woods and simple designs. My choice was based not so much on a passion for Scandinavian furniture as a revulsion for the antiques which overflowed Grandma Chesterton's house and Weatherly Plantation. Everything had club feet, threatened to break if you looked at it cross-eyed and sported more ornately carved whorls than your average fingerprint. I wanted simplicity and I got it. But three years later, I had to admit that not one piece of it was truly comfortable. It would be heavenly to have a huge overstuffed couch to flop onto at the end of a wearying day.

So I wandered down Clark Street, window shopping and planning a new decorating scheme. I stopped at an Art Deco shop, a pleasant little place where I often dropped by to pick up a knickknack or peruse the jewelry selection. For two years I had coveted a lamp in the window, a vastly overpriced glass airplane globe. Buying it now would certainly be simpler than replacing my furniture, and cheaper too. I was about to whip out my checkbook when a masculine voice directly behind my left shoulder announced, "Now *that* is decadence."

I turned in some annoyance to find a short pudgy fellow with shoulder-length dark brown hair and granny glasses. He wore jeans and a plaid wool jacket, open over a Grateful Dead T-shirt. His dark brown eyes were dancing behind the wire-rims. I was outraged that he dared make fun of me.

"Now what would *you* know about decadence?" I sneered.

He grinned disarmingly. "Not nearly as much as I'd like to."

I was boxed in now. I couldn't buy the fool lamp without losing face and I couldn't walk away without making him feel he'd influenced me.

"This lamp," I announced haughtily, "just happens to be an exquisite representation of its period."

"So what? I'm a pretty exquisite representation of my period, but nobody's paying megabucks for *me*."

"Maybe you're not worth it."

"Oh, I'm worth it," he assured me. "But the price of that lamp would feed a welfare family for a month. Not that you're likely to know about things like that."

I thought about the Fletcher School and my students who routinely stayed home on snowy days because their only pairs of shoes were tennies riddled with holes. "I know plenty about welfare families," I answered stiffly, wondering how I could get the hell away from this rude boob.

"I bet. Let me guess what you know. They all drive Cadillacs and there's an able-bodied man lurking under every ADC mother's bed and there are plenty of good jobs to go around if only they weren't so damn lazy."

"I take it you're an expert on welfare?" I queried poisonously.

"Expert enough, rich lady. I'm a social worker in Cabrini-Green."

I shuddered. Cabrini-Green was one of the worst projects in Chicago.

"You don't see any airplane lamps in Cabrini-Green," he continued. I was ready to slug him. So all right, I had dressed up. You don't, after all, get much respect from sofa salesmen when you're decked out like a cotton chopper. But this guy had no right to assume such a holier-than-thou attitude, merely because I happened to cast an avaricious eye upon an overpriced room accessory. Which was, as it happened, an exquisite representation of its period.

"I hope that you're more tolerant with your clients than you are with people you meet on the street," I said. He looked at me a bit askance, probably because I had properly used the buzzword *client*. I decided to give him the other barrel while I had his attention. "We could do with a little bit less white condescension in the ghetto."

"*We?* Listen, I don't know quite what you're talking about, but I don't run into the likes of you in Cabrini-Green."

"And for very good reason," I shot back. "I'm too busy working in Lawndale to spend much time hanging around other projects."

"Good God," he said sheepishly. He was quiet for what seemed like a very long time. Consternation suddenly lined his face. I loved every second of it. "You work in Lawndale?"

"I teach at the Fletcher School," I informed him smugly.

He extended his hand. "I'm Andy Lamont, and I'm really an asshole. I apologize."

I took his hand and shook it firmly, careful to anticipate the minor soul grip he had in mind and end with the appropriate thumb twist. "Laurel Hollingsworth. Are you always an asshole?"

"Only when I'm on a diet."

I forgave him immediately. Two minutes later we were on the way up the street for a beer at the Ramblin' Banana. There I learned that he was a native of Calumet City, a graduate of the U of I Circle Campus and a grizzled four-year veteran of the Welfare Department. We got along famously. He looked nothing like my fantasies of Mr. Right and I'm sure I bore no resemblance to his Dream Girl. But we certainly had a lot in common, and by dinnertime I felt I'd known him for years. Since he'd already blown his diet for the day, we went down to Luigi's for pizza and more beer before going back to his place to watch *Hud* on TV.

Andy shared the lower half of a large two-flat just west of the fashionable part of Lincoln Park with two other guys, neither of whom was home. The furnishing was late Salvation Army with psychedelic black-light posters plastered all over the living room and mohair strung in cobwebs, which glowed when the black lights were turned on. A long-haired black tomcat slept in one corner of the living room and the whole place smelled a lot like cat piss.

Andy produced an ornate brass hash pipe right after we arrived and we quickly got very stoned on some great Lebanese blonde. Then we ate popcorn and drank Tab and listened to his John Prine and Steve Goodman albums. We never did turn on the movie.

"You know," I said, waving a stoned arm listlessly around the room, "this place reminds me of the crash pads where people lived when I was in college. It's like the sixties never ended."

"That's me," Andy acknowledged cheerfully. "The village anachronism. I miss the sixties. The seventies are already half over and nobody's even noticed. Sometimes I'll see all these guys waiting at the bus stop in suits with briefcases and I want to start yelling, 'Hell no, we won't go!' "

"They'd flag down a cop and have you carted off in a straitjacket."

He rolled over on his stomach and propped his elbows on a huge pillow with a torn Indian print cover. "But they were the guys who were yelling right along with me. I guess they were just being cool and fashionable back then. Me, I've always had a lot of trouble being cool. And fashionable always seemed hopeless."

I laughed. "It was fashionable to be a social worker for a while."

"Yeah, until everybody realized social workers get paid shit. Then they all got haircuts and straight jobs. I'll tell you what I really miss. It's that spirit of being in a big crowd where everybody feels passionately about something. That old protest march fever. Turmoil and excitement and hope. One day I woke up and it had all turned into suspended animation."

"I know. It's as if the people who still care about changing things are all floating around in a weightless chamber full of whipped cream. Now and then we connect with somebody long enough to do something mildly significant. But most of the time we're just bobbling and floating through clouds of whipped cream."

Andy shook his head. "You're wrong. This is a chemical age, Laurel. It's Cool Whip." We both laughed. "When did the sixties end for you?"

"When a friend of mine got into something so big it ruined her whole life." It just slipped out. But after deflecting all of Annie's questions a scant twelve hours earlier, I had no desire to get into the Prentiss Granger story again. I hurried on before he could become inquisitive. "Actually, I suppose it was Kent State. It happened right before I graduated and it really seemed like the end of the dream. How about you?"

He considered. "Well, Kent State was a biggie, no doubt about it. But the one that really tore me up was when Fred Hampton was murdered in his own bed. And I suddenly realized that the leaders I believed in were never going to be safe." We sat silently for a while as he refilled the hash pipe and passed it.

"At least we have Watergate," I sighed. "Though lately it's all started to seem almost anticlimactic. Like too little, too late."

He shook his head. "It's not too little. It's the scandal of the century, Laurel. But maybe it is too late. Sometimes, like when I saw you looking at that lamp today, I think we've all sold out. I start wondering how much longer it'll be before I cut my hair and slide into the personnel office at Con Edison."

"It doesn't sound to me like you're ready to do that anytime soon."

He shook his head. "I don't know. Sometimes it seems like it would sure be nice to make some money." He grinned then, and waved a lazy arm around the room. "Of course, that would mean I'd have to give up all this."

I laughed. "Maybe what we ought to do is set up a service for people on the verge of packing it in and going straight. Hunt up some leftover hippies to staff it, pay them in hash brownies and call it the Whole Earth Hotline."

"Or the Society for the Prevention of Creeping Republicanism."

I took another toke from the hashpipe and considered. "Nope, too long. Maybe it just ought to be Misfits Anonymous."

Chapter 12 _____

Perhaps what happened in San Francisco was inevitable, but you would have to stretch a lot of points to make that argument believable. The fact is, we were getting careless and sloppy. It's just that simple.

Pren had finally split from her hiding place in the wilds of California and gone to the Bay area to await the birth of her baby as Barbara Bellamy, young divorcee. She was fiercely determined to have the kid. "If I'm going to be out here in the world alone," she argued, "I'll feel a lot less alone with a child. It will give some kind of shape and purpose to my life." She could not be dissuaded and eventually I stopped trying. It was, after all, her life.

But in moving to the city and forsaking her official connections to the underground, she no longer had access to the extensive above-ground support system she had grown accustomed to. The parting from her fugitive friends had been an acrimonious one, and they would sooner sign on as Red Squad field agents than lend her any assistance whatsoever. On the heels of the SLA barbecue in Los Angeles, this struck me as needlessly churlish. But I guess nobody really wanted to stick their necks out farther than necessary to preserve their own tender hides. Increasingly I was feeling the same way myself.

To simplify matters we decided that I would fly to San Francisco from Chicago. We would live as tourists for a week, staying away from her apartment and repeating the anonymous out-of-towner act we had so successfully executed the previous summer.

From the moment I stepped off the plane, everything seemed slightly alien. When I had been here before, I met up immediately with Pren and Wilt, and we went straight home to Berkeley at night. Now, however, it was midday and I was intensely aware that I was alone in a strange and teeming world. The airport swarmed with irritating young religious solicitors, Moonies and Children of God and other blank-eyed riffraff, determined to sell me incense and give me flowers and divest me of my last dime. I saw Hare Krishnas with ponytails and saffron saris and couples swathed in unisex white robes with matching turbans.

My instructions were to go directly to Fisherman's Wharf, and I gawked with glee as my cab carried me past gingerbread-encrusted Victorian houses painted mauve and lemon, crimson and gold, red, white, and blue. On the side of a building, somebody had spray-painted FREE THE WATERGATE 500.

We'd never made it to the wharf on my previous visit, and I was startled to find it flooded with the same sorts of folks who swarm into the French Quarter of New Orleans. All that was missing were the artists selling Elvis on velvet. I wandered about for a while, halfheartedly checking to see that I wasn't followed but not really considering the possibility very likely. After a couple of walkaway crab cocktails, I bought a loaf of sourdough bread and tucked it beneath my left arm, my "all's clear" signal. Following instructions, I strolled down toward the pier where the sightseeing boats were docked. Within five minutes, I felt a tug at my sleeve.

"A crust of bread for a poor, pitiful mother-to-be?" came the plaintive whine of Prentiss Granger.

I laughed and turned to hug her. For the second time in as many years, I was shocked by her appearance. She was fat. Had I not known she was pregnant, I would merely have thought that here was somebody who had communed too closely with a lot of pastry and potatoes.

Her hair was still mouse brown and still clipped in the abominable pixie cut of the previous summer. Her face had changed, however. Her cheeks bulged unnaturally and her eyes were slightly sunken beneath the puffy new flesh. She wore a loose turquoise smock over baggy white double-knit pants, the kind with an elastic waist and a sewn-in crease.

She realized that I was staring and grinned. "The perfect disguise, no? Even my own mother wouldn't recognize me."

I didn't know whether or not I should say anything about her shocking weight gain. But she was way ahead of me.

"I'm entering a Shelley Winters look-alike contest," she said. "What do you think my chances are?"

"Excellent. But maybe you should go for the Cass Elliot competition. Then you can wear a flowing tie-dyed velvet caftan."

"Just what I always wanted. Tie-dyed velvet. That's terribly passé, you know. Years out of style."

"Well, listen to Miss Fashion Plate. That fetching little ensemble looks like the Lane Bryant catalog to me. What's the plan?"

"We're registered for the next four days at the Holiday Inn Fisherman's Wharf," she said. "In other words, just over there. I thought we could do some tourist stuff, if you like. It's probably safe enough and we never did before."

I looked around us. Within fifty feet stood a scruffy hippie with gingham-patched jeans and greasy blond hair hanging loose to his waist, a leisure-suited Rotarian with sunburned bald head, an Oriental family jabbering like finches in some exotic tongue and a pair of nuns in modified street habit. One of the nuns was drinking a Coors.

"One of the most interesting tourist things would seem to be merely *watching* the critters. Is this normal?" I swept a hand around vaguely.

Pren laughed. "The definition of *normal* in California is always subject to interpretation. Listen, since we're here already and it's kind of clear, let's take a boat ride around the bay."

So we climbed into the tourist boat and it was, as advertised, a fascinating tour, though I felt rather nervous when we hovered near Alcatraz. It reminded me a little too clearly who I was with.

I relaxed totally, however, once we got to the hotel and sprawled on our respective double beds to catch up on all the gossip. I drank Heineken with my sourdough bread and Pren consumed an entire quart of milk, part of a rigidly pure pregnancy diet that eliminated junk food, alcohol, tobacco, drugs, caffeine, white flour and refined sugar.

"I figure last time was a trial run," she explained, "and I gave away the test product anyway. But this one I intend to keep and I'll be damned if I'm going to make any avoidable mistakes. Like coffee or liquor or dope. I have the next four months all planned out and there's only one item on the agenda. My baby."

We woke early the next morning to thick, chilly fog that shrouded buildings and people with mysterious wisps and clouds. As fog drifted casually through the streets, the day seemed terribly romantic and clandestine, altogether in keeping with an underground liaison.

We caught the cable car for Chinatown in midmorning, a marvelous ride which offered an entirely new perspective on public transportation. But I forgot the cable car altogether the instant we first stepped onto Grant Avenue.

I was absolutely mesmerized. There were so many places to look and things to see that I longed for ball bearings in my neck. Fortunately, Pren was patient and in no apparent hurry. She trailed dutifully along as I wandered in and out of strange little groceries crammed with exotica. Odd dried vegetation was festooned above jars of unrecognizable fruits. Golden roasted ducks dangled behind meat counters and slightly ominous things bobbled in open vats of brine. Peculiarly shaped fruits and vegetables were arranged in neat colorful displays.

We meandered through gift shops too, admiring exquisite cloisonnette urns and intricate cork sculptures from Fukien. Pren was particularly intrigued by the concentric rotating balls painstakingly carved from single solid balls of ivory and I was entranced by a full-sized elephant tusk carved into an entire complex microcosmic world of trees and animals and pagodas and people.

Before long, Chinatown's hole-in-the-wall restaurants took precedence over art and culture. I was absolutely ravenous. When I mentioned this to Pren, she grinned expectantly and led me around a corner into a place called the Hong Kong Tea House.

The enormous restaurant bustled with what seemed to be thousands of Chinese men, women and children. Dozens of people waited in a large lobby for seating in the cavernous dining hall. We joined them, watching Chinese women wheel around carts of what Pren identified as dim sum, exquisite little morsels with the capability to tempt at twenty yards. As each waitress wheeled her cart along the aisles, diners would flag her down and remove little plates of goodies from the tray. At the end of the meal, Pren explained, they simply added up the number of empty plates on a table to compute the bill.

It sounded like a splendid system to me. I began to seriously consider the possibility that God might be Chinese.

True to Pren's promise, we were seated in fifteen minutes, near the back of the room. I automatically reached for the menu on the table, but found it printed entirely in Chinese. Soon the waitresses were streaming past. Pren's caution in identifying each item in advance saved me at the last minute from a confrontation with some scrumptious-looking french-fried duck feet.

I was munching merrily along, taking two plates at a crack of particularly interesting looking items, just in case they wouldn't pass my way again. I didn't even try to keep a conversation going and wasn't paying much attention to Pren when I heard her speak quickly in a low urgent voice.

"Don't look up. There's a guy just outside the front window that I saw yesterday when we were at the wharf."

I didn't see much initial cause for alarm. "So? We're hitting all the tourist spots, aren't we? Seems like of course we'd run into some of the same people."

"This guy was carting around a 500 mm lens. And he was hanging around before *and* after we took the boat ride."

Suddenly my appetite was gone. Convulsive terror seized my guts. "What do we do?"

"I'm going to split," she said. "Slide a ten out of your purse under the table to leave for the check. Now, listen. I'm going to go right around this corner past the kitchen as if I were headed for the ladies room. It's a blind exit. Then I go through the kitchen and out back. When I get up, you start looking around, casually but very carefully, to see who's interested. I think we can assume that the guy up there by the front window will be, but there might be somebody else here. I want to know who. About four minutes after I leave, you slide the money on the table and follow me. Just go through the kitchen and down the alley to the right. Once you get to Grant, run as fast as you can toward the towers downtown. Be in Union Square at five forty-five during rush hour and I'll find you. Got it?"

I nodded. "What if I can't find you again?"

"Same time, same place, next two days. After that, go back to Chicago. Don't go back to the hotel. For anything. Are you all right?"

I must have looked as shaky as I felt. "Sure. This is probably a false alarm anyway."

But the look on her face said otherwise. I wiggled the money out of my pocketbook and held it folded in my hand. Pren stood up and wandered nonchalantly away from the table. As she did so, I swept my gaze lazily around the room and froze in terror. Sitting against the wall about twenty-five feet away was a man I had seen at the airport when I first got off the plane. I doubt that I would have even noticed him had he not so quaintly resembled John Dean. He hadn't seemed interested in me, but he was waiting at the gate when I arrived and I never did see him greet anybody.

Now he rose slightly from his seat. Clearly he was hesitating, wondering if Pren were merely going to the ladies room. I willed him to sit down, to relax, to take another bite of fried duck foot. Then, in a heart-stopping moment, our eyes met. I could see him panic. He leaped up and bolted for the back of the restaurant in pursuit of Prentiss Granger.

Molten lead rolled up and down my esophagus. She hadn't had enough time to get away.

He charged down the aisle between the tables of merrily munching Chinese, right at me. Meanwhile, a waitress approached my table with a cart fresh from the kitchen, loaded with woven reed steamers and plates of little hot dogs in biscuits. I jumped up, threw the ten on the table, grabbed the cart from the startled waitress and pushed it as hard as possible down the aisle toward the man. He sidestepped to avoid the cart, collided with a busboy carrying two pots of hot tea and they both seemed to fall in slow motion across a round table full of flabbergasted Chinese businessmen in conservative gray suits.

But by then I wasn't watching anymore. I took one fast glance at the front of the restaurant, just enough to see that the guy Pren had pointed out was now inside the restaurant and closing in on us fast.

I ran like hell toward the back and flew through the kitchen. I was vaguely aware of dozens of slender men chopping and deep frying and steaming and assembling dim sum by the thousands. I hurled a bushel basket full of cabbages back toward the door of the dining room and caught a fast glimpse of them rolling in many satisfying directions. Then I scooted out the back door.

"FBI, freeze!!"

I heard the stentorian order behind me clearly, but it never occurred to me to stop. God knows why. I'm the world's biggest coward, after all. I guess I must have realized subliminally that they wouldn't want to shoot an unarmed fat girl in the kitchen of a Chinese restaurant, even if there weren't any risk of accidentally knocking off a few cooks. Out in the alley, Prentiss Granger was about half a block away. I hurtled toward her as fast as I could, yelling wildly.

"Run, run, RUN!!!!"

* * *

We tore down the alley, Pren slightly in the lead. I hoped to hell that she knew where she was going, because we were both comically fat and I knew that I wasn't going to be able to keep up this pace long at all. She turned and led us down to Grant Avenue, pausing enough to let me catch up to her. We ran down the street, threading ourselves through clots of gawking tourists and elderly Chinese ladies shopping for dinner with baskets over their arms, all of the same people who had seemed so picturesque and charming an hour earlier. Now they were only obstacles and camouflage. For the first time in my life, I yearned to have black hair, yellow skin and thickly lidded dark brown eyes.

I followed Pren as fast as possible. She seemed to be in much better condition than I, doubtless from all those months of exercise and military drill at Fugitive Farm. I lost sight of our pursuers, but it was almost impossible to keep running, avoid collisions and monitor what was happening behind us.

Finally Pren ran into a small grocery store. I followed her through the inside, ignoring the startled cries of the elderly proprietors who were, in any case, speaking Chinese. We dashed through into the alley, where Pren collapsed against the side of a building, clutching her stomach. For the first time I thought about the baby.

"You all right?" I gasped.

She nodded. I tried to touch her shoulder but she brushed me away. "I can't run any more. Do you think we lost them?"

"I don't know. I think so, though." I leaned back against the wall. "Now what?"

"Christ, I don't know." She was still holding her stomach. "Let me think. See if that door over there is open."

It was an alley entrance to an apartment building and it was unlocked. We slipped inside and sat on the linoleum floor, hidden from sight. I told her what had happened after she left, about the guy from the airport. Her brow knotted in anger, fear and confusion. I was happy to oblige when she asked me to be quiet.

As I waited for Pren to work out our battle plan, I wondered how on earth they had discovered us. We had been so *careful,* I thought. I *knew* I had lost my Chicago tail in Marshall Field's before going to the airport. Could it be plain dumb bad luck that somebody had spotted her? That didn't seem quite plausible, given her current excess poundage. If I could barely recognize her, it seemed unlikely that a stranger working only from photographs of yesteryear would be able to. And that still didn't explain how the John Dean clone happened to be waiting at the San Francisco airport.

When Pren started to talk again, her breathing was much slower and she was no longer clutching at her abdomen, both good signs. But there was still real fear in her voice, fear that didn't disappear when she dropped her tone to a barely audible level.

"We can't go back to the hotel," she said. "If they've been on us since yesterday, they know we're there. Hope you didn't leave anything there that you mind losing."

I thought about the paltry contents of my navy blue tote bag. "Nothing. But your money's still there, isn't it?"

She grimaced. "Yeah. You'll just have to send me more. They'll get the car too, and from that I don't know if they can trace me back to the apartment or not. I don't think I left anything in the car and it's registered in Daly City. But I'm not sure. Damnation! At least I used a new name to register at the hotel."

We waited another ten minutes or so while she plotted and fumed. Then we walked through to the front of the building, and slunk along the sidewalk waiting for an empty cab to pass. One came by almost immediately. "Thank God for the tourist industry," Pren murmured.

Pren had the cab deliver us to a downtown office building. The pharmacy and gift shop on the ground floor had an open pay phone at the rear. I followed Pren as she strode through the store, slipped a dime into the phone and dialed. In a sudden flash of the past, I became aware again of her odd memory for numbers. If Prentiss Granger got busted, I thought, at least she wouldn't take anybody down with her. She'd never carried an address book in her life. I knew perfectly well that she had memorized all the phone numbers where she called me in Chicago. I'd been willing to bet that she also knew the numbers of Weatherly Plantation, Grandma Chesterton's house, and every dorm at Duke University.

"Laura?" Pren cooed gently into the phone. "It's Barbara, from Lamaze. Not so good, really. You know that problem I told you about? Well, I can't really talk right now, but the problem is back in town. I'm afraid to go home and I've got my cousin here from Atlanta. Could we possibly crash at your place tonight?" She turned and gave me an upraised thumb and a big grin. "Super. Listen, we're downtown right now. How about if we meet you after work and ride out with you? Terrific. Bye, now."

She was beaming after she hung up. "We might just make it after all. Now we need to kill three and a half hours. If I'd realized we were going on the lam, I'd have told you to bring a good book. This part gets very, very boring. Want to go to the movies? We could see *Chinatown*."

I laughed despite myself. "How about *Barbara Doesn't Live Here Anymore?*"

"Indeed she doesn't. In fact, for all practical purposes, Barbara Bellamy doesn't exist anymore. Pity, I was growing to like her. Anyway, the theater near here is showing *Godfather, Part II*. So I guess we get to see what the FBI ought to be doing instead of chasing expectant mothers through minority neighborhoods. And eating dim sum on expense account."

But we never made it to the movies. Instead we spent the afternoon outfitting ourselves in a series of boutiques. Even as we frantically fled the long arm of the law, we acted like Junior Leaguers out for lunch and a little shopping, giggling and trying on all sorts of stuff. We ended up with two abbreviated new wardrobes, paid for by check on Barbara Bellemy's account. The clothes were dowdier than I would have liked, but Pren pointed out that as political fugitives, we would hardly be expected to look like refugees from the K Mart mark-down bin.

Pren's friend Laura was waiting for us in the lobby of a shiny glass and steel office building at five-thirty. Laura was small and dark, with a shock of wildly curly jet black hair, deep brown eyes and a rich Mediterranean complexion. She was pretty and sophisticated and very pregnant. Pren had told me she was an accountant for a Japanese megacorporation.

"This is my cousin Lou Ann from Atlanta," Pren said as we piled into a cab with our miscellaneous bundles. "Lou Ann, Laura Berg. Laura, I'm so *grateful* to you for taking us in this way. He's just an animal when he's drinking. I can't stop him and I didn't know who else I could turn to." Pren's cover story for Lamaze involved a vicious estranged husband who beat her horribly.

"Barb, you're welcome anytime, I told you. In fact, if you want to move right in, that's fine with me. I still say you ought to call the police on that swine."

"I did once, I told you, and he was just sweet as pie till they left. Then he broke my rib. Actually, Laura, I'm afraid the only way I can get rid of him is to move back home to Atlanta. I think that I'll go back with Lou Ann when she leaves tomorrow."

"If you change your mind, there's plenty of room. Barry won't be home from Brazil for at least three months. He's not even sure he can get away when the baby's born. That damn hydroelectric plant is ruining my marriage. This one, driver. The blue with white trim."

Laura's house was one of those wonderful Victorians near Japantown, and it resembled nothing so much as a giant Wedgwood plate. The house had been divided into six apartments. Laura's was two large rooms, both with high ceilings, beautifully ornate woodwork and spectacular parquet floors.

They fixed dinner while I flipped through the record collection, which ran heavily to female vocalists. I selected Roberta Flack's *First Take* album and uncorked the bottle of wine I'd bought as Roberta purred into "The First Time Ever I Saw Your Face." The reminder of Mike Donovan didn't hurt quite so much anymore. Or maybe I was just totally numb from the dizzying events of the afternoon. I lay there on a beige velvet sofa reviewing the dreadful events of the day. In the kitchen I could hear Pren and Laura exchanging niggling pregnancy details. I lifted my glass in a silent personal toast to freedom and proceeded to polish off the entire bottle.

When I woke up the next morning, at first I had no idea where I was. I knew only that my head ached horribly and my eyes were watering in some kind of allergic reaction. I was in a sofa bed beside somebody who was turned away and covered by blankets.

And then it all came to me in a sudden horrific flash. For the first time in my life, I too was a fugitive. I was on the run from the law and I was scared half to death. How could Pren live this way?

Laura cashed a check for Pren before leaving for work, which brought our total assets to just over ninety dollars. Then we spread newspaper on the kitchen floor and set to work on our *Glamour* beauty makeovers. Had the stakes not been quite so high, it might have been fun. "This reminds me of getting ready for fraternity rush back in Wognum," Pren said at one point. But somehow fraternity rush seemed very far away.

Since Pren's hair was already so short, she decided to perm and dye it rather than attempt any further trimming. I read the directions on the Toni box carefully, breaking into uncontrollable laughter at one point as I recalled those svelte girls in gold lamé who used to get home permanents on one side of their heads during the Miss America Pageant. Then it was my turn. Prentiss Granger, head bristling with ridiculous pink metal curlers and reeking of chemicals, cut six inches off my hair.

The time was at hand. I was about to learn once and for all if blondes had more fun.

The kitchen had the petrochemical stench of Baton Rouge before we got finished, but the results were pretty amazing. Pren now sported a reddish-brown three-inch natural and my hair was about four inches all over, still riotously curly but now a pale creamy blond. At least when I was arrested, nobody would recognize me.

As Pren carefully adjusted her new shoulder-length black wig, I tried to think of us objectively as two strangers. This objectivity was no help. Everything appeared quite bleak and hopeless when viewed realistically. We had ninety-four dollars, no transportation and no destination. I could only hope that we at least had a plan.

Alas, the plan Pren finally unveiled seemed preposterous. But I didn't argue when she said we really should leave at once. I was, however, responsible for an unplanned but not altogether unexpected delay. Other people may leave their hearts in San Francisco. I left my breakfast.

Chapter 13 _____

We stole a car and drove to Portland.

It certainly sounds simple enough when reduced to the bald statement, and I don't doubt that there are people for whom such matter-of-fact pronouncements are perfectly routine. Grand Theft Auto, however, was a brand new experience for me.

The actual heist was disturbingly simple. Pren removed the plates from Laura's husband's Lancia, garaged behind the house for the duration of his South American sojourn. Then we took all our hair-care garbage and other trash out to the alley and dumped it in a galvanized can halfway down the block. We left a note of thanks for Laura on the kitchen table, filched a coat hanger and hit the bricks, carrying our tacky new wardrobes in brown paper grocery sacks. We strolled in fairly aimless patterns through the neighborhood while Pren searched for our ideal getaway car. I kept breathing deeply and swallowing hard and reminding myself that I wasn't the one they wanted anyhow. It didn't help at all.

Finally Pren found a car which met her requirements of good gas mileage and relative obscurity. It was a dark green 1970 VW Beetle, parked on a side street and dusted over with a couple of days' worth of city street grime. She didn't even need the coat hanger to get in. The wind wing wasn't locked. As she expertly fiddled beneath the dash and made the connections to start the engine, I wondered whether this were a routine occurrence for her, but I didn't trust my voice.

In an alley behind a dry cleaner's shop, Pren switched the plates and tossed the ones off the VW in a paper bag in a Dumpster. Then we hit the road.

"There's no need or reason for you to come with me," Pren said for the hundredth time as we snaked up and down the San Francisco hills. Her plan was to drive clear down the peninsula and around the Bay through San Jose, rather than risk apprehension crossing any of the bridges. If they had photographs of us, a reasonable assumption given our friend at the wharf with the 500 mm lens, it would be simplicity itself to station a couple of agents on the Golden Gate and Oakland bridges.

"I want to," I said. "This was all my fault and I'm not going to abandon you." Ever since we figured out how it happened that the cops were on to us, I'd been suffering from excruciating guilt. I desperately wanted a chance to somehow redeem myself for my appalling previous stupidity.

"It wasn't your fault," she repeated. "You were set up. And I can manage by myself, believe me. All I have to do is drive. I just need to stay awake and be anonymous. That's not such a problem."

"Forget it. I'm coming along. I'm not about to go scurrying back to Chicago for a long meaningful chat with the FBI, my friend."

She grimaced. "I can hardly blame you. We'll have to work out your return in steps, I think. Kind of like decompression. That way we can set you up to be reasonably clean too. Don't worry."

"I couldn't not worry to save my life."

Pren shook her head. "But that's where you're wrong, Lou Ann." We'd decided that Lou Ann was as good a name as any for me. I actually rather liked it, better than Penny anyway. "Your life isn't in danger. Mine is. The worst that can happen to you is accessory on the car theft and you can always dump that on me. I'm afraid that once they get hold of me, they won't care at all who you are. Sorry."

It didn't seem like anything to apologize for. And it also didn't ring quite true. Nobody had paid much attention to whether or not Patty Hearst was in that Los Angeles house before the SWAT teams torched it, after all. And if they didn't care about a kidnapped heiress, they sure weren't going to hesitate to wipe me out. But I kept my mouth shut.

Once we reached the central valley, it was very hot, a stunning contrast from the chilly fog of San Francisco. We shed layers of our hideous doubleknits, down to ungainly little shells. Pren complained about the wig and how sweaty her head was, but she didn't risk taking it off. My own new haircut felt good, actually, though I still jumped in shock and wonder each time I caught my blond reflection.

We drove late into the night, stopping only for gas and food. Now and again for maybe three seconds I forgot why it was we were chugging up the center of California. All it ever took to remind me was a single glance at Pren with her dreadful Dynel wig and scarf, her unattractive puffiness and soft full tummy.

I noticed that Pren seemed to know northern California pretty well. She was able to point out upcoming landmarks and natural wonders, which made me speculate that perhaps we were near her former hideout. She had finally acknowleged that it was located somewhere north of San Francisco. She just hadn't quite explained whether she was talking Marin County or Alaska. It gave me an odd shivery twinge to think of that little fugitive den humming along at that very moment through the routines of a bright summer day. Somebody would be milking the goats, perhaps, while others hoed the vegetable garden, kneaded sprouted grain bread and assembled plastic explosives. Your basic scene of communal warmth and harmony, save for the arsenal of Uzis, AK-47s and maybe a missile launcher or two.

Our route was meandering and indirect, with a six-hour nighttime stop in the mountains, so it was late the second night when we finally pulled into Portland. Pren stopped at a twenty-four-hour truck stop outside town and disappeared to make phone calls. When she returned to the car she was beaming, shooting out that same self-satisfied grin I recognized from moments of personal glory dating clear back to her selection for the Parker Academy Homecoming Court in 1963.

"Bingo!" she said. "I'll have to work out the long-term stuff later, but we've got a place to crash tonight at least."

I was totally lost and confused by the time we pulled into a driveway in a quiet residential neighborhood. I waited in the car while she went up and knocked on the door. A moment later she was back and we slipped inside a run-down frame house with tightly drawn shades. Inside I blinked a few times as I quickly cased the place, discovering rather to my surprise that it was quite pleasant. The furniture appeared to be homemade, not the ubiquitous cable spools and bricks and boards of ordinary counterculture dwellings, but actual complicated chairs and a rather odd sofa and end table unit built into one corner. A large oval braided rug appeared to be fashioned entirely from old blue jeans and the curtains and upholstery were all blue and green batik.

A somber-looking young strawberry blonde gave me a visual inspection so thorough I was tempted to inquire whether she'd like to examine my dental work. Pren introduced her as Margo, a name I assumed to be as phony as mine. There was something mildly unsettling about Margo, but I didn't realize what it was until her roommate Elaine emerged from the back of the house.

Elaine had closely cropped black hair, permanently furrowed brows and a sturdy muscular build. I had never met any lesbians before, at least not that I was aware of. This was clearly a week of endless firsts.

"No way anybody can see into the cellar," said Elaine without any preliminaries. She had a lovely lilting voice, which seemed a great contradiction to her burly appearance. "You'll be safe there for at least a couple of days." She eyed me suspiciously. "And what about—"

"Lou Ann will leave tomorrow," Pren announced. Lou Ann felt a bit miffed at this, but held her tongue. "Do you suppose one of you can get her to the airport?"

Margo nodded. "Give me the keys and I'll put your car in the garage."

Pren laughed. "I seem to have somehow misplaced the keys. Want me to go start it?"

"Not necessary," Elaine replied. "I can do it." She went outside and a moment later I heard the engine roar back into life.

Meanwhile, Margo led us down to the basement. It was dank. There was no other way to describe it. I was surprised not to find moss on the unpainted concrete walls. On the floor lay one elderly double mattress, mottled with a lot of rather suspicious stains. Margo left to get bedding for us and I shuddered involuntarily.

"Be polite," whispered Pren.

I laughed. Etiquette seemed to be the last thing in the world I needed to worry about. Not going crazy was a far more serious concern. But it was ridiculous, no question about it. And so I laughed. And laughed and laughed and laughed. Every bit of pressure and madness from the past three days poured up and spilled over in a sudden bout of hysteria. It felt wonderful.

But it didn't last for long. One minute I was laughing hysterically and the next Pren had me by the shoulders, shaking me hard. I snapped out of it instantly when I saw the worry in her eyes.

"Sorry," I apologized immediately. "Just a mild case of water on the brain." I looked around, curiously eyeing the furnace, a vast contraption with tentacles reaching across the room toward various corners of the ceiling. I could tell already that when I woke disoriented the next day, it would seem to be an enormous extraterrestrial monster come prowling for a succulent breakfast. "Not exactly the Holiday Inn at Fisherman's Wharf, is it?"

"I promised you an adventure, didn't I?"

"The last adventure I recall you mentioning was a drive to Berkeley."

She smiled and I suddenly noticed how tired she seemed. "Next time, Lou Ann. Next time we'll really do it properly." She glanced at her watch with a slight frown, then looked back up. "And I figure that will be about March of 1997, when it's finally safe for me to hit the Bay again." We both laughed and the awkward tension was gone.

Margo returned with pillows and blankets and some lovely floral percale sheets, which Pren and I instantly recognized as coming from the Granger Mills luxury collection. Such linens seemed far too grand for that scurrilous mattress and wildly out of place in that dank, chilly basement. I was actually rather touched. This seemed to be the residence of capable people, folks who could hotwire an engine, construct a sofa and take in a radical fugitive on fifteen minutes' notice. I was quite happy to turn Prentiss Granger over into their competent hands. Mine was the easy role, when you shifted perspective a little. All I had to do was go back to Chicago and stonewall the FBI. They were the ones who had to find Pren a new home, identity and Lamaze class.

The next morning, I hugged Pren good-bye at the house, realizing as I did so that it might be years before I could safely see her again. I felt an enormous void opening in me, and I didn't look back when I walked out the door.

Margo drove to the airport without saying more than a dozen words and dumped me at the terminal. I took a deep breath, picked up the tattered BOAC flight bag Elaine had donated and walked inside to pick up Lou Ann Baxter's ticket to Salt Lake City.

Pren and I had worked out my agenda together. We decided I should use our dwindling cash to go someplace and check into a hotel under my real name for a few days before returning on a traceable flight to Chicago. That would provide an alibi for part of my absence, permit me to pay by credit card, focus the feds on a misleading location and allow me some time to reconstruct my mental health.

Salt Lake City was my idea. I needed a place where they didn't have to roll up the sidewalks at night because nobody had put them out to begin with, where the toss-up for an exciting afternoon was between the Mormon Tabernacle and the Donny Osmond Miniature Golf Course. I wanted no surprises.

And in Salt Lake City I got none.

Four days into my Salt Lake City sojourn, Martin Luther King's mother was gunned down while playing the church organ in Atlanta. My own nervousness suddenly seemed a little hollow. I bought a box of hair color that approximated my own natural shade and ended my brief but eventful fling as a blonde. Then I squared my shoulders and flew to Chicago. It was never going to get any easier, and there was no point in postponing it any further.

Five minutes after I emerged from the cab and entered my apartment building, the FBI knocked on my door. I insisted that they slide the warrant under the door, but it appeared to be entirely in order. I was to be taken into custody as a material witness for aiding in the flight of a federal fugitive and my apartment was to be searched for evidence relating to the whereabouts of one Prentiss Louise Granger.

I knew the apartment was clean, so I didn't worry much about that. The only incriminating material I ever kept there was the key to the safe deposit box and that was currently with Pren in Portland.

"Mr. Sanford wants to speak to you personally," explained the G-man who stashed me in a little interrogation room with the obligatory mirror on one wall and no furnishings save a table and three hardback chairs. "He's on his way here from San Francisco."

"I want a lawyer." I was beginning to sound like a parrot.

The G-man shook his head. "You're not under arrest. Until that happens, we can question you legally for twenty-four hours."

Before I could protest again, he left the room and locked me in. There was nothing I could do but sit and worry and wonder and check my watch for the hundredth time. I tried not to think about FBI agents sorting through my underwear drawer and making note of my tampon preference. Around 6:30 they gave me a dry ham sandwich on white bread with a smear of bright yellow mustard, accompanied by a Styrofoam cup of battery acid masquerading as coffee. Otherwise, everybody left me alone.

At 8:45 a snarling young man collected the refuse from my alleged dinner. "I'd like a chance to really take you apart," he muttered darkly, in a tone that suggested vivisection.

I was still a little unnerved when the door opened again and Special Agent Melvin Sanford strode in with a big warm smile on his craggy face. "Why Miss Laurel," he drawled, "I was expecting to run into you out in California. Everybody been takin' good care of you?"

I'd seen *Kojak*. I knew a mean cop, nice cop routine when I saw one. I also knew Mel Sanford pretty well by now. "I want a lawyer," I said. "I have the right to counsel."

"Well, of course you do," he answered, settling down at the table in the center of the room, directly across from me. He laid a large briefcase between us on the table, snapped open the latches and left it closed. "After you're arrested and booked. But we haven't charged you with anything. You must be a mite confused. We just want to ask you a few questions."

"I want a lawyer. I get a phone call, Mr. Sanford. Everybody in America knows you get a phone call when you're arrested."

"But you haven't been arrested, Miss Laurel. You're a material witness, that's all. We haven't charged you with so much as jaywalking." He lifted the lid of his briefcase and removed a manila file. He opened the file in such a fashion that I couldn't tell what was in it, smirked, then closed the file and left it lying on the table. He drummed his fingers gently on the file. "San Francisco's right pretty this time of year, don't you think?"

"I'm sure I wouldn't know."

He frowned. "That's funny. This photograph was taken Tuesday afternoon in San Francisco Bay, and I'd say it's a most remarkably flattering likeness of you." He pulled an eight-by-ten glossy from the file and slid it across the table to me.

I picked up the picture, careful to keep my expression utterly blank. Oddly enough, it *was* a flattering likeness. I was facing the camera smiling broadly. Beside me, also beaming, stood Prentiss Granger. "That isn't me. But I still want a lawyer."

He shook his head rather sadly. "No question but that it's you, Miss Laurel. From the time you left your apartment on Tuesday morning till you ran out of the Hong Kong Tea House, we had you covered every minute."

"If I wanted to take a vacation to San Francisco or anyplace else," I began carefully, "there's no reason why I couldn't do that. Which is hypothetical anyway. That isn't me. I wasn't in San Francisco."

Mel Sanford took the picture away from me and slid it back into the folder. I could see now that there were at least a dozen other photographs in there.

"Miss Laurel, I respect your loyalty to your friend, I honestly do. Indeed, I have a lot of respect for you all the way around. You seem to be a good, hard-working girl doing a thankless job and making a mighty fine business of it. Not a single solitary soul we've ever talked to has spoken of you in a negative fashion. If it weren't for the fact that you're protecting somebody who is a dangerous wanted criminal, wanted as an accessory to murder, in fact, I suspect that you're the kind of girl who'd never have occasion to sit and talk to the law in this fashion. You strike me as a lady, Miss Laurel, but you're a lady caught up in a right dangerous situation. This isn't any game."

A lady. I was rarely accused of being a lady these days. And I'd grown up in a veritable sea of southern bullshit. I wasn't about to be taken in by anything as transparent as this.

"I want a lawyer. I have a right to make a phone call."

"Not just yet, Miss Laurel. You make yourself right at home here. Can I have one of the boys get you some more coffee?"

"You can get me a telephone, dammit!"

"Comes a time, Miss Laurel, when it's downright silly to be so stubborn. Now suppose I just have one of the boys run out and get us a little something to eat, some fried chicken, maybe, or a pizza. You like pizza?"

He knew perfectly well that I liked pizza. He'd been monitoring my dining habits for over two years. I kept quiet.

"Never did take too well to Italian food myself, actually," he continued. "Give me good old-fashioned southern cooking every time. Fried chicken, a nice mess of collards, biscuits and gravy, now that's my notion of a mighty fine supper. 'Fraid the only place up north I ever count on decent biscuits and gravy is home with my little wife Wanda doing the honors, though. My little Wanda used to make the best biscuits in Americus, Georgia. Always told her that was why I married her."

All this folksy familiarity made me gag. Did he really think that after all this time I'd break down and spill my guts just because he conjured up images of supper in the South?

"What about my phone call?"

"In good time, Miss Laurel, in good time."

"In good time, Mr. Sanford, the South will rise again, or so my dear granddaddy always used to tell me. I'm afraid I can't wait that long. I want my phone call now."

He was quiet for a moment. "You know that Donovan boy is living up in Vancouver now? Kind of surprised me, him leaving the country that way."

I said nothing, concentrating on keeping my face utterly void of expression. I had no intention of allowing him to pick the scab off *that* wound and I was shocked that he would be so direct about it anyway. Even so, it was nice to have a line on Mike again. Pren had been baffled as to his whereabouts, though of course she didn't have the full resources of the United States government behind her.

When it became quite clear that I wasn't talking, he led me to a similar room down the hall. This one had a mirror too, and three hardback chairs around another metal table. It also had a green vinyl sofa. He locked me in and I flopped down in utter exhaustion. Sooner or later they *had* to let me make my call.

They let me go to the bathroom once when I banged on the door, then locked me back in the little room. I never did get anything more to eat that night, not pizza or southern-fried chicken or even another dry ham sandwich. I was horribly hungry. And while I swore I wouldn't fall asleep, it happened anyway. In the middle of a decidedly X-rated dream about Mike Donovan and New Orleans, the door clicked open and the welcome aroma of freshly brewed coffee filled the room. It was 8 A.M.

The coffee was far above standard for such occasions, and I theorized that perhaps Wanda Sanford had been deputized to cater a confessional breakfast. I half expected a spry little lady in a flour-dusted calico apron to pop through the door, bearing a basket of piping hot biscuits fresh from the oven.

No such luck. Breakfast turned out to be Egg McMuffin. It stuck in my throat as we went around and around again. By now they had traced me to Salt Lake City and the Hilton, no difficult task. I envisioned platoons of eager young field agents calling Mormon attention to the possible presence of a dangerous fugitive in their midst. By now there were probably troops of Boy Scouts going from door to door seeking clues to the whereabouts of the Debutante Revolutionary. By now her picture was probably hanging beside every cash register in Utah.

It was during what passed for breakfast that Mel Sanford brought up the money for the first time. "You left behind a little cash in San Francisco, didn't you, Miss Laurel?"

"I'm sure I don't know what you're talking about."

"In the room at the Holiday Inn. We found nine thousand nine hundred sixty dollars in cash. Your fingerprints were on that money."

"I've never been fingerprinted. You're making that up."

He smiled. "As it happens, Miss Laurel, I do believe we have a set on file. Seems to me we lifted them off some photographs you handled on a previous occasion when we were together."

The rotten sneaks. I knew that the money was clean, however. It couldn't be traced to me or anybody else, save by those damnable fingerprints. If, indeed, they could take fingerprints off money. I wasn't so sure. And it would be a lovely way to try to trap me.

"I want a lawyer. I believe I may have mentioned that before."

He hammered at me for quite a while, but I didn't say a thing. I just smiled enigmatically now and again and periodically inquired about my phone call. I felt a lot better now, actually, knowing that Mike Donovan was still alive someplace in the world. Assuming that Mel Sanford hadn't just made it up, a possibility I didn't want to consider too hard.

Finally, just after 2 P.M., I was taken to an outer office to make my phone call. There were three secretaries typing busily away in that office and none of them even looked up. Two were in their thirties, dressed more or less in current fashion. The other was a stereotypical office battleaxe, complete with a white tailored blouse that buttoned up the back.

I called Maxine Lockford's real estate office. I was afraid she might be with a client or out showing a house, but I got lucky. She answered on the second ring.

I'd been rehearsing the call for quite some time. I didn't want to waste any time or reveal anything, but it was important that she understand how serious matters were. I plunged ahead without pausing. "Mrs. Lockford, it's Laurel. I need your help. The FBI has me under arrest and I've been here almost twenty-four hours. I want a lawyer, but this is the first phone call they've let me make."

She was calm, businesslike and unsurprised. "Why now?"

I'd thought that one through too. "They have a picture they claim is of me and Prentiss Granger in San Francisco."

"I see." God love her. I bet she didn't even blink. "Tell me where you are and I'll get somebody there as fast as possible. Want anybody in particular?"

"I've never been arrested before. I'll trust your judgment." I told her where to find me and she promised to take care of everything. I felt much better now that somebody responsible knew where I was. For nearly twenty-four hours, nobody in the world had known my whereabouts except the Federal Bureau of Investigation. Some people would find that reassuring. It scared the hell out of me.

An hour later, back in the interrogation room, Mel Sanford still sat facing me across the table. The photographs of the Bay cruise were scattered around us, all unmistakably showing Laurel and Prentiss on a carefree sightseeing jaunt. I was growing quite weary when one of the young agents opened the door and beckoned to Mel Sanford. He rose, conferred in a whisper at the door, then left, locking me in again.

Twenty minutes later, he returned. "Your lawyer's here, Miss Laurel. Come along with me."

Out in the main office, Maxine Lockford was leaning against a wall, smoking. The battleaxe's desk was right beside her and the battleaxe was making something of a production out of blowing away the smoke, but the drama was lost on her intended audience. A distinguished-looking man in his late forties perched on the battleaxe's desk. He looked all business, in a beautifully tailored lightweight tan suit and supple Italian shoes. If he hadn't been so well dressed, he might have passed for an FBI agent himself. His coarse short hair was a tweedy blend of sand and silver and his pale gray eyes reminded me of Robert Stack as Elliot Ness. When he stood up as I crossed the room, I was relieved to find that he had a warm friendly smile. I'd never had a lawyer before, other than my father and Lee, and this guy looked like a pretty good first shot. I'd always known Maxine Lockford was a class act.

He stepped across to greet me with extended hand. "Miss Hollingsworth, I'm Larry Cone. We're all set to leave whenever you're ready."

I shook his hand weakly. "I was ready twenty-four hours ago, when they first brought me here."

He frowned and shook his head slightly. "We'll talk about all that later. What do you say we just leave right now?"

I looked around the office at the typing drones, the grubby metal furniture, the two indistinguishable junior agents and Mel Sanford. "I'd say it was about fucking time."

The battleaxe let out an involuntary gasp. It was quite wonderful.

Chapter 14 _____

If there isn't a special suite in heaven reserved for Maxine Lockford, I'm not sure I want to go there at all. I was on the brink of collapse by the time she arrived and I guess it showed. She put an arm around my shoulders as we left the office and it was a joy beyond belief to be able to lean on somebody else for a change. I'd about shot my wad on personal fortitude.

We went first to Larry Cone's office on LaSalle Street, where I formally retained his services. Mrs. Lockford left us alone while I gave him a somewhat abbreviated account of what had happened. I figured there was no reason not to tell him anything that the FBI knew for certain, though I never did specifically state that I was with Prentiss Granger. I ended my narrative in Chinatown and picked it up two days later in Salt Lake City, just as the FBI had.

"They were obviously hoping that she'd lead them to more people," he said, "or they'd have picked you up that first afternoon at Fisherman's Wharf."

I'd spent a lot of time thinking about that one and we had discussed it at length on the ride to Portland. "I'm not so sure. The person they believe to be Prentiss Granger doesn't look at all like the old photographs they have. It might have taken them a while to confirm, or anyway *think* they confirmed, her identity."

"True. But they could still have done that by nightfall and taken you in the motel room. Incidentally, they found ten thousand in cash in that motel room. It had your fingerprints on it. Where did that money come from?"

I shook my head. "I can't say. But the money is clean. It didn't come out of my personal accounts or anything and it can't be traced to me, except for what they say about the fingerprints."

"A significant exception."

"Can they actually take fingerprints off money?"

He grimaced. "They can get fingerprints off damn near anything. There's a new technique where they can lift them from the inside of a glove and they're working on another to take them off human flesh." He paused and concentrated a moment. "Seems to me that when Prentiss Granger went underground, there was a brouhaha about a hundred thousand dollars. If you have that money, it could get rough."

"If I had that money, the FBI would have found it a long time ago. I've been under surveillance for two years now, remember. Don't worry about the money or where it came from. That's all I can say." I figured that once they found the safe deposit box, I'd know pretty directly. All hell would break loose.

When we left Larry Cone's office, rush-hour traffic was already in full swing and it took nearly half an hour to reach my apartment. I expected to find a shambles, but only my darkroom closet seemed to have been disturbed. All of my negatives and contact sheets for the past eight years were missing. I felt horribly violated. Nobody had any right to those negatives but me. There were no relevant pictures on them. The FBI already had all the best pictures of Pren, the ones her family had so eagerly turned over. They didn't need those negatives. My best work was in those files.

I reacted in the only logical, intelligent adult fashion open to me. I burst into tears.

Mrs. Lockford let me cry in the living room while she rummaged through my refrigerator. She was back a minute or two later with two glasses of chilled California chablis and a plate of Jarlsberg cheese and sesame crackers. "I want to get you out of here," she said as she set the tray down. "Do you want to go get your toothbrush and a nightgown or do you trust me to do it for you?"

I managed to assemble my own overnight stuff, but that was about all I had the energy for. Once we reached Evanston, we went right out for dinner and over a big plate of barbecued ribs I told Maxine Lockford the same slightly incomplete story I had given Larry Cone. She listened with attentive concern.

"Dammit," she said finally. "Sounds like you're really in the soup this time, Laurel. But I've known Larry since third grade and if anybody can get you out of this mess, he can. Did Ginger know where you were going?"

I shook my head.

"Well, I can't really blame you for not telling her and I won't say anything about this conversation. Her politics get closer to her father's every day." She hesitated a moment. "Laurel? I never asked before because I didn't want to put you on the spot. But if you can, I wish you'd tell me what actually happened down there in Beaumont. I've tried so hard to understand, and it never made any sense."

Her neck was already on the block and it seemed only fair to tell her. So I did. When I finished, she was brushing away tears.

The next afternoon I went over to Northwestern, dozed through my graduate historical perspectives on education class, then found myself a nice comfortable phone booth where I could sit down. It was time to find out how much of the scenario I had deduced was paranoia and how much was reality. Increasingly I was finding the line between the two blurring.

It was a painful process to systematically examine my friends to determine who had warned the FBI to pay close attention to me, to back up their conspicuous tails with a secondary crew so that when I lost the first I would be too smug to look for further company. But obviously that had happened. One agent put me on the plane at O'Hare and the John Dean clone picked me up in San Francisco.

The obvious choice was somebody who knew I was leaving town, but the only person I'd told of my projected absence was Millicent Baer, who picked up my newspapers and mail whenever I was away. She was a little old lady who lived down the hall from me with a wretched little Chihuahua named Tortilla, fifty million house plants and a kitchen full of cast iron trivets that say things like ALL GOOD THINGS COME TO THOSE WHO WAIT. I trusted her because she had come to me in outrage on each of the four occasions when representatives of the law visited her on my account. Millicent Baer's parents and two sisters had died in Auschwitz and she maintained a very low opinion of law officers who came in the night to whisper ill about one's neighbors.

I left for San Francisco on a Tuesday. The previous Sunday I had dropped by Millicent's to tell her I'd be gone for about a week starting Wednesday and that I'd slip my mailbox key under her door before I left. I said I was going home to Louisiana but that I wanted a boy I'd been dating to think that I was going on vacation with another boy. The morality of even considering such an illicit vacation shocked her a little, but she found the intrigue rather appealing and promised not to breathe a word to anybody.

And so I eliminated Millicent Baer. If she'd snitched on me, I was willing to adopt Tortilla, that's how sure I was she was innocent.

I scratched Andy Lamont off my mental list mostly because he had been out of town for nearly three weeks, down near Indianapolis staying on his grandmother's farm. At the time he left, *I* hadn't even known I was going to San Francisco, so it wasn't likely that he'd know.

My teaching buddy Kathy Lundquist was in Stockholm with an Exchange Program for the summer, and it took me only a brief while to conclude that Ginger would not have done such a thing. She was clerking with a prestigious LaSalle Street law firm that summer and was madly in love with a fellow clerk from the U of I law school downstate. On the rare recent occasions when I'd encountered her, she was so totally engrossed in this torrid love affair that it was all she could do to remember my name.

I supposed there was a chance that somebody from one of my summer school classes was on to me, but I didn't see how and couldn't remember any action that might have created suspicion. I'd never given out my unlisted phone number to anybody and had spoken only of where I worked, not where I lived.

And I hadn't seen a soul from the Fletcher Primary Center since we exploded in our various directions on the last day of class in June.

Which left Annie Vanderwoek, my friend from cooking class. I remembered with belated perception a minor incident which occurred the Monday night before I left. I was carrying my garbage down the hall when I ran into Millicent and Tortilla heading out for their evening constitutional. Millicent gave me a big broad wink and stage whispered loudly, "Have fun at your parents' house!" I laughed and turned just in time to see Annie Vanderwoek rounding the corner of the hall, with a strange, mildly puzzled expression on her face.

Of course Annie overheard Millicent. And as if to test me, that night Annie proposed an outing to Lake Geneva for the upcoming weekend. I hastily manufactured a date for the auto races with Andy Lamont. I couldn't remember mentioning Andy's Indiana trip to Annie, but she could have easily called him to check. And discovered that he wasn't due back in town for another two weeks.

Annie Vanderwoek, who heard Millicent Baer refer to an upcoming absence of mine, who preferred to come to my place or meet me somewhere for dinner or the movies and had only once invited me to her own apartment, who was "not allowed" to take personal calls at work, and who had appeared out of nowhere at the second session of my Italian cooking class and actively sought out my company.

Yes, it had to be Annie Vanderwoek, a woman I had grown to love and trust. Annie had waited patiently for somebody else to make the first reference to Prentiss Granger and then jumped all over it.

Annie Vanderwoek had sold me out.

First I called Hope College in Holland, Michigan, identifying myself as a personnel officer for IBM, checking the credentials of a secretarial applicant. Hope College had no record of her in any class between 1964 and the present. Then I tried Holland information, seeking the Vanderwoek Bulb Farm. There was no such thing. There were five different Vanderwoeks listed and I called every one of them. Nobody had any knowledge of a woman named Anne Vanderwoek.

That night I called Annie and invited her to join me for dinner the following evening. I thought she sounded a little nervous, but she agreed to meet me at my place after she got off work.

I took a certain immature pleasure in watching her squirm. She was edgy when she got to my place at six and two fast glasses of wine didn't mellow her out very noticeably. When we were choosing a restaurant, she was extremely deferential. She must have been going out of her mind with anxiety, wondering what I knew or suspected. I loved every second of it.

I chose a Szechuan restaurant which had recently opened nearby and burbled on a bit about Chinese regional cooking and how I had happened to recently learn about dim sum. I watched Annie closely and saw her fidget even more. So she knew about Chinatown. Then she knew it all. Good. That would make it more fun.

In my high school and college biology classes, I had discovered a rather inexplicable interest in dissection. Instead of being squeamish about the innards of fetal pigs and cockroaches, as I would have expected to be, I was absolutely fascinated. I felt just like that now.

Annie tried to keep the conversation light by talking about some woman in her office who had just been evicted because of her twenty-seven cats. I was having none of it.

"Why don't we go up to Holland next weekend?" I asked brightly, as we waited for our fortune cookies. "I've wanted to see that bulb farm for a hell of a long time now."

Annie wiggled uncomfortably in her chair. "Next weekend might not be so good," she mumbled. "My mother's been kind of sick these last few weeks."

On two previous occasions when we were scheduled to visit Holland, both trips had been canceled at the last minute due to illness in the Vanderwoek family. Sickly lot, those Vanderwoeks.

"Then how about the weekend after?"

She nodded without looking at me and just then the waitress came with a plate of fortune cookies and the check. I picked up a cookie, cracked it open and extracted a narrow slip of paper.

"Be wary of false friends," I pretended to read, with one eye on Annie and the other on the slip of paper. I watched a wave of shock pass down her body. "You will be betrayed by someone you believe you can trust."

I crumbled the fortune in one hand and looked across the table at Annie, whose eyes had grown wide and whose face was the color of a steamed Chinese dumpling. She was wringing her hands together and casting nervous glances everywhere except at me. "I should have gotten this fortune about two weeks ago, shouldn't I?" Her eyes widened but she remained silent. "Why'd you do it, Annie? Maybe I can understand a little better if you can only tell me *why.*"

"Do what?" Her voice cracked unexpectedly.

I stifled a chuckle. "Report on me to the FBI."

"I didn't. I don't know what you're talking about."

"Bullshit. Mel Sanford told me everything." I saw her eyes flicker at the mention of his name.

She looked down into her lap for a long time, then brought her bright blue eyes up to meet mine. "I didn't have any choice. They made me."

I remained the Woman of Steel, scalpel poised to determine just what made this particular specimen tick. I said nothing.

"I really do care about you," she said finally. "It wasn't easy."

"Well, it wasn't too damn easy on me either. So what did they have on you, anyway, that would make you do this? Who'd you kill?"

"Not here," she said, looking around nervously. "I'll tell you everything but this place is too bright. Can't we get out of here?"

"We could go to my place," I suggested poisonously. "So the rest of the folks at the office can listen in and save you the trouble of writing out a report."

"Please don't. Please."

So I paid the check and we went down the street into a dark quiet bar. In a booth at the rear, Annie Vanderwoek told me her story. It wasn't even a very noble one. She'd been busted with her boyfriend on mail fraud charges, on twenty-three counts of offering nonexistent merchandise through small ads in the backs of magazines. The checks from customers were never large, but there were always plenty of them. Annie and her boyfriend made offers that were literally too good to be true. And by the time the authorities in Philadelphia or Kansas City or Seattle were looking for one disreputable fly-by-night mail-order house, Annie and her beloved were setting up another scam halfway across the country.

All of which was fine until a snoopy landlord in Omaha happened upon a pile of uncashed checks Annie left out on the kitchen table, along with the accompanying orders for—and I loved this part—reducing shorts guaranteed to trim off pounds in minutes. Three months earlier the landlord's wife had been stung ordering a similar item from a box in Tallahassee. He called the cops.

Annie was granted immunity as a prosecution witness against her boyfriend with the understanding that the government might call upon her later to help in other matters. It had, and she was nicely remunerated for her efforts. My tax dollars had paid for that wooden shoe of Christmas tulips.

When I was sure she had nothing more of interest to say, I told her the FBI could pick up my bar tab and I walked out.

I never saw her again.

Chapter 15 _____

Even the resignation of Richard Nixon couldn't bail out that miserable summer for me. Never before had I bottomed out so totally emotionally.

There was, at first, a great deal of fuss and to-do about aiding and abetting, fugitive murderers, grand juries and the like, but Larry Cone was able to deflect most of that. I began to understand why Mafia chieftains so highly prize their *consiglieres;* the cost might be ridiculous, but the service they provide simply can't be measured in monetary terms. For example, I have no idea how long it might have taken me to shake loose my negative files and contact sheets without Larry Cone. I'd probably still be waiting, leaving hostile messages for Mel Sanford. But Larry Cone got them back within two weeks. True, they were horribly disorganized and there were ugly fingerprints on a lot of negatives, but at least nothing seemed to be missing. It was rather like being reunited with a dear relative who's been missing in action behind enemy lines.

As soon as I got everything in relative order, I set up my darkroom and spent a rainy weekend printing every negative I had of Prentiss Granger. I cadged a couple of joints from Andy Lamont, laid in provisions, turned off the phone and utterly indulged myself.

When I finished printing all the pictures of Pren, I tacked them all over the walls of my apartment, grouping them by Pren's various phases: prep school hell raiser, darling daughter, coed grind, concerned liberal, radical activist. But after a few days I grew tired of cohabiting quite so intensely with the ghosts of the Debutante Revolutionary. I took down all but half a dozen of my favorites, and those I framed. The rest I burned.

I worried quite a lot at first about the legal repercussions of being positively identified in the company of Prentiss Granger, but Larry Cone proved invaluable. He was able to fully exploit the twenty-four hours I had been held incommunicado, as various prosecuting attorneys grudgingly conceded that the FBI had done a merry tapdance all over my constitutional rights. In that sense, I was extremely lucky. I never did end up behind bars. But there was a lot of other rotten stuff going on, enough to make the victory ring rather hollow.

For example, I was mysteriously reassigned to a fourth grade at the Sawyer School, a jolly little hellhole on the near South Side where rival teen-age gangs had been leaving bullet-riddled bodies lying about like so many discarded dolls. Nobody at the Board of Education cared to accept credit for the transfer, but everybody agreed that it was a fait accompli, quite irrevocable and that I might just as well get used to the idea. I was permitted to go to Fletcher and retrieve my personal belongings under the watchful eyes of the building custodian. I took along Andy Lamont for brawn and moral support, but ended up leaving almost everything behind. It seemed the least I could do.

Throughout all this my family was not what you might call wildly supportive. Mel Sanford wasted no time in getting word to Daddy of my alleged criminal activities and Daddy reacted as enthusiastically as he might have greeted the news that I'd contracted genital herpes.

Nevertheless, by the end of July I was desperate to go home to Louisiana, where I could regress and pretend I was eleven again, a chubby innocent hanging around Cloretha's kitchen seeking handouts. I sought the simplicity and solitude of the former life where I had not been obliged to consider such matters as grand juries, capricious ghetto reassignments or birthing babies.

So naturally two days after I got home, Grandpa Hollingsworth died. It was certainly no surprise to anybody, inasmuch as he hadn't been out of bed in sixteen years, but it certainly blew my idea of quiet retreat all to hell and gone. Instead of being permitted gentle sanctuary, I was suddenly on display as a Bereaved Relation, with attendance at all funerary functions mandatory. And there were many, many funerary functions. Departed Hollingsworths are sent to the Promised Land in style.

People I hadn't seen or heard of in fifteen years popped back into my life and you can bet your camellia garden each and every one of them had been following the Prentiss Granger story for years. I felt pretty hypocritical about it, but the only way I was able to evade the questions was to feign intense grief at the passing of Grandpa Hollingsworth. I found myself talking a lot about what a fine, gallant man he had been. There are a lot of fine, gallant men in the South. They're the ones who live their entire lives wishing it were the nineteenth century.

All of my family assembled for nearly a week. Don came up from Baton Route and Little Eddie was over constantly from St. Francisville. Lee, of course, already lived right there in town. All came complete with wives, children and properly mournful expressions, which didn't fool me for a second.

I was appointed Governess at Large, with primary responsibility for seven raucous children between the ages of three and fifteen. It was a treat to be around kids who were reasonably polite, properly clothed, adequately nourished and passably educated. I was thrilled to discover that against all odds, several of my nieces and nephews had turned into avid readers, actually bringing along their own books. We baked cookies with Cloretha, played games, told stories and took nature walks around Weatherly.

It was really quite a lot of fun and I felt a certain nascent longing, the desire to have a child of my own, a son or daughter to rear and teach and love. I could understand a little better why Pren had decided to have and keep her baby this time. I also knew that the desire for filial encumbrance would pass within a week. It had happened before.

Beneath the genial dignity of wakes and services and reminiscences, an undercurrent of destiny and greed was swiftly flowing. It had long been a matter of public record that after Grandpa Hollingsworth passed to his eternal reward, Mama and Daddy would move out to Weatherly. At long last Daddy would attain his birthright and Little Eddie would waddle up to the position of Dauphin. But at 287 big ones, with hypertension he generally ignored, Little Eddie might easily predecease Daddy.

Which raised a lot of interesting questions about succession.

By logical succession, Little Eddie would have taken over Daddy's house in town, but he and Don were firmly entrenched in their respective hometowns and careers. This gave Lee first refusal on my parents' house and he jumped on it. Then, to my utter astonishment, I was informed at dinner one night that I was slated to take Lee and Jane's place when they moved.

"Now, Daddy," I explained patiently, "we've been through all this a thousand times before. I don't *live* here. And even if I were going to move back to Louisiana, which I don't have the slightest intention of doing right now, I already own a perfectly good house in New Orleans."

He stared at me a long time, then sighed deeply. "Well, all right then. But you ought to at least stop throwing away good money on rent up there. It's downright perverse of you not to get yourself a little place and start building some equity."

"You're right," I agreed so suddenly he dropped his praline in surprise. He beamed at me, visions of country cottages and duck ponds and black daily women swimming in his head.

When I returned to Chicago, I enlisted Maxine Lockford's assistance in Operation House Hunt. She talked me out of a co-op apartment, pointing out that I could rent out half a two-flat for enough to virtually cover my mortgage payment. I could get more room in an older building, enough for a permanent darkroom and a real dining room and a guest bedroom and a big cheerful kitchen. Suddenly I felt horribly cramped in what had always seemed a quite spacious apartment.

Within a month she found me a newly restored turn-of-the-century brownstone two-flat, three blocks off the lake on a quiet residential street. She introduced me to a congenial banker who arranged a reasonable mortgage and produced a young German couple delighted to rent the upstairs apartment immediately. On the day I signed the papers Maxine (as I was calling her since our relationship had become professional as well as personal) took me to a celebration dinner on the ninety-fifth floor of the Hancock Building. It's no wonder she has an office full of sales awards.

Somewhere on the planet during the first week of October, Prentiss Granger was scheduled to give birth to her second child. I could only hope that it was a safe and uneventful delivery; there certainly was no way to chat with her obstetrician or wire flowers. I hadn't spoken to her since we parted in Portland in June. I didn't know where she was or what name she was using.

The safe deposit key had been returned one Sunday by an unfamiliar woman who slipped in beside me at a matinee of *Conrack,* delivering instructions to fetch $20,000 by the following weekend. At considerable inconvenience, I managed to get the money and at the appointed assignation in the ladies room at Pizzeria Uno (my choice) I passed it along to the same woman. This had been right before I went to Louisiana.

But I still wasn't able to speak directly to Pren. I gave the courier a new code word, "Nightmares" and a list of four new pay phone numbers where Pren could reach me. But then I went down South and by the time I returned and found a copy of *Fear and Loathing on the Campaign Trail '72* in my accumulated mail, the assignation it arranged was long past. There was no further word and it was not until much later that I learned a copy of *Been Down So Long It Looks Like Up to Me* went inexplicably astray in early September.

Right around the time I estimated Pren to be huffing and puffing away in labor, I moved to my new home in an unseasonably chill and blustery wind. Andy Lamont proved invaluable throughout the entire move, forever ready to lend a hand, pack a carton, lift a chair, run out for a six pack.

Andy had become, through a process so gradual I barely noticed it happening, one of my closest friends in the world. It was a new experience having a male friend and I rather liked it. Men had always been adversaries of one sort or another before. They were brothers who patronized me or friends' beaux who tolerated me or strangers who ignored me. They rarely treated me as a thinking, feeling human being.

But Andy not only treated me as a person, he seemed to regard me as a Woman of Commitment Making a Difference. He was proud of my teaching accomplishments and could understand the frustration and anger I so often felt. We found ourselves alternating support and appreciation for each other's thankless jobs. When his ADC mothers were driving him bug-eyed with their eternal pregnancies and oddly misplaced priorities, he knew he could explode at me and I would understand and fix him a special dinner and soothe him through the crisis. When my students made me so furious that I yearned to kill every human below the age of twenty, he always knew where a Marx Brothers retrospective was playing. When we both felt totally discouraged by the hopelessness of making any significant difference, we could get drunk together and blot out our respective ghettos. We could say things to each other that would have sounded callous and racist to anybody else and know they would be understood and forgiven.

There was an unspoken agreement between us that we were friends who would not be lovers, and that helped too. Andy was forever getting crushes on the wrong kinds of women and I nursed him through the inevitable hurts and rejections. I even told him a little bit about Mike Donovan, and though I tried to make light of the affair, I knew he understood the depth of my pain. He even managed to make me laugh a little about it, which represented a quantum leap forward.

Indeed, being able to laugh with Andy was one of the most rewarding aspects of my life. He was a natural clown who could so uncannily impersonate a ghetto pimp teetering along on silver platform shoes that I'd laugh till my sides hurt. He was a ready audience on whom I perfected many of my best stories and routines. His working-class background was so different from mine that merely in the process of recounting our separate life stories we spent what seemed like months in helpless laughter. We would regularly get stoned and listen to the *National Lampoon Radio Hour,* howling at tributes to "El Allende, the Dead One" and the exploits of Craig Baker, the nineteen-year-old Perfect Master from Champaign-Urbana.

That fall I was the one making the heavy withdrawals from the favor bank, however. My fourth-graders at the Sawyer School could not read, compute or in some instances write their own names. Several of them already carried knives. They did not understand a classroom without corporal punishment and for the first two months I struggled daily with discipline problems.

And when I came home sweaty and exhausted and infuriated at the end of each day, Andy's support and encouragement was all that kept me tough enough to go back and face it again.

That fall was one of the busiest, most frantic periods of my life, between the Sawyer School and moving. I had grossly underestimated the complexity of taking possession of real estate, the hassles of buying appliances and waxing floors and haggling with utility companies. I left several rooms totally unfurnished at first, despite Mama's offer to ship me some of the excess furniture accumulated in the St. Elizabeth Shuffle. I declined with polite shudders; the last thing on earth I wanted was a bunch of pippy-poo end tables and rickety side chairs and fussy porcelain lamps with fringed shades.

When I had finally settled in, I discovered that the combined exertions of moving and the Sawyer School had melted away nine pounds. I decided that my weight was the one remaining part of my life I still controlled, and that it was time to slim down for good.

Andy and I joined Weight Watchers together, and while he pooped out quickly, I persevered. I learned to immediately stuff any leftovers down the disposal, drew upon my lifelong perusal of weight loss guides to construct my own foolproof diet and stripped the larder of my huge new kitchen to the bare essentials.

Andy cooperated fully. He'd been through enough diets himself to know the agony that can be caused by watching an unfeeling friend pour butter on the popcorn or mound Reddi-Whip on a banana split. He always made it a point to eat before he came over, bless his pudgy little soul.

He was also kind enough not to snicker as he helped me assemble an exercise bike, which I set up in one of my empty little rooms, and sometimes he came over and used it himself. He complimented me often on the progress I made, and from one fatty to another it was glorious encouragement indeed.

All in all, things were swimming along rather nicely. And then a big fat toad got dropped into my garden. Right before Thanksgiving, a letter arrived from Shirley Granger, with a return address in Columbia, South Carolina. Her mother had been through two major cancer operations in the past eight months. She would have written herself, but was no longer able to manage a pen.

Iris Prentiss Granger was dying. And she wanted only one thing before she left this world: to see her daughter Prentiss again.

I called Shirley from a pay phone on Saturday morning, noting as I left the house that I had company again. She picked up the phone breathlessly on the seventh ring. "Hello?"

"Go to the phone booth," I instructed tersely in a very southern accent. "Take a lot of change with you. Leave right this minute and call this number." As I spit out the ten digits, I fervently hoped that Shirley possessed at least a fraction of the quickness and cunning so evident in her father and sister.

"Wait!" she wailed. "I don't have a pen. And I can't leave now anyway. My hair's wet." It was a very small fraction, if it existed at all.

"Put on a goddamned hat," I snapped. At least she hadn't asked who was calling. I wasn't sure, however, if that was because she knew or because she just hadn't gotten around to it yet. It had often been hard for me to believe she was blood kin to Prentiss Granger. *"Now* do you have a pen?"

"Yes'm."

I chuckled involuntarily at her automatic manners, then recited the number again and hung up. I had long ago memorized the numbers of several convenient booths I didn't ordinarily frequent, in preparation for just such an emergency. It was pretty damn chilly as I paced down Broadway, but my shadow and I were both warmly dressed. The phone Shirley would be calling hung on an interior wall of a struggling little natural foods grocery, where a fellow with two braids was packaging millet behind the counter. I wandered up and down the aisles, remembering fondly the winter I had worked my way through *Beard on Bread* and *The Tassajara Bread Book.* Those days were gone forever.

When the phone rang, I grabbed it before the pigtailed clerk could even move. "Yes?"

"I'm in a booth," reported Shirley Granger. I was proud of her for not identifying herself.

"What's the number?" I wrote it on a slip of paper. "Stay right where you are." I hung up and left the store, nodding pleasantly to my shadow as we set off again.

I walked three blocks toward the lake to Narahara, a Japanese restaurant where I knew the phone was inside the ladies room. I fed a bunch of quarters into the phone and sprawled in a large comfortable armchair.

She picked it up on the first ring. "Yes?"

I was pleased. If she could at least mimic, there was hope.

"This might *possibly* be a clean connection," I told her cautiously. "But we can't assume that it is. Please be very careful what you say."

"Isn't this all a little silly?" I could practically see her perfect little face pouting prettily.

I tried to disguise my irritation. Did she really think this was a game? "For the past two and a half years, my phone has been tapped. My mail arrives late, sloppily resealed, even solicitations to help save the lives of baby seals. I'm not paranoid. I'm just realistic. Now. Tell me about your mother."

She gulped a little bit. I realized suddenly that her mother was dying and that the situation would probably have been pretty hard on Shirley even if she didn't have a sister on the lam. But her voice only caught a couple of times as she reported briefly on the course of what was clearly Iris Granger's final illness. It didn't sound too likely that she would survive until Christmas. Shirley thought that the only thing keeping her alive was a dream of seeing Pren again.

When she finished, I spoke gently. "I'm sorry. And I really mean that, Shirley. But I don't know what to tell you. I don't have any idea where Prentiss is. And even if I did, they're hoping that I'll lead them to her. I'm being watched all the time. We can assume that they read your letter to me and we can also assume that they've known about your mother's illness for a long time. They'll be watching me like crazy. They'd be stupid not to. Does your father know you wrote to me?"

"No. Mama made me promise not to tell him."

"But he must suspect if she's been talking about it. Listen, I can make some phone calls, but for all I know, she might be in Abu Dhabi. You must have heard about San Francisco."

Shirley barked a short, bitter and most unladylike laugh. "Of course. It was all Daddy talked about for months. I was living at home last summer, you know."

"Tell you what. I'll put out feelers. But don't count on anything. Would it help if I came and saw your mother? I could tell her that it's impossible. Maybe it would help if it came directly from me."

Shirley was quiet for a moment, then spoke softly. "I was going to ask you to come anyway. But I didn't know how you'd feel about it after last time."

"I'll come," I answered quickly. "I can stay at a hotel in Spartanburg and sneak over during the day. I'm a very good sneak. But remember, this conversation is probably being monitored anyway. So they'll know and tell your father. I'll call you later this week at home, as if we hadn't spoken today."

"What do I tell Mama?"

"That I'm going to try to get a message to her daughter. And that if she wants me to succeed, not to tell her husband. Okay?"

"Okay."

After I hung up I dialed Jason Abernathy's office in San Francisco. I didn't really expect to find him in on a Saturday, but I guess radical attorneys work pretty hard. He remembered my name immediately, from when Larry Cone had spoken to him back in August. I explained the situation, well aware that his office line was probably monitored.

"So what do you want me to do about it?" he asked.

"Just put the word out, that's all. I'm going to call a bunch of folks anonymously and just leave a basic bare-bones message. I figure she must have been in touch with somebody."

"Don't be so sure," he warned. "If she's really burrowed in, could be she's gone solo, particularly if she managed to glom onto some cash. She's not very popular in a lot of circles where she would have been welcome once upon a time."

"I know. But can't you at least try?"

"Sure. But if you want to find her fast, maybe you should get the sob sisters on the story. You know, *Mother of Fugitive on Deathbed*. They're a prominent family and God knows Prentiss is a media favorite. I'd guess the only reason that kind of story hasn't already hit the wires is that the old fart is sitting on the local media. He's got enough clout to do that."

"In South Carolina, he's got enough clout to kill a reporter, not just a story."

Jason Abernathy laughed. I wondered what he looked like when he was laughing. I'd seen his photographs in newspapers and magazines, but they were always very serious, as if he carried the entire burden of the radical left on his narrow shoulders. I suddenly realized that most twenty-six-year-old women were not on joking terms with important criminal defense attorneys in Texas, Chicago and San Francisco.

After getting Jason Abernathy's assurances that he'd put the word out, I hung up, went back into the chilly late morning and walked around for two hours. I figured at the very least, I could give my operative a little exercise while I planned my strategy. Might as well keep my tax dollars at work.

Eventually I hopped on a downtown bus and lost him in Marshall Field's. Then I took a series of cabs to different hotels on the off chance that they had a double tail on me. When I was satisfied that I was alone, I dusted off my sense of irony and caught one last cab to the Conrad Hilton, where it had all begun six years earlier.

I went into the Haymarket Restaurant for a salad and some wine while I compiled a list of likely people to contact about Prentiss Granger. I knew very few of them personally, which made the project simultaneously easier and harder. I listed everyone I could think of who had known or worked with Pren since her senior year at Duke. There were a lot of names, but I knew I had very little chance of finding many of them. Even if they weren't politically oriented folk with assorted reasons not to list their names in phone books, the odds were enormous that most of them had moved a dozen times since I'd last known their whereabouts.

Andy and I had discussed this rootlessness of our generation just a few weeks earlier, as I settled into the house. "You know," he said, "you're about the only really interesting person I know who hasn't moved five hundred times in three years. And taken up half a dozen different occupations."

"You could look in the mirror and find another."

"I suppose. But really, think about it. People our age fall into one of two camps. Either they're totally straight and boring, or they spend every waking moment trying to figure out who they are and what they're doing and why."

"If you start taking on the accouterments of adulthood, you've got to act like a grown-up. And when you start accumulating *things,* it's a lot harder to just up and split for Key West or Vermont."

"Actually," he said, "it's probably a good thing for the economy that so many of us are like that. The antimaterialist wave of the sixties came along just in the nick of time. Imagine what a mess there would have been if everybody had tried to settle down and work right out of college. There never were nearly enough jobs for everybody. If all those Ph.D.s hadn't gone off to wait tables and grow organic rutabagas, there might actually have *been* a revolution."

But there hadn't, I reflected now as I added Bob McCoy's name to my growing list of one-time true believers.

When I had my lists organized by state and city, I got several pounds of change from the cashier and started working the bank of pay phones in the lobby. I allowed myself to think frequently about the 1968 Democratic National Convention and the ghosts of dreams abandoned and denied, which still clung to the lobby. The Conrad Hilton was a good place to call from. It gave an otherwise noxious task a certain delusion of historical significance.

I used a totally standardized procedure on every call. Without identifying myself in any way, I asked for and was connected with the person I sought. If that person wasn't home, I asked to leave a message. Then I spoke fourteen words: *Prentiss Granger's mother is dying of cancer. She wants to hear from her daughter.* Message dispatched, I hung up immediately.

I disguised my voice for everyone, attempting to sound like a long-distance operator from Mobile. I wondered, as I dialed folks like Lana Armstrong Layton and Marcy Miller, whether they would know immediately who was on the line. Frequently I was unable to locate people, particularly those Pren had known in the Bay area. The VETRAGE crowd had evaporated. There was a Marylou McCoy in Berkeley but no Robert. I found Adam Gerard in Atlanta. I referred to "Barbara Bellamy's" mother when I called Laura Berg in San Francisco. I saved the most obvious people till the end, Elaine and Margo in Portland and Mike Donovan in Vancouver.

Yes, that's right. I called Mike Donovan. If Mel Sanford was obliging enough to supply his current hometown, the least I could do was follow a perfectly logical lead. I was actually fairly certain that Pren had gone to Canada. I knew she could buy papers if she wanted, that the apparatus for assuming a permanent identity was all set up and that she knew just where to find it. I had left her less than three hundred miles from the border. So Mike was indeed the most logical choice. He might well know where to find her.

I almost hung up when I heard his voice answer the phone. It was a strangely clear connection, as if he were upstairs in the hotel rather than a continent away. I took a deep breath, said my fourteen words and smashed down the receiver.

It's funny how you can be getting along just fine, all scarred over, and then *BLAM!!!* that scab just gets blasted away and you have a raw, oozing wound all over again.

Chapter 16 _____

By the time I called Shirley on Tuesday night at home, I didn't need to suggest that she contact a South Carolina sob sister. The story was already running in newspapers from Bangor to Honolulu. After all, everybody had loved the Debutante Revolutionary before. There was no reason not to make a fuss over her again. And the story was a natural accompaniment of the events of the day. The Watergate Seven were standing trial in Washington, eight Kent State National Guardsmen had just been acquitted and Rusty Calley was once again on the streets.

"I didn't realize that girl reporter was actually going to write it all up like this," Shirley wailed. "Daddy is absolutely furious with me, but I didn't tell her anything she didn't already now. She seemed like such a nice girl too."

"It wasn't your fault. Jason Abernathy gave it to the press."

"Who?"

"He's a lawyer in San Francisco who didn't know where Pren was either. Do you still want me to come?"

"Oh please, Laurel," she begged, and so I made my reservations. I didn't want to have it on my conscience that I let Mrs. Granger die without knowing that her missing daughter was healthy and happy.

My connecting flight from Atlanta was delayed and I didn't reach the Spartanburg motel till very late on Friday night. I was too frazzled to sleep very soundly, so it was quite early on Saturday when I called Azalea Acres. To my intense relief, Shirley answered the phone.

"It's clear, Laurel, but hurry, please. Daddy's gone off to the mill this morning and Mama's nurse has the day off. Just drive around back to hide the car. If Daddy finds out I did this, he's going to absolutely kill me."

This December, I noticed, there were not any Christmas decorations. Shirley was out the back door and at my car by the time I had the engine turned off. As before, she appeared to have stepped off the cover of *Mademoiselle*, but this time her hug seemed quite genuine and it wasn't so difficult to return it. She assured me that her father wouldn't be back for several hours, until midafternoon at the earliest.

I was not prepared for the physical deterioration of Iris Granger. She seemed to be already quite dead. She had lost an enormous amount of weight, leaving folds of skin flapping loosely off her forearms and hands. Her brown eyes were sunken deep into the new furrows on her face and she wore a lace kerchief over what was obviously a wig. Replacements for her missing brows had been drawn in carefully.

She lay propped amid lace pillows on Iris Rose, the top of the line of the Granger Mills luxury sheet collection. I recognized the sheets from Marshall Field's; I always tried to keep abreast of new offerings from Granger Mills, though I refused to purchase them.

"Thank you for coming, Laurel dear," she whispered. Her voice was still mellifluous, though it had grown very faint. I wondered fleetingly if she ever drank anymore, if that nasty habit had departed after her first few bouts with chemotherapy. "Shirley is quite certain that Major Granger has no idea you were coming."

"Don't you worry about him," I soothed, moving nearer and taking one of her frail hands. Until I saw her I was uncertain just how much I could risk telling her. At the back of my mind I carried a slight wariness, a paranoid suspicion that my secret visit might simply be part of an elaborate ruse cooked up by Mel Sanford and/or the Major to get me to spill the secret goodies.

But this was obviously a dying woman. I made an immediate decision to tell her as much as I possibly could without incriminating myself or jeopardizing Pren's freedom.

Mrs. Granger lay in the same large bedroom she and the Major had shared in earlier days, still decorated in gold and cornflower blue with a wide bank of windows overlooking the presently dormant rose garden.

Despite the enormous size of the room, it seemed incredibly close and stuffy. A lot of hospital equipment was lying about, much of it disguised by fabric covers, as if to suggest, for example, that the oxygen tank was simply an oversized blender. Three space heaters were going full blast and it must have been ninety degrees. I began to swelter almost immediately, right around the time my nose started itching from the pollen in a dozen elaborate floral arrangements.

The place seemed like a dress rehearsal for the wake, complete to soft classical music playing from a radio on the dresser.

I rummaged in my purse for an antihistamine, stripped off several layers of Chicago winter clothing and settled in the chair beside her bed. Shirley showed me the buzzer to use if I needed help, quietly excused herself and closed the door as she left us alone.

Then I told this dying mother about the daughter she had never really known.

As I spoke, Iris Granger fixed her gaze on a picture on the nightstand beside her. Out of an ornate sterling silver frame smiled Prentiss Louise Granger, age eighteen, freshly graduated from the Greenwood Academy. Since that seemed to be the juncture where her mother had completely lost track of her, I began my narrative at Duke in the fall of freshman year, explaining how Pren's belief in racial equality and her extensive knowledge of military history had combined to draw her into the political activism that changed her life forever.

Vietnam and civil rights protests seemed very far away in that stuffy bedroom full of flowers, and at times I wondered if I were making any sense to her at all. But I forged on anyway.

I picked through the events of our college years, skipping such unpleasantness as the affair with Bob McCoy, the abortion and the Days of Rage. The picture I painted was rather a pretty one, really, of an idealistic and patriotic student distressed by her country's foreign policy and anxious to use any nonviolent means possible to change public opinion and the course of history. I laid heavy emphasis on Pren's academic achievements, which even as I recounted them struck me as awesome. As I explained just exactly how difficult it was to become a Phi Beta Kappa, I thought of the appalling waste of brainpower being perpetrated by Prentiss Granger's forced exile from society. Dammit, she was somebody who could have been and should have been making a difference. It was *wrong* that she had to hide and sacrifice all that potential.

I wondered if I might be tiring Mrs. Granger, but she shook her head firmly when I asked and begged me to continue. So I moved Pren to the Bay area after graduation and explained how she became involved with VETRAGE. I also revealed to her mother just how deeply Pren had loved Wilt Bannister, fabricating an intention to marry because it seemed both logical and appropriate. This new information touched her enormously. Tears poured quietly down her cheeks and she gripped my hand even tighter. And then I told her Pren's version of the shoot-out in Beaumont.

She made me go back over the Beaumont story several times, clearly puzzled and confused at the discrepancies among the media image of what had happened, the Major's interpretation via the FBI and the reality as recounted by the young woman who was actually on the scene. She wept again as I described Pren watching the man she loved blown away before her very eyes. Then I told her firsthand about the travesty that had passed for Randy Hargis's trial and how Pren had subsequently concluded there was no way she could ever hope to turn herself in and receive justice.

I told Iris Granger, as gently as I could, that there was no way in the world her daughter could ever come to visit her.

"But that Alpert girl came back," she whispered.

"That's different. She was wanted on so much less serious charges."

"Bombing is a serious charge." I was amazed that this invalid who had never cared about the world beyond Azalea Acres was so well informed.

"True. But you've got to believe me. If there were some way that Pren could come back, she would. You know, you were right a year ago. I did come here because she sent me." At that the sobbing began again, and I backed off a bit, announcing that Pren had assured me by phone of her continued superb health although (alas) I had been unable to confirm her condition in person.

Iris Granger wasn't buying it. She had seen the pictures from San Francisco and she thought that Pren looked perfectly horrible. I remembered Pren standing at Fisherman's Wharf announcing. *Even my own mother wouldn't recognize me.* How sadly wrong she had been.

"Well," I replied, choosing my words carefully, "Pren was always one of the most gorgeous girls I knew, even prettier than Shirley. For her to avoid being noticed requires a lot of work and plenty of camouflage. I reckon you produced two of the prettiest girls this state has ever seen. I have to keep pinching myself when I look at Shirley, she looks so much like a fashion model."

As if on cue, the beautiful Shirley Granger knocked gently on the door to announce lunch. Behind her lumbered Willie Mae, carrying a massive tray and wearing an equally enormous smile of greeting.

And there we sat, the three of us and our chicken salad, when Major Granger stomped up the stairs. I don't know why we didn't hear his car come in. Maybe it was the classical music or maybe I'd just stopped paying attention. At any rate, when I heard that unmistakable clomp approaching, it was like being bitten by a virulently venomous snake. I went into instant and total paralysis. For a desperate moment I considered lunging into the clothes closet, but there wasn't enough time even if I'd been able to move.

He swept open the door, stopped just inside the sickroom, and sent that familiar piercing gaze around the room. "I had a feeling we'd be seeing you again, young lady," he told me. Then he turned to the bed and his tone softened to a gentleness I hadn't believed him capable of. "And how are you feeling this afternoon, my dear?" He crossed the room in three strides, leaned down and kissed her wizened forehead.

Iris Prentiss Granger stared her husband straight in the eye, then beamed the warmest smile I'd seen on her face since I arrived. "I am feeling better than I have in months, John. I am tremendously touched that Laurel came to visit me."

He didn't look at me at all. "Then I'll leave you to your girl talk. Shirley, come with me."

Shirley's eyes widened but she said nothing as she stood and followed her father out of the room. My breathing didn't seem to stabilize for quite some time after they left.

When they were gone, Mrs. Granger closed her eyes for several minutes and I wondered if perhaps she had fallen asleep. Then she opened them again and smiled the same warm wide gentle smile she had given her husband. "I really meant that, Laurel dear, what I told Major Granger. I know I'm not going to last much longer and you've given me something I desperately needed. You are a kind and generous girl to come to me this way. If God wills that I never see Tissa again, I will be more able to bear the pain because you were here. Now, tell me about yourself. And your dear family."

So I prattled on a bit about the Hollingsworths in general and Laurel in particular. I didn't really have to give much thought to what I was telling her, so I was able to concentrate fully on any noise coming from behind the bedroom door, like machine gun fire when Shirley went before the firing squad. Alas, there was nary a peep for a full twenty minutes. Then I heard the Major clomping up the stairs again and braced myself.

His entrance was an exact repeat of his previous one. "I have sent Shirley to Spartanburg to retrieve your possessions from the hotel," he announced without preamble. "I will be most honored if you will spend the night with us here tonight."

I gulped and cast a side-long glance at Mrs. Granger. She looked as surprised as I felt. "I'd be happy to, sir. If you're certain it's all right."

"Anything that makes my darling Iris happy is not merely all right, young lady. It is absolutely imperative."

And so it happened that I got drunk with a retired military officer from the West Point Class of 1938 on a chilly Saturday night two weeks before Christmas in a study full of military history books in a pseudo-Georgian mansion in a small mill town in South Carolina.

God knows I didn't plan it that way. And neither did the Major, I'm sure. I think it was just that he had been under so much pressure for so long with his wife's illness and suffering that he no longer trusted his view of the world so absolutely. Into that chink I was more than willing to drive a little personal wedge. I was discovering, to my intense surprise, that I had actually *missed* the Major over the past four years. I remembered how much I enjoyed his presence in my adolescence, when we were silly teen-age girls on prep school vacation, how he always treated me with at least casual respect. Of course I knew that this was because he so cherished the intelligence of his daughter Tissa. Tissa who played chess by mail and was delighted to join him in the game room for fiercely intense rounds of Gettsburg or Blitzkrieg. Tissa who had spent so much of her youth closeted with ponderous historical tomes. Tissa who had accompanied him on a military tour of Europe in her thirteenth summer, visiting Omaha Beach and the Meuse-Argonne and that fateful field near Anzio where the Major had left his right leg in 1943.

The Major never did go back to the mill that afternoon. After I left Mrs. Granger for her afternoon nap, I slipped into Pren's old bedroom and sat by the front window, looking out over the peach orchards and trying to sort out the jumble of memories. But I wasn't there long before Shirley wound up the driveway in her burgundy Monte Carlo. Within five minutes of her arrival, she was knocking on my door, conveying the Major's compliments and asking if I could see my way clear to join him in the game room.

I took several deep breaths and followed her downstairs.

He had a tumbler of bourbon in one hand as he fiddled with the little soldiers on one of his war tables and he didn't look up at first when I came in. But as I stood there just inside the door, shifting my weight nervously, he suddenly pivoted to face me. "I won't bite, young lady. Come in and keep me company."

He led me into the study and refilled his glass from a George Dickel bottle on the sideboard. "Suppose I ought to offer you a drink," he said, almost to himself. "Girls drink in public these days, don't they? Libbers do, leastways. You a libber, Laurel?"

"I 'spect you'd consider me one," I told him. "In any case, yes, please, I'd like a drink. And this is not exactly my idea of public, except maybe for Public Enemy Number One. Me."

"Nonsense!" he thundered, handing me a glass and pointing to a brown leather chair beside the fireplace. As I perched nervously he lowered himself into the matching chair opposite mine and raised his glass. "To the past."

I clinked glasses, considering the irony and appropriateness of the toast. Here we sat in the largest private collection of history books I had ever seen, remembering past images of the girl who used to be here with us and the woman upstairs who would never really be here with us again. The present had nothing at all to do with Granger, South Carolina, and the waning days of 1974. Everything that really mattered was imprisoned in the amber of the past.

"It was good of you to come," he told me, after a few minutes of mildly uncomfortable silence. "Iris has seemed to lose all interest in everything these last few weeks. I was shocked when Shirley told me that she sent for you behind my back. Iris should know that I wouldn't deny her anything. Particularly now."

"I'm sorry she's so ill," I responded lamely. "I was happy to come if I could reassure her at all. This must be terribly difficult for all of you."

"I'd cut off the other leg and both arms to get that lady well again," he said gruffly.

I couldn't help myself. I burst into tears. The sentiment was so fierce and yet so credible, so violent and yet so caring. I believed him absolutely. Even so, as he passed me a handkerchief and discreetly looked away into the fire, I realized that I had committed a serious judgmental error in permitting myself to fall apart at such minor provocation.

I tried, therefore, to regain ground. "Sorry about the waterworks," I laughed, soon as I trusted my voice. "Guess my new automatic sprinkling system went off by accident, what with sitting so close to the fire."

He smiled and we were back on track. We must have been there for two hours, sitting by that toasty peachwood fire, drinking bourbon and reminiscing about old times. He did most of the reminiscing, actually, and most of the drinking too. I had no intention of losing control, so I nursed my drink carefully. Gradually I began to feel less trapped. We didn't talk about Pren at all, and we sidestepped almost all current events as well, save for his occasional mention of the imbecilic clayheads at OSHA and the EPA and one passing vitriolic reference to Jerry Ford's damn fool communistic amnesty program. That one made the hair on the back of my neck stand up, but he launched immediately into a discussion on Llewellyn's enthusiasm for the Point.

I finally pleaded exhaustion and begged for a nap, getting his solemn assurances that Shirley would rouse me in plenty of time for dinner. When she did, two hours later, it seemed like a whole new day, which was fine by me. I needed one.

We were an awkward three at dinner, a feast so high in calories that I had to will myself not to think about the damage I was doing to my diet. Obviously Willie Mae had knocked herself out in my honor—" 'Bout time we had a good eater around here," she had greeted me earlier—and I was delirious with joy at the prospect of such a spread.

Since I was not about to be the one who broke the taboo by mentioning the name Prentiss under the roof of Azalea Acres, I decided to grab the conversational ball and hang on to it for as long as possible. The Major seemed quite willing to laugh even at my B material as I told tales of house hunting and moving and dishwasher installation. Shirley had never really understood my humor, so I threw in a few bona fide jokes for her benefit. I swear I don't know when I found the time to eat, I was running my mouth so fast. A veritable one-woman show, it was. Lily Tomlin, move over.

The last traces of banana coconut cream pie were gone and we were on our third cups of coffee when Major Granger abruptly invited me into the study for a brandy. And that, of course, was that. After a full day of avoiding Topic A, we were finally going to confront the reason for my presence.

I went to bid good-night to Iris Granger, whose nurse had now returned and was coaxing her to finish a little sliver of pie. The nurse was a surprise, a lovely young redhead from Columbia who managed to give the impression that carrying bedpans was merely an amusing break from her customary duties as curator of the local art museum. The Major had to be paying her a bundle.

And then it was back to the study. My brandy was poured and waiting and it was not an insubstantial portion. It was also not even half as large as the one the Major was swilling. But even so, I managed to get quite totally smashed that night.

My memories of the evening are still slightly on the foggy side, with occasional clear patches. In one of those, I remember shamelessly pumping Major Granger for all of the gory details about his war injury and evacuation, an inquisitiveness I would never have permitted myself sober but one he actually didn't seem to mind a bit. In another I listened with rapt fascination as he described the annoyance and expense of getting "that slimy Bolshevik kike" Murray Levin out of Granger Mills. Murray Levin, it seemed, had all sorts of unacceptable ideas about brown lung and union representation, but he was not averse to turning a huge profit on his investment. In still a third, he reported on the unsuccessful South Carolina gubernatorial bid of the retired General Westmoreland, into whose campaign the Major had evidently pumped a fortune at the behest of their mutual good buddy Strom Thurmond.

And it was the Major's wistful references to Strom's wife Nancy that formed the inevitable segue to our discussion of Pren. Because Nancy Moore Thurmond had been a sophomore ADPi when Pren and I first went to Duke. Somehow over the years she had come to represent everything the Major would have preferred for the life of his own daughter.

And once he was on the subject, it was impossible to stop him. He went on at interminable length about where he had gone wrong raising Prentiss. I couldn't have stopped him even if I'd wanted to and actually I didn't really want to. A lot of what he was telling me was totally new information, glimpses into a childhood unlike any other I had ever observed or heard of. He was laying a lot of the blame for her later disobedience and disgrace on the fact that he'd raised her too much like a boy, an allegation I found absolutely incredible.

"Listen," I said finally, "you're doing yourself a tremendous disservice.

You raised a daughter with intelligence and a conscience and integrity, even if you disagree with everything she stands for now. Don't keep punishing yourself. Remember the good times."

I'd swear his eyes were moist when I staggered off to bed.

And because of our resuscitated friendship, it was Major Granger who insisted that I receive a copy, air mail special delivery, of the cassette which arrived the Tuesday morning after my visit, postmarked San Francisco and addressed to Iris Prentiss Granger.

Mama, it's a really terrible thing to learn that your mother is seriously ill by reading the newspaper, and I don't know quite how to respond to your desire to see me without hurting your feelings. I can't come, Mama. There's no way I'd be able to get to you without being intercepted, particularly since everybody in the country will be waiting to see if I show up. The fact is simple enough. I'm a fugitive and I will be for the rest of my life. There isn't any way I can expect to come back without being slapped in jail forever for something I had no real part in.

And I swear to you, Mama, it was all a horrible accident and mistake, that business in Beaumont. I was just in the wrong place at the wrong time. It's a horrible ugly mess that's been blown all out of proportion, but I'm stuck with it.

I'd like to see you at least as much as you want to see me. I've been thinking a lot lately about the bond between a mother and daughter and I'm not sure that we ever really took full advantage of the joys that should have been part of that bond. I regret that, a lot. I guess we got the patterns all set up wrong when I was young and there never seemed to be a way to get out of them after that. And, of course, I was always so close to the Major. It seemed like whenever he and I weren't together, I was studying.

Looking back, I'm not sure quite why I felt I had to learn so much, but I still find myself learning new things out of habit and a real desire to keep growing mentally. There's a certain risk in my kind of existence, beyond the obvious danger of being discovered and arrested. It's the risk of mental atrophy because there's so little way I can use the things I know.

But this is getting a little bit far afield from the purpose of this tape. I think I know the kind of scene you evision, Mama, with me coming into your bedroom and a lot of hugging and reminiscing and looking through the old photo albums, unless the Major burned all my pictures or something. Well, it wouldn't be like that at all. What would happen is that I'd be arrested and carted off to jail, probably up to Spartanburg because I'm supposed to be so dangerous. It would take Governer West maybe three seconds to sign an extradition order and they'd have me on a plane for Texas. I probably wouldn't even get to see you and there certainly wouldn't be any time to sit around and chat. I'm as sorry as can be that it's like that, but this wasn't my idea.

I do miss you, Mama, and I miss the house in Granger and Shirley and Llewellyn and Willie Mae and the others. Sometimes I sit and remember how beautiful it used to be when the peach orchards were in blossom and how tranquil and magnificent your rose garden used to be. I think of you in the rose garden on that little kneeling pad inspecting for aphids or walking along with that white basket over your arm cutting flowers for a bouquet. There are lots of those memories, Mama, good ones, and I savor them. Nobody can take them away from me.

I can't really forgive the Major for the way he's cooperated with the people who are trying to find me, but I do think that I can understand his reasoning. His behavior is consistent with his generally reactionary political beliefs and nothing is ever going to change them, I'm quite sure. If he hadn't taught me to think and question and analyze, I suppose I might have just accepted those ideas myself. And even though he probably feels that everything backfired on him, he should be proud that he taught me to stand up for what I believe in.

I'm thinking about you all the time, Mama, and I wish you comfort and peace and freedom from pain. Pay heed to your doctors and don't ever forget that even though I can't sit beside you, I'm with you in spirit.

I love you, Mama.

Chapter 17 _____

Two weeks later I got a present that I hadn't bargained on. On the Thursday before Christmas, Mike Donovan broke twenty-six months of silence. With a phone call from his parents' house in Bridgeport.

"I'd like to see you," he said. "I can't get away tonight, 'cause I just got in this afternoon and they're killing the fatted calf for me at this very moment. Any chance you're free tomorrow night?"

I had already accepted three invitations for the evening to follow. "I'm wide open," I answered without hesitation.

"I'll pick you up at seven, then, and we can go to dinner. Okay?"

"Sounds great." I gave him the address, hung up and collapsed onto my bed. So much for resolutions and good intentions and playing hard to get. Teddy bear tricks had never been my forte, anyway.

At seven the following evening, I had been ready for over an hour, munching nervously on carrot and celery sticks. I was scrubbed and scented with squeaky clean shiny hair. Since the impromptu haircut in San Francisco, I'd been wearing it relatively short in a modified natural. This was both becoming and a lot less trouble than trying to wrestle out the curl as I had for so many years. I had also spent forty-five minutes applying makeup so it looked as if I were wearing none. I wore snug and stylish black wool slacks with a matching sweater yoked in white and lime.

The pants were brand-new, an early present to myself because—Halle-lujah!!—I had shrunk an entire size. What's more, it was my second size reduction since starting the diet. I was no Bianca Jagger, to be sure, but I was no longer Totie Fields, either. I was, in fact, the lightest I had been since I was thirteen years old.

But pleased as I was with my appearance, I was still a dithering wreck by the time the doorbell rang at seven-fifteen.

He looked magnificent. His cheeks were all ruddy and a cream-colored wool stocking cap was pulled down over most of that thick dark hair, but the eyes were still sparkling and full of deviltry. As he came inside and shut the door behind himself, I panicked, wondering how I was supposed to greet him. I was starting to extend my hand when he came closer, gave me a hug and kissed me on the end of the nose. Then he backed off, removed his heavy dark green wool jacket and grinned at me. "You look fantastic!" he said. "You're a real sight for sore eyes, my love."

"Twenty-four hours in Bridgeport and he's brimming over with blarney." I was proud to be able to respond so flippantly.

He laughed. "Glad to see you haven't changed." He pulled off the stocking cap and ran his fingers through his hair. It was cut shorter now than I remembered. "This neighborhood sure has, though. I barely recognized it, coming through."

"How long since you've been here?"

"Three years."

"Well, no wonder! This part of town is just abooming, lad. Want something to drink?"

We were seated in the living room by now, him on the sofa and me on a side chair. He looked straight at me as he answered. "How about a Ramos gin fizz?"

My heart all but stopped. He had been drinking Ramos gin fizzes on the last day we were together in New Orleans, on the patio at Brennan's. "You're nine hundred miles too far north," I answered as lightly as possible. "Second choice?"

"Beer if you have it, or wine."

I went to the kitchen, poured his Heineken into a frozen mug and gave myself a generous serving of white wine. In a fit of uncontrollable nervousness, I inhaled the wine, realizing as the icy liquid jolted down my throat that I was fairly weak from hunger and could probably get smashed without even noticing. I poured a smaller portion in my empty glass and returned to the living room. And when I once again saw the physical evidence of Michael Brian Donovan leaning back comfortably on my very own sofa, I suddenly realized that this could turn into a very strange evening.

He raised his glass. "To New Orleans." We clinked glasses and drank demurely, just like a movie from the forties. Just like, dear God, just like me and the Major two weeks earlier. My life really *was* getting very weird all of a sudden.

"Nice place," he observed, waving an expansive arm. "Lived here long?"

"I just bought it in October."

He smiled gently. "It must be nice. Did you sell that place in New Orleans?"

Oops! Now I was going to sound like some loutish representative of the landed gentry. "No."

He was nice enough to let me off. "Show me around? The nickel tour?"

I stood up. "Three cents. Some of the rooms aren't furnished."

As we walked down the hall and in and out of various rooms, he stayed quite close to me. He was wearing some sort of very virile cologne which wasn't, thank God, musk oil. I chattered brightly about the house and my adventures in moving, routines which by now were some of my smoothest and funniest material. He loved it. He laughed and chuckled and guffawed and never got more than a couple feet away from me. I purposely didn't show him my exercise room.

At one point, as we stood in the kitchen, he gently laid his hand on my shoulder. I all about swooned. I had thought all day about how cool and distant I should be, but it was quite hopeless. I didn't want to be the least bit distant from him. I wanted to be as close as two people could get. As soon as possible. I felt weak and melty and I got us in and out of the bedroom in about three seconds out of fear that I might suddenly drag him onto the bed and make a total fool out of myself.

The restaurant he proposed for dinner had been closed for a year and a half. "I always seem to find myself in your hometowns," he said with a grin. "You better choose." So I suggested Narahara, the Japanese restaurant from which I had called Shirley Granger. I called and reserved a private booth for eight-thirty.

"How do you like Vancouver?" I asked, once the dinner arrangements were out of the way.

"It's a wonderful city. I'm inclined to stay there just as long as they'll let me. But how'd you know I was there?"

"Mel Sanford told me."

He raised his eyebrow. "The hell he did!"

"I believe he was trying to get a rise out of me. It didn't work."

He looked around. "We probably shouldn't talk here."

I laughed and waved a hand. "Oh, it should be safe enough. I have a debugging service. Honest. It's sort of like hiring a cleaning service or a handyman, I guess. Once a week, a guy shows up and makes a sweep through the house with a lot of odd equipment. My lawyer found him for me. I believe that most of his other accounts are in the Syndicate. I'm sure I seem very eccentric to him. He must think I'm a hopeless paranoid."

"Hardly. Paranoia's a healthy condition for somebody who lives your life."

We walked to the restaurant. It was a crisp, cold night with a few snow flurries in the air. Mike took my arm as we went down the front steps and never did let go when we hit the sidewalk. It was wonderfully exciting to be walking with a Dream Lover through Christmasy streets full of decorated store windows and blinking lights and glowing tree shapes behind apartment and brownstone windows. It was so nice, in fact, that I didn't even mind being followed by the shadow who had reappeared with the news of Iris Granger's illness.

When we were ensconced in our private booth at Narahara and had ordered, Mike lifted his glass of sake and looked at me. "It gave me quite a start when you called."

Oh, dear God. "What do you mean?"

He mimicked a drawl. "Prentiss Granger's mother is dying of cancer. . . ."

I held a hand up. "Please! Stop!" There was audible pain in my voice. Prentiss Granger's mother was too painful a part of my life to be spoken of irreverently at the moment.

He was instantly contrite. "Sorry, Laurel. Forgot myself for a minute. Anyway, it startled me when you called."

"You knew it was me? How?"

"Who else could it be? Anyway, there's a certain way you say 'Prentiss' that's very distinctive. I was sorry that you hung up right away."

"I had a lot of other calls to make. Let's not talk about it right now, okay? Or Pren either for the time being. Tell me about Vancouver, instead."

And so he did. It sounded like quite a wonderful place, actually, all islands and greenery and progressive-thinking people. And we talked about the ongoing Watergate trials and a lot of other neutral topics. We never did discuss Prentiss Granger.

When we finally left the restaurant it was nearly eleven, we were quite tipsy on sake and the snow flurries had gotten organized. There was about half an inch of snow on everything and it was coming down fast and furious. As we hurried through the relatively quiet streets, I wondered rather frantically what would happen when we got back to my house. There was no way I could win, I supposed. Either he wouldn't make a pass at me, in which case I would be mortified and crushed. Or he would. Then I would have to be either weak and willing or strong and stupid.

He made it very easy, rubbing his chilly hands together when we were back inside. "How about a fire? I was once a helluva Boy Scout. And maybe you could find us something warm to drink?"

Once again we were back in the forties movie, and it couldn't have happened to a more deserving lady. By the time I assembled two hot buttered rums, he had quite a nice little fire roaring in the living room. We sat down in front of it and sipped our drinks and the next thing I knew we were making love right there on the living room floor in front of the fireplace.

Mike stood in the doorway of my bedroom, dressed and nearly ready to leave. "When are you going to Louisiana?"

Christmas was the following Wednesday and I held Sunday morning reservations. "Tuesday," I answered, praying I could wiggle my way up a waiting list on some obscure flight and get home on time.

"Great. I don't suppose I'll get lucky twice in a row, but could I see you tomorrow night?"

"Well, I was supposed to go out to Maxine Lockford's for dinner, but she called this afternoon and canceled. Said she has a horrible case of the flu." Two questions, two lies.

He smiled. "Wonderful. I'll call in the morning." He crossed to the bed, where I sat wrapped in my eiderdown quilt, and kissed me. "Don't get up. I'll lock it on my way out. G'night, Laurel. *Feliz Navidad.*"

"*Joyeaux Noël,*" I answered, and then he was gone. I snuggled in the rumpled warmth of the bed where we had retreated when the living room grew too cold, even with the raging fire. I felt warm and happy and exhausted and was quite certain I glowed with pleasure.

It was the first time I had slept with anyone in my new home. It was, in fact, the first time I had slept with anybody *period* since I had been with Mike in New Orleans. I would, however, have cut out my tongue before admitting that, knowing how terrified he'd be to find that he totally dominated my sex life. And in any case, mine was not an unwelcome celibacy. I never even liked exposing my corpulency to my doctors, much less strangers. And nobody I knew seemed very promising love affair material, clandestine or otherwise. I did not count Gerald Howe, the twerpy Science Mobile teacher who persisted in asking me to join him for "cocktails." Andy Lamont was my dearest male friend in the world, but it would have felt like incest to sleep with him. And most of his friends were as sensually appealing as orange D-Zerta. So I slept alone and kept to my own devices, so to speak.

The next morning I called Maxine, discreetly explained the situation and begged to be excused. I wait-listed myself on eight different Christmas Eve flights and called my parents. I told them some college friends were in town unexpectedly, that I'd be arriving late Tuesday and would rent a car to get home.

Mike called at noon to report he'd be eating an early dinner with some old neighborhood buddies he was spending the afternoon with. "But listen," he said, "I have a feeling this is going to turn into a real long day. It'll be nice to have an excuse to cut out early."

"You can't leave a party they're having in your honor," I told him bravely, trying to avoid letting loose a scream of anguished pain which could have been heard in Bridgeport with no electronic assistance. "It's okay. I don't mind."

"Well, I do. You're leaving soon and I need to talk to you. These folks will still be here after you've left. Some of 'em haven't been out of Bridgeport in thirty years. I can get to your place by nine-thirty."

I wasn't going to try to argue him out of coming to see me, no sirree. "That'll be fine. See you then."

Mike was half an hour late and a little bit loaded. "I've been drinking Schlitz for seven hours," he announced. "What I really need now is coffee. I don't suppose there's a cappuccino joint around here somewhere?"

"Your number just came up. Let me get my coat."

We didn't talk much as we walked down Broadway, escort in tow. And he didn't bring up the meeting with his old friends till I pushed, after we were sipping our cappuccinos.

His old friends, he told me, were not quite as he remembered. The experience had proven most unsettling. "They kept sneaking looks at me as if I were strange, or different!" I noticed that the faint traces of his Chicago accent were far more pronounced after his sojourn on the South Side. "I don't feel strange or different. I feel normal, dammit! They're the ones stuck in their petty little lives and they don't even know there are other possibilities."

"A lot of people don't want other possibilities. They're threatened by them. They want everything to stay the same. Forever."

He shook his head. "I just forgot. It's so easy to get caught up in these little circles we live in so that you just plain don't remember how many people disagree with you. Like Kevin Dougherty, a guy I've known since I was in the second grade. Tonight Kevin said he thought Richard Nixon got a bum deal. Goddamn it, Laurel, how do you cope with idiocy like that?"

"You don't. You just let it roll right off you. I was at home last summer when the Trickster resigned, and the local newspaper editorialized that he was a coward not to stay and fight it out. My family runs the ideological range from John Birch Society to White Citizens Council. My father refers to my students as pickaninnies. The Hollingsworths think the Trickster's an incredibly brave man. Hell, he declared war on cancer, didn't he?"

His laugh was bitter. "And won the same glorious victory in that war that he did in Asia."

"Of course. But I don't try to discuss it with my family. I'd have better luck convincing them that Russell Long is a KGB agent. You just have to cover your ears and pretend it isn't happening. I don't really believe you can change people's opinions anymore."

We argued about what could and couldn't be changed, then, a warm, exciting and totally freewheeling exchange which reminded me of college. The cappuccino perked us both up.

After a while, he leaned across the table and lowered his voice. "I never quite got around to it last night, but one of the reasons I wanted to see you was to deliver some news."

"Let me guess. A grand jury just met in Tulsa and brought in a fifteen-count indictment against me."

"Sorry, not just yet. No, this is good news for once. You're a godmother. Of a little girl who was born on September twentieth. I don't know what her name is."

I tried to keep my expression totally blank and my tone extremely nonchalant. "Oh, really?"

He took my hand across the table. "Yes, *really*. I'd have thought you'd be a little more excited."

I gave his hand a squeeze and whispered. "I am. Of course. She's in Canada?"

He shook his head. "No place near. Don't know precisely where she is, actually. Somewhere in the Southwest. I drove her to Albuquerque last August and—"

I interrupted in shock. "You did *what?*! How? What happened?"

"She tracked me down and sent a friend to cajole me. Wasn't really doing anything at the time anyway. So I dropped out of sight in Vancouver and picked her up a couple days later in Portland. I left her in Albuquerque. She was just intending to stay there till she had the baby and then move someplace else permanently."

"So how do you know it's a girl?"

"The code was a postcard of either a man or a woman, dated when the kid was born. The picture on the card was Annie Oakley, as a matter of fact. And the entire message was 'Chickamauga.' That's a Civil War—"

"I know all about Chickamauga, thanks. I grew up in the Deep South, remember? Chickamauga was some rebel general's finest moment. Longstreet, I think, though I daresay it no longer matters. How very typical of her to pass the date along that way. Miss Military History rides again. Well, I appreciate you taking the trouble to tell me in person."

"That was my instruction, babe. To get word to you, but only in person. After San Francisco, she was awfully wary of any other way."

I thought of Prentiss Granger, Yenta at Large, setting up my preChristmas assignation, and sent a prayer of gratitude and thanks silently flying across the continent.

"So she told you about San Francisco?" He nodded. "It was pretty horrible. I thought they had us for sure."

"I believe she mentioned something about you hurling cabbages at FBI agents in the kitchen of the Hong Kong Tea House."

I laughed. "It sounds like a Mel Brooks movie when you put it like that. But it sure didn't seem like one at the time."

"Tell me about it."

"I thought Pren already did."

The Irish eyes twinkled and the blarney flowed like honey across the table. "She can't tell a story the way you can and you know it, Laurel. She's a thinker, not a talker."

And so I told him all about our San Francisco adventures. It was the first time I had ever been able to tell the entire story to anyone and it felt really nice to be able to finally share it. I felt much better now that I knew Pren and the baby were all right. *I've been thinking a lot lately about the bond between a mother and daughter,* she had said in the tape to Iris Granger. I should have known then.

I told him about Iris Granger and my strange interlude with the Major two weeks earlier. He looked at me in surprise. "I thought you told me the old goat was a despicable Bircher who's been trying to sell out his own daughter for years."

"Well, I did. And he is. But I like him anyway. Think of him as another permutation of your friends in Bridgeport."

We went back to the house and we made love again. This time it was even nicer, since the strangeness and fear of the previous night had worn off. I wasn't really expecting anything beyond Tuesday, but I figured I might as well accumulate one hell of a nice memory while I had the chance.

"Big day tomorrow," he told me as he dressed to leave. I was still in bed, with the covers bundled up around me. It was damn cold all of a sudden. "For the first time in ten years, yours truly is attending eight o'clock mass. I told my mother I'd go *once* now and then at midnight Tuesday and that was that. So she decides it has to be sunrise. Then around eight hundred seventy-three of my relatives, down to great-uncles and fourth cousins, will appear for Sunday dinner at high noon. And as soon as I can get away after that, I'm going out snowmobiling with a couple of the guys I saw today. Want to come along?"

I'd have been willing to accompany Mike Donovan to a demonstration of medieval torture techniques. "Sure. Sounds like fun."

And indeed it was. His friends were nice enough, and their wives seemed almost jealous of me. They appeared to have pretty dismal lives, full of new cold-water detergents and Engelbert Humperdinck. I didn't mind a bit if they thought Mike and I were in love. It was at least half true.

And so the last few hours went. Mike was charming and sexy and clever and a wonderful audience. I don't think I've ever had quite as nice a Christmas present as his appearance that December.

And I even made it to Louisiana by Christmas, though it was a cliff-hanger for sure. I took my bag out to O'Hare at 7 A.M. on Tuesday and hung around every waiting flight until 3:45 when at the very last minute I was allowed aboard a 727 for New Orleans. It was long past dinner when my rental car wound up the long Weatherly drive, but I had made it home in time for Christmas.

And that night as I lay in my nineteenth-century bed, I thought of Mike Donovan, nine hundred miles to the north at midnight mass with Hizzoner da Mare. I thought of Iris Granger, six hundred miles to the east and two weeks from death. I thought of Prentiss Granger, a thousand miles to the west with her infant daughter.

And I thought of Laurel Hollingsworth, the girl she had been and the woman she had become. She was smart and shrewd and skinny and competent and rather to my surprise, I found I liked her.

Book Three

*The difference between selling out and pragmatism
is whether you're passing judgment on somebody else
or justifying your own life . . .*

—L. David Fairbanks, Jr.

Chapter 1 _____

"If you had tried to tell me ten years ago that you and I and your illegitimate daughter would be riding through Taos in a six-year-old Chevy pickup the day before the American Bicentennial—and that the reason we'd be in New Mexico was because you were a federal fugitive on murder charges—I'd have sworn you were completely bonkers. I must be getting more flexible in my old age. Somehow it seems quite reasonable."

As we jostled down the quiet road toward the Taos Indian Pueblo, I looked past Melinda Cartwright, age twenty-two months, at our driver, Mrs. Janet Cartwright, née Prentiss Granger, CB handle Lucky Lady. The resemblance between the two was startling. The limpid brown eyes were identical, as was the deep golden hair, cut in similarly tousled styles with feathery bangs. True, Pren's came straight from the bottle, but it looked every bit as natural as the chestnut mane of yesteryear. In fact, she looked absolutely terrific. She'd lost every gram of extra weight from her pregnancy and was tanned darker than I could ever recall. Best of all, since denim represented haute couture in the Southwest, she was back in blue jeans again, having burned, or rather melted, every polyester item she owned.

She laughed. "I'd never have suggested it. And if I'd thought at all about where I was going to be today, I'd have said the Northeast, teaching introductory history somewhere while I finished my dissertation for Harvard or Yale." She pushed the radio button and the plaintive wail of

Willie Nelson filled the cab. I winced. No matter how convincingly Pren explained that country and western music was the logical accompaniment to the southwestern ethic of space and independence, it still sounded like the same caterwauling I'd hated my entire lilfe.

I adjusted the volume. "At least here nobody's making a big fuss about the Bicentennial. I swear, I burned out on it before the year even started. If I see another bicentennial jockstrap or roach clip, I'm likely to defect to Moscow. Why, I didn't even like *Bicentennial Nigger,* and you know I think Richard Pryor's the funniest man alive."

She shrugged. "There's no reason for anybody to care here. Two hundred years is practically current events. The Spanish were all settled in long before the Pilgrims ever heard of the *Mayflower.* And the Indians have been here eight hundred years, since before the Crusades." She turned into the parking lot at the pueblo. "Ready to play Ugly American?"

It was a role for which we'd evidently have a huge supporting cast. The parking lot was jammed with station wagons and campers from Iowa and Texas and California. Paunchy men in plaid Bermuda shorts posed bored children against a backdrop of Winnebagos and the incongruously rising pueblo. As we picked our way among the broken beer bottles and discarded Coke cans, I felt ashamed to be disrupting what should have been a serenely private Indian morning.

There was an undeniable beauty to the five stories of dusty adobe framed against a vibrant azure sky and majestic Taos Mountain, but still I felt incredibly intrusive. I couldn't decide which offended me more, the loud gawking turistas or the pandering curio shops offering utterly uninspired craft items. I wasn't even interested in the local flat bread, fresh from outdoor clay ovens. I tried to read the impassive faces of the few Indians we encountered, unsuccessfully.

"I'm hungry, Mommy."

"Okay, honey, we'll go eat. You don't mind leaving, do you, Lou Ann?"

"I thought you'd never ask."

We drove down a narrow road up into the mountains. "It's a shame I can't take you to one of the more interesting Indian communities," Pren apologized. "but I really think it would be better to keep our vacation separate from what I'm doing on the reservations."

What she was doing was compiling an oral history of the Navajos from interviews she'd been conducting throughout the Southwest. "I don't really mind. I'd hate to blow your cover. But God, Janet, that pueblo seems so hokey somehow."

"It wouldn't if you got rid of all the junky souvenirs and yahoo tourists. It's just too accessible. Once you get back into some of the more remote areas everything is a lot more authentic. You saw those transcripts I brought along. It's an entirely different world."

"Doesn't it make you nervous being out in the open that way?"

She howled. "Out in the *open*? Lou Ann, there's no way in the world that anybody's going to know who I am. I've talked to a couple of guys who are younger and more political, but most of the people I've seen are truly out of another world. The closest they get to modern civilization is booze. And anyway, when I talk to them it's all focused on *their* lives and histories, not mine."

"Don't try to tell me you just sauntered onto the reservation, cool as a cucumber, and whipped out your tape recorder without even thinking about who you were. 'Cause I won't buy it."

"Of course not. But the only time that was rough was at the beginning, when I didn't know exactly what I wanted to be doing there. I guess I had visions of whipping the old reservation into tip-top shape and getting everybody nice and organized. Which of course was ridiculous. It took me a long time to realize that the best thing I could do for these people was also the one thing that was easiest for me, as a historian. To let them tell their own stories. Once those stories get exposed, then maybe other people will be interested enough to do the nitty gritty."

I shook my head. "Well, maybe the interview part doesn't expose you, but you can't tell me that nobody's going to notice when you publish a book. Even as Janet Cartwright."

"Come *on*! It's just a little university press. And it's hardly the kind of book that winds up on paperback racks in airports. Outside the Southwest, nobody'll ever be aware of the book, much less its author. Well, here we are. The rest is on foot."

She strapped Melinda into a papoose carrier on her back. I carried a backpack filled with food, lagging behind shamefully as Pren and Melinda charged up the trail. I considered myself reasonably fit and was still relatively skinny, but I thought I'd expire of exhaustion by the time she rounded a final bend and we came out onto a ridge overlooking the Sangre de Cristos.

"My God, this is magnificent!"

She twisted out of the carrier and let Melinda down. "I was hoping you'd like it. I used to come up here when Melinda was a baby. Of course, she weighed about sixty pounds less then."

Some two years earlier, Pren had arrived in Albuquerque as the pregnant widow of an Allentown, Pennsylvania, shoe salesman killed in a head-on collision with a drunk driver. Because her parents had died several years earlier in a plane crash and she was quite alone, Janet Cartwright had decided to flee her painful memories and begin life anew with her expected baby. A few months after Melinda's birth, the Cartwrights moved to Tucson, where they presently lived in a rented adobe bungalow in a middle-class neighborhood.

As we unpacked chorizo, queso fresco and ice cold Dos Equis, I offered a small prayer of thanks that Pren had passed out of her vegetarian phase. Melinda lustily gobbled corn chips loaded down with salsa, her taste buds far more inured to the fiery peppers than mine.

"It's so great to feel safe with you," I said between bites. "You know, I still have nightmares now and then about San Francisco."

"So do I. But you're right about the safety. Once I started working on the book, I started to feel I *was* a different person. Plus I think that Melinda has really given me a new identity in more than just the obvious way."

Melinda beamed at her name, never missing a stroke as her little hand pumped corn chips into her mouth.

"She's a wonderful child. I can't tell you what a treat it is to see somebody doing the mother job properly for a change." I came in contact with far too many students whose home life was absolutely unspeakable, and those parents trying to raise their children properly were still cramped by poverty and ignorance and crime.

"It doesn't feel like a job, but in a sense I guess you're right. Till I started the book, I didn't do a damn thing except take care of her."

"Well, it shows." And indeed it did. Melinda possessed a remarkable disposition. She didn't seem to be bothered by anything. She was cheerful, inquisitive and extraordinarily verbal, a little girl who just might grow up and change the world. And sure enough, when it was time to leave half an hour later, Melinda knew without being told that we would carry out all our trash.

*   *   *

I had told Pren I felt safe, and two years after the nightmare in San Francisco, the government seemed to have forgotten me altogether. I still sneaked out of Chicago under a phony name, of course, and had arrived in Albuquerque via Seattle. And I still had Marty Delvecchio sweep my brownstone monthly for electronic bugs. But it was mostly just force of habit by now.

Even so, I automatically checked to be sure we weren't being followed later that evening when we left our Santa Fe motor court. We had dinner at a charming Mexican restaurant where Pren claimed to have once seen John Ehrlichman, then went back to the motel and turned on the TV so Pren could get the latest details on the Israeli commando raid into Uganda. Melinda conked out almost immediately.

"God, this is so exciting!" Pren's eyes fairly glistened. "It's exactly the kind of military raid I used to fantasize when I played war games with the Major. I bet he's getting a hell of a kick out of it too."

I wrestled with a bottle of wine and the corkscrew on Pren's Swiss Army knife. "I just wish they'd gotten Idi Amin while they were at it. He's such a giant blot on the image of obesity."

Actually, my interest in what went on in the nation and the world had dwindled sharply over the past couple of years. The current events of the sixties had been pivotal to our lives in a way that those of the seventies were not. I no longer felt that things that happened outside my own narrowly proscribed world really mattered. It had been possible to genuinely loathe and despise both Lyndon Johnson and Richard Nixon, but it was difficult to muster any reaction more intense than indifference to Jimmy Carter or Gerald Ford. When the issue was whether my friends and relatives would be asked to die in Southeast Asia, I could feel directly involved in a way that I couldn't about Angola.

So when Pren carried on about national or international affairs, I had a tendency to tune her out. I lay back on the bed sipping my wine, thinking how nice it was to hear her prattle on again. It was almost as if it were 1967 again, before we had fears or enemies or limitations. The San Francisco experience had left the sort of nasty acrid aftertaste you get from inferior brands of diet soda, and it was nice to finally wash it away with fine zinfandel.

I did, however, perk up when she started sputtering about the trial and conviction of Patty Hearst. That was one story I *had* followed, with almost religious zeal.

"It's ironic," she growled, "that a family with enough money to buy a platoon of defense attorneys for their prodigal daughter gets screwed for picking the one who's supposed to be at the top of the field. A pair of legal aid lawyers fresh out of law school could have done a better job. Every inch of the way, F. Lee Bailey blew it."

"It wasn't the easiest case to defend," I reminded her. "There were a few awkward little details, like that missing year and a half and spraying bullets into that store in L.A. and kidnapping that kid in L.A. and the guy who saw her pick up her ammo at the Hibernia Bank."

"Regardless, it was a travesty. I hope to God that if I ever stand trial I can at least count on my lawyer to do his job. If they ever catch me, I want Jason Abernathy."

"If they ever catch you, you'll run your poor lawyer ragged."

"Maybe so. But at least I won't rat on my friends. Hey, look! It's midnight. Happy birthday, America."

I raised my wineglass. "To the land of the free, and may you stay that way forever."

After huevos rancheros the next morning, we took Melinda down to a nearly deserted park near our motel. While she dug in the sandbox, Pren and I sat on a nearby bench. I was already sweaty at nine A.M.

"What are you going to tell Melinda about her father?"

"That he was a shoe salesman in Allentown, Pennsylvania."

I wrinkled my nose. "Do you think she'll be satisfied with that?"

"She'll have to be. I certainly can't tell her the truth."

"Not ever?"

"Not ever. I'm locked into this identity now, after all. And unless something happens so that I have to change that, there's no reason for her not to believe who we are."

"Don't you ever wish you could share her with her father?"

She looked at me with a strange expression. "Are you trying to worm his name out of me again? You promised you wouldn't."

"I know. And I'm not, really, though I have to admit that I'm absolutely dying of curiosity. I don't see why you can't tell me."

"Because nobody can ever force you to say something you don't know, that's why. But I don't guess it would hurt to tell you a little bit about him. He was the guy who owned the land where I was hiding out in Northern California all that time. He wasn't even really very political, which was a big part of his appeal to me. Everybody else I was with during that time was so goddamned kinetic, they practically crackled when they moved. That was why I started doing all the farm chores, to be by myself. Being with him was nearly the same as being alone, 'cause he hardly ever said a word. The silence was so pleasant I got to be a lot fonder of him than I probably would have otherwise."

"Well, if he was so apolitical, I don't understand how he happened to be harboring the likes of you. Particularly since I seem to recall you saying once that he'd been an MP."

She stretched languidly. "Listen, I've told you too much already. I wasn't in love with him, I never even considered telling him I was pregnant and I don't really miss him very much. Don't try to make this into a giant love story, 'cause it wasn't one. My giant love story had an incredibly unhappy ending, remember?"

"I'm sorry. It's just that you know how nosy I am. And when I can't know something about your life, I'm always tempted to fantasize it as being glamorous and exciting."

She grinned wryly. "Yeah, it's been real glamorous. Hell, the only really glamorous boyfriend I ever had was J. J. Webster and look what happened to him. And I fully expected that he'd be working out tax scams, or maybe doing a little PR for a few select clients like Gulf and Exxon."

But it hadn't quite worked out that way. A year and a half earlier, J.J. had appeared on my doorstep one Saturday with a sleeping bag and an exceedingly vague itinerary.

His timing couldn't have been better. I'd just finished losing all my weight, felt genuinely pretty for the first time in my life and had embarked on what would shortly develop into a program of rampant promiscuity. I was so thrilled to have him around that it took me a while to realize just how badly he had worn over the years.

J.J. had graduated with a C minus average, a $75,000 bequest from his recently deceased grandfather, a draft number in the high 280s, and rejections from six law schools. So he hopped on Icelandic and spent half a decade in Europe, mostly in Amsterdam and Morocco. There were a few half-assed efforts at setting up some sort of import business, but mostly J.J. just drugged out. At one point he went to India and studied meditation with Swami Somthinorother, but it never quite took.

And when the money ran out, he decided to retrace his past and discover where he'd missed the connection that would have given his life some meaning. It was a noble enough quest, but it got pretty tedious after about the fourteenth telling.

"Was J.J. a good lay when you were in college?" This was the first occasion I had ever had to make a qualitative sexual comparison with somebody who was a relative authority on the subject.

Pren laughed. "I'm sure he thought he was! But no, he was not exactly your basic sex machine. Why? Has he turned into Warren Beatty?"

"*Au contraire*, my dear. Even when I was a total novice, I always had the impression that the sex act was supposed to last longer than five minutes."

"Same old J.J.! Actually, as I recall, J.J. had a maddening tendency to get so loaded that he couldn't make it at all."

"Sounds like he hasn't changed much. He can put away a fifth of vodka in twenty-four hours, and not seem very drunk until he throws up on the sofa." The fact of the matter was that J. J. Webster had been a colossal disappointment. He was still handsome, but anything resembling a soul had long since drowned in a sea of alcohol and drugs. "You know what made him the maddest?"

"What?" Pren actually didn't sound as if she cared.

"When I told him that even if I knew where to find you I wouldn't tell him. He just went berserk when I told him that. And then about a week after he left, they busted Cameron Bishop in Rhode Island, just a hop, skip, and a jump away from the Webster summer home on Block Island. For that matter, didn't they get one of the Berrigans on Block Island, too?"

Pren shuddered. "Please, must you remind me of all that? I still go into cold sweats when I remember that horrible time when they were busting everybody. Bishop and Saxe and Swinton, three separate busts all in the space of a month! I couldn't even calm down by reminding myself that they were all in the Northeast and I was thousands of miles away. I stayed in my house for an entire month."

"The worst one for me was when they got Patty and the Harrises. Not just because they'd done such a great job of hiding, but because it was going to free up a whole lot of G-men with plenty of experience seeking fugitives. I was scared to death they'd start looking for you."

"The thought crossed my mind as well. An average of once every forty seconds. Actually though, what got to me even more than that was that interview Abbie Hoffman did from underground with TVTV and *New Times*. I figured that would bring down every fed in the country. It was such an incredibly arrogant thing to do."

"But you said you feel safe now."

She grimaced. "Oh, sure. Face it, nobody cares anymore. The revolution's all over and our side lost. Just look what's happened to all our stalwart leaders. Eldridge was designing pants with cod pieces and now he says he's a born-again Christian. Tom Hayden's running for the Senate. Rennie Davis sells insurance and shills for the Guru Mahara Ji. I always really liked Rennie too. He was one very bright boy."

"I don't see how he can be so bright if he worships that disgusting little lardass." I had followed the career of His Pudginess, the Guru Mahara Ji, with considerable interest. "How can any intelligent person take him seriously? I mean, here's this grotesquely fat teen-ager asking his followers to send him blenders and crockpots and toasters!! It's just too absurd. I saw a PBS special on the Divine Light Mission. You know what Abbie Hoffman said about him?"

"That if this guy is God, it's the God the United States of America deserves. I saw it too. That's a wonderful line. I always thought one of Abbie's strongest points was his phrasemaking."

An ice cream truck jangled by and Melinda dashed over. "Popsick?" she chirped hopefully. We got three Bicentennial Freezes, alleged blueberry and raspberry and vanilla swirled on a stick.

"Melinda, come back here," ordered her mother. "Finish that before you get back in the sandbox." Melinda dutifully plopped at our feet and lustily sucked at her treat. Pren nibbled hers for a moment, then abruptly chucked it in a nearby trash can. "I don't want to know what's in that, but I have a feeling you could probably change one ingredient and end up with nail polish remover."

"Melinda swing?" She had finished her popsicle and wrapped the stick in the paper. Pren took it from her while I stood up.

"I'll swing you, honey, come on."

She screamed with joyous glee as she rocketed upward into the air, her peals of laughter ringing like a miniature carillon in the clear hot morning air. When she finally tired of swinging and went back to the sandbox, I found Pren angrily tearing apart a weed. Her jaw was set and she looked furious.

"What's the matter?"

"Shit!" She hurled the tattered remains of the weed away and began ripping at another. "I've been thinking about how ridiculously my life is being wasted. Having you here has brought a lot of stuff to the surface that I thought I'd already worked out. I'm just starting to realize how mad I am about the way I have to live. What we were just saying about how the revolution's over. Well, it sure isn't over for me. I'm stuck here in a part of the country where I'd never have chosen to live voluntarily. I had to give up all my plans and ideas for the future. I don't even have anybody to talk to here. No friends that I'd have picked if my life were normal. What in the name of creation am I doing with my life?"

"You're raising a great kid. And putting together an important book."

"And I couldn't have done that otherwise? I'm *stuck,* dammit. Trapped in a life and time that doesn't even exist anymore. I could raise a kid anywhere. And I'm doing the book almost by default. It sure wouldn't have been my first choice, if I still had the luxury of real choices. Everybody else gets to do exactly what they want and I'm mired in 1972 forever. You could call me the ultimate Vietnam casualty."

I was really disturbed by the bitterness in her tone. "If you feel that strongly, why don't you go back?"

She shook her head defiantly. "We've been through that a thousand times. Limited as this life is, it's better than spending the next twenty years in a Texas prison. And I never even accomplished anything while I had the chance."

"Oh, come *on*! You did plenty, more than a dozen other people. There was VETRAGE. . . ."

"*Was* VETRAGE. At least you've got the tense correct. There's nothing left of that anymore. Wilt and Randy are dead, I'm in exile and Mike Donovan's probably off somewhere chasing girls."

I didn't want to even think about Mike Donovan, much less discuss or try to defend him. "Well, the war's over anyway."

"Terrific," she snarled. "The war's over. Hundreds of thousands of people are dead and most of Vietnam looks like the back side of the moon. And for what? I found myself screaming at the TV set last year when the Americans were leaving Saigon. . . . All those mobs of people being kept out of the embassy they used to work in. Embassy attachés feeding American dollars into the shredder. Now *that's* a tidy metaphor for the war if ever there was one. Though I guess the crashed C-fiveA full of stolen Vietnamese babies was at least as good. Nobody even noticed, they were all so damned glad to have it over with."

"Well," I pointed out mildly, "you can't have it both ways. You can't complain too much about *how* it ended as long as it did. And there *were* some good things that came out of it all."

"Like what?" she snapped. "Improved technology for handling traumatic amputations?"

"The war politicized a lot of people who probably wouldn't have ever thought about any kind of social issues otherwise." One prime example I could think of was Laurel Hollingsworth. "It brought together our generation."

"Sure, for a little while. But that unity disappeared when they changed the draft law."

"It brought together something else," I reminded gently. "You met Wilt Bannister."

She was quiet for a moment and began picking apart another weed, more carefully this time. When she spoke again her tone was softer. "That's true, I suppose. But I like to think I would have found Wilt anyway, somehow. You know, this may sound crazy, but I still talk to him. Sometimes I feel like he's hanging around keeping an eye on me. He'll go away for a while but then when I particularly need or want him, I just feel like he's there. I like to pretend sometimes that Melinda is Wilt's daughter. Is that too macabre?"

I shook my head. "I don't think so."

"I feel like he's with me when I do those Indian interviews, kind of sitting behind me suggesting questions and ideas. And I can feel him wondering what ever happened to all the hopes and dreams everybody had. I suppose there's a chance he would have burned out or turned narcissistic the way everybody else seems to have lately, but somehow I doubt it." She leaned back and shielded her eyes as she stared up at the sky. "This period is so politically *sterile*. The seventies strike me as being like a black hole. That black hole sucked up all the light and energy and hopes and dreams from the star that was the sixties."

"It swallowed some bad stuff too. Nixon's gone, for starters."

"That's true. And so are those horrible puppet governments in Southeast Asia. And with executive privilege stripped away, look what was left: COINTELPRO, enemies lists, anti-Castro plots, Allende, Lumumba, Diem, Trujillo . . ." Her voice trailed off and she was silent a moment. Then she shook her head. "But nobody really cared. They were all too busy planning their next orgasms. When we were in college, I used to think that the world would change, that we could *make* it change. But maybe that whole period was an aberration. I have a feeling that if I were to see Duke today, I'd hate it. It would be just like it was when we were freshman, only in blue jeans."

"Well, it's certainly like that at Northwestern. The primary concern seems to be getting into graduate school. Not that there's anything wrong with that, I suppose, but they're so boring. They don't seem to believe in anything. In a way, those kids remind me of Ginger. Now there's somebody the sixties never touched."

"Ah, yes. Good old Ginger Lockford, pride of the Evanston tennis courts."

"Please. Ginger Lockford-Robertson. She's hyphenated now, remember?"

"Of course. How typically Ginger to straddle the fence that way. Not enough guts to keep her name and too superficially hip to change it."

I felt suddenly defensive. Ginger might not have ever met Pren's standards of political action, but she was still a good friend of mine. "Maybe she was just ahead of her time."

"Because she was never burdened with idealism? I don't know. Of course idealism didn't work out very well for most of us, so I guess maybe it's not surprising that those younger kids today are so cynical. And of course they *are* young. Llewellyn's age and even younger, and I suppose I'll always think of him as a little kid. He was only fourteen the last time I saw him, worried because his voice cracked at the wrong times and his friends were taller than he was. Not that Llewellyn would ever have really had a chance to develop a social conscience anyway, the way the Major probably clamped the lid on him after I left. It'd be interesting to know what he wanted to do with his life. I'd bet anything it wasn't the military. But he never had that defiant streak I do. So he'll end up as a career officer, living in some God-awful base housing in Germany, till the Major decides it's time for him to come home and take over the mill."

Chapter 2 ————————————————

But it didn't quite work out that way for Llewellyn Granger.

In early September, barely two months after my visit to Santa Fe, Shirley called me, sobbing uncontrollably. Her story took a long time to tell, but it was depressingly simple.

John Llewellyn Granger IV had been found guilty of an honor code violation and expelled from the U.S. Military Academy. Four hours after his expulsion, he checked into a Poughkeepsie hotel, addressed a short note of apology to his father, stripped, and stepped into the shower. Then he inserted the muzzle of a .38 caliber pistol in his mouth and pulled the trigger.

So once again I found myself at a funeral in Granger, South Carolina. Shirley hemmed and hawed and boohooed when I asked her what I could do to help, but she managed to get out a nice convincing "Yes, please" when I asked if she wanted me to come. The Major was by now quite accustomed to living alone, it having been a year and a half since his wife's death and over a year since Shirley married her banker beau and moved back to Columbia. But the lonely months seemed to have aged him beyond all proportion, or perhaps his vitality had been suddenly drained with the death of his one last hope. In any event, he hugged me when I arrived, the most touching gesture I could ever remember him making.

This was a beaten man, no doubt about it.

There was no public funeral. I was, in fact, the only nonrelative present at graveside, except of course for the servants and one discreet FBI agent. The Major's wretched sister and brother-in-law were down from Connecticut and Aunt Nell was up from Columbia, drenched in lavender cologne and positively swathed in mourning. Shirley's husband John devoted his full attention to the physical support of his very pregnant and emotionally distraught wife.

It was, in short, one of the creepier gatherings of my adult life.

I cried, though not so much for Llewellyn. Face it, I'd never really known Llewellyn. When Pren and I were teen-age buddies, he was an energetic little boy who was always off squirrel hunting or climbing in the peach orchards. Through our college visits he kept quietly in the background as Pren and the Major argued the politics of the day. I had no idea what he had wanted or expected from life. I could not recall a single truly significant conversation I had ever had with him.

But I did know that the attrition rate of the Granger family had gotten a little frightening. When I wept, it was for Shirley who understood nothing and for the Major who seemed to be beginning to understand everything just a little too well. He seemed haunted and, for the first time ever, almost unsure of himself. I considered the very real possibility that he might follow his son's example, even mentioning the possibility surreptitiously to Shirley's husband John.

"I think you're probably overreacting just a bit, Laurel," he replied condescendingly. "Major Granger's a fine, strong man." Then he put his arm around me and gave me a little hug, reassurance for the silly female who thought big tough men had emotional reactions.

And so I dropped it. If Major Granger could be regarded as anybody's responsibility, it was certainly his, not mine.

Pren, however, saw my point instantly when we spoke by phone a week later. "So who's keeping an eye on him?" she demanded.

"Shirley for a while. She was going to stay out there a couple of weeks. But she's in her seventh month already and John wants her to go back to Columbia."

"Even in her prime, she'd be useless in an emergency."

"I know. But you know there's no way to stop him if he decides to do it. I'm guessing he'll be all right if she just sticks around for a week or so. You know, continuity of the family, baby on the way, that sort of thing."

"I suppose." Pren sounded very doubtful. "It's just the part about him hugging you that has me a little worried."

"It was only twice."

"That's twice more than he ever hugged *me,* even when he was being my good pal before I got pregnant the first time. The guy has always been your basic iceberg."

It took time to settle her down. Llewellyn's death had clearly shaken her and she projected a vague, impotent despair. It was twenty minutes before she calmed down enough to chuckle proudly when I asked her how Melinda was.

"Precocious as always. She's into architecture and engineering right now. Jerry got her a set of cardboard bricks and she's been building play houses."

"Jerry Ford or Jerry Rubin?"

She laughed. "Jerry's a divorced engineer who lives down the block. He's very sweet on me and he's trying to purchase my affections through Melinda. Melinda adores him. I think he's a bit of a jerk and certainly a mental lightweight, but horny's horny."

And long after the conversation ended, that was the remark I kept flashing back on. *Horny's horny.* It certainly summed up my own recent history succinctly enough. Ever since I'd gotten skinny two years earlier, I'd been trying to prove my own attractiveness to myself by seducing any jerk who so much as nodded hello.

I had discovered a Basic Truth: Women can always get laid. The selection may not be too terrific, but if tumescence is the only requirement, it's not the least bit difficult to find. Since the converse is not true, I can only assume that this is God's way of making up for giving us those lower salaries.

It had all been rather thrilling at first. After a lifetime of social awkwardness, suddenly I found myself Desirable. Anytime I wanted, I could hit one of the local singles bars, down a couple fast screwdrivers, make a minimal amount of banal converstaion and wind up in bed half an hour later. I felt compelled to somehow make up for all the time I had lost, and I rather liked the anonymity of it all. And for a while that was enough.

Then, toward the end of this odyssey of sexual exploration and discovery, I began dating a former fraternity brother of Ginger's husband. Norman Freeman was a financial planner for a chain of nursing homes, with too-short hair and thick horn-rimmed glasses. His body, however, was slim and unobjectionable and would probably have been quite appealing had it not been attached to Norm's head.

Norm liked softball, steaks cooked medium well and *Sports Illustrated.* He listened to Barry Manilow and secretly idolized Steve McQueen. His conversation was littered with Bizspeak and he was forever prioritizing in public. His idea of dinner at home was boiling a couple of Oscar Meyer weiners and slathering them with French's mustard. And his performance in bed was not much more imaginative.

Norm's persistence was flattering, and I tried not to think about how dull he really was. But I also continued my search for the perfect orgasm until a nerve-racking encounter with a real Neanderthal forced me to consider just what I was doing with my life.

He was a semi-epsilon moron named Neil who worked for the phone company and I picked him up at a bar on Broadway. I didn't really notice the little bag he carried in from his car until we were in my bedroom. Then he opened it up and started pulling out handcuffs, leather thongs and even, God help me, a leather mask.

"You've got the wrong idea altogether," I told him, trying not to sound as terrified as I felt. "I think maybe you'd better go home."

"You know you'd like it," he said, running his hand down my back. I twisted away from him and lunged across the bed toward the alarm button I had wired to Andy Lamont's apartment upstairs. When the German couple's lease expired, he had moved in and we'd rigged a two-way alarm system, almost as a joke.

"What are you doing?" He pounced on me on the bed as I pushed the button. His crushing weight pinned my legs and I prayed that Andy be home. I heard footsteps upstairs and shuddered in relief.

"I called for help," I gasped. "You'd better get out of here."

He rolled off me, gave me a thunderous look and slapped my face, hard. "Dumb cunt bitch!"

My ears rang as I slipped past him and ran to the front of the house, arriving at the door just as Andy began knocking loudly. "You need help, Laurel?" he called, lowering his voice two octaves to sound more menacing.

"Call the police!" I yelled, flinging open the door. I knew that Neanderthal Neil could make hamburger out of Andy.

But Neil was at the door now too, zipped up and carrying his horrifying little bag. "Fuck your fat friend, bitch," he sneered at me as he roughly pushed past us both. He stumbled out the front door and I collapsed in Andy's arms in tears.

The next night, Andy took me to a new Indian restaurant that had opened nearby. "I'm worried about you," he said gently. "That guy could have killed us both last night. I think you're out of control, Laurel. Isn't there anything I can do to help?"

"You can mind your own goddamned business!" I huffed. "I don't need any fucking morality lectures from you." Then I stalked out.

But as I curled up with Joni Mitchell and a bottle of chablis in front of my fireplace later that night, I had to admit he was right. I *was* out of control. Seriously. And I realized even in my fury that I was lucky to have a friend like Andy who cared enough to notice.

So much later, after his stereo was silent and I was sure he was asleep, I crept upstairs and slipped a note under his door. "I'm sorry," I wrote. "Let me make it up to you tomorrow night with Chicken Paprikash." And once I had made my peace with Andy, I decided to do the same thing with myself. I took a vow of celibacy, Norm excepted, and promised never again to fuck anyone I had just met.

And because I had religiously adhered to these vows, I was already putting on weight again.

I pounded on Andy's door, ashamed at myself for being thankful that he had the flu and was too sick to go to work. "It's Florence Nightingale, open up."

He looked like hell when he pulled the door open, wearing a brown plaid wool bathrobe with moth holes running in a jagged line down the front. His hair stuck out at odd angles and he wasn't wearing his glasses. His nose was red and swollen and his whole face seemed puffy. "Where's my chicken soup?"

"Oh, God, Andy, I'm sorry. I forgot completely. I'll go get you some right now."

He grabbed my arm. "Wait a minute. What's the matter?"

"Lie down, you're making me nervous. You look horrible. You want to know what's the matter, I'll tell you what's the matter." I was gabbling like a parakeet. "You remember Joe Jefferson, that student of mine that I used to talk about all the time?"

He collapsed on the couch. "The pint-sized one who kept the green afro comb in his hair all the time?"

"Yeah. Well, I won't be talking about him anymore. Somebody shot him to death last night. He would have turned thirteen next Tuesday."

"Oh, my God! What happened?"

I sat down on a giant pillow. "They aren't exactly sure, but the general consensus is that it was drug related and not an accident."

He closed his eyes and didn't say anything. That was one of the nicest things about Andy. He knew when to shut up. Finally he opened his eyes again and blew his nose. Beside him sat a nearly empty box of Kleenex and a nearly full wastebasket. "I'm sorry, Laurel. I know he meant a lot to you."

I nodded silently and felt tears roll quietly down my face. Andy moved to comfort me but I held him off with an outstretched hand. "I'd love to cry on your shoulder," I sniffed, "but I don't want to get sick too. I have enough problems."

"Let me fix you a drink. I've got gallons of orange juice that you brought me yesterday and I think there's some vodka."

I shook my head. "No, that's all right. I'm supposed to be taking care of you, remember? And I couldn't even remember the damn chicken soup. I'll go get it now. I'm all right, really. And I'll even stick around to entertain you for a while after you eat. I'm at least as interesting as *Hollywood Squares*."

He cocked his head and gave a twisted smile. "On your good days, anyway."

I threw the Kleenex box at him.

Four days later I was the one in bed with a hacking cough. Andy had rigged my speakers to play in the bedroom and we were listening to *Hasten Down the Wind*, a new addition to Andy's collection of erotic album covers. Even as we listened he was fondling the cover. And I rather enjoyed the album myself. Ever since I'd learned that Linda Ronstadt was a former fatty, my opinion of her had escalated significantly.

"The only good thing about being sick," I sniffled, "is that you almost always lose a few pounds. It's been so hard keeping my weight down since I stopped, um, bringing home strangers. I guess what it comes down to is do I want to be a skinny slut or a fat lady? I'm too oral to give up both sex and food. But what a depressing choice."

"At least you get to choose."

"But that's not what I want to choose from! Why can't I find a decent man to settle down with? Why can't you find a decent woman to settle down with? Where the hell are all those great people who are supposed to be out there somewhere?"

He shook his head. "I don't know. It's really a shame we can't just fall in love with each other, isn't it? It would all be so tidy. And we'd each be getting such a prize."

"I would, anyway." I let loose a horrible cough that shook the bed. Then Andy started hacking too. We sounded like the seal cage at the zoo.

"Oh, c'mon, Laurel, don't be so glum. And don't start into that garbage about how worthless you are. That's ridiculous! You're pretty, you're skinny and you're the best cook I've ever known in my life. You do a great job in a difficult profession doing important work. You teach people how to *read.* That literally and permanently changes their lives. Plus, you're practically finished with a master's degree."

"And Joe Jefferson is dead, so it doesn't matter anymore that I taught him how to read. I get so tired of seeing all my work get washed away. The longer I stay at any one school the more depressing it gets. I have them for one year and then they get thrown back into this horrible system based on fear and repression. I can never get used to the way they beat students in these schools."

"If it's really that hard on you, then for Pete's sake get another job. You've got enough experience now that you could probably get a suburban gig if you put a little effort into it. It might be kind of a nice change for you, to mingle with the socioeconomic hotshots, producing titans of industry. Maybe even an astronaut or a congresswoman."

"Oh, Andy. You know I don't want to do that."

"Well, look, you're practically done with the master's. You can get an administration job once you have it."

"If I wanted to work in an office, I could find something more interesting to do than shuffle dental records and issue tardy slips."

"Well," he said, "let's look on the bright side here." He gave an impish grin. "When all else fails, you can always interface with Norm."

"There's a lot to be said for Norm," I defended halfheartedly. "He never wears gold chains or musk oil and he always lets me choose the movies. Plus he's the closest thing I've run across yet to the kind of person I always assumed you were supposed to marry."

"Nuts," said Andy. He coughed furiously for a moment. "He's not good enough for you. He's boring, Laurel; you've said so yourself. At the very least, you should hold out for a guy who's a decent audience. Norm doesn't have the vaguest idea what things I say are supposed to be funny. He waits to see if you're going to laugh."

I couldn't really argue with this. "Well, don't worry. Norm doesn't want to marry me, thank God. He's just like every other man out there, scared to death of permanence. Welcome to the seventies, the decade that brings you disposable razors, douches, diapers, lighters and relationships."

Health restored, I pondered solutions to my sorry state of alienation and anomie. I could take est, quit my job, adopt a minority baby, make an unfortunate marriage, move to another city or follow the example of my President and become a born-again Christian. Instead, I took the easy way out. I went to the pound and brought home a puppy.

Acquiring a dog might not seem an earthshaking life change to most folks, but I was pushing thirty pretty hard without ever having assumed responsibility for so much as a pet rock. I named the dog Apicius after the famed Roman gourmet, but within three days I was calling him Bubba. Bubba was a casual blend of black-and-white patches, with thick, long, luxuriant hair. His feet and floppy ears were enormous. It was love at first sight.

Bubba became my immediate slave and constant companion. Each time I left a room he moaned as if his heart would break. My return from such far-flung locales as the front porch was invariably greeted by wagging, jumping and frantic whimpers of delight. A bit of Puppy Chow and a daily walk by the lake seemed a paltry price for such fidelity.

I boarded him with Maxine over Christmas, but took Bubba home with me the next summer. Note how I say "home" when in fact I had been a year-round resident of Chicago for a solid six years. I voted in Cook County, paid taxes to the State of Illinois and worked for the Chicago Board of Education. For all practical purposes, I considered myself a Chicagoan. But of course that wasn't really true at all. I was still a southerner, and Louisiana was still home.

I felt just like my students that spring, waiting for the year to end, though the concept of going "down South" carried considerably more freight for them. Everywhere I had taught in Chicago, I encountered scores of children whose only tangible connection to the world beyond their housing projects was an occasional visit to relatives who had stayed behind in Mississippi, Arkansas or Louisiana. On these trips they were exposed to such marvels as fresh milk, fireflies and mules which might be ridden for hours. They gathered eggs and picked blackberries and went joyously barefoot, save on Sunday mornings. They didn't notice that the shotgun shacks where their aunts and grandmothers lived lacked paint, screens and frequently windows. They had no way of comprehending the depth or intensity of the racism their kinfolk grappled with daily in this superficially ideal natural wonderland. They knew only that compared to the filth and danger and horror of their squalid northern lives, this seemed surely to be heaven.

Andy and I threw a big party the weekend after we got our respective master's degrees, his in social work and mine in education. I was also celebrating, very privately, the appearance of Janet Cartwright's *Voices of the Navajos,* which had been published three weeks earlier. It was a damn fine book in the tradition of Studs Terkel, haunting interviews masterfully edited to provide a rich glimpse inside the Navajo world. I was jealous of Pren for having written it. Shattered though her life plans may have been, she was still coping and producing.

But me? I could live where I wanted and do the work I wanted and pursue whatever interests struck my fancy. And still I felt totally dissatisfied and unconnected. The strongest links in my life were to Mike Royko, *Mary Hartman, Mary Hartman,* and *Saturday Night Live.*

Was it so terribly selfish and unrealistic to think there should be more?

Chapter 3 —————————————

I honestly believed that going to Louisiana for the summer would solve my problems.

Mine is the same love-hate relationship that afflicts all southern expatriates, which is why we endure muggings, burglary, sketchy garbage collections, rudeness, filth, blight, decay and frigid interminable winters. It's always when the car's been stolen or a neighbor raped or the delicatessen owner shot in the course of a $17 robbery that we think fondly of the little hamlets in which such behavior would be unthinkable. As we wait for the tardy bus, the surly repairman or the brusque impersonal dentist, we reminisce about what always, in such moments, is perceived as "home."

But set us down in the backwater towns of our youth and we'll be stir crazy in twenty-four hours, guaranteed. In the oppressive silence we yearn for the reassuring lullabies of ambulance sirens and jackhammers. At the local catfish joint we gratefully accept more iced tea and hush puppies, dreaming all the while of scallopini and rifstaffel. Passing the only movie theater in town, we shudder at GP double bills held over for the seventh week.

We desperately twirl the radio dial in search of powerful faraway stations and sigh deeply as the last TV station signs off with "Dixie" at half past midnight. We flip through seventeen pages of birth notices, garden club schedules and photographs of puppies in the local newspaper before discovering a two-paragraph report on the war in the Middle East.

When the fourteenth person inquires solicitously about our divorce/boyfriend/operation, we yearn for the rude anonymity of city neighbors who neither know nor care about such personal affairs. We recoil in guilty horror from the racist exploitation of the hometown blacks, anguishing at their servility, complacence and resignation in the face of appalling discrimination. We cringe at gross rednecks scratching their butts while they swill Rebel Yell and plan next week's hunting expedition.

We feel stifled. We chafe under attention we thought we missed. We wonder what on earth ever possessed us to think we missed such narrow-minded, bigoted provincialism. When we finally flee back north, it's with the absolute conviction that nothing could ever cause us to repeat such a dreadful mistake.

And six months later, we're ready to do it all over again.

Of course my trip was not a total bust. Bubba made an instant hit with everyone, then fell passionately in love with the rolling hills and endless woods of Weatherly Plantation. Bubba, indeed, proved a good deal more popular than his mistress. He did not correct elders who referred to "pickaninnies" and "niggers," he did not refuse food placed before him as too fattening, he did not question for a moment his singular good fortune at having come to visit this little microcosm of nirvana.

Would that I could have adjusted as easily and graciously as my dog. I knew within twenty-four hours of my arrival that I'd made a massive mistake, but I was determined to stick it out for at least a month. I did compromise, however. I drove over to Baton Rouge one afternoon and called Pren.

"Oh, c'mon," I wheedled. "We'll have a great time! You know, the only time you ever came to see me when I lived in New Orleans, you were only here overnight. In fourteen years we've never gone to the French Quarter together."

"Well, I suppose it might work," she said doubtfully, and I knew I'd won. "Melinda and I could stay in a hotel somewhere, I suppose."

"I'll get you reservations at the Provincial, right in the Quarter. It'll be our best vacation yet, I guarantee."

The recently widowed Earline greeted me in New Orleans with the by now quite common concern that I "wasn't eating enough." I marveled again that everybody in Louisiana seemed to feel I was a likely draft choice for anorexia nervosa poster child. And after dutifully inspecting the premises under her watchful eye, I excused myself to take a brief nap. I couldn't tell Earline that I was performing what had grown to be almost a mystical ritual each time I visted the house.

I would lie on the bed and visualize Mike Donovan in the room with me, standing in the doorway, straddling the dressing table stool, lying beside me with his devilish tongue tracing patterns on my trembling flesh. Then I would sob my heart out. It was quite a satisfying little routine, actually, sort of a semiannual purgative.

But this time it didn't happen. Prepared though I was to wallow in the exquisitely painful memory of Mike Donovan, I realized with a jolting shock that I neither loved nor hated him anymore. I didn't resent his popping in and out of my life so callously and abruptly.

I felt as if a lever had suddenly flipped somewhere deep inside my heart. I still cherished the memories of the time we had spent together, those hours in Beaumont and New Orleans and Chicago when I felt that surely no princess had ever experienced greater joy. But I no longer detested his arrogant assumption that he could saunter in and out of my life without even the slightest attention to my feelings. I rather pitied him. He was just a simple jerk, same as all the rest of us.

The next afternoon, I sent Earline off to visit her daughter and grandchildren for the week, then went home to await the arrival of the Cartwrights, *mere et fille.*

Unfortunately, Melinda touched down at New Orleans International with the sniffles and twenty-four hours later she was flat on her back with a stuffy nose, elevated temperature, and hacking cough. I scouted out a pediatrician who prescribed antibiotics and told the anxious mother that although her daughter was in no immediate danger, she ought to stay in bed for at least three days.

"I'm taking her home," Pren announced as we left the doctor's office. "If you think I'm going to spend three days cooped up in a motel room with a sick child, you're crazy. We can catch a plane tonight."

"But you can't," I wailed. "You just got here. There's got to be some way to work this out. Just let me think for a minute."

It took a little longer than that, but eventually I produced a plan that Pren agreed to, an odd reversal to all those times that I had waited anxiously while she plotted and fumed. Thanking the inspiration which had led me to send Earline to her daughter's, I went home and had all the locks on the house changed. Then I went at dusk to pick up the Cartwrights. Pren and Melinda hid beneath a sheet in the back seat once we got out of the Quarter. Melinda seemed too groggy from her medicine to really notice anything amiss.

It was quite dark by the time I drove up the driveway and straight into the garage, parking the car in the usual spot, closing the garage and entering the house alone. Ten minutes later Pren rapped gently at the back door and I let them in.

"I'm going to be moving soon," Pren confided that night after Melinda was finally sleeping quietly. Their suitcases remained packed and we kept the curtains drawn, but I felt quite certain of our safety. I'd already made my courtesy calls on the neighbors and Earline wasn't due back for four days.

"I believe I've heard that before. At approximately four-week intervals." Our pay phone to pay phone assignations were by now as regular and predictable a part of my life as my own menstrual cycle.

"No, this time is different. I've picked the town out and everything. We're going to go to Bisbee. It's an old copper mining town way down in the southeasternmost corner of Arizona. I'm planning to do another oral history, of miners, and buy a house there."

"Fugitive Murderess Takes on Mortgage, read all about it."

She laughed. "Won't even need to do that, actually. They closed the mine and the area's economically depressed. You can get a nice little place cheap for cash, and unless you've been playing the ponies, I still have some cash."

"You mean you're really going to do it?"

"You bet. There's a pretty good-sized colony of retired hippies down there, so it has the advantages of a small town without the narrow-mindedness of a place like Granger or St. Elizabeth."

"Seems to me you're more likely to get caught in a small town. Everybody spends so much time taking care of everybody else's business."

She shook her head. "Not in the Southwest. They really respect privacy out there. Most people go to those little towns to get away anyway. That part of the country is where the folks who had nowhere left to run ended up. Like me. And apart from that, it's absolutely beautiful. The mountains are magnificent. It's enough to make me want to believe in God."

"You could send Melinda to Sunday school."

She laughed. "Bisbee is precisely the kind of town where nobody's going to make a hullaballoo if I don't."

Melinda was much better in the morning, well enough to lie on the living room sofa while Aunt Lou Ann read her favorite stories to her. And Aunt Lou Ann found the experience thoroughly enjoyable, even as Mrs. Cartwright relished the break from her maternal duties. I was truly delighted to find Melinda so comfortable and content with her books, but even more thrilled that she never once inquired about television.

I fixed dinner again that night, a splendid ratatouille from the glorious vegetables available in the Louisiana summer. Melinda ate some too, and actually seemed to like it. And she gobbled her hush puppies as if she'd been born and bred in Macon. It was nice to cook for Pren and Melinda, and not just because I was able to resurrect some of my favorite bread and dessert recipes. It was nice because the three of us somehow seemed like a family, in a way that my own family never actually did.

We put Melinda to bed early, then sat in the huge formal living room with the elderly air conditioner roaring. Pren settled in Granddaddy's old leather armchair, then waved a hand around the room. "You know, this place is really ridiculous. No offense."

I sat opposite her in a direct line with the air conditioner. "Why should I be offended? It was like this long before it was mine. I'd like to sell it, or at least rent it out, but the only time I ever mentioned it to Daddy he informed me that the Hollingsworths do not sell their birthrights or lease their homesteads to strangers, unquote."

"I bet it's worth a fortune. You know, I've been thinking a lot lately about how different my life would have been if I hadn't ever had money. Yours too, for that matter."

"Well, we wouldn't have met at Chadwick, that's for damn sure. We'd have learned to do dishes at a more tender age."

She shook her head. "No, seriously. If my father had worked at the mill instead of owning it, I'd still be in South Carolina."

"You'd have gotten out."

"Perhaps. But certainly not the way I did. I wouldn't have had the luxury of studying history, or worrying about social issues. I'd have been struggling along trying to make ends meet, just worrying about survival. We were all so arrogant back in the old days, figuring a little black power philosophy would change things for people. They didn't need philosophy. They needed food and education and decent jobs. And think about you. If Jasper and Mary were your parents, you'd be lucky to be scrubbing floors in Baton Rouge."

"Rufus is in college."

"Rufus is in college because you're paying for it, Lady Gotrocks. Not just because he's intelligent and has a promising future. He's living off your charity, a rose by any other name. And look at me. Even if through one chance in a trillion I'd been born poor and still ended up as a white radical, I'd have been destitute underground, waitressing or something. I wouldn't be wandering around the Southwest compiling oral histories. Sure, it's been a challenge building myself a new life, but I had money to do it with. Neither one of us has ever had to really scramble for economic survival."

"Agreed. But surely you aren't trying to say that money brings happiness? I've spent too much of my life miserable to buy that for a second."

"But you've always had the *knowledge* that money can't make you happy. A lot of people spend their whole lives waiting to find that out."

"Somehow I don't find that too comforting."

"You know," she said flatly, "I get a little tired of hearing you whine about how miserable your life is. You don't have to stay in teaching if you don't want to. You don't have to stay in Chicago if you don't want to. You've got all the choices in the world and if you're really as dissatisfied as you say, I don't think that just finding a man will solve your problems."

"Now wait a—"

She held up a hand to stop me. "Come on. You *know* you're thinking that Prince Charming could change everything for you."

"And what if I am?"

"Dammit, Lou Ann, would you rather be living fifty years ago? You'd have found a man then. Or rather some man would have found your family and they'd have turned you over to his custody. Never mind if you didn't like him or had other ideas. There's more genuine freedom now than there's ever been in history, particularly for women. So if you want to—"

Just then a doorbell rang. We both froze. It rang again and then I heard a sound that catapulted my heart right up beside my uvula. Somebody was turning a key, trying to open the front door. That meant family. They all had keys, with carte blanche to use them as often as they liked.

And I would have to answer.

I walked out toward the front door. "Who's there?"

"Laurel?" It was my brother Lee. "Open up, we're sweltering."

Dear God. Lee and his wife Jane had been off somewhere at a national bar association convention. I could hardly refuse them admission. I thought fast. "Lee, you'll have to wait a second. I was in the shower and I'm absolutely starko."

I knew that would shock him into momentary silence, and I didn't wait for him to compose himself. Pren had already run upstairs and I followed her at a dead heat. She was gathering Melinda's toys and smashing them into her carrying bag. "Where can I get a cab?" she asked breathlessly.

"Nowhere around here without calling. Tell you what. Take all the stuff and Melinda out to the garage. I'll tell them I was on my way out and leave within half an hour. I can get you out of here then."

I was a little breathless when I swung open the huge front door, but that was to be expected of somebody racing to dress after being snatched from the shower. I'd even thought to dampen a few curls by my temples for dramatic effect.

Lee was red-faced and annoyed as he carried in two enormous suitcases, but sweet Jane chattered apologetically. "We didn't realize you'd be here, Laurel. It's so rude of us to just burst in on you this way. But the plane was late and you know how upset my stomach gets flying anyway, so we thought we'd just spend the night here and drive home tomorrow."

By now Lee had the luggage in. "What's with the lock, Laurel?" So much for warm sibling greetings. He was sweating profusely.

"I lost my keys in the Quarter the other day and changed it. You're lucky I was home." It couldn't hurt to remind him just whose hospitality he was accepting. "Earline's off visiting her daughter." I frowned at my watch. "And I was on my way out myself. I'm meeting some school friends and I'm late already. So I hope y'all won't mind if I rush off on you. We'll have lots of time to visit next week when I go back to Weatherly. Unless y'all can stay over a couple of days?"

Jane shook her pretty head. She was a former Shreveport belle who had met and married Lee while he was in law school. "That's sweet, but I really want to get back to little Lee. I've missed him so terribly." Little Lee, who favored his father and was already substantially overweight, was staying out at Weatherly with my parents.

"It's up to you." I shrugged. "Help yourself to anything in the fridge. And now, if you'll excuse me. . . ."

I went upstairs and made a lightning inspection for incriminating evidence, finding one of Melinda's barrettes on the bathroom floor. I turned on the shower briefly to wet the tub. When I came back downstairs, Lee was sipping a large tumbler of bourbon and Jane was on the phone to Weatherly. I called out good-nights and fled.

Pren and Melinda were in the back seat of the car. "Duck down now, honey," Pren warned as we backed out the driveway. Anybody who happened to notice the car leaving would have observed that Laurel girl from Chicago heading off somewhere alone as usual. Not until we were several miles away did Pren stick her head up.

"Where to, my lady?"

"The motel nearest to the airport. It's too late to get out of here tonight, but we're splitting on the first flight in the morning. Enough is enough."

We found a motel, put Melinda to bed and settled in a pair of fairly uncomfortable chairs. "Now where were we?" Pren asked.

"You were telling me I whine all the time and that I'm expecting to be carried away by a knight in shining armor." I was still a bit miffed, actually, and I didn't try to hide it. "You may have noticed that I got you away tonight without the assistance of any man."

"And I'm grateful," she answered gently. "It could have been a real disaster. But you know, that's exactly the point I was trying to make. You're competent and self-sufficient. You don't need a man just for the sake of a man."

"I didn't say I needed one. I don't mind admitting that I *want* one, though. I get lonely. I get depressed. My work's not exactly cheerful, you know."

"But it's important."

"Important work doesn't keep you warm at night. And neither do the jerks you meet in bars." I considered a moment. "Maybe you're right. Maybe I *am* just whining. Hell, I even find myself getting jealous of Ginger sometimes. She may be a total sell-out, but she's got a great husband and a high paid, high status job she loves. She could be a *Savvy* magazine cover girl."

Pren snorted. "You're worth ten of her and don't you ever forget it."

Chapter 4 _____

My jealousy of Ginger had been, it developed, a trifle premature. A week before I was due to leave Louisiana, she called me at Weatherly. "Dale wants to marry his secretary," she announced matter-of-factly, "and I wondered if I could stay at your place till you get back?"

I was flabbergasted. "My God, of course, Ginger! I had no idea. Are you all right?"

"Oh, I'm fine," she said cheerfully. "A bit surprised, but not really, if you follow me. I just need a bed for a few days till I can get my own place. Dale's staying in the co-op. He wants to buy me out."

"Listen, I'll call Andy right now. He's got the key. Help yourself to anything. He wants to marry his *secretary*?"

"Uh huh. Apparently she understands his needs better than I do. Hell, a secretary's *job* is to understand your needs. That's what she gets paid for."

"I just can't believe it. Is there anything else I can do? I could come back early if you want."

"Don't be silly," she answered. I wasn't surprised. Ginger was not prone to hysteria. Once when she was smashed she had told me quite seriously that her emotions were like wisdom teeth. About every five years they gave her a little trouble.

By the time I got home, she had been through a week of informal counseling from Andy Lamont. And Andy was, after all, a pro. She seemed just fine and certainly looked terrific. Her newly permed hair was a riot of silky black curls. Mostly she was surprised at how much time she had on her hands.

"I'm astonished," she confessed, "at how much time a relationship that doesn't even really exist can take up." A week after my return she had found an acceptable apartment and moved out again, but she was still by often to see Andy or me. "The thing I miss most," she explained woefully, "is having somebody to talk to at the end of the day, somebody who understands and cares about my work."

Clearly this left me out on two counts. Ginger was a shining light in the litigation department of her massive LaSalle Street firm, defending heinous megacorporations against legal assaults by consumers, struggling little companies, the federal government and assorted other n'er-do-wells. She steadfastly denied any moral qualms and sadly I believed her.

I really felt quite dreadful that her marriage had failed, even though I never particularly cared for Dale. It was a horrible shock to learn that simply looking like a perfect couple was insufficient. I don't know why this surprised me. By now I knew a lot of people who were divorced. Everything seemed to have gone topsy-turvy from the time, a scant twenty years earlier, when miserably unsuited couples stayed together for the sake of propriety. Now the minute something went wrong in a marriage, everybody went dashing to a lawyer. There was no attempt to work out anything but a property settlement.

Perhaps I was unfair to Ginger. Maybe she did feel a stronger sense of loss and pain than she projected. But if she did, she wasn't sharing it with me, or with Maxine, who was generally philosophic about the whole matter, having shed her husband long before it was trendy.

Maybe she was finding real solace with Andy. M.S.W. in hand, he had left Cabrini-Green to become the assistant director of an agency dealing in job training for the physically handicapped. He'd cut his hair, changed the granny glasses for soft contacts and bought himself a couple of suits. Though undeniably short and perennially pudgy, he was really quite attractive.

More to the point, however, Andy had just been through an unhappy love affair himself, eight months worth of screaming fights and smashing crockery and storming down the stairs in the middle of the night. If he and Ginger wanted to mope around, listen endlessly to *Hotel California* and feel sorry for themselves, it was fine by me. They were saving two innocents somewhere from having to endure it all.

*   *   *

The last week before school started, I made a two-day turnaround flight to Tucson to deliver the money Pren needed to buy her house in Bisbee. And I hadn't even unpacked my bag when two unexpected events occurred almost simultaneously.

First I got a call from Rob Marner, one of my former education professors, wondering if I'd be interested in a staff position at an experimental inner city school for which he had just received minimal foundation funding.

"It would gild the lily to even call it a shoestring operation, Laurel," Rob apologized. "But it's really a wonderful opportunity. I can't pay you anything near what you're making with the Board. But when I started making up lists of teachers I'd like to have, you were the very first person I thought of for reading. Also the second, third and fourth."

"You've got students and everything?"

"Fifty-five of them. Some of them are regular students, like George Tyson's three kids. He's the fellow with the soul food restaurant who's donating the space. And some of the other kids are real problems, nonreaders, troublemakers, kids who've just about been thrown out of public school."

I thought about the freedom, flexibility and volunteer classroom help Rob had promised. "How soon do you need to know?"

"I know it's short notice," he apologized again, "but could you possibly tell me by Monday?"

There seemed no point in waiting. "I can do better than that. I'll tell you right now. Sign me on."

Then I got up and hand carried my resignation downtown to the Board of Education. I felt terrific.

The second event was a good deal more confusing. My phone rang the following evening and it was Mike Donovan.

"I'm here in town," he announced, "and it looks like I'll be around for at least six weeks. Max Cleland hired me to help coordinate the new counseling program for Nam vets. Any chance I could talk you into dinner tomorrow night?"

I took a deep breath and reminded myself that I no longer loved or hated him. "That sounds like a great job, Mike. And sure, I'd love to see you. But why don't you just come here about seven and I'll fix dinner?"

"You always could read my mind. I just thought it would be a little presumptuous to call up and invite myself. There is one little thing, though." I waited for him to announce that he was bringing his fiancée. "Could you possibly not serve boiled potatoes? I've been at my folks' place for three days and I think I've exceeded my potato ration for the next seven years."

I opted for easy flash. I dusted off my wok, made a fast raid on the National and started chopping ingredients. Even if I didn't love him anymore, I wanted him to carry away a warm memory of at least the meal.

He was dressed casually when he arrived from work, in jeans and a pale blue knit pullover shirt. His gorgeous black hair was shorter than I'd ever seen it, but of course he looked terrific. He had a bouquet of cut flowers in one hand and a bottle of champagne in the other.

"What's the occasion?" I asked, after his perfunctory kiss of greeting.

"There needs to be a reason? How about this: I'm meeting a beautiful lady for the first time in a couple of years and I wanted to celebrate."

"Lovely sentiment," I replied blithely, "but I don't quite buy it."

He grinned. "Okay, then, how about this one. Not that the other isn't true, of course. I just found out that my divorce will be final next week."

I was genuinely confused. "I thought your divorce was final five years ago."

"That one was."

Oh, dear God. "You mean . . ."

He nodded sheepishly. "Blew it again. But I can't say that I'm very sorry and I sure can't say it was anybody else's fault. Seems I'm not cut out for the double yoke, but the romantic in me just won't quit." He started to peel away the foil from the champagne. "Think you could rustle up a couple of glasses?"

He followed me to the kitchen, poked approvingly at my little piles of cleverly chopped ingredients and filled the glasses that I gave him. "To old times and good friends," he said, lifting his glass. Then he started to drink.

"Wait a second. I have a toast of my own. To terrific new jobs."

And it was the terrific new jobs that we talked about while he sat at the butcher block table watching me stir fry, in rapid succession, mushroom rice, velvet chicken and shrimp with almonds.

I listened spellbound as he told me all about his VA position. I had never seen this kind of animation in him before, and I found it thrilling that at long last he was again doing something worthwhile. That to me has been one of the major tragedies of our generation: The people who could have helped make a difference frequently didn't bother, or never quite got around to it.

"It's a strange progression," he conceded, as he sipped his coffee after dinner. Not so much as a grain of rice remained from what I had estimated as ample to serve four. "From the U. S. Army to the Vietnam Veterans Against the War to VETRAGE to the VA. Nobody'd ever have been able to make me believe I'd end up as a VA lackey."

"Hardly a lackey. And anyway, isn't this what you wanted all along from the VA? To have guys like you in there calling the shots?"

He nodded. "Of course. It's just that I never thought the guy like me would actually *be* me. Just like I bet you never thought you'd get excited about going to work for peanuts over a chitling joint."

I laughed. "True enough. Listen, let's walk down to the lake. Bubba hasn't had his run today." Bubba had taken an instant shine to Mike and was lying quietly at his feet. Now he jumped up, tail wagging furiously, and ran to the hook where his leash hung. He was back in two seconds with the leash in his teeth.

Mike patted his head. "Just hold on one second, Bubba, while your mistress and I abuse a controlled substance." He pulled out a joint so thin I would have sworn it was nothing but a Zig-Zag wrapped toothpick.

"That looks potent. Hawaiian?"

He shook his head. "Even better. It's Mendocino County sinsemilla, from California."

"Mendocino County who?"

"Sinsemilla. It means without seeds. It's kind of a radical feminist approach to marijuana culture. They kill all the male plants so none of the females' potency and energy will be diverted into reproduction. I like to think of it as an example of Yankee ingenuity triumphing once again over nature." He lit the joint, inhaled shallowly, then passed it across the table to me. "Easy," he warned.

But naturally I didn't listen. I took a nice strong toke and felt my lungs implode.

Two more hits and I didn't feel like ever moving again, but Bubba started whimpering and dragging his leash forlornly around the table. Mike and I both laughed. He looked like he was auditioning for a dog food commerical.

Once I released Bubba on the beach, he charged off to begin his normal exercise regimen, a series of hell-for-leather sprints that continue either till I call him or he drops, whichever happens first. We sat down on the rocks and I stretched my legs.

"How's Prentiss?"

It startled me to hear her name, and I jumped a bit. Mike laughed. "We're all alone, Laurel. It's safe. I work for the Veterans' Administration, not the FBI."

I was horribly embarrassed. "My God, Mike, I didn't . . . you didn't . . . My God, I'm so stoned." I paused for a moment to recall what we had been discussing. Oh yes, Prentiss Granger. "She's just fine, Mike. She looks wonderful and she seems fairly happy and her daughter is an incredible child."

"Is she still in Albuquerque?"

I shook my head. "But I think she's planning to stay down in that part of the country indefinitely." By now, I reasoned, she might actually be an Arizona homeowner.

"She working?"

I chortled. "She published a book not long ago, under her new name. It's an oral history of the Navajos and it's gotten some nice reviews. I'll show it to you when we get back."

He gaped. "Son of a bitch! She published a *book*?!? What incredible nerve. And energy too. That woman never could keep from working, even back when some of us were trying to make laid back into an art form. What's her kid like?"

"Melinda? The spitting image of her mother. And incredibly bright."

"Melinda." He rolled the name. "A beautiful name. I'd like to see her, and her mama too. Next time you talk to Prentiss, ask her if she'd like company sometime."

"Of course. I'm supposed to talk to her soon, as a matter of fact . . . *BUBBA!!!*" He had taken off at a dead run after a frisky little standard poodle and was on his way to Evanston. He halted at the sound of his name. "Bubba, *come!*" He hesitated a fraction of a second, glanced once wistfully at the poodle, then ran straight to me. "Good boy," I told him enthusiastically, rubbing his ears.

"What a dog!" Mike said. He scratched Bubba's ears too. Then he put his arm around me as we both bent down over the dog and kissed me on the forehead. "And what a woman!"

I stood up quickly. I intended to summon every particle of willpower

I could find to avoid sleeping with him. I was tired of him thinking he could waltz in and out of my life every couple of years when the mood moved him. And since he seemed to have gone through an entire *marriage* since we were last together, I was even less inclined to make it with him.

I pulled Bubba's stick from my pocket and pitched it out across the beach. Bubba raced after it, brought it back and presented it to Mike. He ran out on the beach with Bubba at his heels, hurling the stick twice as far as I could. After half an hour they returned, exhausted. Mike crumpled onto the rock beside me.

"It's good to see you again, Laurel. Dammit, I've missed you."

Not enough to call or write, I thought. I said nothing.

He moved closer. "You know," he said wistfully, "there's nothing I'd like better right now than to go back and lick whipped cream off your body for dessert."

I avoided his eyes, not quite trusting myself. "I'm not sure that would be such a good idea."

"Oh, it would be a good idea, all right. But it's, um, not a physical possibility right now. I, uh, seem to have contracted a social disease."

I couldn't help myself. My eyes shot straight to his groin.

He laughed. "No parts missing or anything. Not like those nasty little strains they used to have in Nam where one day you go to take a leak and it falls off in your hand. It's just a plain, garden variety dose of the clap. For which I'm being amply punished, I assure you."

I moved back slightly and looked him straight in the eye. "Well, I bet you sure kept the folks down at the public health service busy. They probably had to take on an extra field investigator, just for your case."

He grimaced. "Please. What did I ever do to deserve a reputation like that?"

I grinned at him. I was surprised at how much I was enjoying this now. "Plenty. But mind you, I'm not complaining."

We started back. "So how long are you going to be in town? Till your parents start driving you crazy?"

"That happened after five minutes. No, I'll be here till the end of October probably. My schedule's kind of erratic though. I figure I'll get a motel room, before I permanently alienate the folks."

"You could stay at my place." It was my voice and I heard it with astonishment. He stared at me quite intently but with no particular surprise, which annoyed me a little. "Don't worry, I don't have designs on you. But there's an extra bedroom and if you're going to be gone most of the time you won't get in the way. I only ask one thing."

"And that is?"

"That you don't bring your women back here."

He laughed. "You make me sound like a real incorrigible. I tell you, I'm here on business, Laurel. Believe it or not, I can work hard when I want to. And I think I like the idea of staying at your place too. I'm reasonably tidy and I don't leave the cap off the toothpaste."

Where he got the idea he was reasonably tidy I will never know. For the next seven weeks life became a continuous housekeeping battle. He left dishes and glasses everywhere, dropped odd items in even odder places and seemed totally unfamiliar with the operation of a vacuum cleaner, broom or mop. I could easily understand why his most recent wife, a Vancouver nurse he described as "compulsively anal retentive," had given up so easily. He was, quite simply, a slob.

But I won't pretend it wasn't fun having him around. He took me to see *Julia* and stroked my hand gently as I sobbed through nearly the entire movie. He cooked a few meals, rather ineptly, but with such apparent enthusiasm that I cheerfully chomped my burnt pot roast without complaint. He was somebody to talk to when I came home each night from school and he seemed as interested in my work as anyone I knew, even Andy.

He was pleased with his job, the modification of an extant general counseling service to accommodate the special needs of the Nam vets. Pren was terrifically excited when I told her about it, worrying only that he might be too easily co-opted. I assured her that I considered the possibility highly unlikely.

"That's what they all say," she sniffed, "and the next thing you know they've signed on with IBM."

"Oh, I don't think so. He's too lazy unless he really believes in something. But if you don't mind, I'm not going to try to defend him. I'm trying very hard not to even like him very much. I'm absolutely terrified that I'm going to fall in love with him again. Even if he does leave his underwear wadded all over the bathroom."

But it didn't happen, not even after he got a clean bill of health, brought home a magnum of champagne and seduced me so effortlessly that I was embarrassed.

I was damn proud of myself.

Chapter 5 _____

I find it absolutely terrifying how quickly time passes as I age. Sometimes I realize that entire months have vanished without my ever noticing them. It is entirely possible, I fear, that by the age of sixty or seventy, time whirls by in positively kaleidoscopic fashion, leaving the helpless Homo sapiens at the vortex of this cosmic swirl, wondering not merely what year it might be, but also what decade.

I don't know exactly where in my life things started to accelerate, but as I approached my thirtieth birthday, I was seized by a blind, despairing fear that there was scarcely any point in putting the birthday candles away once I blew them out, so quickly would I need them again. I was old, life was nearly over and I had achieved nothing. I was washed up. All that remained was to flip a coin. Heads I'd open a vein, tails I'd stick my head in the oven and if it landed on end, I'd cross the Dan Ryan on foot at high noon.

"Nonsense!" snorted Prentiss Granger, when I confided my anxiety. "When Jane Fonda was thirty, she was shooting *Barbarella*."

"Yeah, and when Joan of Arc was thirty, she'd been charcoal for ten years."

There did not appear to be any hypocrisy in her impatience with me. Pren had complacently turned thirty a year earlier, though Janet Cartright celebrated her birthday several months afterward. Maybe it was that hiatus between the private fact and the public reality that allowed her to accept it so calmly, or maybe she was just a genuinely mature person and I was a silly little twit, even as she suggested.

"I've been hearing the same sorry crap for years now," she told me impatiently. "It's always the same. 'Oh, woe is me, my life is coming to a close and I've accomplished so little.' Well, you'll notice that you don't hear a lot of bellyaching about the big three-oh from the people who are actually doing things, accomplishing things. Which is one reason I'm surprised to see you reacting like this. You ought to know better than to allow yourself to be tryannized by the calendar."

But actually, I think she was wrong, and I was heartened to realize that at long last I could disagree with her without automatically assuming my own position was in error. The fact of the matter was that turning thirty was a tremendously significant milestone.

I moaned obnoxiously all through my alleged birthday celebration dinner with Andy at a sleek nouvelle cuisine place near the lake.

"It's this damned prolonged adolescence," I explained seriously. "We've put off assuming responsibility so well we don't know *how* to be adults. We're a generation of goddamned selfish Peter Pans. This has got to be the most pampered and overeducated and solipsist generation in history, Andy. I hate us all. People who ought to be reproducing themselves for the good of the species think abortion is birth control and that childbirth was only worthwhile when their mothers did it."

"I'd ask you to marry me and have my child," he said as the waiter brought our entrees, "but I doubt that's what you had in mind." The waiter left and he stared glumly at the artfully arranged morsels on his plate. "Is this all?"

I lifted my fork. "Nouvelle cuisine is based on minimalism, Andy. Unlike everything else in current society. You and I are throwbacks to still care about trying to make a better world. We're the brontosauruses of the seventies."

"A charming analogy to use at dinner," he muttered. "Actually we were ahead of everybody. Long before the world started jogging and drinking light beer, we were already watching our weight."

We ate in silence for a few minutes before I spoke up again. "Do you realize," I asked in sudden horror, "that a lot of people die before they're sixty? That means we're already middle-aged."

He shook his head. "Not me. I'm fahrevah yunnng."

I laughed despite myself. "Forever young indeed. Bob Dylan's building a goddamn mansion in Malibu and his wife says he beats her. The music world was only political when it was fashionable. The new issue of

Rolling Stone has a full-page ad for diamonds. *Diamonds,* Andy. It sure seems like a hell of a long time since Mario Savio got up on that car in Berkeley and warned us not to trust anybody over thirty."

"You've got to be more flexible," he admonished. "I've decided it's best not to trust anybody wearing a T-shirt for a ten-kilometer race or any kind of blue jeans with somebody else's name on the ass. And to run for the nearest exit any time somebody starts explaining how an M.B.A. will give meaning and substance to their life."

Only my work kept me sane during that period of depression, but my work actually compensated for a lot. Rob Marner, the rising young education prof who had finagled the funding for our demurely named Taylor Street School, had assembled quite a lovely little educational institution atop one of two booming Heart 'N' Soul restaurants.

As Director, Rob Marner spent half his time at the school and the other half off playing Distinguished Professor. I was the reading teacher, Dana Goulding covered arithmetic and science and Marsha Deviver was responsible for everything else. Dana had been teaching in slums long enough to call it a career, first in Philadelphia, then in Milwaukee and now in Chicago. He was gentle, patient and good-natured. Marsha was black, twenty-four and sharp as a razor. I fully expect her to be heading up the Department of Education someday.

We erected mobile partitions and adapted flexible time periods. As much as possible, each child moved independently at his or her own pace and there was a continual hum of activity throughout the day. We had four full-time aides and the students' parents and grandparents came in to help according to their interests and abilities. When it became apparent that several of these women (and they were nearly all female, those assisting relatives) were virtuallly illiterate themselves, I set up an after-school reading program for parents that became a roaring success. At first shy and uncomfortable about their educational weaknesses, the women soon grew closer in their shared accomplishments. At Christmas they bought a huge ornate card for "A Wonderful Teacher" and all signed it carefully. When Loretta Johnston stood and read the syrupy verse inside aloud, I cried. Three months earlier Loretta's six-year-old daughter had been reading at a higher level than her mom.

I put a lot of my own money into materials and became an expert scavenger as well. Maxine Lockford donated an old typewriter, a sewing machine, an aquarium and four church banquet tables. I nagged Ginger till she gave us a dozen magazine subscriptions and wrote out a check for science materials. Andy was most generous of all, providing not just learning materials but also priceless contacts and references to people who would give us more. And in Bisbee, Arizona, Prentiss Granger assembled an Indian Awareness Kit so comprehensive that it filled three cartons.

I wrote letters to national corporations, foundations, Congresspeople and hundreds of local businesses, eating the postage costs. When Maxine discovered that I was actually typing these requests myself, she volunteered first the use of an electric typewriter at her office and then the assistance of her secretary. At her mother's insistence, Ginger also turned over a stack of typing to her own secretary. I particularly savored this, since her firm's notion of *pro bono* work seemed to be suing the gas station which had refused to come out in a midwinter blizzard and extricate a senior partner's Lincoln from the snowbank in his Hinsdale driveway.

So why, if I was doing such wonderful work, Making a Difference, so to speak, did I feel like lying down on the railroad tracks? God only knows, but I became fixated on death and actually mourned Hubert Humphrey, finding it far easier to cherish him in death than it had been to stomach him in life.

"Hubert Humphrey? Did I hear you say you feel bad because *Hubert Humphrey* died? There must be something wrong with this connection." Pren had used the same tone to correct my political ignorance when we were college sophomores.

"If you can just forget about Vietnam for a minute, you have to admit he had a pretty remarkable life. He was always in the vanguard on race, back when it was plenty unpopular."

"I think it asks a bit much to 'forget about Vietnam for a minute.' He was a wishy-washy whore, too busy sucking up to Lyndon Johnson to even consider what was right. Saying that Humphrey was all right except for Vietnam is like saying Hitler was all right except for the Holocaust."

"That's ridiculous!" I was actually angry. I didn't need her to tell me what I should be thinking politically anymore and I hadn't for years. "That sounds like something Bob McCoy would have said in 1968."

She was quiet for a moment. "As a matter of fact," she conceded softly, "that *is* something Bob McCoy said in 1968. Verbatim. And I guess I'd have to admit that you're at least half right about Humphrey, overall. But I'm telling you right now, if Richard Nixon kicks, I don't want to hear any mournful sighs out of you."

"The Trickster? I solemnly swear that I'll eat every page of the White House transcripts if a single word of praise should ever pass my lips."

"Every page?"

"Unabridged. Eighteen-minute gap and all."

By the time I visited Bisbee the following July, Prentiss Granger had thoroughly settled in. Her little cottage clung to the side of a steep hill and was reached by a long precarious wooden stairway. But the climb was well worth the trouble. The onetime miner's shack was painstakingly restored and beautifully decorated in the warm purples and browns of the desert mountains. Navajo blankets, Hopi pottery and Papago baskets were displayed everywhere, set off against whitewashed walls and newly laid red tile floors. The furniture was handcrafted redwood, deceptively simple and designed especially for her by a local cabinetmaker, another sixties refugee who had settled in Bisbee.

Pren seemed surprisingly at home in this colony of mellow, laid-back sorts, though it seemed slightly odd to me to find so many people my own age leading such indolent lives. Of course many of the young locals were artisans and craftsmen, and obviously could ply their trades anywhere so long as they had outlets for the resulting stained glass, wood carvings, paintings, jewelry, leather goods, and clothing. But a lot of others did absolutely nothing.

Pren had made friends almost despite herself. There was a lovely young Nordic blonde named Deirdre who fashioned intricate silver and turquoise jewelry for outlets in Phoenix and Tucson. Deirdre's daughter Jennifer was just a little younger than Melinda and the two little girls played together constantly.

Pren had a boyfriend too. John Washburn was an exceedingly gentle carpenter who had done the structural work on Pren's house and fallen hopelessly in love with her before the first nail was hammered. I liked John. He had a huge bushy anachronistic beard, the kind his urban counterparts had trimmed down to tidy Vandykes. He was friendly and quiet and extremely devoted to Melinda. He had packed his high draft number after Kent State and left Indianapolis, drifting to Colorado, then south to Santa Fe, and finally south again to Bisbee, always seeking greater isolation.

I was initially nervous about being so openly in town and meeting so many people, but I soon realized that Pren's new identity was secure. A published historian had plenty of credibility in a town where the primary occupation seemed to be hanging out.

I went along with her one afternoon to the dilapidated old boarding-house where she was interviewing retired miners for her new book. The Copper Quarters was an odd, rickety place, where water stains on the hallway walls had peeled the wallpaper down through six layers. As we passed open doors of shabby rooms, the feeble old men inside would cast toothless smiles in her direction as they waved and croaked out greetings. She stopped for a moment in a large room at the end of the hall and spoke with four frail fellows playing poker for matchsticks. When she introduced her cousin, they regarded me with gruff suspicion that belied their fragile frames.

"It takes them a while to warm up to strangers," she apologized, as we climbed the sagging stairs to visit old Lefty Ballard. But I was entranced by the rapport she had built with these old-timers, and spent a spellbound two hours in a quiet corner while she led the grizzled octagenarian through a rambling recounting of his own saga of western restlessness.

As we rose to leave, he turned to me for the first time. "That's a good girl," he said, pointing an arthritic finger at Pren. "Helped me get straight with the Social Security."

"They get abused a lot by bureaucrats," she explained as we walked down to Deirdre's house to pick up Melinda. "And a lot of them don't even realize the benefits they're entitled to. So I fill their forms out and make a lot of phone calls. It's hard sometimes to get them to accept that the government owes them anything. They've got a lot of macho pride. But wasn't old Lefty a sweetheart? They've all got such incredibly interesting stories. I was afraid when I started that there might not be enough material to do the job properly, but I'm finding it's just the opposite. There's one old fellow here who left Brooklyn in 1911 to go chase Pancho Villa and he's been roaming around ever since. I think I could get a whole book just out of his story. God knows how I'll ever pare it down."

"They're like hippies from yesteryear, aren't they?"

She nodded enthusiastically. "Exactly! Which is one reason the miners and the new kids in town manage to coexist so well, I think. They may not like to admit it, but these old-timers really understand what it feels like to run away."

We drove down to Mexico and I was intrigued at how easily Pren was able to enter and leave the country at the tiny border checkpoint. We ate stunningly good Mexican food at one small restaurant in town and remarkable vegetarian dishes at another. I adored the Copper Queen Hotel in all its faded splendor.

Melinda was delighted to see me again and I was astonished at how much she had grown. She shared all her favorite books with me and her reading speed and comprehension were superior to that of many adults in my Taylor Street School literacy program. Her curiosity and imagination were absolutely boundless. She was fascinated by fairy tales and mythology and had created a fantasy world for herself populated by princes and dragons and turreted castles. John Washburn had built her a small castle of scrap lumber where she retreated for hours on end with Jennifer. She drew intricatrely complicated pictures of her imaginary kingdom. Her pictures showed a significant talent, and it seemed to me that she might easily become a professional artist one day. Pren agreed. "When she's older, I'm going to see about lessons for her. For right now, though, I just want to let her follow her instincts. She's got so much natural talent, I'm afraid lessons too early might stifle it."

We took Melinda over to visit Tombstone, a strangely hokey little town some twenty-odd miles down the road. I loved Boot Hill, where Melinda scampered gleefully around the deadpan markers for GEORGE JOHNSON, HANGED BY MISTAKE; JOHN HEATH, LYNCHED and other odd townspeople who met strange and violent deaths thousands of miles from their birthplaces. And these were not people who moved because they sought a change in climate either. They were people who fled, most often in the middle of the night.

My planned one-week vacation turned painlessly into two with a quick call to Andy. And then on the eighth night of my visit, after Melinda was in bed and we were sitting listening to an old Simon and Garfunkel album, Pren shocked me.

"What would you say," she asked carefully, "if I told you I was thinking of turning myself in?"

I stared. It was years since I had even considered the possibility. And she had always been steadfastly, obstinately opposed to the idea. "I thought you swore you'd never do that."

"I've said a lot of things. And I certainly meant that when I said it before. But I've been thinking a lot lately about the future. And it seems so limited, somehow. I love doing those books, and I want to keep on doing them. There's a real thrill I feel in capturing history through the actual people who lived it. Not the politicians, or the warmongers, or the dates and places. The little people, the ones who are actually participating in an event or a culture or a time. But I've got to face facts. The more I do, the more visible I become. And to get into some of the subjects that I'd really love to tackle, I'd be exposing myself incredibly. I'd like to do a really first-class Vietnam book, for example, all in the words of the guys who were there. And you know I could never get away with that."

"But—"

She waved a hand to still me. "Wait. The thing is, times have changed. It's 1978, six years since Beaumont. If I'd been caught and tried back then, they would have thrown away the key. But the political climate's a lot different now than it was then. Even in Texas. I'm sure I'd have to do some time, if only to jusitfy that Randy was guilty the way they said he was. But it probably wouldn't be that long, and once it was over, I could really be free again. I could live wherever I wanted, and do the kind of work I want, without always having to worry about someone finding me out."

"What about Melinda?"

She smiled gently. "That's where you come in, Aunt Lou Ann. She'll be old enough to start school in another year. And she really does love you. I was thinking maybe you could keep her while I was gone."

While I was gone. While Prentiss Granger wore a shapeless cotton shift in a hot dry Texas cell. My mind was reeling. Of course I could keep Melinda. That was the easiest part. But I kept feeling the malignant hostility of that courtroom in Texas where Randy Hargis faced the law. And remembering the dogged persistence of Mel Sanford. Everyone had put so much time and effort into hating her and trying to find her that they'd hardly roll out the welcome mat now.

"God, I don't know what to tell you. I see what you're saying, and of course Melinda'd be welcome, but it still makes me nervous to think about it."

She grinned. "Me too. Which is why I thought I'd get an expert opinion. How'd you like to go to San Francisco with me and talk to Jason Abernathy?"

Chapter 6 _____

As the plane touched down for my third visit to San Francisco, I felt my calmness melting away. It had all seemed so reasonable back there in Bisbee. We would slip into town, stay at a hotel and perhaps even do some of the sightseeing we had planned on our last, aborted visit four years ago. But now I found myself dripping sweat, casting anxious eyes on even the pesky religious robots trying to sell me their wretched plastic flowers.

Pren was coming in on a separate flight. By the time she reached our room at the Miyako Hotel in Japantown, I was already halfway through a bottle of Napa Valley pinot chardonnay.

"Not a hitch," she reported cheerfully. "God, it's great to be back here! Not that I don't like Bisbee, but I sure do miss the stimulation of a real city. This would be a great place to raise Melinda. She'd be exposed to so many different people and ideas."

"Let's not put the cart before the horse. Even if your plan works, her first city will be Chicago, remember."

"Say," she exclaimed, pacing excitedly back and forth. "I just thought of something. She could go to your school, couldn't she?"

I giggled. "She'd have to desegregate it."

"So? From everything you say about that school, she'd get a terrific education there. And have the services of the best reading teacher in the Western world."

I poured more wine. "Flatter me some more and I'll buy you dinner. Unless you want me to go see Jason Abernathy right this instant."

She shook her head. "He can wait. After I see him, I want to be able to leave town immediately. And it would be too much of a waste to just duck in and out like that. Nobody knows we're here, and I really don't think anybody's going to recognize me out of the blue. So let's take a day or two and just play first. Rent a car and take a sentimental journey."

Which is exactly what we did. We spent the next three days systematically exploring the Bay area. We walked by the Pacific Heights Wedgwood plate Victorian where I had become a blond for one tumultuous week. We skipped the boat tour of the Bay, but strolled the streets of Chinatown, where I found myself suddenly nauseated outside the Hong Kong Tea House. And we located the Berkeley storefront which had once served as national headquarters for VETRAGE. It was now a hot-tub emporium.

"This really is an incredible place," I mumbled with a mouth full of Tekka Maki at a sushi bar near our hotel. "California. Where else could one governer be Ronald Reagan and the next Jerry Brown?"

"It was Jerry Brown's birthright. He and his daddy are like liberal bookends around the Reagan administration. His sister's a politico herself, down in L.A. She's so hip she uses Brown Rice as her surname."

I laughed. "Everybody's so *involved* in things. And there are so many things to be involved in."

"True enough. One thing about San Francisco, no matter how bizarre your interests might be, you can always find a group of people doing the same thing. Feverishly. There's even a program out here somewhere to help rich people shed those nasty guilt pangs over excessive wealth. And not by giving it away either."

"But giving it away is so much more fun than hoarding."

"That's easy for you to say."

"I know, I know. I don't have to live on my hundred and fifty bucks a week from the Taylor Street School. But I really do love being able to help support the things I believe in. I just can't understand the mentality that celebrates money for the sake of money."

"To your everlasting credit," said Prentiss Granger. "But tomorrow you're going to have to spend a little anyway. And retain a new attorney."

I arrived unannounced at the tangerine and lemon Victorian where Jason Abernathy practiced law at 9:15 the next morning, but he hadn't gotten in yet. So I squirmed in the waiting room, idly flipping the pages of *Mother Jones* and *The Progressive* and watching the receptionist, a beautiful young black woman with fifteen-inch corn rows that must have taken an entire day to braid. She typed furiously while I waited, stopping only to answer the phone. Her phone had an oversized mouthpiece so nobody could hear what she was saying, a nice little security precaution.

At 9:38 Jason Abernathy strode through the door. He wore jeans, a light beige sweater and a tired expression. I recognized him immediately, of course. The shock of silver hair and the deep-set brown eyes were familiar to anyone who paid even the most remote attention to the legal travails of the American left. He nodded to me and picked up a stack of messages from the receptionist. He riffled through them, then turned and crossed the room in two bold strides, hand extended.

"So you're Laurel Hollingsworth! At long, long last we meet! Sorry I wasn't here when you got in, but I had a meeting."

I was amazed that he remembered me. It had been nearly four years since I had spoken to him and I knew that they were years filled with labor strikes, politically oriented murder trials, Supreme Court challenges to questionable legislation and all manner of Significant Things. As I followed him into his office, I felt suddenly more confident.

I assumed that his office was bugged. "I'm bringing you privileged information," I said carefully, "for you to keep in a safe place indefinitely. You're supposed to examine it in my presence and then stash it."

He hefted the envelope I handed him. "Shouldn't take long."

"Think of it as my nickel. I've got to hire you myself now. Privilege and all that."

He smiled. "You're right, of course. But don't worry about that now. I was just hoping you wouldn't be bored."

"I once spent twenty-four hours in a room half this size wondering when Mel Sanford was going to slap me in the hoosegow so I could finally have my one phone call. There wasn't even a copy of *Masters of Deceit*. At least here there's something to look at besides gray steel and a two-way mirror."

He laughed, and just as I'd always imagined, he had a wonderful, practically reckless laugh. At last I'd achieved the goal of seeing Jason Abernathy laugh in person. I suspected that it might not be so simple to attain world peace and universal literacy, my other two aims.

"How is old Mel Sanford?" he asked. "Heard from him lately?"

I shook my head. "No more than usual. He calls about every six months or so to quote me the law on aiding and abetting, but I haven't seen him in the flesh for years. I'm not even sure where he's stationed anymore."

"Washington," sneered Jason Abernathy. "Called to the home office about a year ago. I understand he damn near got indicted himself, with Pat Gray and Felt and Miller, for wiretaps trying to find the Weather people."

"Almost doesn't count. And I'll feel a lot better when that envelope is safely locked up."

"Sure thing." He opened the envelope and pulled out Melinda's birth certificate. He looked up, surprised, and smiled at me. I beamed back, nodding cheerfully. Next he read the Last Will and Testament of Prentiss Granger, a holographic document bearing a complete set of her fingerprints beneath the signature. In it she left all her possessions to Melinda and Melinda to me. I had been shocked when she first showed it to me, but she waved an airy hand. "Don't worry," she reassured me breezily, "I'll live till I'm ninety. It's just that there's been a bit of bubonic plague around these parts lately, and if I turn into a medieval anachronism and public health statistic, I want a guardian on record. I couldn't bear to think of Melinda being raised by some Hughes aerospace engineer in Phoenix or, worse yet, my father. You're the only one I can trust."

When he'd read through the will, he put it and the birth certificate back in the envelope and sealed it into a larger envelope. He wrote a number in the upper left-hand corner, then stood.

"I'm going to put this in the safe. Care to watch?"

I shook my head. "I trust you."

He was halfway around the desk. He leaned backward in a mock swoon. "If only I could get all my clients to feel that way."

He was back in less than five minutes. "C'mon, I'll buy you a cup of coffee."

We walked a block and a half to a charming little café where I ordered cappuccino and Jason Abernathy asked for a cup of Red Zinger. I must have looked surprised, because he grinned crookedly. "Heart," he explained. "Had to give up caffeine and cigarettes or give up breathing. Turned out to be a tougher choice than you'd think. You know, it's a funny thing, you showing up today. I was just thinking about our friend yesterday, hoping she was all right."

"She's more than all right. She's here in town and she wants to see you."

"Oh yeah?" He didn't even blink. "When?"

"At your convenience. She can't exactly drop by the office."

"True enough. Tell you what. A friend of mine has an apartment building near here that has a vacancy right now. I'll get the key and she can meet me there. Say tonight about nine-thirty?"

"Fine. Are you sure it will be safe?"

He sighed deeply. "Laurel, I've been skulking around meeting clients in secret since the McCarthy hearings. This place is perfect. And ever since I started dropping Freedom of Information Act claims on the feds, they've been damn careful to leave me alone."

My heart was racing as we climbed the back stairs to the apartment that night, but the halls held only an aroma of baking cookies. At our quick knock on number seven, Jason Abernathy swung the door open. He bolted it behind us.

"So, it really is you," he told Pren as she pumped his hand. "Seems like forever since you were helping me on that D'Amico case." He turned to me. "Dick D'Amico was a vet who got himself into a pile of trouble trying to blow up a troop train in Oakland back in 'seventy-one. VETRAGE was in on the case, but it was your pal here who did most of the work." His explanation sounded weary, and I suddenly realized what a heavy personal toll his quarter century of defending unpopular causes and people must have taken on him. "Here, have a seat."

He motioned to a mangy dinette set, the only furniture in the dingy little apartment. "We better drink these before they get warm. The refigerator's shot." He opened three cans of Olympia and passed them around as we sat at the table. The back of my chair wiggled alarmingly. "Now. What can I do for you?"

Pren spoke for the first time. "You can tell me what might happen if I decide to come back."

He leaned back, then moved suddenly forward. Apparently his chair back was no more secure than mine. "Hmmmm. That would depend. I'd have to talk to Marty Wheeler and see what life's like in Texas these days, but I can probably give you a pretty good idea. First of all, if you turned yourself in, you'd look a lot more reasonable and contrite. Much better than if somebody discovered you on prints after a drunk driving charge, say. The next thing would be what you've been doing lately. You must have been laying low or I would have heard something. When I was trying to get a line on you when your mother was sick, the trail was stone cold. And I rounded up all the usual suspects. Been up to anything responsible lately? You wouldn't perchance be a director of the Bank of America?"

Our laughter echoed hollowly through the apartment.

"Afraid not," said Pren. "But I did publish a book last summer."

He didn't even look surprised. "It can't have been *Memoirs of the Debutante Revoluntionary,* or I'd have heard. What kind of book?"

"It's an oral history based on a bunch of interviews I did on reservations in the Southwest. *Voices of the Navajos.*"

"*Voices of the Navajos.* . . . *Voices of the Navajos.* That sounds familiar." He brightened suddenly. "Wait a minute! Does it have a blue cover? With an old Indian wrapped in a blanket on it?"

Pren smiled in obvious pleasure. "Yep."

"I *know* that book. That was *you*? I didn't read it myself, but my wife's got it. Native Americans are a special interest of hers. She liked it too. I can remember her talking about it." He rubbed his hands together in apparent satisfaction. "Nice work. And good for our case too. I'm liking this better every minute. The main question, though, is what they've got on you in Texas. And that's a little rougher. Marty Wheeler and I once spent a long liquid evening talking about Randy's trial. He said he felt like a gladiator facing the lions back in Rome, armed with an Exacto knife. But . . . that was years ago. And Randy *did* kill a cop. You were just driving, right?"

Pren was looking increasingly doubtful. "Yes, but—"

He waved her silent. "Just answer the questions, that's your first lesson. Don't volunteer anything. Now. You were outside when Randy and Wilt were in that gas station, right?"

"Yes."

"Did you know that Randy had a gun with him?"

"Sure. Randy never did anything without having a gun with him. Wilt used to swear he kept it in the soap dish when he took a shower."

Abernathy frowned. "We might," he said thoughtfully, "be able to get into the whole Vietnam-syndrome issue, but I'd hate to try a test case based on that in Texas, even now. Let's just get back to the bare facts. You knew that Randy was carrying a gun. Was it registered anywhere?"

"Nope. Randy thought gun registration was subversive. Even when he was borrowing money for beer, he kept up his NRA membership."

"But based on your knowledge of Randy Hargis, a man you knew very well, there was nothing *unusual* about him carrying a gun."

"Absolutely not." She spoke forcefully, and I could see that she was picturing herself on the witness stand.

"Fine. Now why did you stop at that gas station?"

"It wasn't a gas station, really; it was a little grocery place, a convenience store that happened to have gas pumps too. We stopped there to get some beer."

He scowled slightly. "Too bad it couldn't have been something like aspirin. Or tampons. Beer isn't the greatest thing for people who are driving to be buying, after all. Although I do know that driving *while* drinking isn't a crime in Texas, just driving while drunk. Were any of you drunk?"

She considered. "Randy might have been. He was in the back seat as we were riding along and I wasn't really paying attention to how much he drank. He had a cooler back there and just kept slugging it away. Although that wasn't unusual either. Randy drank a lot of beer."

I nodded unconsciously as I recalled my Thanksgiving in Berkeley. I always pay close attention to refrigerators and I knew for a fact that he had gone through almost three cases in four days.

"Was Wilt drunk? Or you?"

She shook her head. "Wilt hadn't had a beer in hours. And I hadn't had anything at all that day."

"All right. Now, why did you wait in the car when they went inside?"

She shrugged. "Why not? I didn't want anything. And I could tell by the fan in the window that it wouldn't be any cooler in there than it was outside. I just wanted to keep moving and get out of Texas. Randy had been acting real funny all day and some guys had hassled him when we had lunch."

Abernathy perked up. "Hassled him? How?"

"Well, Randy had a ponytail, you know. And a big chip on his shoulder. There were some punks in a pickup truck, teen-agers. They were giving him wolf whistles and it really pissed him off. It took Wilt a long time to calm him down."

"Was that the only time anybody bothered him for his appearance?"

She shook her head. "No. There was some gas station attendant out in West Texas earlier that day. He kept calling Randy 'Miss' while he was filling the tank. But if what you're driving at is was Randy frazzled by the time we hit Beaumont, the answer is absolutely yes. I don't think he ever got over being kicked out by his parents. And being in Texas again was bringing all that back. He was talking a lot that day about how his old man had a lot of nerve telling him he wasn't a patriot when he lost his foot over in Nam proving he was. And about how his father hadn't even been overseas in World War II, so what did he know about combat, anyway?"

"Okay. We have Randy acting, shall we say, a little unstable. You stop for beer. You're waiting outside. Did you hear any sounds from inside while you were waiting?"

"No."

"Now tell me exactly what you saw when Wilt and Randy came out." I saw a wave of tension sweep through her body. Abernathy reached over and patted her hand gently. "I know it's hard," he soothed. "But we have to sort out the facts."

She set her jaw and spoke as if reciting. "Randy came out waving his gun in one hand with a six-pack in the other. Wilt was right behind him. He said, 'Randy, for God's sake, *no! Come back!*' He was trying to grab Randy's gun hand. Then an old guy in khakis and a T-shirt ran out carrying a sawed-off shotgun. Sixteen gauge. A green Chevy pickup pulled into the lot just as the guy with the shotgun came out of the store. A young guy jumped out of the pickup waving a forty-five and hollering for everybody to hit the deck. Randy started to fire at the young guy and Wilt dove onto Randy's gun hand. Randy's shot went a little bit wild and winged the young guy's shoulder so he dropped the forty-five." She was getting paler now and speaking very quickly. I held my breath, knowing what came next. "Then the old man with the shotgun fired one barrel." She paused and took a deep breath. "That shot killed Wilt. It also got Randy in the right arm and side a little bit but he grabbed his three-fifty-seven with his left hand and shot the young guy, who was trying to go for his own gun that he'd dropped. The old guy tried to fire the other barrel and it didn't go. Jammed, I think." She stopped, looking utterly drained.

Abernathy patted her hand again. "Did the young guy in the pickup identify himself as a police officer?"

"No. He just kept yelling, 'hit the deck.' "

"All right. What happened next?"

"Randy jumped into the car, screaming at me to split. I had the keys 'cause I'd been driving the last stretch. And I split."

"You didn't wait to see how Wilt was?"

"Wilt was very dead," she said flatly. "There were pieces of his head all over Randy's shirt."

"I'm sorry," he said gently. "I had to ask. Did you feel any physical fear from Randy when he started yelling at you to leave?"

"Not really. Randy never scared me. He was always a little strange, but he worshiped Wilt and I was Wilt's lady. He wouldn't have hurt me any more than he'd have hurt Wilt."

"Even after a scene like he'd just been through?"

She shook her head firmly. "Even then. Particularly then."

"Well, then. It's a matter of record that you separated from Randy pretty quickly, because they found him the next morning by himself. Did any other illegal activity occur while you were still with him?"

She offered a rather wan smile. "I broke the speed limit some. But that was all."

He started to sit back, remembered his rickety chair and leaned forward on the table instead. "That sounds," he said slowly, "like a fairly good case for you. Of course with a jury you can never tell. Now, about the charges. There are federal charges of flight to avoid prosecution, but generally in a situation like this those would be dropped. That's probably particularly true right now with so much heat on the FBI and those wiretap indictments. The Texas charge was accessory to felony murder. That's a capital offense, and Randy *was* convicted before he died. However, I don't think any prosecutor would seriously seek a death sentence in a case like yours. And there would be your testimony about how it wasn't intended to be a robbery. You might be able to plead out to a lesser charge. But if it goes to trial, you'll have to take the stand. Now granted, there isn't all that much against you when you put it into a simple fact situation. But you've been gone for six years. Once you take the stand, you can be open to all sorts of other questions. That was what crucified Patty Hearst. And I know who you were hanging around with when you were first underground. If you had a lily white track record then, I'm J. Edgar Hoover. So think carefully before you answer my next question, and for God's sake omit the particulars because I don't want to hear them. Now then, is there any other criminal activity that you're aware of for which there might be witnesses or hard evidence against you? Anywhere?"

I thought of the Presidio bombing, of the car she had stolen in Beaumont, of the car *we* had stolen in San Francisco. And I knew there had to be plenty more besides. I held my breath again.

"No," she answered firmly, looking him square in the eye.

"Well, then," he said, opening another beer. "I'd say you're in reasonably good shape. I'll have to talk to Marty, of course. And you've got to realize there's no way we can get you off totally. Maybe in a more progressive jurisdiction, but certainly not in Texas and there's no way to make this anything other than a local crime. A jury could end up throwing the book at you, no matter how respectable you seem now. And a judge might be even worse. There'll almost have to be a sentence, with a chance of getting it suspended because you're leading a really upright life. That Navajo book will certainly help."

"I'm working on another one right now."

"Oh, really? More Navajo?"

She shook her head. "Miners. Old guys in western mining towns. Actually, I'd kind of like to get it finished before I do this. In case I have to go away for very long."

"When will you be finished?"

She cocked her head. "Hard to say, exactly. I've got most of the interviews done already, but transcribing them takes forever. I'd say another seven or eight months, anyway. And of course it will be another year before it's published."

"You're not in any danger of being discovered right now?"

"I don't think so."

"Well, then, it might make sense to finish up this project before you go in. Just the manuscript, not getting it published. That will happen plenty fast when they find out who you are. But I'd say that if one serious book looks good on your record, two would look incredible. Of course I couldn't advise you to wait as your attorney."

"Of course not. Actually, I'd rather wait a while anyway, till my little girl starts school. Then I won't mind so much if I have to ... go away for a while. What do you think?"

"I think it's your decision."

She looked at him, looked at me, then looked back at him. "Then let's make a date for next summer."

Chapter 7 _____

"I just don't understand," I wailed. "It's all so horrible and pointless. They're going to spend eight million dollars to bring back all those hideous bloated bodies? Why the hell didn't they just give them the eight million in the first place? I bet nobody would have gone to Guyana then."

Andy sighed deeply and leaned back further into his chair. He was plenty tired of listening to me carry on about the People's Temple by now. He had somehow managed to maintain a calm and balanced attitude toward the entire Jonestown Massacre. "They should have known better when he asked them to go to a country whose only previous claim to fame was Devil's Island."

"I don't see how you can joke about it. How could anyone poison their own *children*? I have dreams, Andy, horrible dreams every night where these tiny little bloated bodies dance in a circle around a huge swollen corpse wearing black glasses. They keep singing *Why? Why? Why?* in little echoing voices and then one of them jumps up and pulls off the glasses. There aren't any eyes, Andy, just huge yawning holes that suck all those little bodies in."

"Laurel, you've just got to snap out of this." I could tell from his tone that his patience was wearing thin. "Now, come on. They're showing *The Producers* out at Northwestern tonight. I think we ought to go."

I shook my head. "You go. I couldn't possibly."

"Want some cheese and crackers?"

"I suppose."

"You *suppose?* You mean you're off your feed? This is more serious than I realized!"

"Forget it, Andy. It won't work. You can't cheer me up."

And indeed he wasn't able to. I moped, I whined, I walked about in a spooky haze for weeks. I even left Thanksgiving dinner at Maxine's early. I felt the anguish even more acutely at work. My students were so like the Jonestown children, boys and girls who were passed over when life's advantages were distributed. But as I looked at them and saw their precious smiles, their wonderful energy, their enthusiasm and joy, I felt myself hardening inside. How could anyone kill children like these in the name of God?

"That's what makes me the maddest, I think, that it all happened in the name of religion."

"Laurel, *please.*" Andy looked up from his chicken enchiladas and poured more beer into both our glasses from the pitcher. "Can't we get through one meal without discussing Jonestown?"

"I'm sorry. I'm really obsessed, aren't I? It's just that I've been thinking about this religion angle and I'm amazed at how many horrible things in history have come out of some bozo's interpretation of God's will. The Inquisition, for example. Hanging witches in Salem Village. Dozens of hideous wars. I mean, what does God think when Tex Watson and Charles Colson and Larry Flynt go around calling themselves born-again Christians? It's enough to make a body yearn for the Reverend Billy James Hargis."

"Who?" Andy sounded both puzzled and mildly interested. I guess he thought this changed the subject, so it was worth pursuing.

"You mean you don't know about the Reverend Billy James? He used to travel the South with his road show when I was a kid, explaining how sex education was a communist plot and niggers were an abomination unto the Lord. The main thing that distinguishes him from all the other two-bit religious hustlers is that God got even. Two of his most promising protégés married each other, and on their wedding night they each tearfully confessed that they'd known their spiritual leader. In the biblical sense."

Andy roared. "Boy, do I love it when hypocrites get it between the eyes. Or in this case, I guess you could more accurately say between the legs."

*   *   *

The *Chicago Tribune* ran an article on the Taylor Street School in early January, a huge glowing spread on page one of the Tempo section. The headline read COMMUNITY SUPPORT HELPS EXPERIMENTAL SCHOOL FLOUR-ISH and just below it I was pictured with one of my reading groups. It was a flattering picture and an even more flattering article, which I promptly dispatched to everyone I ever met.

Then two days after I mailed the last of my bulky manila envelopes, the snows began. At first I was excited by the blizzard. We'd be snow-bound like the Bobbsey Twins, having a marvelous adventure. Twenty inches fell in forty-eight hours, and Andy and I turned our tiny front yard into a sophisticated snow fort guarded by a giant snowperson. We had plenty of food and a full tank of fuel oil, though we argued con-stantly over where to set the thermostats.

"There's an energy crisis Andy, remember?"

"You're damn straight there's a crisis. I'm wearing three sweaters and still freezing, that's what the crisis is. You should have called John Wayne Gacy and had the place insulated if you weren't going to use the furnace this winter."

I threw a copy of *Gourmet* at him. "That's a horrible thing to say! What's the matter with you?"

He stood up and started swinging his arms from side to side, like a baboon. He whirled his head around in a circle and twirled his eyes si-multaneously. "Stir crazy," he muttered in a funny voice. "Stir crazy." Then he jumped me and we rolled across the floor, laughing.

In point of fact, however, Andy *was* stir crazy. Everything in Chicago had ground to a halt. It was a full week before they finally plowed our narrow side street, a week with no newspaper or mail delivery, no Taylor Street School, no job training for the handicapped. We were stuck.

I caught up with all my magazines, reread *Shogun,* scrubbed the house from ceiling fixtures to baseboards and worked in the darkroom till I ran out of photographic paper. We watched a lot of TV, and I noticed that for all of his fashionable feminism, Andy seemed quite engrossed by the current spate of tits-and-ass shows, clones of *Charlie's Angels* in which trios of beautiful morons presented themselves as flight attendants, TV researchers, everything but brain surgeons. Perhaps we hadn't come such a long way after all, baby.

One night while Andy was watching Farrah Fawcett pretend to be an unsuccessful hooker—a concept so mind-boggling I was forced to leave the room—he suddenly yelled. "Hey, Laurel, come quick!" I dashed out from my bedroom and found Jimmy Stewart aw-shucksing his way through a Firestone commerical. Andy had nearly totaled his car when a new Firestone blew out several months earlier, before anyone knew there was an epidemic of defective tires. "Mr. Smith Takes a Dive!" he chortled.

Mr. Smith gave way to Cathy Rigby offering sanitary napkins as large as her thighs. "Why is it," Andy asked, "that people can't buy anything without a celebrity endorsing it?"

I shrugged. "Nothing really works anymore. If you're paying attention to *who's* selling something, maybe you won't notice that it isn't worth shit."

"Oh, I don't know," he answered earnestly. "That roach powder worked pretty well, just like The Champ said it would. God, I'm hungry," He suddenly jumped to his feet. "I just remembered something important!" He dashed out the front door and rumbled up the stairs. Two minutes later he was back, waving two bags of Pepperidge Farm cookies. "Bordeaux or Milano, milady? I forgot all about these. It's my survival food, in case of natural disasters or World War III. Surely a blizzard qualifies as a natural disaster."

"Absolutely," I agreed, reaching for the Milanos. "In fact, I'd say there's some sort of low-level chemical poisoning affecting the entire United States lately."

"Please, Laurel, no more Jonestown talk. You promised."

"Who said anything about Jonestown? Have you been paying attention to what's been happening this week? Some wacko hijacked a plane to get Charlton Heston to read a statement. The Shah of Iran abdicated. Richard Nixon went back to the White House and the first Red Chinese official ever to visit this country was there. So was John Denver, singing 'Rocky Mountain High.' *John Denver.* Patty Hearst's sentence was commuted. It snowed in Los Angeles. And a sixteen-year-old girl shot up a schoolyard in San Diego because she 'didn't like Mondays.' I tell you, I'm afraid to watch the news anymore."

"Don't worry," Andy assured me. "After all that, nothing else could possibly happen."

But he was wrong. On the ten o'clock news that night we learned that a Chicago snowplow driver had gone berserk, utterly demolishing dozens of cars and crushing a person inside one of them. The reason? He "hated his job."

*　　*　　*

My spring vacation retreat to Bisbee seemed timed perfectly as a retreat from all this madness. And I was desperately anxious to see Pren and Melinda again. Pren was in the final stages of the miners manuscript and it was time to do some serious planning for her return to the world. She'd been sounding a little hesitant lately, which concerned me. Martin Wheeler had long since reported back to Jason Abernathy about his talks with the Beaumont prosecutor. The DA was unwilling to make any concessions in advance of her surrender, but both of the lawyers regarded that as a formal position that could easily change once she surfaced. The store manager was still in Beaumont, but one of the two old ladies who'd been witnesses against Randy was dead and the other was in a nursing home.

And Pren seemed to be getting cold feet. "I really need to talk to you in person," she said on our last call before the trip. "Maybe it's just as well that you think the world's falling apart. It'll make Bisbee seem more seductive. And bring plenty of film. The desert's just starting to come into bloom and I want to get some good shots of cactus flowers to hang in my cell."

It all sounded quite splendid. Bisbee might not have been ideally suited for a lot of things, but it was a dandy place to retreat from reality.

So what happened? The day before I left, Three Mile Island blew its top.

When Pren picked me up outside the Holiday Inn in Tucson, she was grinning. "Remember *On the Beach*? If this is Armageddon, and the look on your face says you think it is, you'll probably get a few more days just by being here. And I'm up for celebrating too. I just sent off the manuscript yesterday and I'm itching to play."

We stopped several times along the highway to shoot pictures of the cactus flowers which were, as she had promised, magnificent. "Just think," I said as she clowned among the saguaros, "pretty soon I can take pictures of you too."

A strange look crossed her face. "Let's just stick to Melinda for now, all right? I can't wait to show you how well the pictures you took of her last time turned out. Not that she looks anything like them anymore. I can't believe how fast she's growing."

Melinda was overjoyed to see me, running screaming from her play castle and all but plummeting down the steep staircase. Her hair was cut very short and had gotten notably darker, so that it was nearly the same shade of chestnut that her mother's had been when we first met. Melinda looked, in fact, like a miniature version of that Chadwick junior of yesteryear, who now looked like somebody else altogether.

Pren thanked the neighbor who had watched Melinda and the three of us walked down to Deirdre's. We left Melinda with Deirdre and Jennifer and went on down to the Copper Kettle, one of Pren's favorite hangouts. The Copper Kettle was a casually restored saloon, almost self-consciously primitive, with only a country and western jukebox as concession to the twentieth century.

John Washburn was already there and he rose laconically to kiss Pren hello and hug me. It still seemed odd to see her as part of a couple again, particularly with somebody as apolitical and laid back as John. But they always seemed comfortable together, and of course it wouldn't be for much longer.

John was with a group of half a dozen other folks I had met the previous summer, all but one of them male. There were also new faces, one belonging to an interesting-looking guy with bright red hair and a beautifully proportioned body. I soon attracted his specific attentions and he identified himself as Fred Langren, an itinerant potter originally from Spokane by way of Seattle, Portland, San Francisco and Denver. Fred had recently blown into town and was not yet decided on whether to make Bisbee his permanent domicile, as much as anyplace had ever been his permanent domicile. He seemed, as we talked, to be the sort of fellow who spends his entire life in a state of indecision.

He had cousins in Atlanta, my alleged hometown, so we played a little do-you-know. I rather enjoyed my occasional role as Lou Ann Baxter, vacationing Atlanta teacher, and particularly relished sharing the inside scoop on what Jimmy Carter had *really* been like as governor.

Fred claimed to love my drawl and he was very attentive. He laughed at my brand new routine about radioactive Hershey bars from the plant just down the pike from Three Mile Island. "Even the almonds glow in the dark," I intoned in my best Don Pardo voice. "Perfect for those midnight snacks!"

Pren seemed restless, but I paid little attention, concentrating on getting drunk and blotting out the world. It was, after all, Saturday night, and the world was likely to blow up any second.

The jukebox was playing country and western, which I still didn't like much, but after a gallon or so of Budweiser, damn near anything sounds good. The bar filled up as we ate dinner, and before I knew what was happening, I was actually dancing with Fred Langren, some odd cowboy dance that I never got straight but which was still a lot of fun. He had his arm around my waist when we went back to the table and it felt quite comfortable there.

Pren apologetically explained that she really had to get Melinda to bed, and Fred promptly offered to see me home. "By all means stay if you like," Pren told me, and with Fred's hand on my thigh, that seemed quite a pleasant prospect. Then Janet Cartwright and John Washburn bid everyone a merry good evening. I noted, as they left, that Pren was still quite sober, an automatic act of fugitive caution.

I was no fugitive, however, and had no such constrictions. I was absolutely blasted by the time Fred and I stumbled into the deserted streets. Freezing though I was, I declined the offer of his jacket. It seemed a lot nicer to have his arm around me instead, and when he stopped to kiss me, I felt warmth and desire surge up uncontrollably. It was a long time since I'd gotten laid and I swear if it hadn't been so cold, I'd have ripped his jeans off right there on the street corner.

Instead I pulled myself reluctantly away. "Not tonight," I whispered. "I've gotta get back."

"How about tomorrow then?"

If I hesitated even a second it was only because I was so drunk I feared my speech would slur. "You're on."

He kissed me again at the foot of Pren's stairs, then helped me make the agonizing climb. John was gone, but I could see Pren through the window, lying on the sofa. The soft strains of "Slow Train Coming" seeped gently through the wall. Fred kissed me once again and I all but fell into the room. It was looking like this might turn out to be just the vacation I needed.

That forlorn hope was shattered the next morning as Pren and I washed the breakfast dishes. Melinda was out playing in her castle with Jennifer.

"I've got a problem," Pren said abruptly, "that blows a great big hole in our plans for this fall. I'm pregnant."

"Oh, no!"

She nodded her head grimly. "Oh, yes."

"Does John know?"

"Nope. If I told him, the first thing he'd want to do is march off to a justice of the peace and get married. Which is not exactly in my game plan. And neither is this."

I sat down at the kitchen table and opened a beer. It was bound to be five o'clock somewhere in the world. "You're sure."

She joined me at the table and poured herself a glass of milk. I flashed back to the Holiday Inn at Fisherman's Wharf and her pregnancy diet before Melinda's birth. "I'm sure. Believe me, after all this time, I don't have any trouble recognizing the symptoms. I've been down this road before. Four times, counting now."

I pointed at the milk. "And you're going to keep it?"

She shrugged. "I honestly don't know. But of course I can't take any chances with the baby's health."

So she was thinking of it as a baby already. "You could turn yourself in anyway."

She stared at me indignantly. "Are you crazy? You think I'd have a baby in *jail*? Not that actually having the babies has ever given me much trouble. But I don't think you get the state of the art in prenatal care in Texas prisons. And it would be too horrible to go through with it and then have the baby just snatched away from me. I've been through that once before. And don't tell me that I'd get the baby back eventually. Of course I would. I suppose I might even be able to talk you into taking it once it was born, until I got out. Is there day care at your school?"

I nodded. "The mothers who come help bring their babies, but it's not really official." Then I suddenly burst into tears.

"Hey, take it easy. This is a problem, but it's not any kind of tragedy."

"I had it all planned," I sniffled. "Everything was going to work out so well."

She patted my shoulder. "And it still will. I haven't absolutely decided to go through with this. We could end up right on schedule, just the way we worked it out." Her tone sounded doubtful.

"But?"

"But I just don't know. I really *would* like to have another kid. I think Melinda's probably the single most important thing I've ever done with my life. And I find myself wondering a lot lately about what happened to my son. There was a time when I could just forget about him from one of his birthdays to the next, but now I think about him almost every day. He's nearly fourteen now, believe it or not. And if he looks at all like his daddy, he's bound to be a heartbreaker."

"His mama ain't exactly ugly either," I reminded. "And if he got your brains, he's probably already at M.I.T."

She actually seemed embarrassed. "That's sweet. But you know he's probably never going to leave Georgia. I always figured he was adopted by some nice conservative couple in a small town. Which makes me responsible for putting another redneck into the world."

"The jury's still out on environment versus genes." By now I was feeling better. I blew my nose and managed the ghost of a smile. "And you're still plenty young enough to have more kids. We *know* you don't have any fertility problems!"

She laughed. "That's for damn sure! I swear, sometimes I think a guy could beat off into his handkerchief in the next room and I'd still end up pregnant. But what if they really send me away for a long time? I could be too old when I get out."

"That doesn't seem very likely. And there's amni— amnio— whatever that stupid word is. I never did figure out how to pronounce it. There's tests."

"Amniocentesis," she enunciated carefully. "Sure. There's that. But that doesn't make any decision any easier now. And there's one other thing I haven't told you. John knows who I am."

I gaped. "How?"

"Somebody told him."

"Somebody told him," I repeated flatly. "This is like one of those wooden Russian dolls that you keep opening and finding smaller dolls inside."

"I know. And it complicates things, because I don't have any way of knowing who else might be on to me and not saying anything. You see, folks around here really value privacy. But the people who told John are gone."

"Oh, terrific. Where'd they go, the police academy?"

She chuckled. "Hardly. It was Bob and Carol McIntosh. I don't know if you ever met them." I shook my head. "They've gone back to New York. It was too desolate here for Carol. She kept wanting to walk down Fifth Avenue and get her tail pinched. Anyway, I talked to them after John confessed he knew my guilty secret, and I don't think they're any danger to me. Carol remembered me from VETRAGE days in Berkeley. She had a brother who came back from Nam a para in a chair and for a while she was working in the movement. Her brother killed himself and she went back to New York. And then a couple of other places before here. But as I said, Carol won't tell. I'm convinced of it."

"If she knows and John knows, somebody else could. Easily."

"I'll have to risk it, at least for now. Of course, like Jason said, it'll be much better if I turn myself in instead of getting picked up."

We were silent for a while, listening to Melinda's shrieks from the playhouse as she admonished Knight Bainbridge to mind his manners.

"If you really want to have this baby," I said slowly, "I could take it right after you delivered." I thought about colic and two A.M. feedings with a mild internal shudder. Somehow I had always thought that when that time arrived for me, I'd have a husband to help shoulder the burden. And that the baby would be my own. "When would that be?"

"December."

"That's not so far away." I pictured the Bide-a-Wee diaper truck pulling up outside my brownstone in a blizzard. "But what about John?"

"I won't marry him. Definitely not. He's only a diversion, much as I like him. But I guess we could tell everybody here we were married. I don't think he'd like that very much, but I can usually get him to do what I want."

"He'd probably want to keep the baby when you went away. And if he's the acknowledged father, he'd have pretty good grounds."

She flinched. "I hadn't thought of that. And I wouldn't want it either. Maybe I could leave here and go somewhere else just till I have the baby. That way John would never need to know."

"And he wouldn't tell when you left? A man scorned . . ."

"John is a fundamentally simple person. I'm sure I could find a story he'd believe, and tell him I was coming back. And then, when the baby and Melinda were safe in Chicago, I could march up the courthouse steps in Beaumont free and clean. It would be a rotten thing to do to him, I suppose, but I've done rottener things before. One of the basic truths I've had to accept about myself is that I'm not a very nice person."

"So where does that leave us?"

Melinda and Jennifer suddenly dashed into the room. "Knight Bainbridge won't listen anymore," Melinda announced seriously. "I had to send him to the dungeon."

Pren looked at me over their bobbing heads. "It leaves us in Bisbee, Arizona, where you're on a vacation of debauchery. Now didn't you say you were supposed to meet Fred Langren for lunch?"

And so I did. And by the time I went back to Chicago, Pren had made her mind up. She would leave Bisbee and have the baby before turning herself in. It was simply a question of finding a congenial new locale.

Chapter 8 _____

Two months later, I was on my way out the door late on Saturday afternoon when the phone started ringing. The moment I picked it up and heard the hollow echo of long distance, I knew instinctively that something was wrong. And when I heard John Washburn's faint twang ask tentatively for Lou Ann, I knew that something was quite dreadfully wrong. I sat down abruptly, anxious to head him off before he said anything traceable.

"John? Don't say a single unnecessary word, all right? Has something bad happened?"

"Yes."

"Are you at a pay phone?"

"Yes." His voice was so faint the booth could have been in Guam.

I thought fast. We had celebrated his birthday in Bisbee the previous April. "Listen carefully. I want you to give me the number of the booth where you are. But I want you to give it to me in code." He started to protest and I cut him off brusquely. "Just shut up and listen. I want you to subtract the number for the month of your birthday from each number before you give it to me. Like if you were born in January and the first three digits were seven two oh, you'd tell me six one nine. And never mind the area code. Understand?"

There was a moment's silence. "I guess so. If you're sure this is necesssary. . . ."

"I'm sure, dammit! Now hurry. Give me the number and I'll call you back within five minutes."

I made it to the nearest booth in two and a half and he picked up the phone on the first ring.

"Sorry I had to put you off, John, but I'm sure you understand. Now tell me what's going on."

"There was a fire."

My heart crash-landed at my feet. "Oh, dear God! Janet? Melinda?"

"Melinda's fine. She's with Deirdre. But Janet's hurt pretty bad. I'm in Tucson. They brought her up here to the burn unit."

The burn unit. "John, what happened? Was it the house?"

"No, it was the Copper Quarters, that old boardinghouse where the old geezers live." I flashed on the rickety old building, with its sagging stairways and peeling wallpaper and decrepit tenants. "She was down there when the fire started, and she helped a lot of the old guys get out. It was so old and dry, it went up like kindling. Fifteen of them didn't make it out at all."

"Oh, *no*! *No!!*" I realized I was moaning. Fire. *Burns. The burn unit.* The beautiful face and body of Prentiss Granger trapped in an inferno. "How badly is she hurt?" For a moment I heard only hollow, echoing silence. "John?"

"She's not that badly burned," he said, and relief flooded over me. "But when the building came down, she was halfway out. A lot of stuff crashed down on her. I got there just as the building collapsed, and I helped pull her out. It took three of us to dig down to her. I thought she was dead. She came to for a second just as they were putting her in the ambulance and told me to call you. Knew your number right off the top of her head. Then she passed out again."

I had to ask. "Her face?"

"No. The burns are mostly on her legs. But the doctors are scared, Lou Ann. I am too. I think you'd better come."

I pictured the body of my oldest and dearest friend trapped beneath timbers as a holocaust raged around her. Tears rolled down my cheeks as I fought to regain control.

"I'll be there just as soon as I can get to the airport. Listen, John, this is very important. You've got to keep the reporters away. This will be news, and we can't have them find out who she really is."

"I'll do my best," he answered fiercely, and I felt confident that no snoopy reporters would get anywhere near Janet Cartwright. I got directions to the hospital and hung up.

And then my body swung into overdrive. I managed to get a plane reservation on a flight leaving in an hour and a half. I fairly flew back to the brownstone, planning all the way. Andy was away for the weekend, but I managed to reach him at his parents' in Calumet City. I told him only that I'd been called out of town on an emergency and that he'd have to feed Bubba for a day or two. I reached Rob Marner and told him that my brother and his family had been seriously hurt in an automobile accident and I had to go home to Louisiana. Then I threw odd items in a suitcase, cleaned out my emergency cash reserve and flagged down a cab for O'Hare.

At the Tucson airport I bought the local paper and found a photograph of the raging fire on page one. I could barely even recognize the building. Sixteen elderly men had been killed when the building collapsed and three others had succumbed to burns and smoke inhalation. Eleven people were still hospitalized. Three victims were in critical condition, including Janet Cartwright, the author of *Voices of the Navajos*, who was credited with saving dozens of lives in the first crucial moments before the entire building went up. It was believed that a carelessly discarded cigarette had caused the blaze.

By the time I got my rental car to the hospital, visiting hours were over. An officious gray lady began giving me a little lecture about hospital regulations and I just exploded. I have no idea what I said to her but the next thing I knew I was holding a tearful John Washburn in my arms. Behind us, double doors led to the nameless horrors of the burn unit. As the door opened and a doctor emerged, I heard a bloodcurdling howl of pain, barely identifiable as human. John grabbed the doctor's white coat and he stopped to talk to us. He was a long lanky fellow with a slight twangy drawl and a weary gentle expression.

"She's just back from Recovery," he explained. "We have her here instead of Intensive Care because of the burns, but they aren't the worst part of the problem. ICU's full anyway. There was a bad auto crash on the interstate. The surgery was successful as far as it went. She's got some pretty serious internal injuries, and I'm afraid she miscarried." I saw John's expression of pain turn to disbelief and I touched his arm. I knew Pren hadn't told him about the baby. "There'll have to be more surgery later, when she's stronger. She's got broken ribs and a punctured lung and some pretty serious hemorrhaging. But she's still alive. That's the important part for right now. She's young and she's in excellent physical condition. If she can make it through the next seventy-two hours, we can all breathe a little easier. But the burns are a special problem. She's burned over thirty percent of her body, and she's extremely susceptible to infection right now. I think we'd better all keep praying."

"Can we see her?" My voice sounded hollow and distant.

"She's not conscious. But you can go in for a few minutes if you gown up first. Remember, we've got to fight the infection."

John went in first, emerging moments later ashen beneath his beard. He collapsed blindly into a chair as I dressed in a baggy green gown and mask and followed the nurse into Pren's room.

She lay utterly still, with half a dozen different tubes and wires protruding from her body. All manner of awesome machinery blipped and whirred and monitored her faltering life signs. I fell into the chair beside her bed sobbing helplessly as a gowned nurse fiddled with the machinery.

Until now, I had somehow managed to convince myself that it really wasn't that serious. But her lashes and brows were partly singed away and faint beads of sweat lay on her brow. Her skin tone was oddly surreal, a soft deadly gray with a flushed red overlay from the heat of the fire. I tried without success to tell myself that the bouncing green lines on the machines proved she was alive and fighting. And I prayed for the first time in years.

John and I spent the night in that waiting room, and I assured him I knew nothing about a pregnancy. Neither of us slept, but neither of us was awake either. An authoritative clock on the wall claimed that time was passing, but I found it difficult to believe.

In the morning I found the Business Office and forked over a thousand dollars cash on her account. Business then shunted me over to Admitting, where an animated little gray lady wanted to know all sorts of things about her family medical history. Since I was calling myself next of kin, I made up a bunch of hooey and at last they left me alone.

I spoke briefly with Deirdre, then told Melinda that her mother was a very brave woman and the doctors were helping to make her better just as fast as they could. Stung by the force of my own lies, I brushed off a couple of reporters who wanted to know more about the heroine of Bisbee's worst fire in sixty years. John and I tried to eat breakfast, then brunch, then lunch. Each time we left our food cold and untouched on the heavy white institutional plates.

In the early afternoon she regained consciousness and they let me speak to her for a few minutes. Her color was still terrible and her eyes were filmy. I had to lean within inches of her face to hear her labored whisper.

"I really did it this time," she rasped.

"You're going to be fine." I made my voice be cheerful. "Just hang on and concentrate on getting better."

She shook her head slightly from side to side, then cringed in pain. "I'm dying."

"Nonsense!"

She squeezed my hand. "No bullshit, Laurel. There isn't time."

"Look, the burns are bad. I won't lie to you. And you were kind of smashed up when the building fell. But your doctors are really first rate. I've talked to them. You're gonna make it, I promise you. It'll just take time. And your cover is still okay."

"The baby?"

I shook my head slowly.

She looked waxen as her lashless eyes blinked. "Melinda?"

"Melinda's with Deirdre and Jennifer. I just talked to her and she said to tell you she loves you and get better fast."

I saw tears well up in her eyes and I felt my own moisten too. "It all went so wrong," she said weakly. I didn't know if she meant the fire or the shoot-out in Beaumont or maybe her entire life.

"It will get right again."

She closed her eyes. "I'm so tired. And I hurt so bad."

I had to leave her then, but every hour they let one of us see her for five minutes. She was asleep or unconscious all through the afternoon. I made John go out for food at one point, just because he was so anxious and edgy. But the burgers he brought back tasted like sawdust and the fries were even worse.

Seventy-two hours, the doctor had said. Somehow we made it through twelve, twenty-four, thirty-six. I never left the hospital. I spoke frequently to Deirdre, who was holding down the fort in Bisbee. By dinnertime on the first day, Deirdre reported that Melinda was refusing to eat. I spoke to Melinda again and explained that her mama had specifically asked her to do everything that Deirdre said. Two of John's friends came by the second evening, bringing him a change of clothes.

I left John with his friends and found a pay phone in the hospital lobby. I needed the comfort and reassurance of somebody I could trust absolutely. I fed coins into the phone and called Andy in Chicago.

"Andy?" My voice sounded weak and faltering. "Andy, it's Laurel. I need to talk to you. This is going to sound crazy, but you know that place where we had dinner last Thursday?" It was a new sushi bar on Broadway, two blocks from the brownstone. "Could you go down there now? There's a pay phone outside. I'll call it in ten minutes."

He sounded unsurprised. "Sure, no problem. Are you all right?"

"No." I was starting to cry. "No, I'm not. Please hurry."

When he answered the pay phone I had pulled myself together somewhat. But at the sound of his voice the tears returned. "I don't know how to explain all this, Andy. It's kind of a long complicated story and I'm not really sure where to begin."

"If it has anything to do with friendships, very *old* friendships, I think I can save you a little time. I already know a lot about it, Laurel."

I was too shaken to think clearly. "But how ... I don't understand...." I had never told Andy about Pren.

He spoke gently. "I notice things, Laurel. I notice paranoia and mysterious disappearances and unexplained absences and photographs on walls. Also, Ginger has told me a lot of stuff over the years."

"Then you *do* know. Oh Andy, I should have told you all about it years ago, but I—"

"Never mind that. You don't need to apologize. But whatever is happening now, you sound awfully upset. Tell me how I can help."

"You can listen, Andy." And then I spilled out everything, the fire and Pren's injuries and Melinda and how frightened I was that she was going to die. He listened patiently, asked the right questions, took it all in with gentle understanding. Until I spoke to him, I hadn't realized just how terrified I was.

"Would you like me to come?" he asked when I had finished. "I couldn't do much but—"

"No," I answered. "I appreciate the offer, really I do. But I'll be all right. I just had to talk to you."

"If you change your mind, I'll be on twenty-four-hour call. If I'm not home, I'll be at work. You know the number. And Laurel, even if you don't want me to come, keep calling me. Don't try to carry this one alone."

I felt better than I had for thirty-six hours when I went back upstairs to rejoin John Washburn in our vigil.

*   *   *

When sunrise came a second time, they told us that despite massive antibiotics, infection had taken hold. And in midmorning there was a sudden flurry of activity in the burn unit. The doors swung open and shut and figures in white bustled in and out with grim determined expressions on their faces. I stopped a nurse who thus far had been kind and friendly.

"Is this it?" I asked, surprised at the reasoned calm in my voice.

"It may be," she answered, and I pushed her aside. Inside the room two doctors and a nurse were clustered around her bed. They didn't see me approach till I was right beside the bed. Pren's filmy eyes were staring in my direction but I wasn't sure she could see me till she spoke.

"Laurel?" The faint voice rose from the pillow. I could scarcely hear her and leaned closer, taking her hand and doing my best to stay out of the way.

"I'm here. Everything is all right."

"No." It was barely a whisper.

"You'll have to step outside," one of the doctors told me brusquely.

"Like hell I will," I retorted and I saw the faint glimmer of a smile pass across Pren's face. "I'm right here, baby. Hang on."

"I can't," she answered weakly. "I'm sorry."

They were her last words.

I would like to report that what followed was a merciful blur, but I can't. Each detail etched itself painfully and permanently into my consciousness and I doubt very much that I will ever be able to forget any of it. But for Pren's sake, and for Melinda's, I made myself be strong. I cried briefly with John, and each of us was allowed to go inside alone and say our private good-byes. Then I sent him home to Bisbee and braced myself for the torturous ordeal ahead.

I took a room at the Holiday Inn and called Jason Abernathy. I was clipped and precise as I told him what had happened. "I want to be able to take Melinda away," I explained. "I think you'd better come and help." He put me on hold just long enough to instruct Dartanya to make his plane reservations and by the time I hung up I knew his flight number and arrival time. Then I looked up Federal Bureau of Investigation in the phone book.

The tired-sounding young G-man who answered the phone was not about to tell me how to reach Mel Sanford. "All right," I snapped. "Listen closely, because I'm not going to repeat this. My name is Laurel Hollingsworth. I have positive information about the whereabouts of Prentiss Granger, as in the Ten Most Wanted List. In exactly one hour, I'll call back and expect a number where I can reach Mel Sanford." Then I hung up.

I left my suitcase at the hotel and drove my rental car to Bisbee. In my call to Deirdre I had asked her not to tell Melinda until I arrived. Now it was time to assume the responsibility I had so lightly told Pren I was willing to accept. My vision blurred frequently on the hundred-mile drive to Bisbee, but I kept my foot to the floor and reminded myself that I could manage.

The hardest part was over. I had watched my best friend die.

I carefully repaired my makeup just outside town and drove directly to Deirdre's house. I was pleased that Deirdre had turned out to be so tough. One never knew, I supposed, just who could handle the rough stuff and who couldn't. John Washburn, he of the bristling beard and tough facade, had fallen all to pieces. But fragile little blond Deirdre greeted me dry-eyed and calm. Even as Melinda ran to hug me, Deirdre took Jennifer by the hand and walked right out the front door.

I had been wrong. The hardest part was not over. The hardest part looked at me plaintively now out of Prentiss Granger's deep brown eyes.

I took Melinda gently on my lap, wrapped my arms around her tightly and told her that because her mother had been so brave during the fire, God had called her to heaven to be one of his most important angels. I don't think she quite understood at first, but she was nearly five and the gravity of the situation over the past two days had been quite clear all along.

"You mean she's dead," she said very softly. And then with a sudden little yowl that broke my heart, Melinda buried her chestnut head in my breast and sobbed. They were not the tears of a little girl. They were the tears of a little woman. And my own tears, which flowed freely once again, made it impossible for me to talk. When at last I could control my voice, I explained that I had promised her mother I would love her and take care of her for always.

We were still seated like that when Deirdre returned. She had left Jennifer with another friend and was prepared to mop us both up if necessary.

"I want to go lie down," Melinda announced in a clear little voice, and I carried her into Deirdre's bedroom.

"You just rest here, honey," I told her. "I have to go away and talk to some people, but I'll be back soon."

Deirdre had coffee water on when I came back out. "I just can't cry," she told me. "It just doesn't seem possible."

"It's very possible. And it's not over yet." I told her then just exactly who Janet Cartwright had been. She listened wide-eyed without interruption. And the first thing she wanted to know was what would happen to Melinda. I explained about the will and Jason Abernathy's scheduled arrival in Tucson. I remembered suddenly that the hour deadline I had given the FBI was long past. So I walked up the hill to the house Prentiss Granger had strolled out of on her way to visit old friends at the Copper Quarters.

Turning Deirdre's key in the lock, I almost expected to find Pren lying on the sofa reading. But the house was empty. Horribly empty. As I walked across the living room toward the kitchen and the telephone, I saw my cactus flower photographs mounted on the far wall. I noted with professional dispassion that they were really quite good. I would have to take them to Chicago with me. And then I really broke down.

When at last I could cry no more, I sat at the kitchen table and called the FBI. I could tell from all the clickings on the line that the call was being recorded and traced, but that no longer mattered. They gave me a number in Washington and told me Mel Sanford was waiting for my call.

He answered the phone himself and I heard his breath intake sharply when I informed him that the Most Wanted List no longer numbered ten. To his credit, he quite obviously believed me and in fact he was meticulously polite, offering personal condolences I could tell were sincere. I expected that there might be some difficulties, I told him, and I wanted him to come to Tucson in person.

"Done," he said.

"And one more thing, sir. I'd like to tell her father myself."

"Well, Miss Laurel, no point in me bothering him until I have a positive identification anyway. You go right ahead. I'll be in Tucson by morning at the latest."

The phone rang six times at Azalea Acres before anybody picked it up. It was nearly suppertime in South Carolina, and as I had hoped, the

Major was already home from the mill. He greeted me quite cheerfully at first. For the past few years I had made a point of calling regularly on occasion just to wish him well. We were on relatively good terms. I hoped that he would remember that as I proceeded to shatter his little fiefdom once again.

I just did it straight. There was no need to be coy, or even circumspect. "I'd appreciate it if you'd sit down, sir. I'm afraid I have some rather bad news for you."

"If you can tell it, I can take it. Go ahead, young lady."

"It's Prentiss, sir. I'm afraid she's dead. But she died a hero. She saved the lives of a lot of people who might have been killed if she hadn't been so brave." Old people, I thought, as I felt the sting of tears rising again. People whose lives were nearly over anyway. While hers was just beginning. I pushed those thoughts away. "You would have been proud, sir." There was only silence at the other end. "Are you there, Major?"

"I'm here, young lady." His voice sounded curiously empty. "Now suppose you tell me just what's happened."

If he could be tough about it, so could I. I explained where she had been living, and what had happened the previous Saturday at the Copper Quarters.

"She burned to death?" I heard his voice strangle at the image of his daughter, his beautiful perfect daughter, seared and disfigured.

"It wasn't the burns. She was hit by a lot of debris when the building collapsed." I was crying again, but kept my voice calm. "It was the infection and internal injuries that killed her. I was with her at the end. There was nothing anybody could do."

"Burned," he repeated in a dull, numbed voice.

"*NO!!*" I answered sharply. "No. But sir, Major Granger, there's something else I have to tell you. She has a four-year-old daughter."

At that I heard a wrenching noise which could have been a sob or could have been a gasp or might have been the beginning of a coronary occlusion. "Are you all right?" I asked anxiously.

"As right as I can be, with the news you're giving me. Prentiss left a child, you say? A little girl?"

"A wonderful little girl, Major. Her name is Melinda and I know you're going to adore her. I'm only afraid there may be trouble taking her away from here." I explained about the will and Jason Abernathy and Mel Sanford homing in on Tucson.

"Would it help if I came there myself?"

I was stunned by the question, but it took me only a second to realize that his presence would simplify everything enormously. "It certainly would, but you'd have a hard time getting connecting flights, at least not until tomorrow."

"Young lady, I can be on a chartered jet in one hour. You just sit tight and tell me where to find my granddaughter."

The Major was truly wonderful. He arrived after Jason Abernathy and before Mel Sanford came in the next morning, which gave us time to get the documentation in order and present a unified front. The child welfare people had been making noises about putting Melinda in a foster home, but Mel Sanford took care of them. I knew that two FBI agents had been dispatched to search Pren's house but I also knew they'd find nothing because I had searched it first. There had been no incriminating evidence at all. Her secrets had died with her.

By the time Mel Sanford called a press conference that afternoon to announce the death of Prentiss Granger, her father and daughter and I were on a private plane bound for South Carolina. We arrived just in time for me to catch the *CBS Evening News* and watch the life of Prentiss Granger pass before me on film. It was a slow news day. They gave her nearly three minutes.

I'm not sure how long we'll stay here at Azalea Acres, but I do know that it's very strange to be here again. Shirley and her husband John live here now, with their two kids, and John works at the mill. In a way, that's a blessing, because the house seems much fuller than it has for a long time.

Melinda seems to like the Major and he is hopelessly smitten with her. Perhaps he sees her as a way to make up for the mistakes he made with Pren. I've tried to tell him that it doesn't matter anymore, any of it, but I'm not always sure that he hears me.

We buried her this afternoon beside her mother and Llewellyn, with camera crews from all three networks and a dozen southern stations held at bay by hired goons the Major brought in from Spartanburg. We all cried as the coffin sank finally and irrevocably into the ground, but Melinda held my hand very tightly and she wiped away her little tears on my sleeve and by the time we got back to the house, she seemed to be all right. She doesn't have a lot in common with Shirley's two daughters, who are both younger and quite inexperienced at anything beyond the nursery of Azalea Acres. And she's very southwestern in odd little ways I hadn't considered. She's still getting used to being around black people, for example. And she's absolutely amazed at the lushness of the vegetation.

I'll be glad to get her out of here soon, though. I won't make it back to the Taylor Street School for the end of the year, but I don't have to worry about losing my job, not at the salary I make. So there will be all summer to adjust to being a sudden mother before Melinda starts school in the fall. We'll have to go back to Arizona at some point to retrieve the Cartwright family goods and see about selling the house, but that can wait. For now the important thing is learning how to be a mother. Already I find it very different from being a teacher or an aunt. I have a lot to learn, but I think Melinda will be a very good instructor.

And some day, when she's old enough to really understand, I'll be able to tell her what an extraordinary woman her mother was.